# BEDTIME

Blaze stood looking down at father and daughter, thinking how different Hunter looked in repose. The harsh lines around his mouth were relaxed, as were the lines around his eyes. You are a handsome devil, she thought, and wished that things were different between them. A derisive half smile curved her lips at the impossible thought. Her husband had formed his opinion of her and nothing was going to change it.

She gently shook Hunter's shoulder and for a moment the softness remained on his face when he opened his eyes. But when he recognized her through his sleep-fogged eyes, the old hardness settled over his features again. "Bedtime," she said shortly, and carefully lifted Becky off his lap. In so doing, the back of one hand brushed against the bulge of his manhood. He jumped as though he had been scalded with hot water. Blaze gave him a curious look and walked on into her bedroom, Becky was still sound asleep.

Hunter swore softly under his breath as he grew hard and stiff. There would be little sleep for him tonight.

# NORAH HESS

# BLAZE

**LEISURE BOOKS**  **NEW YORK CITY**

*To Bruce Barrett,*
*the owner of the real horse SAINT.*

A LEISURE BOOK®

April 1997

Published by

Dorchester Publishing Co., Inc.
276 Fifth Avenue
New York, NY 10001

Printed in the United States of America.

# *Chapter One*

*Wyoming, 1868*

"What do you think is gonna happen to her now?" a rawboned woman in her midforties asked her husband as they sat eating the noontime meal that had been prepared over an open fire.

Jake Hackett slid a glance from the corner of his eye toward the wagon pulled up alongside his own. The bright autumn sun shone on a tangled mass of red-gold curls framing a tearstained face. The girl sat Indian fashion in front of her own small fire. A few hours ago the men of the wagon train had buried her grandfather, her only remaining relative.

Elisha Adlington, aged seventy-two, had died in

his sleep last night, leaving the girl on her own for the first time in her life.

Hackett looked back at his wife. "I don't know, Rose," he said before shoveling a spoonful of beans into his mouth. "Only one thing seems clear at the moment . . . she can't go on with the train. Those were the rules when we started on the trail back in Missouri—every wagon must have a man handling the team."

"I hardly think that rule should apply to Blaze," Rose pointed out as she got up and pulled a blackened coffeepot from the edge of the fire. She filled two tin cups with its contents, and then handed one to her husband as she pointed out, "She's been handlin' the team more often than her granddaddy ever since they joined us in Utah. I don't know why she can't continue. She may look delicate, but there's strength in her slender arms."

Hackett took a cautious sip of the steaming brew and then answered, "There's gonna be a meetin' at the council fire a little later. The men will decide on it then. But I'll tell you now, most of the men favor leaving her here at Fort Laramie."

"That's a cryin' shame," Rose said indignantly. "How do they expect a young girl to make a livin' here among rough trappers, rougher mountain men and women with low morals?" Rose paused to catch her breath. "There's only one way she'll survive and you men know it."

"She wouldn't necessarily have to work in the saloon. If she wasn't so unfriendly and standoffish, any number of men would be more than willin' to marry her."

"Hah!" Rose snorted. "I haven't seen any decent husband material hangin' 'round the fort. Like I said, there's just dirty mountain men and crude-mannered trappers. The girl would be better off joinin' up with the whores. At least she wouldn't be worked to the bone day and night."

"You're right," Jake had to agree, "but most of the men in our group are afraid she couldn't handle her team in an emergency. Any number of things might happen—a thunder storm, or a snake spookin' the team. Then there's the danger of gettin' caught in a buffalo stampede. Or what if her wagon lost a wheel, or one of the mules broke a leg, or drowned in a river crossin'?" Jake shook his head. "Ain't no use arguin', Rose. The men have families to think about. They want to get to Fort Bridger before winter sets in and they're afraid the girl will hold them up, keep them from gettin' settled in before the snow falls."

As Rose frowned into the fire, unable to come up with another rebuttal, Jake finished his coffee and stood up. "I'm gonna amble over to the council fire," he said. "I see the men are beginnin' to gather."

Rose looked up at her husband and asked anxiously, "You're not gonna vote against the girl, are you Jake?"

"You know I wouldn't." Jake patted his wife's brown hair, which was pulled back in a tight bun at her nape.

Mrs. Hackett watched the slightly built man walk away, a softness in her eyes. Her mate of twenty years was a kind man and would never willingly leave an orphaned girl on her own in a rough place like Fort Laramie. But—she sighed inwardly—he was in the minority.

As Rose washed the few dishes and utensils used in making the meal, she glanced often at the wagon a few yards away. The girl still sat staring into the flames of her fire. The motherly woman would have liked to console Blaze Adlington, but the stiffness of the slender body said as clearly as words, "I want to be alone."

Rose understood that as she settled back down in front of her own fire to await the return of her husband. People had different ways of handling grief, she thought. Some liked to wail aloud their heartache, some sought company and sympathy, while others wanted to be alone with their grief. Some didn't even shed tears. They did their crying inside.

Nevertheless, Jake Hackett's wife wished that she could comfort the lovely young woman who was suffering so. She had been drawn to Blaze from the start. The one disappointment in an otherwise satisfactory marriage was her inability to have children.

As she listened to the carefree voices of children at play, Rose sat in thought, wondering and worrying about the outcome of the meeting that was to decide Blaze Adlington's fate.

\*   \*   \*

It was solemn group of men who had gathered around the council fire that afternoon. The task they'd undertaken was not an easy one. For the most part they were good, decent family men, and as such, their minds were troubled that they were going to vote against the girl. But in their view she could not continue to travel with them.

"Well, men, you all know why we're here." John Jackson, the wagon master, opened the meeting when all the men were seated. "I'm sure you've given serious thought to what we should do about the young Adlington woman's plight."

When he was answered with a mumbling of *ayes*, he continued. "I know it will go against the grain to vote for leaving Miss Adlington behind, but we must first think of our famlies. I can see no other way of handling it."

"Maybe she could sell her wagon and team and ride with another family," one man suggested. The wagon master gave him an amused look.

"Would your wife want a beauty like Blaze Adlington sharing the wagon with you?"

The man grinned sheepishly. "She wouldn't allow it for a minute."

"Nor would any of the other wives," Jackson said.

"Me and Rose would take her in if we wasn't so crowded in our wagon already," Jake Hackett spoke up. "It's packed to the top with things Rose couldn't bear to leave behind. But I'm agin' leavin' the girl in this god-awful place with the kind of men and women who live here. Nothin' good would come of it and you know it."

Jackson nodded agreement. "We're all aware of that, Jake, and don't think for a minute that we enjoy doing what we must, but Miss Adlington is too fragile a female to handle a team of mules all the way to Fort Bridger. As it is we're running a little behind schedule. Every time her wagon breaks down through mishandling we could be held up for days that we can't afford to waste."

"I guess you're right," Jake agreed reluctantly, "but it don't seem the decent thing to do."

There was a stirring in the rear, and then two young men rose and stepped forward. They were brothers, James and David Wilson, and had been traveling horseback with the wagon train since its beginning.

"Do you fellers have a suggestion?" Jackson asked.

"Yes," replied the younger one, who was somewhere in his midtwenties. "Me and James will drive the wagon for Miss Adlington."

There was a muttering of protests, and the wagon master, shaking his head, said, "It wouldn't be seemly for a young woman to travel alone with two young, single men. People would talk."

"Let them talk," the younger brother said sharply. "What could be worse, a little gossip or an uncertain future here with whores and rough men?" His gaze swept over the men who stared back at him, a thoughtful look on most of their faces. Encouraged, he added, "If you think we have it in mind to sleep with her, put the thought from you. You have our word of honor that that is the last thing we would do. We will never touch her in that way."

Jake Hackett leaned forward and studied the clear-eyed young man. "Come to think of it," he said slowly, "you two are the only young fellers who ain't been tryin' to court the single women in the train. You ain't woman-hungry, that's for sure."

"We're not," David assured him. "We're only interested in filing on our land the same as the rest of you."

"Well—" the wagon master stood up—"let's go put your suggestion to Miss Adlington. She might not be willin' to travel with two single men."

Blaze Adlington was unaware that at that very hour strangers were deciding whether or not she would be allowed to continue on with the train or be forced to stay behind in the rough outpost. She was only aware that the grandfather she had adored had passed away in his sleep the night before.

He had been too old to start the trip across country, she thought guiltily. He had done it for her. He had wanted her to get as far away as possible from the outlaw gang and its leader, Garf Mullen.

She shivered. The man could very well be following the wagon train right now.

Blaze had grown up in many different outlaw camps, a motherless, wild and lonely child. When her father was around he'd done his best for her; he was a loving and protective man. But he was often gone with the gang to rob banks or trains. For many weeks at a time they would be on the run from the law. One time they were gone for three months before they thought it safe enough to venture back to their camp in the High Unita Wilderness.

It had been Grandfather Elisha who had always been there for her, soothing her through lightning storms, bandaging scraped knees, taking her fishing. Later, as she grew older, he taught her how to handle his Colt expertly.

A tender smile curved her lips as she remembered how, on her sixteenth birthday, he had given her her own Colt.

Suddenly, unbidden, another man slipped into Blaze's mind. Another male who had been there for her at a very important time.

Hunter Ward.

She remembered the first time she had seen him up close. He was tall and handsome, with cold, steady, alert eyes, firm lips and coal black hair that hung in loose waves to his shoulders. He wore a black woolen shirt with a blue neckerchief, and well-worn chaps covered his legs.

She had been sitting on the porch of their rough little cabin when she saw him coming through a haze of heat about a quarter of a mile away. She had frowned and sat forward when he pulled in his mount and swung stiffly out of the saddle. Why didn't the fool ride on? she had wondered. Strang-

14

ers were rare, and never welcome in the outlaw camp. She was surprised he hadn't been spotted yet and sent on his way by a spray of bullets kicking up dirt under his horse's hooves.

She watched him walk toward camp, the reins dangling over his shoulder, the exhausted stallion trailing behind him. His consideration of his mount surprised her. The outlaws rode their horses until the poor things were ready to drop.

He was almost at the main cabin where the men ate and slept before he was spotted by the others. She had wanted to follow Grandpa when he left to see what the stranger was about, but was told to stay put. "Stay here, honey. I don't like the looks of that feller. He's got the face of a lawman to me."

Although Garf had finally accepted Hunter's reason for wandering into their camp, Blaze had strong doubts about him. She felt that lurking behind his genial, easygoing manner there was a ruthlessness that could outdo even Garf Mullen's.

She had been sitting between Sid and Rusty, two members of the gang whom she had known for years, when she first met Hunter face-to-face. The evening had been chilly and each man had wrapped an arm around her to keep her warm. The stranger's gray eyes had searched her face, then dropped to the male arms holding her close. When he looked back at her face, a slight curl of contempt had twisted his lips. Blaze remembered how she had blushed, realizing for the first time that what was normal for her old friends to do might be misinterpreted by a stranger. This man

Hunter thought she was a camp woman, strictly there to see to the men's carnal wants.

Then anger had washed over her, and lifting her head defiantly, she'd leaned closer to Rusty. The stranger had looked at her only one more time that night. He hadn't tried to hide his contempt when her father caught her hand and pulled her to her feet, saying, "Come on, honey; let's go to bed." She had felt the bore of his hard gaze on her back as she and her father passed into their cabin.

She hadn't slept well that night. In her mind's eye she recalled the cold looks the handsome man had given her. And adding to her distress was the fact that tomorrow morning her father and the men planned to ride out to rob another bank. She worried herself sick every time he rode away. There was always the chance of his being shot and never coming home again.

And what would become of her if that happened? Garf was becoming more and more brazen in his attentions to her. Poor old Grandpa would try his best to protect her against the man, but the outlaw paid no more attention to him than he would a pesky fly flitting around his head.

As a result of her poor sleep, when she and her father stepped out of the cabin the next morning, she knew that she didn't look her best. Her eyes were red rimmed and her face wore a strained look.

As they joined the men for breakfast her gaze went straight to that of the stranger. His sneering lips told her what he thought of her haggard appearance. She had scowled at him, then accepted the plate of beans and salt pork Shorty handed her.

She sat down next to Elisha and her father; Mullen sat down on the other side of her. Blaze had just picked up her fork when Mullen growled at her father, "Go sit somewhere else."

The camp grew deathly quiet, breakfast forgotten as everyone watched Luke jerk to his feet and grind out savagely, "Go to hell, Mullen."

Breaths were held as Mullen came to his feet, his hand hovering over his pistol. "You'll go there first, mister. I want the girl and I intend to have her."

"Like hell you will." Luke brushed aside his jacket, clearing his own gun and holster. "She's not for the likes of you."

"She's for anyone who can take her away from you, and I mean to do just that."

As the two men had faced off, Elisha pulled Blaze to her feet. While she stood white faced with fear for her father, the stranger edged up to them and said in an undertone, "Take the girl and slip out of here as fast as you can."

Elisha grabbed Blaze's hand, and as they dashed away Garf barked, "Go for your gun." Two gunshots rang out almost simultaneously. Blaze looked back and saw her father on the ground, Garf still standing. She gave a distressed cry and tried to dig in her heels to run back to her father.

"Come along, honey," Elisha said, his voice husky as he dragged her forward. "You can't help him. You've got to save yourself."

They sped on to the cottonwood grove, where the saddled horses waited to carry the outlaws to another bank holdup. Elisha boosted Blaze onto Garf's stallion. "He's the fastest of the bunch," he said. "I'll take Luke's roan. He's the next-fastest." Before he mounted, however, Elisha ran to the cabin. When he hurried back, he carried his saddlebag with his meager life savings in it.

With tears streaming down her cheeks, Blaze gathered up the reins, and as they thumped their heels into the horses, sending them tearing away, two more shots rang out. A hurried look over their shoulders showed Garf on the ground and the stranger, his smoking Colt in his hand, holding the rest of the men at bay.

"Do you think Garf is dead?" Blaze called to Elisha over the noise of their mounts' pounding hooves.

"He's lyin' mighty still," Elisha called back as the horses thundered on and their riders listened for more shots. None rang out.

In the three days Blaze and Elisha had ridden before they came upon the wagon train, they wondered out loud many times why the stranger had shot Garf and what had happened to the rest of the gang.

The emigrants had made them welcome, and Blaze and Elisha had traveled with them along the Utah trail.

After a while Elisha began to complain that he was tired of riding horseback, that he was about to get saddle sores. One day at a small outpost on the Platte, he bought a wagon from a farmer and covered its top with canvas on a tall frame. He fashioned two straw-filled pallets, bought eating utensils, pots and a skillet, a water barrel, and a tar bucket to keep the wagon wheels moving smoothly. He then purchased supplies and had a blacksmith look over the wheels and axle. His last act was to purchase two mules from the same farmer who'd supplied the wagon. He and Blaze had found it much more comfortable sleeping in the wagon as they traveled. The wagon train covered fifteen or twenty miles a day, depending on whether they rolled over prairies or labored over mountains.

Blaze and Elisha kept mostly to themselves, and they were closemouthed about where they'd come from. Elisha had cautioned her that the less people knew about them, the better. Although he hadn't taken part in any of the gang's holdups for years, the law might still consider him an outlaw.

As they bounced along, Elisha and Blaze had planned their future. They would live like decent folk from now on, never having to watch over their shoulders again. "I'll find work on a ranch," Elisha told her, "so we can be together."

A fierce pain jabbed her at the memory of Elisha's words. She couldn't believe that she would never see him again, never again know his kindness, his gentle teasing. She didn't remember her mother or grandmother. Typhoid had taken them both when she was four years old. Her father had never remarried, but there had been a succession of women in his life. Some had been truly kind to her, but there had been others who only pretended affection when he was around. Grandpa, though, had always known the pretenders and they soon disappeared from camp.

She took a deep, ragged breath. She would have to go on without him, try her best to make his dream of a new beginning come true.

When Blaze saw the group of men coming toward her, she dashed the tears from her eyes. They look so stern, she thought uneasily. When they stopped at her fire and gazed down at her, she tilted her chin aggressively and demanded coolly, "What can I do for you, gentlemen?"

The wagon master shifted his feet nervously, thrown by the unfriendliness in her tone. He had expected to find her crying and worrying about what was to become of her. He cleared his throat and said, "Well, miss, it's this way. We men have been thinkin' on what to do about you."

Puzzled, Blaze stared up at Jackson a moment, then, rising to her feet, asked aggressively, "What do you mean, do about me? You don't have to do anything about me. Although Grandpa is gone, I intend to go on as before."

Avoiding her eyes, the wagon master shook his head. "I'm sorry, miss, but we can't let you go on alone. You know our rule. Every wagon has to have a man handlin' the team."

Blaze narrowed angry green eyes at Jackson. "No one ever told me that. I've been doing most of the driving ever since Grandpa started ailing so much. Why didn't you stop me then?"

As the men squirmed uneasily, Jackson blushed guiltily and muttered, "I guess we didn't notice."

"Bah! You didn't notice." Blaze snorted. "You even remarked a couple of times on how well I handled the team."

"Look, honey." Jake laid a hand on Blaze's shoulder, talking over Jackson's fumbling denial that he couldn't remember ever saying that to her. "There's only one way you can continue on with us."

"Oh? And how is that?" Blaze asked suspiciously.

"David and James Wilson have offered to drive your wagon," Jake explained. "They'll look after you, shoot fresh game and such. If you don't take them up on it, the vote is that you can't continue on with us."

Blaze stared unbelievingly at Jake. Would these men actually ride off and leave her here alone in this dungheap of a fort? Surely not. She and Grandpa had had the same dreams and plans as they did.

The stony looks on the men's faces said that they would leave her. Did she want to depend on these two brothers to get her to her destination? She directed her gaze to the Wilsons, taking time to search their faces. She was good at reading faces. She'd had to be for a long time. So many different kinds of men had come and gone in the outlaw camps over the years, and very few of them had been honorable ones.

Blaze was impressed with the brothers, however. She liked the way they held her gaze, not looking away for a second. Not even the younger one, who was blushing like a schoolgirl. She knew intuitively that she would not have to fight either one of them out of her bed. And truth be told, she added to herself, she'd be glad of their presence. There were other single men in the wagon train who she didn't trust at all.

She nodded at the brothers and gave them a genial smile. "I'll be thankful for your help." She paused a moment. "But I must tell you up front, I don't know spit about cooking."

"That's all right." James Wilson returned her smile. "I'm a fine cook. David shot a couple of sage hens today. We'll have them for supper."

When the three fell to talking among themselves, planning how they would travel together, the men left them to go to their own wagons. Their relief that they wouldn't be leaving the girl behind tomorrow morning showed on their faces. Unlike their womenfolk, they thought that Blaze Adlington was a fine young woman. They had seen the tender care she had given her ailing grandfather and felt that it was no one's business if the Adlingtons mostly stayed to themselves.

The wives and daughters, however, had taken a different view of the situation. They claimed that the young woman thought she was too good to fraternize with them, even as they admitted in their hearts that they had not given the young beauty any encouragement to do so. Blaze Adlington's exceptional good looks were a threat to the other single girls. The men knew that tongues would wag now that she would be traveling with the two most handsome men in the wagon train.

Most everyone had sought their beds, either in a wagon or on the ground, as Blaze and the Wilsons ate their late supper of tender roasted fowl and potatoes that had been roasted beneath glowing coals. After a cup of strong coffee, Blaze sought her pallet in the wagon, and the brothers rolled up in their blankets beneath it. Emotionally exhausted, Blaze fell asleep almost immediately.

The next morning in the gray light of dawn, the wagon master shot his gun into the air, alerting the travelers that it was time to rise, eat breakfast and be ready to roll out at sunup. In a matter of minutes, smoke was rising from small campfires and men were hitching up wagons.

By the time Blaze washed her face and brushed her hair, David had the team and wagon ready to pull out, and James had flapjacks and crisp salt pork ready to be eaten. When Blaze finished her cup of coffee she visited the small cottonwood grove where her grandfather had been laid to rest.

Kneeling beside the rock-covered mound, she laid down the bouquet of wildflowers she had picked, and, wet eyed, she whispered, "I'll make our dream come true, Grandpa."

When Blaze returned to the campsite, David was sitting on the springboard seat of the wagon and James had just finished tying the two mounts

to the tailgate beside the horses she and her grandfather had ridden. He smiled at her and gave her
a boost up to sit beside David.

The sun was just peeping over the horizon when
the call came to roll out. When it was their turn to
fall in line, David flicked the reins over the mules'
backs and the wagon began to roll.

David wasn't one to talk much as they put miles
and days behind them, but Blaze didn't mind. She
was deeply immersed in studying the country they
moved through. Surely there was no other place
in the world as beautiful as this land of rugged
mountains, green valleys and winding rivers.

She was watching a bald eagle hunt for fish
along the Snake River when David said, "The Indians call this country Big Sky."

"I can see why they would," Blaze said, and then
asked, "Where are we?"

"We've been in Montana Territory about a week
now."

It was a great relief to all the day they reached
the Sweetwater River at Independence Rock. The
wagon master had said that they would rest there
for two days. When camp had been set up, many
of the travelers climbed the rock to scratch their
names, along with the hundreds of others already
etched into the stone. Sometime later, after Blaze
had scrubbed the brothers' dirty clothes as well as
her own on the rocks in the river, she was about
to do the same, but then stopped to reconsider.

She decided that it was best she didn't. She

didn't want to advertize the fact that she had passed through the country, in case Garf Mullen was still alive and was looking for her.

After the grateful travelers' rest, the wagons rolled southwest to the Continental Divide at South Pass. There they rested again for two more days, and it was there Blaze finally became aware that the women were shunning her and whispering behind her back. When she mentioned this to Rose Hackett, who was still as friendly as usual, the plump little woman told her frankly that it was because she was traveling with two single men.

At first Blaze could only stare at her friend in stunned surprise. Then slowly she was consumed with anger. "The hypocrites," she said, fuming. "Their husbands practically forced me to travel with David and James, and now they have the nerve to turn their noses up at me."

"Pay them no mind, honey." Rose patted her clenched fist. "They've got nothin' else to do but gossip. Besides, they're jealous that you've got the two handsomest men in the train taking care of you. They say that all you do is sit around like a queen while they fetch and carry for you."

Blaze declared angrily that she didn't care what the women said about her, but deep down she was deeply hurt.

After crossing the Continental Divide, the wagon train wound its way southwest until eventually they drew near Fort Bridger and the general area where they would settle.

Beyond that was the wild and waiting land.

"Fort Bridger is a fur-trading post, the last out-post of civilization," Jack Hackett informed Blaze and the brothers the evening before they arrived. "Though it's not really a fort, we're fortunate that it is here. We can buy supplies when we run out of things."

With a soft smile, Blaze counted her blessings. She had made it to Fort Bridger. Tomorrow a brand-new life would begin for her.

# Chapter Two

The sorrell had come far. Its once shiny coat was sprinkled with dust, its eyes rimmed with it. Its rider's coal black hair and mustache were also dusted with it.

Hunter Ward had been riding for three months and was just as weary as his mount. They were both spent. Now the sun was touching the rim of the tree line and the only grub he had was a sage hen he had shot and the makings for a pot of coffee.

The sun-baked valley he followed wound upward, to lose itself in the cooler regions of the mountains. He decided he would make camp there, among the many boulders scattered about. He could safely build a fire among them, one that wouldn't be spotted by night riders or renegade Indians.

Hunter was about to begin his ascent up the mountain when he spotted a wash of swift, clear water. He loped the stallion toward it, and after the thirsty Saint had drunk his fill, Hunter dipped his nearly empty canteen into the cool stream and quenched his own thirst.

He had ridden up the mountain just a short distance when he found a suitable place to make camp among a jumble of large boulders. It was a perfect spot to build his fire and at the same time be sheltered from the cold air once the sun went down and night fell.

Hunter reined the stallion in beneath a tall pine. Swinging to the ground, he took his bedroll from where he had strapped it behind the cantle. Carrying it to the place he intended to make camp, he spread it between two tall boulders. When he had unsaddled Saint, slipped his bridle off and hobbled him in grass growing at the foot of the pine, he built a small fire and started a pot of coffee brewing. He next prepared the sage hen to be roasted over the red coals.

Twenty minutes later as he wolfed down the tender meat, he thought ahead to when he would reach Fort Bridger tomorrow, and his ranch five miles away.

Full night had arrived while Hunter ate his supper, and after a second cup of coffee, he sought his blankets. As he lay on his back, gazing up at the star-filled sky, his mind was on his ranch, which he had worked on like a slave.

His first act had been to build a tight, sturdy

cabin for his new bride on his five-hundred-acre tract of land. Then had come the backbreaking task of building up a small herd of cattle. It had not been unusual for him to work fourteen hours a day as he herded the longhorns, branded the calves when they were weaned from their mothers, and kept ever alert for wolf packs and night riders who would try to rustle his stock.

The hard lines around his mouth deepened. Jenny hadn't been as enthusiastic as he about the ranch. She had complained night and day about the drudgery and the lack of any entertainment, and that none of their neighbors ever came to visit. Jenny had not been well liked by the ranch wives.

He had wondered about Jenny's sudden uplifted spirits, then thought no more about it. He was only thankful that she had stopped carping and was settling down to being a rancher's wife. He was to learn later how foolish his thoughts had been.

One day while riding the range his horse had gone lame and he'd returned home unexpectedly. He had found Jenny in bed with the drifter he had hired to help him with odd jobs. Stunned beyond belief, Hunter had summoned all his willpower not to shoot the man and throw Jenny out of the cabin.

He had done neither. The drifter had run naked from the cabin, carrying his pants and boots in his hands. Jenny had cried and pleaded with him that she was sorry and that it would never happen again. "It's just that I'm so lonesome here on this godforsaken place, and you're never around except to eat and sleep."

He had thought that perhaps some of the fault lay with him and he had forgiven her. But he hadn't forgotten. Her infidelity festered like an open sore.

Three weeks later he was to receive another jolt. He came home from branding cattle all day, and at the supper table Jenny told him she was expecting. He couldn't help asking himself if the baby was his or the drifter's. A week later when he came home to an empty cabin and found the note on the table, he had the answer to his question. Jenny had written that she had gone to Hicksville to join the drifter.

He knew the small town. It consisted of two short streets facing each other, and the dregs of society lived there. He didn't have the time, or the desire, to go after her.

He hadn't seen Jenny again until that rainy night she showed up at the cabin, ready to give birth to her baby. There had been no comparing the rain-soaked, haggard-looking woman to the pretty girl he had married. With the exception of her protruding belly, she was rail thin, and there were blue smudges beneath her eyes. In her run-down condition her labor had been hard, and he had used what knowledge he had of birthing calves to ease her pain as he helped a tiny little girl into the world.

Two hours later Jenny gave up the struggle to

live, not once looking at her squalling, hungry infant. In desperation, he had gone to the nearby Arapaho Indian village to seek help for the infant. Luckily there was a young woman there who had delivered a stillborn infant two days before, and her breasts were sore with rich milk. Her husband had been killed in a recent battle with another tribe, and her father had gladly, for a sum of money, let him take the young mother home with him.

Hunter then turned his hand to bathing Jenny and putting her into a dress she had left behind the day she ran away from home. He had just finished combing her hair and crossing her arms when the father and brother of the Indian nursemaid stepped into the cabin.

"We have dug a grave for your wife," the father said.

"I am grateful," Hunter responded. "Where did you dig it?"

"Several miles from here beneath a tall pine. A very peaceful place." After a pause, the Indian added, "We went to the fort and told your friend Jim Bridger about your wife. He and your friends will be here soon."

The father and son left then, as silently as they had come. A short time later Bridger and two of his trapper friends arrived in a wagon. They didn't offer him any condolences, for they knew he didn't need them. It was common knowledge that he had lost all feelings and respect for his wife the day she left him for another man.

Jim Bridger said only, "We brought some pine planks to make a coffin." Hunter nodded his thanks and helped carry the boards into the barn. As his friends sawed and hammered, he made arrangements with the fort owner to let the Indian woman have whatever she would need from his store.

"You goin' somewhere, Hunter?" Bridger asked, spitting a stream of tobacco juice at a chipmunk scurrying across the ground.

"Yeah," Hunter answered. "I want to get the hell away from here for a while, Jim."

"Can't say that I blame you. A man can take only so much. Stay away as long as you want to. I'll see that the squaw and the baby get whatever they need."

A couple of hours later Jenny was laid to rest, after Hunter read a passage from the Bible. He thanked his friends for their help, and after telling the woman, New Moon, that he would be gone for a time and that she could get supplies at the fort, he had saddled Saint and ridden away.

Hunter remembered how he had ridden into Utah and become a state marshal; his job was mainly to hunt down outlaws and bring them in. After five years he grew weary of always being on the move, putting his life on the line, shooting it out with outlaws. He yearned to see his ranch again, to run his cattle. He decided that after he had found and taken in the Mullen outlaw gang, he would hand in his star.

It had been quite easy infiltrating that gang, getting the men's trust. But as he waited for the right moment to draw his gun on them, he had suddenly found himself in a dilemma. The men were planning a bank robbery and they expected him to ride with them, take part in the holdup.

The morning they were to ride out he was still trying to figure out what to do when Garf Mullen and another man had gotten into a fight over the camp woman. The leader had shot and killed the man she had spent the night with. As the leader of the outlaws stood over the slain man, Hunter had surprised himself by telling the old man of the gang to take the sobbing girl and ride away as fast as he could.

Then, unobserved, he pinned the star on his vest and ordered the men to reach for the sky. They had gaped at him in stunned surprise. Then Garf, his gun still in his hand, had spun around and aimed it at him. Hunter squeezed the trigger of his Colt a second before the outlaw did. His shot hit the outlaw in the chest just as the man's bullet whizzed past his head.

Seeing their leader on the ground had taken the fighting spirit out of the others. He'd had no trouble tying their hands behind their backs and taking them to the nearest town. After he had turned the men over to the sheriff there and told him where he could find the body of their leader, he mounted Saint and turned the stallion's head toward home.

As the days and weeks passed, bringing him closer to home, he thought often of the woman he'd aided and wondered why he had let her and the old man escape. She was the kind of woman he despised, beautiful and innocent-looking, but hard as nails inside. She sold her body as readily as a farm woman would sell a dozen eggs. However, many nights, rolled up in his blankets, he fell asleep thinking of the russet-headed beauty with eyes the color of new moss and skin so fine it looked dew washed. He wondered where she was tonight.

A cold gray mist hung over the valley the next morning when Hunter descended the mountain. As he rode into Fort Bridger hours later, he noticed a wagon train pulling in. They're a tired-looking bunch, he thought. Then he caught his breath as his gaze fell upon the little beauty who had wandered in and out of his dreams so often.

Shocked, he sat and stared at her, and suddenly she was staring back, fear in her green eyes. A mirthless smile curved his lips. She was afraid he would tell everyone what he knew of her. Should he pretend that he didn't know her? he wondered. He felt sure that was what she wanted. If that was the case, it was fine with him.

But where was the old fellow? Had he abandoned her?

Telling himself that the girl's welfare was none of his concern, Hunter kneed the stallion up to the hitching post in front of the trading post. He stepped down from the saddle, and after looping the reins over the post, he walked into the big main room of the building.

Bridger stood behind the rough counter, and he let out a whoop when he spotted Hunter. "Hunter Ward, by God," he shouted. "We was beginnin' to think that you'd been shot out on the plains somewhere and left for the buzzards to pick at your bones."

Hunter shook the bony hand stretched out to him and laughingly said, "There were a few times when I thought that was exactly what was going to happen to me. I've been chasing outlaws for the past five years. I finally got tired of sleeping on the ground most of the time, and being hungry half of the time. After I brought in the Mullen gang I headed for home."

Bridger reached for a special bottle of whiskey he kept hidden beneath the bar. When he started to uncork it, Hunter said, "I've got to have something to eat first, Jim. My stomach is so empty my guts are sticking together."

"I'll have my cook rustle you up a bowl of stew." Bridger beckoned to a man at the end of the bar who wore a soiled apron wrapped around his fat paunch.

"Is that Indian woman still taking care of the baby?" Hunter asked as he waited for some nourishment.

"Yeah, she's still there. The little one ain't a baby no more, though, Hunter. She's five years old and cute as a button."

"Has the squaw taken good care of her?"

"Seems like. She must be feedin' her good anyway. The little one is real chubby."

"I wonder if the ranch has fared as well," Hunter said. "I guess it's fallen into disrepair since I've been gone."

"I haven't been out that way lately, but when I rode past it a couple years ago it didn't look the same. It looked almost deserted, like nobody lived there. The only sign of habitation was smoke comin' out of the chimney. The only time we see the woman and little one is when they comes to the fort for supplies. Which isn't very often."

The subject of the ranch was dropped when Hunter said, "That's a good-sized wagon train that just pulled in."

"Yeah, and it's not the first one to arrive. For the last two months they've been rollin' in. Those who can afford it stop here first to buy some supplies before headin' out to their claims."

"They're settling around here?" Hunter frowned. "In cattle country?"

"Yeah." Bridger nodded. "The government opened up a thousand acres for homesteading, or whatever a feller wants to do on his claim. The only rule is they have to build on the land and live there for a year. They get title to it then."

"How are you going to feel, having so many people around all the time?"

"I don't know yet. It may work out just fine. It gets mighty lonesome here in the wintertime. A fellow gets tired of listenin' to the trappers and mountain men tellin' their long tales and lies."

Bridger was called to the other end of the bar

just as the cook slapped a bowl of stew in front of Hunter. As he ate the meat and vegetables, he tried to imagine the girl from the Mullen gang claiming a piece of land. With no husband to help her, she would not be able to build a cabin or plow the land. How would she manage? Again, he berated himself for his protective feelings toward her. He should know better than most that youth and beauty could hide a lying heart. Certainly this girl was no innocent. Glancing through a window facing west, he saw that according to the sun there were only a couple of hours before sunset. He had best get on out to the ranch.

"I'll settle up with you tomorrow, Jim. I want to get to my place before dark." Bridger nodded and Hunter pushed away from the bar. As he stepped outside he was jostled by a young man who had a protective arm around his female companion. His lips curled in self-derision. It was the camp woman, and already she had found a male protector, it seemed. Hunter called himself a fool for wasting one moment worrying about her ability to take care of herself.

For the first time in years Hunter found himself relaxing as he rode the familiar path to his ranch. He no longer had to keep a watch on his back trail, to snatch at his gun at every unexpected noise.

His body moved easily with the motion of Saint as he made plans for his ranch. The first thing he would do was to build up his herd. That was if he had any cattle left. Rustlers and renegades might have made off with all of them while he was gone.

When Jenny's child came to mind, he felt a stab of anxiety, but he pushed the thought away. He would think of something, maybe put her up for adoption.

He topped a hill and the westering sun shone on the buildings below. Pride flashed in his eyes as he remembered how carefully he had built the sturdy four-room cabin and barn. The other outbuildings he had added gradually.

Smoke rose from the adobe chimney, but other than that, as Bridger had said, the place had a deserted look. He lifted the reins, and as Saint brought him closer to his holdings, he made out weeds and tall grass growing around the buildings. He was almost upon the cabin when he discovered the narrow path that led to the back porch. Didn't the woman ever use the front door? he wondered as he pulled the stallion in.

He sat a moment, listening for some sound within the cabin. All was quiet inside, and he dismounted and stepped up on the porch. As he stood in front of the heavy door he wondered if he should knock or just walk in. Although it was his cabin, he didn't want to scare the woman. Finally he pushed open the door and stood there, letting the sun shine on him so that the Indian woman could see him.

New Moon's black eyes told him that she recognized him right away. "You have been gone a long time, Hunter Ward," she said solemnly.

"Yes, I have," Hunter said, his eyes drawn to the little girl peeking from behind New Moon's skirt.

He gave a start and sucked in his breath. She had her mother's blond hair, but what he hadn't expected was that the big eyes watching him unblinkingly were the same stormy gray as his own and the small features held the same unmistakable stamp as his. He was gripped with wonder and a heart-pounding joy. The little one was his, his flesh and blood. He came down on his knees and held his arms out to her.

"Come give your daddy a kiss," he said gently.

When the child only continued to gaze at him, not moving from behind the squaw, New Moon pulled her forward and spoke to her in her own native tongue.

*Good Lord*, Hunter thought, appalled. *My daughter doesn't speak English. But then, why should she?* he reasoned. After all, she had been raised by an Indian.

When his daughter shyly came to him, he hugged the warm little body, swamped with guilt and regret that he had missed the first five years of his daughter's life.

"You are hungry?" New Moon asked when he stood up. "Have good stew in pot." She motioned to the cast-iron pot hanging over the flames in the fireplace.

Hunter shook his head. He'd bet anything that the Indian hadn't once used the big black range in the kitchen. "Thank you, New Moon, but I ate at the fort," he said, his hand resting on his daughter's curly head. "I'm going to ride out on the range and have a look at my cattle."

"Hunter Ward has many cattle on his range," New Moon said behind him as he left the cabin.

Swinging onto Saint's back, Hunter left the weed-choked yard, vowing that tomorrow the first thing he was going to do was take a sickle to the growth that was a haven for snakes and other small varmints. He rode over his ranch until darkness was almost upon him, his excitement growing. New Moon was right. Everywhere he looked there were cattle. In his five years' absence his herd had grown to well over two thousand. He must see to hiring some cowhands right away and begin a fall roundup. Thanks to having spent very little of the wages he'd earned as a lawman, he had the money to hire some men. He would go to the fort tomorrow and ask around.

That night, however, after he had coaxed his daughter onto his lap and she chattered away to him in Arapaho, he knew that above everything else he must see to it that his daughter learned her own language. He could tell she was starved for affection from the way she curled up against him and held on to his hand with her tiny fingers. The Indian woman had fed her well, but he doubted if she ever held the child or sang her a lullaby.

Hunter realized suddenly and sadly that the little one didn't even have a first name. Full of guilt, he kissed the tangled, curly hair. His little daughter had fallen asleep in his lap. His first task tomorrow morning was to go to the fort and find a woman to come keep house for him and to teach his daughter to speak English.

As he gathered the child up and walked toward his bedroom, New Moon followed him. At the door he turned around and said, "I'm sorry, New Moon, I'd forgotten that you sleep here now."

The woman shook her head. "I no sleep in here. I sleep on furs in big room. I will now sleep with you. Bring you comfort."

Startled by the woman's offer, Hunter laid his daughter on the bed, then took New Moon by the arm and turned her back toward the door. "I do not need comfort, New Moon," he said kindly. "Continue to sleep on your furs."

From the sullen look that came over the Indian woman's face he knew she was not pleased with his refusal of her body. It was imperative that he get her out of their lives as soon as possible.

# Chapter Three

Blaze stood beside the covered wagon that for now was her home. Upon arriving at the brothers' claim she had parked the vehicle several yards from where they had set up their tent. Tongues would really wag if she shared the tent with them. But being a woman alone, she needed their protection.

She wished she could tell everyone the brothers' secret, which they had shared with her on the trail. If it were known that before winter set in their mail-order brides would be joining them, maybe some of the gossip would die away.

But the two young women didn't want to be known as mail-order brides, so the brothers weren't saying anything about them until they arrived. They would pretend then that they had known the young women for a long time. Right now, they knew so little about their prospective brides, they couldn't even have told what color their eyes were.

Of course, when the brides arrived she couldn't continue to depend on the brothers for protection and food. She would have to move on, but where would she go?

She hadn't staked a claim yet. Although the land was free, it took money to have the land cleared and a cabin built.

A soft sigh escaped Blaze's lips. She had racked her brains as to how she could earn her living. Nothing had come to mind. Her only skills were the ability to ride a horse fast and shoot a gun accurately. Both were men's skills.

Blaze left off her gloomy thoughts when she caught sight of Rose Hackett, her only woman friend, climbing up out of the foothills through the swirling morning mist.

Rose was coming to teach her more about cooking. Today the motherly woman would show her how to put together a venison stew. Yesterday she had taught her how to make skillet bread and coffee and flapjacks for David and James's breakfast. To her surprise she loved cooking.

"Good mornin', Blaze." Rose smiled at her, puffing a bit from her climb. "Do you have the meat cut up like I showed you?" she asked, handing Blaze a cloth bag. "There's herbs and onions and some potatoes in it," she explained.

"I prepared the meat when I woke up," Blaze

answered, leading the way to the rudely constructed table the brothers had thrown together next to the fire pit. She removed the cloth from a big bowl and asked, "Did I cut the meat in small enough pieces?" When Rose nodded that it was fine, Blaze added, "David shot the deer yesterday just at twilight. It was so beautiful, standing there looking at us, I was tempted to clap my hands and scare it away."

"They are beautiful animals," Rose agreed, "but folks have to eat. Now, bring me your flour."

Blaze knelt down and dragged a wooden crate from beneath the table. She took from it an earthen bowl that had traveled with her across country. Grandfather had bought it for her at a small post along the way, paying for it with almost the last of their money. She placed it on the table and Rose scraped the meat into it, then sprinkled the pieces with flour, salt and pepper.

As she made sure each piece of venison was well coated with flour, Rose asked, "Do you have a good fire going under the cooking pot like I told you?" When Blaze answered that she did, Rose ordered, "Then bring along that jar of bacon grease and the pail of water and we'll get this stew started."

Blaze watched carefully as Rose put a glob of grease into the big cast-iron pot, then slowly transferred the meat into it. She began to stir the pieces around with a long-handled spoon until the meat was nicely browned on all sides. She looked up at Blaze and directed, "Start pouring the water in now, but slowly, so that when it hits the hot grease we won't get splattered."

When the meat was gently bubbling, Rose dipped her fingers into the cloth bag she had brought with her and took from it some bay leaves and rosemary. Adding them to the pot, she said, "I brought these spices from my home in Illinois. I also brought along seeds for other herbs. I intend to sow them in my garden patch next spring. To my way of thinkin' a body can't make a decent meal without herbs to make it tasty.

"Now," she said, clapping a heavy lid on the pot, "in about an hour, add the onion and cut-up potatoes to the meat and you'll have a fine supper to serve David and James."

"They'll be thankful," Blaze said. "They come in from work so tired and hungry. They're chopping down trees all day long, clearing the land. I always felt useless, not even knowing how to make a pot of coffee for them."

"Well, we're changin' that." Rose smiled at her. "You learned how to do that yesterday, so let's get that pot keepin' warm by the fire and take it inside. We'll have a cup and chat for a while."

Blaze enjoyed Rose's little chats. There were days when she didn't exchange a dozen words with David and James. They were up and gone before she was out of her wagon, and when they returned home they were so tired they were hardly capable of talking at all. As soon as they finished their supper they mumbled good night and retired to their tent. Even before she started clearing the table she could hear them snoring.

Consequently, her days and nights were long and lonely. She was starved for the companionship of women, especially those of her own age. Always in hiding in some outlaw camp, she had never had an opportunity to make female friends.

She had been close to only one of her father's women. Lucianne had been different from the usual camp followers who made short appearances at their hideout. If not for her, Blaze wouldn't know how to read or write or do sums. She had been heartbroken when Lucianne quarreled with Luke and rode away.

Blaze left off thinking about Lucianne as she filled two tin cups with coffee and asked, "So, any more happenings since yesterday?"

"Well," Rose said, spooning sugar into her coffee, "I can't say anything is new. Everyone is still working themselves to the bone, gettin' their cabins finished, clearin' the land and choppin' wood for the winter months. I swear if Jake could stretch his cords of wood end to end the logs would cover half a mile.

"When I got home from your place yesterday I mixed some clay and grass and added more caulking between the logs of the cabin. The wind can find the smallest crack." Rose looked around the canvas walls of the covered wagon. "This will never hold up this winter, you know. The weight of the snow will cave it in."

When Blaze made no response, Rose said, "Come to think of it, there is a bit of news I heard since talkin' to you yesterday. There's this rancher who's lookin' for a woman to keep house for him and his little daughter."

"He doesn't have a wife, I take it."

"No. I understand she died birthin' the little one. Rumor has it that right after his wife was buried he took off, leavin' an Indian woman to care for the child. He's been workin' for the law the past five years."

"He must have been very much in love with his wife to have gone off and left another woman to raise his child."

"I reckon. Some men are like that, a one-woman man. Maybe he blamed the baby for his wife's death."

"I don't imagine he'll have much trouble finding someone to work for him. I'd think that any number of settler women could use some extra money with winter coming on."

"That's where you're wrong. The wives have their hands full takin' care of their own young'uns and they won't allow their daughters to live with a single man."

Blaze was silent for a moment as she gazed thoughtfully into her cup. Was it possible that if she applied for the job she might get it? Another few lessons from Rose should make her a fair cook. And she wasn't lazy. She wouldn't be averse to scrubbing floors, doing the chores to keep a house clean.

But there was the child. She knew nothing about children. But could they be all that different from adults? "Rose," she asked, "who is this rancher. What's his name?"

Rose thought a moment, then answered, "Hunter something or other. I forget his last name."

After Blaze got over her shock, her lips curved in a thin smile. She knew she must dismiss the hope that she might find employment with Hunter. That one wouldn't want her in his home, let alone taking care of his little girl. And she wouldn't want to be there, either. She remembered all too well the sneering looks and comments she had received from him. One thing had been cleared up for her, though. She knew now why he had drawn on the outlaw gang. He had been a lawman at the time.

Rose heaved herself off the rough bench, interrupting Blaze's grim thoughts. "Get my jacket, honey. I've got to start home," she said. When Blaze brought her the well-worn garment, Rose said, "Keep an eye on the stew; give it a stir once in a while. After you put the potatoes and onions in it, let it simmer another twenty minutes; then rake the coals from under it. Just before it's time for the men to come in from work, make your skillet bread."

"I'll walk with you a piece," Blaze said, grabbing up her shawl. She was not ready yet to lose Rose's company. She'd have nothing to do the rest of the day but sit on a stump watching the squirrels gather nuts and berries for the coming winter.

When Rose and Blaze came to the edge of the clearing where David and James were felling more trees, they paused to say good-bye. "You know, Blaze, I've been thinkin' as we walked along that maybe you could get that job of lookin' after the rancher's cabin and child. You're a fine young woman and it pains me to hear the womenfolk talkin' about you."

Blaze looked at her friend with wry amusement. "And you don't think they would talk about me if I moved in with the rancher?"

"Some would. There's always the gossipmongers who would bad-mouth an angel. But the majority would say that you were doin' an honest job, earnin' your keep. And the little girl would be there."

"I'm sorry, Rose, but I'm determined to make a new life for myself. If I'm to do that, from now on I must guard my reputation." She felt that eventually the gossip about her would die down, but not if she were living with Hunter Ward.

Rose left her then, saying that she would be back soon to instruct her in making a venison roast.

Blaze remained where Rose left her, watching David and James cut down a huge tree. After a few minutes she turned and walked back to the campsite. It was time she peeled the potatoes and onions.

For the first time since his return, Hunter had not risen with the sun. Enjoying his late start, Hunter yawned, folded his arms behind his head and stared up at the ceiling. From the main room of the cabin came the chattering voice of his little daughter, who still didn't have a first name. He simply called her Little One, and the woman called her some Indian name when she spoke to her, which was seldom.

*I've got to give her a name*, he thought, *and get rid of that woman*. New Moon kept hinting that she would like to share his bed and she became more sullen each time he ignored her.

But where was he to find a woman to take over his household and his little daughter? That was the question he'd been asking himself for the past three days. All the settler women were busy with their own homes and families, and none would allow their single daughters to live with an unmarried man. The thought had come to him that the mothers were trying to force him into asking one of their daughters to marry him.

A sour smile curved his lips. Once had been enough for him.

"There's one woman you haven't asked," a voice inside him said. "And she has no mother to say no to you."

"And who might that be?" Hunter asked suspiciously.

"You know who. The one you dream of most nights."

"That one! Never! I would never let my daughter be raised by a whore."

But even as Hunter rejected the possibility, his loins stirred at the thought of the little beauty sharing his home. There was no use in denying it anymore. From the first time he saw her sitting between two outlaws, he had been attracted to her. And that attraction had grown stronger every time he saw her. If he should ask her to be his housekeeper, his child-tender, he doubted strongly if he could keep his hands off her.

When Hunter heard New Moon suddenly break out in a spate of angry words, followed by the sound of a slap, he sat up. The wailing of his daughter had him leaping out of bed.

The scene he came upon brought his blood to boiling. His little daughter sat on the hearth, her small hands gripped tightly in her lap while huge tears rolled down her face. One cheek showed the fingerprints of New Moon's hand. He realized for the first time that his child was afraid of the woman and that this wasn't the first time the girl had been struck.

Hunter picked the small body up, and, holding her against his chest, demanded in a furiously cold voice, "Why did you slap my daughter?"

"She no eat all her mush."

"Maybe she didn't want any more."

"In my village food is not wasted."

"Well then, you eat that lumpy mess and the food won't be wasted." He gave the woman a threatening look as he said, "Don't ever lay a hand on this child again."

The sullen-faced woman made no response, but her black eyes glittered angrily. Nevertheless, Hunter felt sure she wouldn't strike his daughter again.

He sat down in a chair and stroked the girl's tangled curls, speaking soothing words to the little one until her sobs quieted to hiccups and then faded altogether. With her head snuggled on his shoulder and her thumb in her mouth, Hunter stood up and carried her into the kitchen. He set her down at the table, where she watched him silently and curiously as he built a fire in the range and fried a good amount of bacon and scrambled five of the dozen eggs he had bought at Bridger's store the day before.

When Hunter placed the child's share in front of her, she only stared at it, although he could see her swallowing hungrily. When he lifted a spoonful of the eggs to her lips she obediently opened her mouth and accepted it. The way her face lit up as she chewed told Hunter she had never tasted eggs before. Nor bacon either, judging by the way she went after it following her first taste.

Half an hour later, when Hunter prepared to leave the cabin, the little girl clung to his leg, her clutching fingers telling him that she was fearful of his leaving. He swung her into his arms and, stroking her smooth cheek, he gave the pouting New Moon a warning look as he said softly, "Daddy won't be gone long, and New Moon won't ever strike you again." He knew the child didn't understand his words, but he guessed his tone had reassured her, for she made no objections when he placed her feet on the floor and kissed the top of her head.

On his way to saddle the stallion, Hunter met

the carpenter who two days before had started on the bunkhouse for the cowhands he had hired. They were all men who had been let go by other ranchers when their roundups were over. He was late starting his roundup, and a lot of hard work lay before him and the men. It would take them at least a week to cut out the best of the steers, which had become as wild as mountain goats over the past five years.

"I'll have the men's quarters ready around noon, Hunter," Kile West, the carpenter, said after greeting him. "All I have to do is build the beds and hang the door."

"Fine. I'll hustle to the fort and have Bridger send out what furnishings I need. The men will be arriving tomorrow," Hunter said, and walked on to the barn.

As Hunter saddled Saint he thought of the men he had hired. They were good, experienced hands used to long hours in the saddle, lightning storms and blinding blizzards. All were thankful to have employment in the winter months.

A humorous thought lifted the corners of Hunter's mouth. Like most cowboys they would probably be loquacious and full of trickery played on each other. His drover, though, Clay Southern, was none of those. He was a tall, muscular man with a slightly hooked nose and keen blue eyes that held a cold glint. There would be no tricks pulled on him.

Hunter led the stallion outside and swung himself onto its back. He had two errands to run. One he didn't mind, but the other he dreaded like a nagging toothache. He turned Saint's head in the direction of the fort. His first act would be to purchase a couple of tables and a dozen straight-backed chairs, bed linens and a potbellied stove.

It took Hunter only a half an hour or so to attend to his business with Bridger. Then with a long sigh, he reluctantly left the fort and headed in the direction of the Wilsons' claim.

On the ride to the fort he had racked his brains to see if he had overlooked some woman who would be willing to work for him, but he had finally given up. There remained only one other woman he hadn't asked.

The one called Blaze.

It was true she was no better than a whore, but there was something about her that made him think she was a cut above other women who sold their bodies. She was well spoken, with a voice that was almost musical. He hoped she liked children and would be good to his daughter. Somehow, he thought she would be. He couldn't rid himself of the notion that there was a certain innocence, a goodness, about her.

*What makes you so sure she'll agree to work for you?* he asked himself. *She doesn't even like you, and she's sure to know how lonesome a ranch can be.*

Hunter didn't bother to answer himself. He was sure the woman would jump at the chance to get out of her covered wagon before winter set in.

\* \* \*

Hunter heard the sound of chopping as he neared the Wilson place, and he soon spotted the brothers at work clearing a patch of land. They were stripped to the waist, and as the sun glinted on the corded muscles in their arms and shoulders he reluctantly admitted they were fine specimens of manhood. He had heard at the fort how they had driven Blaze's wagon to Fort Bridger, and that she was now living out on their claim. He wondered which one of them slept with her, or if perhaps they both did.

Hunter grew angry with himself for letting his thoughts bother him. Why should he care what arrangements the brothers had with her? There was one thing for sure though: when she started keeping house for him, she could forget about the brothers, or any other man, for that matter. He would have no carrying-on in front of his daughter.

As he guided Saint through the stump-scattered ground, Hunter spotted Blaze bent over a steaming pot, dropping something into it. Her russet curls were pulled back and tied with a ribbon at her nape, and her face wore a rosy glow from the heat of the fire. He thought he had never seen a more beautiful woman, and he had seen many in his duty as a marshal.

The thick covering of pine needles deadened the sound of the stallion's hooves, and he was almost upon Blaze before she became aware of his presence. She looked startled for a moment; then, scowling at Hunter, she demanded, "What are you doing here? I'm sure that you know the men are clearing land down by the river."

Hunter's hooded eyes skimmed over her proud, firm breasts, and he felt a stirring in his loins as he pictured his hand splaying over one of the mounds, his fingers caressing its pink tip.

He mentally shook the image from his mind and hurriedly slipped out of the saddle before he had an arousal that she could see. "I saw them," he said, the reins looped over his arm. "I'm not here to talk to them. It's you I've come to see."

Blaze placed the lid on the pot and, looking up at Hunter, said "I can't imagine what you would have to say to me. As you can see I'm busy right now."

Hiring her wasn't going to be as easy as he'd thought, Hunter realized, and figured he'd better soften his attitude. However, his smile did not reach his eyes as he said, "I'm here to make you a business proposition."

Perplexed curiosity narrowed Blaze's eyes. What was he up to? After a moment she said, "I can't imagine any kind of business we could enter into."

Hunter said, "I'm looking for a housekeeper and someone to take care of my daughter."

Blaze walked away from the cookfire and sat down on the tailgate of her wagon. "I heard that you've been having a hard time finding someone for that job. You must be desperate to want a woman like me taking care of your daughter. Aren't you afraid I'll contaminate her?"

Hunter felt his anger rising. She wasn't going to make it easy for him. His tone was sharp when he said, "She's still too young to pick up any of your bad habits." He let his gaze travel over the sagging canvas shelter. "I have a strong, sturdy cabin that will keep you warm when the winter comes and the snow piles up past your knees."

Blaze was tempted to tell him that she didn't live in the tent, that the wagon was her home. But he wouldn't believe her, she knew, and why should she have to defend herself to him? So, with a toss of her head, she said, "James and David are going to build a cabin before winter sets in."

Hunter shrugged his shoulder contemptuously. "They're not going to have time to build more than a one-room shack."

"You're mistaken. They already have the trees felled."

His only response to her lame remark was a pitying look.

Blaze bit back a bitter laugh. The answer to how she could support herself had just been presented. But could she bear the strain of keeping house for a man whose every look was contemptuous? Also, despite his sneering words and looks, she had seen raw desire in his eyes a couple of times. How long would it be before he wanted her to share his bed? And there was the child to consider. Could she take charge of his little girl?

Hunter shifted his feet impatiently. "Well," he practically growled, "what's your answer? I'll pay you well."

"If I take you up on your offer I'll see to that," Blaze answered smoothly. "But I've got to think on it. Come by tomorrow morning and I'll let you know my decision."

Hunter's face darkened. What was she up to? She should be tickled to death that she was being offered a respectable job and a warm cabin with plenty of good food.

He knew, however, that there was nothing he could do but go along with her. There was no one else he could ask and she knew it. After glowering at her a moment, he said as he swung onto the stallion's back, "I'll see you in the morning then."

Blaze watched him ride away until he disappeared into the forest. She turned back to the stew then, chewing thoughtfully on her lower lip.

# Chapter Four

"Say, this is fine stew." David smiled across the table at Blaze that evening. "You're going to spoil us if you keep cooking like this."

"I can't take all the credit for its tastiness," Blaze hurried to say. "Rose Hackett has been giving me cooking lessons. I'm going to try my hand at roasting venison for tomorrow night's supper."

"Hey, I'll look forward to that," James said.

No more was said for a while as the hungry men fed their appetites. Then James looked up from his plate and said, "We saw that uppity rancher talking to you. What did he want?"

Blaze laughed. "You won't believe it, but he came to offer me a job."

"What kind of job?" James frowned. "I can't imagine he wants you to punch cows."

Blaze shook her head. "He wants me to be his housekeeper, and to look after his daughter."

"Why would he ask you? Wouldn't he want a woman with more experience?"

"According to Rose Hackett, he can't find anyone else to work for him."

"Are you going to take the job?" Both men watched her closely.

"I haven't made up my mind yet. I'm only now learning how to cook a little, and I know even less about children. I doubt if I could please the mighty Hunter Ward."

"If he's desperate enough to get someone to watch his child, he's not going to be too fussy about how you cook," David pointed out.

James chuckled and kept on grinning. "What's tickled you so much?" David asked as he helped himself to more stew.

"I just thought of a proposition Blaze could put to the rancher."

"What's that?"

James looked at Blaze. "Tell Ward that you'll take over the running of his household and the tending of his child if he marries you first."

"Marries me!" Blaze's disbelieving laughter floated into the night. "I'd be the last woman in the world he'd ever marry."

"I don't think so," James said. "You've got him where the hair grows short. He needs a woman in his house and you're his last hope. You might be surprised how fast he'll take you up on it."

"And he wouldn't have to pay a wife wages," David added with a teasing grin.

"He'd like that," Blaze said sardonically. "I'd be his unpaid slave."

No more was said on the subject until the men were leaving the table and David said, "Give some thought to our advice, Blaze. All he can do is say no. If he agrees, you'd have a nice comfortable, secure future. That's more than a lot of women ever get."

"You'd be surprised how many marriages take place without a speck of love between the man and woman," James added.

"And surprisingly most of those marriages work out fine," David said as he followed his brother into their tent. "Just take our example. We haven't even met the women we're planning to marry."

Blaze sat at the table, finishing her coffee, mulling over the advice she'd been given. Even if she got up the nerve to demand marriage from Hunter Ward, she was sure he would give that sneering laugh of his and refuse her. David and James didn't know what contempt he held for her.

Of course she could take his offer of a job and muddle through it somehow. She had been tempted to accept as soon as he asked her. The only thing that had held her back was his low opinion of her. It would be hard to live in the same house with a man who had no respect for her. And once she moved in with him, her reputation would be destroyed with everyone else in the area, too.

Blaze's lips turned down. But what choice did she really have? She desperately needed a job and a place to live. If she demanded marriage of Hunter, at least her reputation would remain intact.

Somehow, that counted for a lot. She was tired of being an outcast, an outlaw's daughter. More than anything she wanted to fulfill her grandfather's dream of a new beginning. Just maybe, marrying Hunter was the way to do it.

Hunter awakened to a drizzly rain. His daughter stirred beside him but didn't wake up as she snuggled closer. He smiled tenderly as he stroked her tangled curls, hair that had never known a brush or comb. His thoughts drifted to the green-eyed Blaze. He wondered what her answer would be. He hoped she would say yes, for, like it or not, she was his last hope.

He heard the mantel clock in the main room strike seven, and he eased out of bed, careful not to awaken the little one. He might as well get it over with, learn what Blaze had decided.

Blaze saw him coming, sitting proud in the saddle. The courage to demand marriage from this hard-faced man almost deserted her. She felt sure he would give that jeering laugh of his, turn on his heel and leave.

She worried the frayed collar of her dress with nervous fingers. Did she want to jeopardize her only chance of living in a warm cabin this winter by making demands of him? On the other hand, how could she sabotage the fresh start her grandfather had wanted for her by ruining her reputation?

She sighed heavily as she heard the sound of a horse's hooves approaching. Still undecided what to say to him, she parted the canvas curtain of the covered wagon and jumped down to the ground. Hunter gave her a curt nod in greeting as he climbed off his stallion.

A tiny frown wrinkled Blaze's forehead. She had planned to offer him a cup of coffee but dismissed the thought as he stood frowning impatiently at her, water dripping off his black slicker.

Giving her a surface smile he asked, "Well, what's your answer? I have a lot of work to do today and I have no time to stand around making small talk. You need a roof over your head; I need a woman to tend my daughter—I'd say this is the perfect solution for both of us."

Blaze knew at that instant what she was going to say to the overbearing man. Lifting her head proudly, her eyes meeting his straight-on, she answered, "I've given your offer a lot of thought." Hunter's look of serene confidence was replaced with total disbelief when she said, "There's only one way I'll keep house for you and tend to your daughter, and that is as your wife."

Hunter's whole body stiffened. "Surely you're joking," he barked. "What you're asking is ludicrous. Why should I marry you?"

Although Blaze cringed inside at his insulting words, she made herself shrug indifferently and say coolly, "Ludicrous or not, that's the only way I'll move into your home."

Hunter glared at her, his stormy eyes saying that he despised her as he said with a sneer, "Why marriage? Won't either of the brothers marry you?"

She forced herself to come up with a plausible lie. "Either one would gladly marry me, but I want something better than this. I like the idea of being mistress of a large ranch. Besides, if I'm your wife, you can't kick me out when you no longer need me."

That Hunter was furious was evident in the way his face became hard and tight. Blaze was a little frightened by the ice in his eyes, but she stood her ground.

"You're a mercenary little bitch, aren't you?" He spun around, his fists clenched at his sides. As she waited for him to mount his stallion he surprised her by turning around and grating out, "All right. You've got me over a barrel and you know it. I'll stop by Reverend Bellows's house and make arrangements. Be ready this afternoon."

With those bitter, angry words, Hunter sprang into the saddle and jammed his heels into the horse's sides. Blaze watched him ride away in the rain, wondering if she was about to make the biggest mistake of her life. The big rancher would make her life miserable. She had seen the threat of it in his stormy gray eyes.

Filled with a chaos of emotions, Blaze scrambled into the wagon, grabbed her slicker, pulled it on and jumped back out into the rain.

As she hurried along to where David and James

continued to work in the wet weather, Blaze wondered if she would have time to ride to the Hackett farm and ask Rose to stand up with her.

She scrapped that idea almost as soon as it was born. Rose lived five miles away. She wouldn't have time to ride there and back. The dreadful man had said that he'd be back this afternoon, and she didn't dare not be ready whenever he showed up. He was so reluctant to marry her, he might just ride away if she wasn't ready and waiting for him. She couldn't risk that. She was surprised at how relieved she felt that he'd agreed to marry her. She had wanted a permanent home ever since she could remember, she realized, and above all she yearned for security. She would sacrifice the love of a husband to have that.

Blaze was wondering what to wear to be married in as she approached David and James in the act of felling a large cottonwood. As she paused a safe distance away to watch the tree come crashing down, she told herself it didn't matter what she wore, theirs was a sham marriage. Certainly the groom wouldn't notice what she had on.

When the ground beneath her feet stopped shuddering and the pine needles and debris settled down, David and James looked up and smiled at Blaze. "What brings you out in the rain?" David asked, leaning his ax against the trunk of the cottonwood that had just been brought down.

"Something that you won't believe." Blaze's eyes sparkled through her rain-wet lashes. "Mr. Arrogant has agreed to my demand for marriage. The wedding is going to take place sometime this afternoon."

"You're joshing us!" James propped his ax next to David's. "He must have put up one hell of a fight."

"Did he ever. My ears are still tingling from the insults he dished out. I guess he really needs a housekeeper and a child-tender."

"Maybe," David said thoughtfully, "but I'm thinking it was more than that. You're very good to look at, Blaze, and it will be no hardship for him to share your bed."

Blaze's green eyes blinked. It hadn't occurred to her that Hunter might want to sleep with her. As her husband, he would have the right to demand it of her.

Blaze shook her head. She would feel like a whore, giving herself to a man she didn't even like, especially one who thought so poorly of her. Before they spoke their vows it was imperative that she make it clear there would be no bed sharing. It wouldn't be honorable to give him that news after they were married.

She looked at the brothers with frosty eyes. "I'll not be sharing his bed," she said sharply. "It's bad enough that he'll be getting free labor. He's not getting my body as well."

"Good for you, Blaze," David said. "Take care of his house and his child and let him take care of his urges somewhere else. He won't have a problem in that department. I hear that women are always panting after him."

It surprised Blaze that she felt a jealous twinge at David's words. Surely she didn't care how many women Hunter Ward slept with, she told herself. Her only concern was that he didn't sleep with her.

While they talked the rain had stopped falling. When the sun broke through a cloud James joked, "Happy is the bride the sun shines on."

"Hah!" Blaze snorted. "I'm not expecting any happiness as a bride. All I'm interested in is a secure future, having a permanent place where I can put down roots and live a normal life."

"Had you and your grandfather traveled around a lot?" James asked.

Blaze nodded. "More times than I care to remember."

When Blaze didn't offer any more information, James respected her obvious wish not to discuss her past life and changed the subject. "We'd better start trimming this tree," he said, picking up his ax. "I expect you'll want to start getting ready for the ceremony."

"I may go just as I am." Blaze skimmed her gaze over the everyday garb she wore: her rain slicker, a faded dress and scuffed shoes.

David chuckled, knowing she wouldn't do that. He went along with her though and said with tongue in cheek, "You might comb your hair, though."

Blaze saw the twinkle in his eyes and had to laugh. "Go chop down another tree," she ordered.

Both men grew sober then. "It's been a pleasure having you around, Blaze," James said. "We wish you the best in your marriage, but if you ever need us for anything, or a place to come to, you know where we are."

Tears glimmered in Blaze's eyes. "You two are like brothers to me. I don't know what I'd have done without you. If ever I can help you, no matter in what way, I'll be there for you."

She kissed each man on the cheek, and with no further words, turned and walked back toward her wagon.

"What do you think, James; will marriage work between those two?" David asked as they watched Blaze leave.

"I've got a feeling it will, after a while. It's going to be mighty rocky at first, though. It's gonna take that proud rooster a while to realize the gem he was lucky enough to marry."

"He'd better damn well treat her right while he's learning," David said as he swung his ax into the cottonwood trunk. "I'll beat the living hell out of him if he doesn't."

"I think that Blaze can hold her own with him." James grinned, picking up his ax.

After giving it a lot of thought, Blaze felt it wouldn't be respectful to God not to look her best in His house.

While she was looking over her wardrobe, choosing her best dress, Hunter was talking to Reverend Otto Bellows.

"Hunter, do you think you're doing the wise thing, marrying this woman?" the preacher asked.

"With the exception of Rose Hackett, the settler women won't have anything to do with her. Can you forget that no one knows anything of her past, that she's been living with the Wilsons almost since she and her grandfather joined the wagon train?"

The old man was her grandfather? Hunter was shocked to hear that. He asked the preacher the same thing he had asked himself. "What happened to the old man?"

"He died along the way. The wagon master said that he was too old to have started the trek across country in the first place."

When Hunter felt a stirring of pity for the young woman who had been left alone among strangers, he reminded himself that she must not have been too broken up over the old man's passing. She had taken up with the brothers to keep her "company" along the way.

He looked at the reverend and said coolly, "It's not a love match, if that's what you're thinking. I don't care if the womenfolk accept her or not. You must know how I've been looking for a woman to take care of my daughter and have had no success. The child only speaks Arapaho, and I'm not at all pleased with the way the Indian woman treats my daughter. I've discovered that the little one is afraid of her. Blaze is my last hope, and the only way I can get her is to marry her."

"What if a few years down the road you meet a woman you fall in love with and want to marry?"

Hunter barked a bitter laugh. "I'm not afraid of

that happening. Falling in love once was enough for me. I won't be bitten by that bug again."

"Do you think this woman will make a kind and loving stepmother for your daughter?"

Hunter nodded his head. "I sense a gentleness in her. She appears to be educated, and in that respect she'll be ideal. She'll not only teach my daughter English but she can also teach her how to read and write."

"Well,"—Bellows sighed—"I see you've made up your mind. Bring the young woman to the church around one o'clock and we'll get it done. My wife Eartha and our handyman can be witnesses if you don't have any of your own."

"I don't and I'm sure she doesn't," Hunter said on his way to the door.

"Remember to change your clothes, Hunter," the preacher called after him. "You're taking your vows in God's house."

Hunter didn't bother to answer as he swung onto Saint's back. Of course he would change into clean clothes, but by hell he wasn't going to wear his suit. He'd been forced into this marriage. As far as he could see, there was no cause for celebration.

Back at the ranch, Hunter set two big pans of water on the stove. As he waited for them to heat he played with his tiny daughter, teaching her a few words of English. He smiled proudly, finding her very bright. She readily caught on to the words he had her repeat after him.

He ignored New Moon, who watched him and the little one with dark disapproval. It gave him great satisfaction to know that by the end of the day the woman would be out of their lives forever.

When steam began to rise from his bathwater, Hunter took the big tub off the back porch and carried it into his bedroom. He noted that New Moon watched his every move, and after he had prepared his bath he closed the door and latched it. He wouldn't put it past her to brazenly come into the room and watch him bathe.

Twenty minutes later Hunter pulled on a pair of woolen trousers, followed by a pair of handcrafted boots that had cost more than a cowhand's monthly wages. After shrugging into a blue flannel shirt, he buttoned it up and tucked the tail into his waistband.

When he finished brushing his hair he started to strap on his Colt. He paused and hung the holster back on the bedpost. A man didn't wear his gun in church.

Feeling naked without his Colt he stepped into the kitchen and took his jacket off the peg beside the door. After slapping the wide-brimmed black hat on his head, he kissed the top of his daughter's head and left the cabin.

As Hunter rode toward the Wilsons' claim, he felt no excitement over the event that would take place shortly. He recalled how anxious he had been to marry his daughter's mother, and a sour smile twisted his lips. The thrill of marrying that one hadn't lasted long.

How long would this marriage last? he wondered. Probably not very long. His bride-to-be was man-crazy, just as Jenny had been. She, too, would soon grow tired of the remoteness of the ranch, of seldom seeing anyone but himself and his daughter. Maybe Rose Hackett would come visiting once in a while, but none of the ranch wives would come around, or the homesteader wives.

Come to think of it, none of the neighbor women had ever come calling on Jenny either.

A long sigh escaped Hunter. If this new wife would only hang around long enough to teach his daughter English, and until she was old enough to be left alone, he would be grateful.

Twenty minutes later Hunter arrived at the Wilson campsite. He frowned down at the quagmire of mud. As he was thinking what the muck would do to his expensive boots, the flaps on the covered wagon opened and his intended stepped down onto the three split logs that had been laid down to make a crude porch.

He stared, and kept on staring. She must be the most beautiful woman in the world, he thought as his gaze ranged over the simple dress she wore. But its simplicity only emphasized the way the bodice clung to the thrust of her breasts, her tiny waist and the gentle flare of her hips. A row of tiny buttons ended at the low-cut neckline, and she had tied a green velvet ribbon around her waist. Her glorious hair hung down her back in loose curls.

If only she were as beautiful inside, he thought.

Dragging his gaze back to her face, he felt angry at himself for being so moved by her beauty. "I see you're ready." he said brusquely. "It's unusual for a woman to be on time. Were you afraid I'd change my mind about tying myself to you if you weren't ready when I arrived?"

"No, I wasn't afraid of that," Blaze snapped, stung that he had guessed her fear. She took the jacket folded over her arm and pulled it on. "We both know I'm your last hope. I'm ready because when I have something unpleasant to do, I want to get it over with as soon as possible."

While Hunter glared down at her, Blaze added the words she'd been dreading to speak. "There's something we must discuss before we make our vows."

"Look, if you think I'm going to pay you wages as well as marrying you, you can discard that idea right now." Hunter's eyes hardened. "I'm not paying you a thin dime."

"I don't want your blasted money." Blaze gave him a scornful look. "Nor do I want you in my bed. I hope you get my meaning."

Hunter's eyes widened a fraction. He hadn't realized until now just how much he had been looking forward to having her in his bed. The thought of her soft curves was infinitely alluring.

But by God, she'll never know that, he thought, disappointed that the attraction wasn't mutual. "The last thing I want to do is share a bed with a wife who has been other men's whore. But put this in your mind and keep it there. If I see the Wilson men, or any other men, hanging around the cabin, you'll be gone so fast it'll make your head spin. If necessary I'll advertise for a woman in another state to come take care of my daughter."

Blaze pushed back the rage that threatened to blind her and managed to say as calmly as possible, "I won't be able to control who comes to the ranch, but they won't be allowed to come inside. And now, here's something for *you* to keep in mind. The first time I hear that you're whoring around I'll pack my clothes and go back to James and David. It's bad enough that the women gossip about me. I will not be a laughingstock among them."

The hard lines around Hunter's mouth deepened. The little witch was driving a hard bargain. Would he be able to adhere to her demands? He wasn't a doddering old man, after all. He sighed inwardly. For his child's sake, he'd do the best he could.

He was silent for so long, Blaze began to think that he had changed his mind about marrying her. She was ready to go back into the wagon when he spoke.

"I agree to your wishes," he said in a hard tone, "but there is one thing I will not tolerate: neglect of my daughter. She's been unloved since she was born and badly needs affection. If she doesn't receive loving care from you, out you go. She's the only reason I'm entering into this farce of a marriage."

Blaze's tone softened a bit as she said, "I admit that I don't know anything about children, but I would never be cruel to a child."

Hunter studied her beautiful, earnest face a moment, then said gruffly, "Let's go get it over with then. I've got work to do."

At any other time he would have seen to the saddling of her mount so that she would not ruin her slippers in the ankle-deep mud. But she had him so riled he couldn't think straight.

As he lifted the reins and Saint moved out, Hunter heard a low, peculiar whistle. He looked over his shoulder and saw her saddled horse come trotting from behind the tent. He watched in amazement as the big, mean-looking stallion came right up to the makeshift porch so that all Blaze had to do was swing into the saddle.

She gathered up the reins and gave him a smile that said, "I don't need you for anything."

Hunter glowered at her, then urged Saint into a ground-eating lope, trying not to think of all he would be missing by agreeing to this marriage in name only.

# *Chapter Five*

Hunter was still in a temper when they arrived at the church. Ignoring Blaze, he swung from the saddle, tied his mount to a cottonwood branch and strode toward the small building. The act told her to get used to such treatment from Hunter Ward. Every chance he got he would let her know his low opinion of her.

There was one thing he didn't know about her, though. She had never been pampered. From an early age she had been expected to more or less look after herself. And that included taking care of whatever mount she had been given to ride at the time. The gang changed horses often so that the law wouldn't recognize them by the mounts they rode.

It had pained her each time she had to give up

one of her pets, and when a young mare was given her, she loved the little animal so, she refused to give her up when Garf Mullen said it was time for new mounts. She wondered what had become of the little mare she had named Beauty.

Tying Garf's stallion beside Hunter's mount, she patted his neck. She had grown quite fond of the stallion, and he of her. He had only been used to the outlaw's rough treatment and he had taken to her gentle touch right away. And he was very intelligent. It had only taken a short time for him to learn to come to her private whistle.

She had given Grandpa's horse to James and David, as well as the two mules that had pulled their covered wagon across country. The brothers had refused to take the animals until she said they were a wedding present.

Blaze hoped that Beauty was in good hands as she gathered up her skirts and picked her way through the spongy mud. She wished she had the courage to ask Hunter if he knew what had happened to her. She doubted that he would tell her, even if he knew.

She would also like to know if his shot had killed Garf Mullen. But she knew if she asked him that he would make some sneering remark that would tell her nothing. In the meantime she would have to live on tenterhooks, wondering if the outlaw was alive and maybe looking for her.

As she walked toward the church she forgot about Garf Mullen. Her nerves tightened. Did she really want to tie herself to a man who clearly intended to make her life hell? Was she ready to commit herself to this hard, ruthless man?

When she could think of no other alternative, she took a deep breath and stepped inside the house of worship.

As she walked across the creaking floor, her skirts brushing against the rough benches on which the parishioners sat every Sunday, her eyes focused on Hunter. He stood with a man and woman in front of the altar, his stance saying clearly that he was impatient to get the marriage over with, to get back to his ranch.

When she reached his side and he remained silent, she held out her hand and said, "I'm Blaze Adlington, Reverend Bellows."

The portly, balding man smiled at her and shook her hand. "But not for long." His eyes twinkled at her. "When you leave here you will be Mrs. Hunter Ward." He pulled the plump little woman forward. "This is my wife, Eartha. She will be your witness."

The kind-looking woman gave Blaze's face a close scrutiny. Then smiling warmly, she said, "Well, the gossipmongers have one thing right. You are a beauty, Blaze Adlington."

Blaze smiled shyly. Realizing that she had a friend in Eartha Bellows, she settled down a bit. She slid a sideways glance at Hunter and saw by the dark look that had come over his face that he wasn't pleased with the warm welcome she had received from Reverend Bellows and his wife.

She was wondering what difference it made to

him whether or not the preacher and his wife liked her when the church door opened and a tall, thin man came clomping down the aisle. A warm smile lit up his face when Eartha said, "Blaze, this is John, our handyman. He's going to be Hunter's witness."

After Blaze and John shook hands, Bellows stepped up on the tall dais and, opening his much-used Bible said, "You can take your places now."

As Blaze stepped forward to stand beside Hunter, his resentment and dislike of her were almost palpable. Her nerves began to tighten again as she waited with gripped fingers for the ceremony to be over with.

The preacher was taking his time, however, giving this unlikely pair the same attention he'd give any couple. But finally he was asking the question that would tie her to the man who stood beside her with clenched fists. "Do you, Hunter Ward, take Blaze Adlington to be your lawful wife, to have and to hold from this day forward, to love and cherish till death do you part?"

There was a long pause, and Blaze wondered if Hunter was remembering the day he'd stood in this same spot marrying the woman he loved. Finally he muttered gruffly, "I do," and she wanted to laugh hysterically. Never in a million years would Hunter Ward love and cherish her.

When Reverend Bellows asked her a similar question, her answer was so low he asked her to repeat herself. This time she spoke her "I do" too loudly.

When Hunter was told, "You may kiss the bride now," he pretended not to hear Bellows, and, leaving Blaze's side, he asked, "Where are the papers we have to sign?"

The preacher and the witnesses looked uncomfortable at his rudeness and gave Blaze a sympathetic smile when it came time for her to write her maiden name for the last time. Finished, she laid the pen down next to the inkwell and turned around.

Eartha hugged her and kissed her on the cheek. "He'll come around," she said gently. "For the most part men remain thoughtless boys. So, in the meantime, while Hunter is growing to know your worth, try to ignore his churlish behavior."

Blaze blinked back the wetness that had gathered in her eyes and said, "Thank you so much for your kindness, Mrs. Bellows."

"Call me Eartha, child, and come visit me whenever you're feeling low." A warm twinkle touched her brown eyes. "If I do say so myself, I bake the best cookies in the area."

"I'll do that, and you come visit me," Blaze said, near tears at Eartha's kindness. "But I warn you, I probably bake the worst cookies in the area."

Eartha's merry laughter rang out. "We'll have to take care of that. I'll share my cookie recipes with you. Now, you'd better hustle along before your new husband goes off and leaves you."

When Blaze stepped outside she found that Eartha's prophesy was almost true. Hunter was several yards down the muddy trail leading away from the church. She was muttering about his behavior when the handyman appeared at her side and boosted her onto the saddle.

"I expect Hunter is anxious to get back to his ranch," he said in apology for her husband's actions.

"Probably," she said, and gathered up the reins. She wasn't about to explain that Hunter's hurry was to put distance between himself and his new wife.

Keeping several yards' distance between the two mounts, Blaze gazed at snowcapped mountains, pine forests and grassy meadows that teemed with cattle. It's a beautiful country, she thought, and hoped that she wouldn't have to leave it for a very long time.

When she brought her attention back to the trail, she saw that Hunter had reined in at the top of a knoll. Riding up beside him, she looked down at a shallow valley.

"My spread," Hunter said, pride coloring his tone.

It was on the tip of Blaze's tongue to correct him, to say, "You mean our spread," but then she thought better of it. He would only give her some scorching answer and they'd be off on another argument.

She fastened her gaze on the buildings below and thought that Hunter had a right to sound proud. Everything looked so neat and tidy, so unlike the tent house where David and James were living. She immediately felt guilty for comparing the canvas shanty to the buildings below. Hunter had been married when he'd erected the buildings, and naturally he had wanted everything to be nice for the woman he loved. There was even a white picket fence enclosing the yard, which had recently known the bite of a sickle.

But strangely, other than the smoke rising from the chimney, there was no sign that anybody lived there until the door opened and an Indian woman stepped out onto the porch that ran the length of the cabin.

"Let's go," Hunter said, his voice tight, making Blaze wonder what had suddenly angered him. Was it because she hadn't praised his ranch? Well, she thought, he'll wait a long time before he gets any compliments from me, when all he has to offer are insults.

They reined in outside the fence, and as Hunter swung to the ground and opened the gate, he demanded sharply, "Why isn't my daughter outside getting some fresh air?"

"Why you bring white woman here?" New Moon ignored his question.

"The white woman is my wife," Hunter answered as he stepped up on the porch. "You can go back to your village now. I won't be needing your services anymore."

An angry, sullen gleam shot into New Moon's black eyes. "No go back to village," she said stubbornly. "Stay here."

"No, you won't stay here," Hunter said impatiently. "My wife will take care of my daughter

82

from now on." He pushed open the cabin door and added, "There are a few hours of daylight left. You'll have plenty of time to get home before dark."

When Hunter disappeared inside the cabin, and the Indian woman remained on the porch, Blaze hurriedly dismounted to follow him. She didn't want to be left alone with the scowling woman. She felt the searing heat of black eyes as she, too, entered the cabin.

The first thing that assaulted Blaze's senses was the dimness of the room, the stale air and the pungent odor of bear grease. As New Moon brushed past her, going to a corner in the room where a pallet of furs lay on the floor, Hunter went through the cabin opening shutters and raising windows. When fresh air and sunshine streamed into the rooms he nodded his head in satisfaction.

Blaze was taking off her jacket when a childish voice cried, "Papa!" and a small body rushed across the room and threw itself at Hunter. She could only stand and stare at the transformation that came over his face as he swept his daughter into his arms. The harsh look on his features was replaced with a softness she hadn't thought possible.

Stroking the snarled blond hair, Hunter said, "Look at the pretty lady who has come to look after you. Can you say hello to her?"

Big eyes the color of Hunter's peeked at Blaze a moment, then were hidden against Hunter's chest.

"What is her name?" Blaze asked, coming

closer, frowning at the condition of the child's hair.

Hunter looked disconcerted for a moment; then he said uncomfortably, "She hasn't been named yet."

"Hasn't been named yet?" Blaze stared at him in disbelief. "How could that be? It's my understanding that she's five years old. What do you call her?"

Hunter looked away from the indignant green eyes and muttered, "I call her Little One."

Blaze studied the delicate little body clinging to the big man, and after a while she said, "Her name will be Rebecca. We will call her Becky for short."

"That's a nice name," Hunter said quietly.

"It was my grandmother's name." Blaze gently stroked a scruffy little leg hanging over Hunter's arm. "Will you let me hold you, Becky?" she asked gently.

When the child made no response, only curled closer to her father, Hunter said gruffly, "She doesn't understand English. I want that rectified as soon as possible."

"What kind of father are you?" Blaze looked at him contemptuously. "How could you go off and leave a strange woman to raise her? How did you expect her to learn her own language?"

Although Hunter knew he deserved Blaze's scorn, he hid his guilty feelings beneath a dark glower as he said sharply, "It's none of your business what kind of father I am. Just do what I was forced to marry you for. Keep my house clean, cook my meals and teach my daughter to speak the white man's language."

Gently untangling the little arms from around his neck, Hunter set Becky on her feet. "I have to get to work," he said shortly and stalked out of the room.

His daughter stood where he had placed her, fear in her wide eyes. Blaze knelt down to her level and said softly, "Are you hungry, Becky?" When she received no answer, only an apprehensive look, Blaze patted her stomach and made motions as though she were eating. She received a shy smile and a nod of the blond head.

Blaze stood up and, taking the little one by the hand, said, "Let's go see what we can find for lunch."

In the kitchen, Blaze found very little in the cupboards, at least nothing that her scant knowledge of cooking could transform into a meal. She was taking down a can of peaches when she felt a tug on her dress. Turning around she saw Becky grinning up at her. "What is it, honey?" she asked, and was pulled toward a door that she had thought led outside. But on opening it she was surprised to find a well-stocked larder.

As her eyes raked over bins of potatoes, turnips, apples, and winter pears, a covered crock and a basket of eggs, Becky, her eyes sparkling, pointed up at a slab of bacon hanging on a hook next to a sugar-cured ham. Blaze took down the bacon and started to leave the small room, but Becky pulled at her skirt again and, nodding at her eagerly, pointed to the eggs.

"So, you like bacon and eggs, do you?" Blaze playfully tweaked her little button nose.

Back in the kitchen again, Blaze cut the smoked meat into slices thin enough to fry. It took her a while because she'd never done it before. All the while Becky sat at the table, smiling and nodding, urging the beautiful woman on. The task was finally done and, setting aside the meat, Blaze tackled the challenge of building a fire in the big black range. Using the same method she had used many times in building campfires, she soon had a fire heating up the range.

Altogether it took about forty-five minutes to make the lunch she finally placed on the table. When Becky attacked the bacon and scrambled eggs like a starved animal, Blaze's first instinct was to wash the girl's grubby little hands. But the child seemed so hungry, she let it go. That could come later, along with a nice warm bath.

Becky had almost cleaned her plate when New Moon came into the kitchen carrying a sack that evidently held her belongings. She ignored Blaze but, muttering something in her language, gave the child a dark look. Fear jumped into the girl's big gray eyes and the little body trembled. Enraged that the sullen woman would take out her anger on a helpless child, Blaze jumped to her feet. Grabbing New Moon by the arm, she practically threw her out the door.

Brushing off her hands, she turned back to

Becky and saw that the little girl wore a wide, pleased smile as she jabbered away in Arapaho. Returning her smile, Blaze said, "That's the last of her. And now I'm going to give you a bath."

As though she understood what Blaze had said, Becky nodded her head vigorously. Tenderness of a sort Blaze had never known before came over her. The little one was so anxious to please. Had the Indian woman treated her badly?

The two large pans of water Blaze put on the stove were soon warm enough for Becky's bath. Blaze found a tin bathtub on the back porch. Bringing it into the kitchen, she poured the water into it. "Now," she said, lifting Becky to stand on a chair, "when I get this filthy garment off you we're going to make you smell sweet and fresh."

Apprehension filled Becky's eyes as Blaze lifted her and set her in the tub. As the water rose past her waist she gave Blaze a fearful look. Blaze gave her a reassuring smile as she dropped a yellow bar of soap into the water. Not wanting to leave the child unattended while she went searching for a towel and washcloth, she reached up under her dress and untied the strings to her petticoat. Tearing a strip off the ruffle when it fell to her feet, she folded the piece and placed it over Becky's eyes. She then took Becky's small hands and placed them over the cloth.

The little one obediently kept them in place and Blaze began to soap her tangled, dirty hair.

After three latherings and rinsings she felt the baby-fine hair was clean and proceeded to bathe

the little body she felt sure had not been bathed very often.

Now, she wondered as she finished drying Becky with her petticoat, what was she to put on the child? Certainly she couldn't wear the dirty rag she had taken off her. She hadn't seen any other little clothes in the cabin. For goodness' sake, the baby hadn't even worn bloomers.

Blaze's anger and disgust grew toward the man who had so neglected this precious little being. She would give him a piece of her mind when he came home.

She pulled a chair up close to the range so that its heat reached the shivering little body and went searching for something the child could wear.

The first bedroom door she opened was obviously Hunter's room; his clothing was strewn about the floor. She walked over to a tall chest and started opening drawers. In the bottom one she came upon a good-sized square of blue silk that she imagined had once belonged to Becky's mother. She thought it strange that this piece of cloth was the only evidence that a white woman had ever lived in the cabin.

In the kitchen she found a pair of scissors, and with Becky watching her every move, she cut a hole out of the material. When she eased it over Becky's head, the little one chortled her pleasure as the silk settled around her body.

Rummaging through the drawer again she found a thin strip of leather and tied it around the small waist to keep the sides together. After she had dragged the tub of dirty water onto the porch and dumped it, she returned to the kitchen.

She dried Becky's hair and combed it with a side comb from her own hair, then set her down at the table, saying, "Now we'll see about teaching you some English."

She began by touching the child's small nose and repeating the word until Becky, a knowing light in her eyes, touched her nose and said gleefully, "Nose."

More than an hour was spent in going over every feature on the small face. When they stopped for the time being, Becky could say and understand the words *lip*, *ear*, *chin* and *hair*. Smiling her satisfaction, Blaze kissed her clean, sweet-smelling cheek and lifted Becky to the floor.

With Becky trotting along behind her, Blaze went to check out the cabin that would be her new home. For a while at least, she silently amended.

Surprisingly Blaze found all the rooms tidy enough, discounting the thick layer of dust covering the furniture and the cobwebs in the corners. All the window coverings hung limp, and she imagined they hadn't been washed from the time they had been hung.

"I can see that tomorrow will be laundry day," she thought out loud, then laughed when Becky nodded as though she understood every word. Blaze ruffled her silky curls and added, "I'll also see about getting you some clothes."

As Blaze had hoped, she found a broom leaning in a corner next to the wood bin. From the dust accumulated on it, she felt pretty sure it hadn't been used in years.

She swept out the two bedrooms and main room, and then with a sigh she attacked the kitchen, the dirtiest room in the house. The Indian woman hadn't been careful about not tracking mud into the house.

Vigorously wielding the broom, Blaze swept trash and clumps of mud toward the open door. She looked up just in time to see Hunter get hit in the shins by two fist-sized clods of dirt.

"What was that for?" he exclaimed, glowering at her.

Blaze ignored him, pausing only long enough for him to enter the kitchen and step out of her way. He opened his mouth to say something, but Becky came bolting into the room calling, "Papa," as she flung herself at him.

The same transformation came over Hunter's face. The hard lines softened and a warm glow came into his eyes. He swept Becky into his arms, exclaiming, "Just look at you!" When she finished hugging him around the neck and leaned back in his arms to beam at him, he said, "That's sure a fancy dress you're wearing."

Her eyes sparkling, Becky touched his nose and said proudly, "Nose."

Hunter swung a surprised look at Blaze, who had resumed sweeping. "Does she understand what she just said?"

Blaze nodded. "Touch the rest of her features."

Slowly, holding his breath, Hunter laid a finger

on the round little chin and Becky responded with a loud "Chin." When with a wide smile he had gone over her face and she clearly pronounced the name of each feature, he laughed and hugged her to his chest.

"I can't believe that she learned all those words in such a short time."

"She's very intelligent," Blaze said, then after a pause added, "And very much in need of clothing. The only dress the child owns was the filthy tunic I tossed into the fireplace. She wasn't even wearing bloomers."

A look of disgust came over Hunter's face. Thanks to his going off and leaving her, his girl had been sadly neglected. Thank God he was getting a chance to make it up to her.

He reached into his pocket and pulled out a roll of money, placing it on the table. "Why don't you take her to the fort and buy whatever she needs," he suggested, wanting to make amends for his earlier neglect.

But Blaze gave him a scathing look. "Am I to take her there in that scrap of silk, with her little bottom bare?"

"Hell, I don't know," Hunter said in exasperation, running lean fingers through his hair. It seemed that no matter what he did, he was damned in Blaze's eyes. "What if I stay here with her and you go to the fort and buy what she needs?"

"Do you mean you'd trust me with all that money? Aren't you afraid I'll take off with it?"

Blaze's tone was sarcastic.

"You wouldn't get far before I caught up with you," Hunter retorted, aggravated by her sarcasm. Why did her disapproval bother him so much? he wondered.

Blaze reached out and took the money from him. Then, shrugging indifferently, she said "I'll go as soon as I finish sweeping."

Hunter had his daughter in his lap, teaching her new words, when a short time later Blaze pulled on her jacket in preparation for her trip to the fort. She was at the door when Becky, with a small cry, scooted off his lap. Running to Blaze, she threw her small arms around Blaze's knees, pleading with her in Arapaho words.

Although Blaze didn't understand the child, it was clear that Becky didn't want her to leave. She picked the agitated little one up and, gazing into the tear-bright eyes, said gently, "I'll be back."

After looking intently back into Blaze's eyes, Becky stopped crying, and her lips curved in a wide smile. She giggled when Blaze gave her a big smacking kiss on the cheek before standing her back on the floor. As she ran to crawl back onto her father's lap, Blaze walked out of the cabin without a glance at the frowning, puzzled Hunter.

# Chapter Six

Deep in thought, Hunter absentmindedly stroked his daughter's clean, shiny hair. He had just discovered a new side to his wife. A child, like an animal, was seldom fooled by an adult. It was plain that Becky had accepted her new stepmother wholeheartedly.

But was that a good thing? he asked himself, half worried and half jealous. Already his daughter was preferring Blaze to him. She would suffer when the woman left them, which of course she would do. The lonely ranch life and the hard work would soon have her clearing out just as Jenny had done.

A disturbing thought struck Hunter, one he quickly pushed from his mind. Becky might not be the only one who would hate to see her go.

He looked down at the curly head resting on his shoulder, the tiny fingers playing with the buttons on his shirt. There was one consolation, though, in this mixed-up affair. In the meantime his daughter would learn to speak English. As for himself, he was too confused about his feelings for Blaze to know how he would feel when she left.

The one thing he did know was that it would not be easy to live in the same house without acting on his growing desire to make love to her.

When Blaze walked into the fort's storeroom, its owner looked up from wrapping a length of material for one of his three women customers.

"Howdy, Mrs. Ward," he said, giving her a gap-toothed smile. "What can I do for the new bride today?"

As one, the three women whipped around and stared at Blaze as though they misunderstood what the old ex-trapper had said. Her shoulders squared and her chin lifted proudly, Blaze approached the counter, returning Bridger's smile.

"I've come for some material also," she said.

Sliding her a sly look, Bridger asked, "Would you like a length of this calico I just cut off for Mrs. Hank?"

Blaze suspected, rightly, that the old man had deliberately posed that question, sensing that she wouldn't like the bright-flowered material and would say so.

She flicked a disparaging glance at the bolt of cloth and said, "No, thank you. It's too gaudy."

She heard the women gasp and she laughed inside. She had finally got back at them a little.

Bridger managed to hide his grin as he said, "Why don't you go over there where I keep the dry goods and pick out what you like?"

Although the shelf holding the dry goods was at the other end of the room, Blaze could still hear the women expressing their opinion of her marriage to the most eligible bachelor in the area.

"Whatever possessed Hunter to marry *her* when he had our decent young girls to choose from?" Mrs. Hank said.

"Well, as you know, he's used to layin' with whores, so I guess it's not surprising that he'd marry a woman who knows all the tricks of pleasing a man in bed," one of the other women replied. "Don't forget that she lived with the two Wilson men on the trail here, then stayed on with them. Don't think for a minute that they lived together as brothers and sister."

"I am surprised, though, that Hunter would want a loose woman taking care of his daughter," Mrs. Hank said.

"I guess when lust hits a man he don't think of anything else," the third woman put in.

Before the three left the store they had declared that the marriage wouldn't last. By spring, they predicted, Hunter would tire of her and kick her out.

Her mind beset with rage, Blaze managed to choose five bolts of small print for little dresses, one of thin white muslin for bloomers and petticoats, and one of soft flannel for small night-gowns.

When she carried her choices to Bridger, he said as he unrolled a bolt, "I hope you didn't pay any attention to them gossipin' old hags. They're just jealous that you snagged the man they had their eyes on for a son-in-law."

Blaze wished that one of the women's hopes had been realized. She wouldn't be standing here now trying to keep her mind on clothing for a precious little girl that Hunter Ward didn't deserve to have.

After a short, bitter laugh, she responded to Bridger's remarks. "I got used to being gossiped about while on the wagon train. When my grandfather died I would have been left behind if James and David Wilson hadn't offered to drive my team. That made the women angry. For some reason they didn't want me traveling with them."

"It's because you're so blasted purty," Bridger said as he began measuring out the first piece of cloth. "If you was dog-ugly there wouldn't be one word said against you."

Blaze silently agreed that the good looks she had inherited from her mother had, so far, been the bane of her life. But, blast it, a person couldn't help how she looked and it shouldn't be held against her. She didn't speak her thoughts aloud, merely stood and watched Bridger continue to measure and cut off short dress lengths for Becky.

"Do you have needles and thread?" Bridger asked as he finished measuring and cutting.

Blaze had plenty of needles and thread, but they

were still back at the wagon along with her clothes. Whether Hunter liked it or not, she had to go get them. She couldn't forever wear the dress she'd been married in. Anyhow, it was now soiled and stained from cleaning the cabin. Also she needed clean underclothing. She wasn't about to go around with a bare bottom like poor little Becky had been forced to do.

She nodded her head in answer to Bridger's question, but added that she would like to look at some buttons and lace.

Bridger reached under the counter and brought up a tray of different-colored buttons. "I have to keep them hidden," he said, "otherwise the Indian women steal them. They like bright colors." He rummaged under the counter again and brought up a roll of narrow ribbon whose previous whiteness now had a slightly aged look to it. "I got this in when the first wagons started coming this past spring. I soon learned though that I had made a big mistake in orderin' the blasted stuff. Them homesteaders are barely able to buy food, let alone fancy lace.

"I'll let you have it cheap if you take the whole lot. I don't see any of the womenfolk around here buyin' any in the near future. Maybe next year when they've brought in a crop of grain and sold it."

As Blaze examined the lace she considered his words. She told herself she didn't care what happened to her nosy traveling companions. But then she thought of the children, of which there were many. She hated to think of any harm coming to them.

"I'll take it," she said after finding the lace strong despite its off-white color. "Becky will like it on her new dresses."

"Is that the child's name? I never heard that Indian woman call her anything. She just mainly grunted at her."

"The little one didn't have a first name until today. My first act as a stepmother was to name her. I named her Rebecca after my grandmother."

"That was right kind of you, Blaze, namin' her after one of your relatives. Who is with the little one now? The Injun woman?"

"No, her father is." Blaze grinned as she added, "Much to New Moon's chagrin, Hunter sent her packing a couple of hours ago."

"I bet she was hoppin' mad at that. She's had it real good the past five years, plenty of food and a good warm cabin. And she didn't take all that good care of the child either. The little girl always looked dirty and I don't think her hair was ever combed."

"How did you learn so fast about my marriage to Hunter?" Blaze asked as Bridger wrapped her purchases in a sheet of brown paper.

"Eartha Bellows was in earlier. She told me," Bridger said, securing the package with a piece of twine. "She was quite taken with you. She said that Hunter won't be able to put anything over on you. She'll be happy to hear how you've taken such an interest in Hunter's little tot."

"Hunter is very interested in Becky also," Blaze interjected in all fairness to her husband. "I'm sure he had no idea that his child was being neglected."

"A bit of warning, Blaze. Make sure you keep a sharp eye out when you're alone. Indians carry a grudge for a long time. I wouldn't put it past that New Moon woman to try to harm you."

Blaze slapped the side pocket of her full skirt. "I always carry my Colt outside the house and I always hit what I aim at. The Indian had better be careful if she tries anything on me." She grinned and added, "Anyhow, she wouldn't be able to slip up on me. I could smell her half a mile away. I just hope that I can get her smell out of the cabin before winter sets in and we have to keep the windows closed."

"Burn some pine knots in the fireplace for three or four days. The pine smoke will eat up the stink."

"I'll do that just as soon as I get home." Blaze picked up her package and turned to leave. Midway to the door it opened and New Moon stepped inside. Her stoic features revealing nothing, she walked up to the counter, the stench of bear grease emanating from her. Bridger looked at Blaze. Shaking her head, she mouthed, "No credit," before leaving the store.

She had just tied the package to the back of the saddle when New Moon came bolting through the door. When she caught sight of the white woman who had ousted her from her comfortable home, a killing look entered her black eyes. Blaze slid her hand into her pocket, curled her fingers around the Colt handle and waited.

The air grew tense as the two women faced each other, black eyes shooting hatred and green eyes coolly alert.

New Moon broke the eye contact first. As she stepped off the porch and faded into a grove of cottonwood behind the fort, Blaze heaved a great sigh of relief and swung into the saddle. She wasn't sure if she could have used the gun on her enemy if necessary. She had shot game many times, but to take a human life would be quite different.

As Blaze nudged the stallion into motion she put New Moon out of her mind and concentrated on pine knots. Where could she find some? Did she dare ask Hunter to get some for her? He seemed so unapproachable.

When Blaze arrived at the cabin, a little nervous that she had been gone longer than she had expected to be, she quickly dismounted, hoping that Hunter wouldn't be angry because he'd had to mind Becky so long. She knew he was needed out on the range. She unstrapped the package from the back of the saddle and pushed open the cabin door.

It was so quiet inside, she imagined that Hunter had taken Becky for a walk, to let her breathe some fresh air. As she laid her purchases on the table she became aware of how neat the kitchen was. The table had been cleared, with only the lamp sitting in its center. There was no cup or glass in the dry sink, and the frying pan she'd used to make lunch had been put away.

She walked over to the stove and felt the coffee-pot. It was almost hot. She hefted it and found that it was full. Hunter had recently brewed coffee. Had he done that with her in mind? Had it occurred to him that she would like a cup of the invigorating brew when she arrived home?

It didn't seem likely, yet there was no evidence that he had drunk any himself. She took off her jacket and scarf and frowned when she hung them on a peg next to Hunter's. If his jacket was there, where was he?

Almost in a panic, she hurried toward the main room, stopping short in the doorway. Hunter sat in his favorite rocker, Becky on his lap. Both were sound asleep. She walked softly across the floor and looked down at the pair.

How different Hunter looks when he's asleep, she thought. The hard lines around his mouth had softened, some strands of hair had fallen over his forehead and his thick lashes fanned out, almost touching his cheekbone. He looks almost boyish, she thought.

She glanced around the room and found it in the same immaculate condition as the kitchen. Even the ashes had been cleaned out of the fireplace and the hearth swept clean.

Blaze looked back down at Hunter and gave a start. His eyes were open and he was gazing up at her. "Hi," he said. "When did you get home?"

"Just a few minutes ago," Blaze answered, flustered at the softness of Hunter's tone. "It took me longer than I thought it would to pick out the material for Becky's clothes."

"I want to thank you for all you've done for the little one," Hunter said.

"It's no hardship to do things for Becky. She's a sweet little thing."

As though hearing her name, Becky opened her eyes and sat up. "Mama," she cried delightedly, using one of the first words Blaze had taught her. Scooting off her father's lap, she ran to Blaze. As she hugged Blaze's knees the look in her eyes seemed to ask, in the way of all children, what Blaze had brought her.

Blaze and Hunter burst out laughing. "Let's go into the kitchen and look through my packages. I believe I saw Mr. Bridger put a candy stick in one of them."

Hunter stood up and followed behind them. "I'm going to join the men now."

"Before you go, do we have any pine knots lying around?"

"There's a pile of them in back of the cabin. What do you want with pine knots?"

"I was told that if I burn them in the fireplace for a few days, I can get rid of New Moon's odor."

Blaze saw by the narrowing of his eyes that he was wondering who had told her this. But he didn't ask and she didn't tell him that his friend Bridger had told her. Was it possible that Hunter was jealous? she wondered.

When she heard Hunter ride away, she tied her shawl around her shoulders and, going outside, she walked behind the cabin. Her eyes were drawn to a large pile of weather-beaten, twisted knots of wood. She imagined they were an accumulation from the logs that had been cut down to erect the cabin. She picked up as many as she could carry. She would come back later with a basket to get more. If she wasn't mistaken, it would take half the pile to rid the cabin of the rancid bear smell.

Reentering the kitchen, Blaze found Becky where she had left her: sitting at the table nibbling on her candy. "You're a good girl," she said on her way to the main room. Most children her age, left alone, would have been running around, getting into mischief. It was plain that from an early age this little one had been taught, through fear, no doubt, to do strictly as she was told. As she tossed the pine knots into the fire she thought angrily how she would like to give New Moon a piece of her mind.

Dusting off her hands and glancing up at the clock, Blaze saw that it was almost six. She ought to start supper, but they'd had a late lunch. Did she have time to cut out one of Becky's dresses first? she wondered. And then there was the matter of riding over to the Wilson claim and picking up her clothes.

She grinned wryly. If Hunter should learn of her going there, he would be furious. He'd specifically told her to stay away from David and James.

Her eyes twinkled with a humorous thought. She would ask her jealous husband to go after her clothing. If he didn't want to make the trip himself, he would have to give her permission to go.

Blaze returned to the kitchen and spread a short piece of material on the table. If she hurried she would have time to begin a little dress before she had to start supper. One thing Blaze was adept at was the use of needle and thread. She had learned their use from Lucianne, the same woman who had taught her how to read and write and do sums. As she took scissors to the fabric, a pair she had found in a cabinet drawer along with other sewing materials, she wondered what had become of the woman who had treated her so kindly.

Having cut out the dress, Blaze took the pieces into the main room to sew them together. Becky sat at her feet, playing with the colored buttons that would go on her dresses. As Blaze's nimble fingers plied the needle she pointed out items in the room, having the child repeat the name for each object.

As the small garment began to take shape, the clock struck seven. Blaze hurriedly folded the dress and set it aside, unable to believe that that the time had slipped by so swiftly. Hunter would be home soon, expecting supper to be on the table.

What was she to prepare? she wondered, entering the larder. After scanning the shelf where the canned goods were stacked, she took down a can each of beans and peaches. Hugging them in the crook of her left arm, she picked out three potatoes from their bin. After carrying everything into the kitchen and placing the food on the table, she returned to the small room to choose meat to round out the meal.

Chewing thoughtfully on her lip, Blaze decided that she would have more luck preparing salt pork than the big piece of ham hanging next to it. As she hurried back into the kitchen, she had visions of the nice meal she could serve her husband.

Feeling quite pleased with herself, Blaze took a knife to the salt pork. When six uneven pieces lay on the table, she took out the frying pan she had used in making Becky's lunch, set it on the stove, and placed the meat in it.

Preparing the potatoes came next, and she cut her finger twice in her hurry to slice them. The sun had already sunk behind the horizon and Hunter would be home soon. She found another skillet in a cupboard and set it on the stove next to the salt pork, which had begun to sizzle. She scooped a lump of lard into the skillet, and while she waited for it to melt, she lit the lamp in the center of the table.

Blaze had just dumped the potatoes into the now hot grease when Hunter pushed open the kitchen door and stepped inside. He looked at the bare table and frowned. Having missed lunch, he was ravenously hungry and his temper was sparked by the fact that Blaze had apparently made little effort to have supper ready for him. She hadn't even gotten around to putting out the plates and flatware. She gave him a harried look when smoke began to rise off the frying meat.

"The meat is burning," Hunter pointed out unnecessarily.

"I know it is," Blaze snapped nervously, near tears, but not knowing what to do about the meat.

"Well, damn it, push it to the side where it's not so hot." Hunter's tone said that an idiot would know to do that.

Grabbing up a cloth to protect her hand from the skillet's hot handle, Blaze moved it as Hunter had advised. She was turning the almost charred meat to cook on the other side when he came up behind her and looked over her shoulder. After giving a disgusted grunt he asked, "Didn't you soak the meat first, get most of the salt off it? And hell, you didn't even cut the rind off."

"Look!" Blaze threw down the fork. "You might as well know now that I have just recently begun to learn how to cook."

"That doesn't surprise me." Hunter snorted. "In your past you took care of your men in an entirely different way."

Blaze felt a sickening lurch in her stomach. What had happened to the considerate man who had walked out of the cabin just over an hour ago? Why had he changed back to his cold, insulting ways? She was near tears. She had done her best, but it hadn't been good enough. Nothing she ever did would please her husband.

Hunter walked to the window, stared out a minute, then turned around. There was a strange reluctance in his eyes when he asked, "Just what was your position in that outlaw camp? Were you a whore to all of them, or just special ones, like the man Garf killed to have you?"

Blaze was so angry she was shaking. She lifted her chin and managed to say, "You'll never know, will you?" When Hunter only glared at her, she said, "I suppose you'll tell everyone where you first saw me."

"Of course not. I don't want everyone thinking that I married a common whore. But get this straight. If I ever hear that you're still spreading your legs, there will be hell to pay."

Blaze had had enough of his insults. The anger that had been building inside her erupted. She took two steps toward him, her arm uplifted to slap his face. But before her hand could connect with his cheek, Hunter caught her wrist in midair. She gasped when he jerked her up against his hard chest.

While she waited to see what he would do next, she felt the heat radiating from his body, smelled the fresh out-of-doors scent that clung to his clothing. There was a queer tightness about him when he ordered thickly, "Don't ever try to strike me again, Blaze. You won't like the results."

"Oh no?" Blaze panted as she struggled to free herself. "If I were a man, I'd beat the hell out of you."

"You think so, do you?" Hunter jerked her closer to him, so close she could feel the hard ridge of his sex pressing against her stomach, startling her. She couldn't believe that though he was raging mad at her he was still getting an arousal. When he said, "Other men have tried it, but none have succeeded," she stopped struggling. She had realized that the movement of her body was exciting him.

She contented herself with saying, "A man will come someday who will beat you into the ground. I just hope that I can watch it and cheer him on."

Hunter drew in a sharp breath, then released her arm and said contemptuously, "If your cooking doesn't improve, you'll be out of here by the end of the week, so I doubt you'll be seeing that beating. Unless, of course, you're planning to have one of the brothers try it."

"Hah!" Blaze rubbed her arm. "Neither one of them would dirty his hands on you."

"Since when have they became so persnickety? They've dirtied their hands on you often enough."

Blaze forgot caution. With fingers curved she sprang at him and brought her nails down across his cheek.

A deathly silence grew in the room as Blaze stared at Hunter in shock. As soon as her hand had connected with his flesh sanity had returned to her. There was a predatory look in the gray eyes that were now the color of storm clouds. She started backing away from him, flinging chairs in his path as he stalked toward her. He merely kicked them aside and continued to come after her.

Blaze's heart was thudding and her pulse racing when Hunter lunged across the table and grabbed her by her arm. Before she could attempt to jerk free he was around the table, both her arms now in his grip.

"Don't you dare hit me," she croaked, fear widening her eyes.

"Oh, I'm not going to hit you. I have something else in mind." His hard gaze fixed on her trembling lips. "I warned you not to strike me."

"You had it coming, saying such awful things to me."

"Is the truth too hard for you to handle?" Hunter demanded. Blaze opened her mouth to give him a rebuttal, and suddenly his mouth was on hers. She stiffened, expecting his lips to ravage hers, to extort his revenge in that manner.

But his lips, soft and firm, were loverlike, Blaze thought, experiencing her first kiss ever on the mouth. When he started tracing his tongue across her tightly closed lips, a thrill shot through her, and unconsciously she leaned into him. He groaned softly as he spread his legs far enough apart to pull her in between them. Her lips parted and he thrust his tongue into her mouth and bucked a hard arousal against her in rhythm with the movement of his tongue sliding back and forth.

When Blaze moaned her pleasure Hunter left her mouth and began to slide little nipping kisses down her throat. When he came to the barrier of her low-cut bodice he nudged the material off one bare breast with his chin. She gasped when he flicked his tongue over the hardened nipple, then closed his mouth over it.

He was suckling her greedily and she was mindlessly stroking her fingers through his hair when Becky came bolting into the room holding up her half-sewn dress.

"Papa," she cried excitedly, pointing at the dress.

Blaze and Hunter sprang apart, both breathing heavily. Blaze pulled her bodice back in place and Hunter fought to regain control of his body. That accomplished, he praised Becky's dress, his face and tone soft as usual when talking to her. "You'll look like a little princess when you wear it."

Blaze could only gape when Hunter turned his attention back to her, his face wearing its usual hard look. She flinched when he said gruffly, "When are you going to put that mess on the table? I'd like to eat before bedtime."

Shattered that their shared kiss hadn't meant anything to him, while it had set her blood on fire, Blaze muttered, "Supper will be ready as soon as I make the bread."

"Don't you realize that you're doing everything backward?" Hunter looked at her as though she were feebleminded. "You should have started the bread before you put the potatoes on. And you'd better stir them before they're burned also."

Tears were fighting to roll down Blaze's cheeks when Hunter picked Becky up and carried her into the main room. With blurred vision she hurried to stir up a batch of skillet bread. While it was frying she set the table. Fifteen minutes later she had supper on the table. She looked down at the burned meat and the scorched potatoes and dreaded calling Hunter to the table. The only thing that was edible was the bowl of peaches, the beans and the bread.

With a long sigh Blaze called out that it was time to eat. When Hunter and Becky were seated at the table, Hunter gave the meal a contemptuous look, and when his daughter reached for a piece of meat he stayed her hand. "You don't want to eat that, honey," he told her. "It would make you sick." He stirred a spoon through the bowl of potatoes, looking for some that weren't half-raw. The few he found he spooned onto Becky's plate; then he added a good amount of peaches and a piece of bread.

"This will have to do you for tonight, baby," he said, apology in his voice. "But you'll have a good supper tomorrow night if I have to make it myself."

With those scathing words ringing in Blaze's ears, Hunter slapped his hat on his head and stomped out of the cabin. A few minutes later she saw his shadowy figure astride his stallion ride past the window. He was headed toward the fort. As she picked through the potatoes, looking for some fit to eat, she couldn't blame him for going somewhere else for his supper. Her first meal as his wife was a disaster.

Later, as Blaze cleared the table and washed the dishes, she knew that she had to do something about her cooking. As she hung up the dish towel, she made up her mind to finish Becky's dress and a pair of little bloomers before she went to bed. Tomorrow they would visit Rose. If anyone could help her out of her dilemma it would be that kind lady.

When she had washed Becky's face and hands and put her to bed in the room next to Hunter's, the one she would occupy also, she went back into the main room and sat before the fire, sewing feverishly on the small clothes.

She was hemming the small dress and reliving what had happened between her and Hunter in the kitchen, how he had made her body throb in a way it had never done before, when a knock sounded on the kitchen door. Startled, she laid the garment down and stood up.

Should she open the door? she asked herself. What if Garf Mullen was still alive and had traced her here? She slipped quietly into the kitchen, and, standing to one side of the window, she peered outside. She relaxed.

It was James, her trunk resting on his shoulder. Delighted that she would have her clothes, even though she'd been unable to ask Hunter to get them, she flung open the door. She was just plain happy to see a friendly face.

"James, thank goodness you've brought me my clothes," she cried.

"I figured you'd be needing a change of clothes by now." James's eyes ranged over her soiled and wrinkled dress. "It looks like I brought your trunk just in time," he said with a grin, stepping inside.

"Where do you want me to put it?"

"Set it on the table for the time being. You might wake Becky if you take it into our room."

"So, the daughter is sharing your bed on your wedding night, is she?" James's eyes twinkled as he let the trunk slide off his shoulders onto the table.

"That's right," Blaze replied with a laugh. "She's much more appealing as a bed partner."

When in the distance the dim lights of the fort came into view, Hunter breathed a sigh of relief. He hoped the company of friends would put a stop to his thinking of the little vixen he had married.

He had made a big mistake back there in the cabin. If it hadn't been for his daughter walking in on them when she did, he'd have seduced Blaze right then and there. Never before had a woman aroused him as she did. He grew hard just thinking about her.

But one of the women at the whorehouse would take care of that, he told himself. Then he remembered his promise to Blaze. If she behaved herself, stayed away from the brothers, or any other man, he'd stay away from whores and such.

*Hell*, Hunter thought, drawing rein in front of the fort, *I'll be going around at half-mast all the time*. He only had to look at—or think of—his wife and he became as hard as a rock.

Dismounting and stepping up on the porch fronting the fort, he pushed open the door that had been closed against the sharp evening air. He glanced down to the end of the bar and nodded a greeting to three of the cowhands he had hired. A few feet separated them from the regular customers, friends with whom he drank and caroused. As he approached them he was spotted and one called out, "Hey, men, here's the new bridegroom."

"What are you doing here, Hunter?" another asked, making room for him at the bar. "Why ain't you home ridin' that little filly you just married and moved into your place?" he asked with a wide grin.

"He's probably had her on her back all day; ain't that right, Hunter?" a tall, lanky friend joked.

All but his hired hands laughed at the men's sallies, and they were thankful that they hadn't as a stillness, thick with threat, came over the room. The chill that grew in Hunter's eyes said that he didn't think the coarse bantering was funny. As one, the men, looking uneasy, turned back to their drinks.

"There's a little nip in the air tonight, huh, Hunter?" Bridger said, coming from the end of the bar to pour him a glass of whiskey.

Hunter nodded. "It was snowing up in the mountains today. It'll be working its way down here any day now." He took a swallow of his drink, then said, "Pour my cowhands a drink, Jim."

As general conversation was struck up, the tenseness left the air and everyone relaxed. It was now understood that the big rancher didn't want his wife discussed in a saloon, even if she didn't have a very good reputation.

When a frizzy-haired whore sidled up to Hunter and asked coyly if she could do anything for him, no one said a word when he answered brusquely "I'm not interested."

Bridger and his friends, however, silently arched their brows at each other.

An hour later, after being served a thick roast beef sandwich, Hunter told his men they could move into the new bunkhouse the following morning, then said good night to his friends.

As Hunter rode along beneath a full moon he tried to figure out why the whore hadn't stirred any desire in him. Even though he wouldn't have taken her to bed, he still should have wanted to.

It wasn't because he had suddenly became impotent, he knew. He had proof of that from the ache that still lingered in his loins. The one that another whore had stirred to life.

Was it possible that the little witch he had married had cast a spell on him? he asked himself. He snorted his disgust at such a foolish notion as a lamp from the cabin shone through the trees. Although she was beautiful beyond belief, his wife had no supernatural powers.

Ready to ride straight to the barn to stable the stallion, Hunter pulled Saint in and peered into the shadows of the two pines growing beside the cabin. He swore under his breath when he recognized the horse tied there as belonging to one of the Wilson brothers.

A film of rage clouded his eyes. One of them was

still fooling around with his wife. "I'll soon put a stop to that," he ground out, swinging to the ground. Hopping up on the porch he banged open the door and stood glaring at the couple, whose laughter froze in their throats.

Blaze gazed mutely at the flaming anger in her husband's eyes. If it were possible, he looked even more forbidding than when he'd stormed away. Swallowing nervously, she motioned to her trunk sitting on the table and said, "James brought me my clothes."

"I see," Hunter said coldly, his fists on his hips. "And what did you give him for doing this favor for you?" He started stalking toward James.

Her heart hammering, Blaze jumped between the two men as Hunter snarled, "That's a poor excuse to come hightailing it over here as soon as you saw me leave, Wilson. As her husband, I would have come after her clothes."

"Yeah, but in your own good time," James derided as he put Blaze from between them. "You're just ornery enough to enjoy making her wait a week or so for clean clothing."

*Oh, James,* Blaze cried silently, *don't antagonize him. He'll cut you to ribbons with his fists.*

She had barely finished the thought when Hunter's fist lashed out, hitting James flush on the chin. He went sprawling backward, taking a chair down with him. But in a flash James was on his feet, his fists held in front of him.

No words were wasted as the two men circled each other, alert to find an opening, to get in a blow at each other. Blaze noted for the first time the bulging muscles straining at the material of James's shirt. Hunter might not find it so easy to whip the young homesteader.

As she fervently hoped that James would be the winner, his fist shot out. It caught Hunter in the mouth, sending him stumbling through the door, which he had left open. Before she could catch her breath, James was out on the porch confronting Hunter as he got to his feet.

Blaze stood in the doorway, watching them circle each other again. Then James lunged at Hunter, sending them both out into the yard, out of her view. She peered through the darkness but couldn't make out who was winning the battle. Finally she saw one figure rise from the ground, leaving the other one lying on his back. When the figure walked toward the horse tied in the pines she knew it was James. Her gaze darted back to the figure sprawled in the mud.

So, she thought gleefully, Mr. Arrogance has finally met his match and I was here to see it. When she saw Hunter stirring, she stepped away from the door. She was picking up overturned chairs and putting them back in place when Hunter appeared in the doorway.

Hunter stood, swaying, disbelief on his swollen and battered face. With a harsh twist of his lips he said, "Well, it appears you have gotten your wish. That damned sod-buster has a punch like a mule's kick."

Hunter's right eye was fast swelling shut, and

though Blaze wanted to bathe his face, tend to the cuts James's fist had put on the handsome features, she didn't make the offer. She said instead, "I don't think you'll be so ready to sling your insults around him again. And so that you're forewarned, David is younger and stronger than his brother. You'd better watch out for him too."

Instantly regretting her outburst, Blaze hurriedly left the kitchen before he could make some insulting comeback. On her way to the bedroom she grabbed up her sewing and took it along with her. Hunter would probably order her to leave tomorrow morning and she wanted Becky to have at least one dress and a pair of bloomers to clothe her little body.

# Chapter Seven

Blaze awakened to the sound of Hunter moving around in the kitchen, and the events of the night before came immediately to mind. Would she get her walking papers today? she wondered. The thought of having to go back to the covered wagon filled her with dread. The evenings and mornings were bone-chillingly cold in the small canvas shelter. She didn't think it was possible to spend a winter in it.

Her eyelids felt gritty as she rubbed them. She had stayed up late finishing the small garments for Becky. She looked down at the child curled close to her side. Already the little one had found a spot in her heart, and it would be painful to lose her.

As Blaze lay staring up at the rafters in the ceiling, thinking back over the months that had brought so many changes in her life, the scent of frying bacon and brewing coffee wafted into the room. Saliva gathered in her mouth. The few potatoes she had eaten for supper had been digested hours ago.

She wondered how Hunter was feeling this morning and what his face looked like. She had heard him on the back porch the night before, washing his wounds before he stamped off to his room. Her lips curved slightly. He'd been mad as a salted gander, Grandpa would have said.

Finally it grew quiet in the kitchen and Blaze dared to relax a bit, to think that Hunter wasn't going to rap on the door and tell her to be ready to leave when he returned from his day's work. She was about to sit up when she heard his footsteps approaching her bedroom and her nerves tensed again. He was going to tell her to clear out of his life after all. She barely had time to close her eyes and feign sleep, when the door creaked open and his footsteps quietly approached the bed.

It seemed to Blaze that Hunter stood over her for an eternity as she made herself breathe evenly in and out. When she was sure she could pretend no longer, she heard him leaving the room and closing the door behind him. A sigh of relief feathered through her lips.

What had he been thinking as he gazed down at her? she wondered. Then she realized that he probably hadn't been looking at her at all. Most likely his attention had been on his daughter.

When the outside door closed Blaze left the bed, making sure the covers were tucked around Becky before she went into the kitchen.

Taking a cup from the cupboard, Blaze filled it from a full pot of coffee and sat down at the table. As she sipped at the strong brew she saw a plate of bacon and scrambled eggs keeping warm on the back of the stove. The sight told her that Hunter didn't have any faith in her giving his daughter a proper breakfast. *I can't much blame him*, she thought, *after that awful supper I put on the table last night*.

Plain and simple, if Hunter didn't tell her to leave today, it was imperative that she see Rose, for she had no idea what to make for tonight's supper.

Blaze had just made her own bacon and eggs when Becky, sleepy eyed and still wearing her makeshift dress twisted around her, walked into the kitchen. She gave Blaze a wide smile and, rubbing her stomach, said, "Eat."

Blaze picked her up and kissed her sleep-flushed face, thinking that the little one was making up for all the time she hadn't tasted American food. She carried her to the sink and sat her down on the drain board. As she gripped the handle of the pump fastened to the sink, she still thought it a miracle to have running water inside a dwelling. Hunter must have loved his dead wife very much to have done this for her.

When the water came pouring out, Blaze wet a washcloth and moved it over Becky's face and then did the same to her hands. Becky grimaced and complained, "Cold."

"Yes, it is cold," Blaze agreed, and gave the little body a hug before lifting her to the floor. "It will wake you up."

Blaze playfully tweaked her nose. "Now go sit down at the table now and I'll give you your breakfast." The child was catching on to English remarkably well, she thought, placing the plate her father had fixed in front of her.

As they ate the morning meal, Blaze pointed out and named knife, fork and spoon to her little companion. Becky quickly learned the words as she finished her breakfast.

Later, when Blaze began to clear the table, she said, "Stay where you are, honey, while I wash the dishes. Then I'm going to dress you in your new clothes. We're going to go visit a friend of mine."

She didn't know how much the little girl understood of what she'd said, but when Becky questioned "visit," Blaze felt that she had understood all but that word. She carefully explained the meaning of the word until Becky nodded her head, and with a wide smile repeated, "Visit."

Blaze had Becky dressed and was brushing her own hair when a knock sounded on the door. Who could that be? she wondered, half afraid as she laid the brush aside and went to peek out the window.

She gave a pleased smile when she saw her friend Rose standing on the porch. She threw open the door, crying out, "Come in, Rose. Becky and I were about to come visit you."

"So it's true what I heard at the fort yesterday," Rose said as soon as she stepped into the kitchen. "You have married Hunter Ward."

"I'm afraid it's true, Rose."

"But how did it happen?" Rose asked as she slipped off her jacket.

"Well," Blaze said, a twinkle in her eyes, "we rode over to the church and Reverend Bellows married us."

"Don't be a smart aleck, Blaze." Rose frowned at her. "You know what I mean. When I mentioned the possibility of working for Hunter, you acted like it was out of the question. Next thing I know, you've up and married him!"

"Don't you see, Rose, marrying him was the only way I could work for him. My reputation would have been blown to smithereens if I'd moved in with Hunter. I would never have been accepted by the womenfolk."

Blaze took Rose's coat from her and hung it on a peg next to her own. When they had both sat down she continued, "The morning after he offered me the job he came riding into camp and demanded my answer. While I was trying to decide what to say, he got real impatient and told me in that arrogant way of his that since he needed someone to watch Becky, and since I needed a roof over my head, it was a perfect solution for both of us.

"And that's when I lost my temper. I told him

123

that the only way I would move in with him was if he'd marry me." Blaze chuckled. "You should have seen his face. You'd have thought he'd swallowed a horsefly."

"I can imagine." Rose laughed, then turned serious. "Maybe . . . you know . . . sleeping together and all, you'll get along."

"Hah!" Blaze snorted. "I let him know right away that we wouldn't be sharing the same bed."

"Not sleep together?" Rose was shocked. "I've never heard tell of newlyweds not sleeping together. It's not natural. A man needs his . . . pleasurin'."

"Well, that proud rooster isn't going to get any *pleasurin'* from this hen."

Rose shook her head. "I don't see how this marriage can last."

"It may not last the day through," Blaze said quietly. "We had a big row last night. James Wilson brought my trunk of clothes over, and before he could leave Hunter came home. He was like a wild man, swearing at James, saying awful things to me. It ended up in a fistfight between them." A wide smile parted Blaze's lips. "I'm happy to report that James beat the stuffing out of my husband."

"Oh, dear!" Rose exclaimed. "Why do you suppose Hunter carried on like that? Do you think he was jealous?"

"I'm not sure." Then Blaze shook her head. "We had made a pact that neither of us would fool around with the opposite sex. I guess he thought

I was breaking my promise, even though James and I explained why he was here."

"Maybe, but I have a feelin' he was jealous of another man bein' around his wife."

Becky chose that moment to come from the bedroom and stand shyly in the doorway. Blaze smiled and motioned her forward. "This is my friend Rose, honey. Let her see the pretty dress I made you," she said when Becky came and leaned against her.

Becky's face lit up. Pulling up her dress until the matching underwear showed, she beamed and said, "Bloomers."

"They're just beautiful, Becky," Rose said warmly. "You look like a little doll."

When the child gave Rose a puzzled look, Blaze explained, "She doesn't know that word yet. The poor little thing has never had toys to play with. I must see to getting her some."

"You'd better put your order in with Bridger before winter sets in. I'm told that once it starts snowing, nothin' moves around here until spring arrives and the snow melts in the passes."

"I'll do it today. She needs a heavy jacket and some boots too."

"Blaze, how come you can sew so well and don't know spit about cookin'?"

"I grew up without a mother to teach me how to cook, and as for my ability with needle and thread, I more or less taught myself." She didn't explain that a prostitute had shown her how to make neat little stitches and that it had been her lot to mend the clothing of a bunch of outlaws, nor that out of neccessity she had always made her own clothing. She had never been allowed to go into the towns the Mullen gang avoided to do any shopping.

"When I heard that you had wed the rancher I thought to myself, Good Lord, all that girl knows how to cook is stew, skillet bread, flapjacks and coffee." Rose reached into the pocket of her white apron and brought out several sheets of paper. "I wrote down some of my favorite recipes for you to follow. They're not fancy, just dishes that men like. Good plain food that will stick to their ribs."

"You must have read my mind," Blaze said as Rose handed her the recipes. "The main reason I was going to visit you today was to have you do exactly what you've already done." She skimmed through some of the pages and then looked up at Rose. "I see I also have to get some supplies when I go to the fort. For instance, cornmeal."

"I thought of that too." Rose reached into her pocket again. "I figured that Indian woman wouldn't have anything in the house to make American food with. So I wrote down everything you'd need."

Blaze ran her gaze over the list and saw several things she wouldn't have thought of. "Rose," she said, "I don't know what I'd do without you."

"Oh, I'm sure you'd muddle through somehow." Rose stood up. "I've got to get home and help Jake with clearing me a garden patch for next spring." As she shrugged into her jacket she said, "When you go to the fort, ask Jim to loan you the catalog he orders things from. I looked through it once and I remember seeing clothing for children. You shouldn't have trouble finding a coat for the little one."

"I hope you're right. The only clothing the child had when I came here was a raggedy-looking deer-skin tunic."

Rose shook her head. "All I can say is that Hunter Ward has a lot to make up to that child. Going off and leavin' her to the care of a heathen Indian."

"Maybe he wasn't thinking straight when he left." To her surprise, Blaze found herself trying to defend her husband. "He was probably full of grief over losing his wife. He might have even blamed the child for a while."

"I wouldn't know, but I guess it's possible."

Rose had her hand on the doorknob when there came the musical jingle of spurs on the porch. She stepped back just in time to keep from getting hit as Hunter pushed the door open. As he stepped inside, Blaze saw the startled look that came over Rose's face. She shot a glance at Hunter herself and understood the reason for Rose's surprise.

Although the swelling had gone from his face, the bruised eye and the cuts on his cheek and chin said plainly that he had been beaten in a fight.

For Rose's benefit, Blaze thought, Hunter's hard look was gone. He looked quite pleasant as he said, "You must be Rose, Blaze's friend."

"Yes," Rose answered. "I just stopped by to wish you and Blaze a happy marriage."

"That's right nice of you, Rose. Thank you."

*You hypocritical polecat,* Blaze thought, *pretending that we have a normal marriage.*

As Rose again prepared to leave she said to Blaze, "Dress the little one up warm for your trip into town today."

"Give me your list and I'll go get what you need," Hunter offered.

Blaze was so surprised that Hunter would do this for her, she blurted out the first thing that came to her. "Thank you, Hunter. Becky doesn't have a coat, so I would have had to wrap her up in a dirty old blanket."

When she saw anger and embarrassment cloud Hunter's eyes, she knew she had unintentionally embarrassed him. She could almost hear him thinking that if his daughter had to be wrapped up in an Indian blanket to ward off the cold, he wasn't much of a father. That was the last thing she had meant to imply. But the look he shot her said that he would never believe any explanation she might give him later on.

Blaze watched Hunter pull a surface smile to his lips and say, "I'll go now. Where is your list?" When she handed him the paper that Rose had given her, he practically snatched it from her hand.

When Rose and Hunter stepped outside, Rose advised Hunter that he had best hitch up his wagon. "That supply order is too large to fasten onto your saddle. There's a month's worth of groceries and incidentals to purchase."

Hunter ground his teeth in silent frustration, sorry that he had softened and offered to make the trip into town. His men would be arriving any time and he had wanted to be on hand to tell them where to hunt for the half-wild cattle that they would drive into the holding pens he had erected five years before. He would lose over an hour making the trip to the trading post.

When he took leave of Rose he was seething inside and condemning his wife to the devil. She had delighted in putting one over on him.

When Rose and Hunter had gone, Blaze sat down at the table and began going over the recipes her friend had left with her. She would try one out for supper.

She settled on a beef roast—a big one, so that whatever was left over could be made into hash for tomorrow's supper.

As he was hitching a team of workhorses to the wagon, it occurred to Hunter that he would have to double some of the items on the list. Meat and flour, for instance. Hardworking cowboys consumed a lot of meat and bread.

That thought made Hunter want to whoop with laughter. *Ah, sweet revenge!* Wait until he told the little vixen that she would be cooking for an additional four hungry men. He would be getting his own back in spades. She'd be too busy and tired to slice her sharp little tongue at him. The fort had come in sight when Hunter saw his cowhands galloping toward him. Their faces wore wide grins as they drew rein around the wagon. "Did you think we wasn't goin' to show up, boss?" Clay Southern, his drover, asked.

Hunter returned the genial grin and said, "I'll be gone for a while picking up some supplies. In the meantime you can start combing the brake for the longhorns up near the foothills. And make sure you stay in the saddle at all times while you herd the cantankerous bastards. You chance being gored to death if you're on foot. They've been running free for five years and are as wild as deer."

"We know all about ornery longhorns," one of the hands said, and with a clatter of hooves they raced away.

Hunter watched them disappear over a knoll, thinking that they were good, tough horsemen. Time would tell if they were equally good at roping and branding.

Arriving at the fort a short time later, Hunter found Bridger standing on a ladder, stocking shelves. The ex-trapper and pathfinder turned his head at the sound of the door opening. Seeing his old friend staring up at him, he climbed down, explaining that a new wagonload of merchandise had been delivered an hour before.

"The driver said he'd be making one more trip and after that not to expect him until spring. I gotta tell the folks if they want to do any Christmas orderin' they're gonna have to do it in the next week or so."

Bridger went and stood behind the counter. "Do you want to purchase somethin', Hunter, or did you just stop by to do a little jawin'?"

"I don't have time to jaw today, Jim," Hunter said. "For the next two weeks I'm going to be too busy to draw a long breath."

"I hope you can get your cattle to market before the snow flies."

"That's my prayer every night," Hunter said, reaching into his vest pocket and pulling out Rose's list. "Can I borrow your pencil a minute? I want some of the items on this list doubled."

Bridger handed him a stub of a pencil and Hunter put a check mark in front of over half of the items Rose had written down.

Bridger ran a glance down the piece of paper and gave a low whistle. "How come you didn't send your cook in to pick up this stuff?"

"I don't have a cook," Hunter answered gruffly. "My wife will be doing the cooking."

Bridger looked up at him, surprise on his homely face. "That's gonna be a right smart bit of work for Blaze, ain't it?"

"She's young and strong. She can handle it," Hunter answered sharply, not liking the hint of censure in the old man's voice.

Bridger let the subject drop, and while he began to fill the order, Hunter ambled around the room looking at the newly arrived merchandise.

There were heavy sheepskin jackets, broad-brimmed hats, shirts and trousers, stacked on a shelf, gloves and boots, most anything a man would need in the line of clothing.

Then Hunter noticed a rack of children's clothing. Rifling through it he found a coat he thought would fit Becky perfectly. It was a bright red-and-white plaid, lined with rabbit fur. It also had a matching attached hood. It would keep the little one toasty warm on the coldest day. He looped the garment over his arm and, making his way back to the counter, he saw children's boots lined up against a wall. He pictured the size of Becky's foot in his mind and chose a pair he thought would fit her.

"Do you have any mittens for children?" Hunter asked the busy proprietor of the trading post.

"Yeah, I got a whole box of them here on the counter. Ain't had time yet to put them out. Go ahead and look through them."

After laying the coat and boots alongside the growing pile of supplies, Hunter chose a pair of mittens that would go with the coat.

When he had laid them on top of the jacket, Bridger reached behind him and picked up a much-used catalog. "It says on the bottom of your list that your wife wants to look through this. Maybe before you take it home you might want to look through it and pick out some Christmas gifts for the family."

Hunter leafed through the book, interested in spite of himself. When he came across a stunning dress that would show off Blaze's figure to perfection, he was almost tempted to place an order. But she was the one who had specified that theirs was to be a marriage in name only. How would she interpret such a gift from him?

As for Becky, what would his little girl want for Christmas? A picture book, maybe, to help her learn English?

Then his eyes caught on a page that was filled with toys. There were dolls, balls, stuffed animals, big hoops to be rolled and sleds. When Bridger had a small mountain of supplies on the counter, Hunter told him to order a sled for Becky.

Bridger laboriously wrote out the order, then, looking up at Hunter, asked, "Is that all? Nothin' for your wife?"

Hunter shook his head and grunted. "Can't think of anything she needs."

Bridger gave him a searching look but said no more. He managed to keep what he was thinking from his face when the catolog was pushed at him and Hunter said, "There's no need to send this along."

When everything was carried outside and stowed in the wagon, Hunter climbed onto the spring seat and picked up the reins. "I'll be sending someone in for more supplies next week," he said and slapped the reins over the team's back.

Bridger watched the wagon roll away, shaking his head. What a damn fool Hunter Ward was.

As Hunter neared the ranch he grew more and more nervous. He knew he would have a fight on his hands when he told Blaze that she would also be cooking for the cowhands. He grimaced. He would also have trouble with his hands once they ate one of her meals.

A glance at the sun told him that it was close to

133

ten o'clock when he drew the team to a stop in front of the porch. He could still get in a good day's work. When he opened the kitchen door and stepped inside, Becky ran to him and threw her arms around his knees. He picked her up and gave her a loud, smacking kiss that made her giggle. He looked at Blaze, who was spreading a large piece of flannel on the table.

"You'll have to move that," he said brusquely. "I need to put some of the supplies there."

When he walked back outside Blaze reluctantly folded up the cloth from which she had intended to cut out a nightgown for Becky. She stood back then and watched Hunter make trip after trip from the wagon, the piles of supplies growing.

When he started carrying in burlap bags of potatoes, dried beans and apples, and storing them in the larder room, she asked, "What did you do, double everything on the list?"

"Mostly. And I added some things that weren't on it."

"But why? That's an awfully large amount of food for just three people to consume. Unless, of course, it's for the entire winter."

After giving Blaze a look, a mixture of unease and challenge in his eyes, Hunter said, "There will be more than three people eating this grub. My four cowhands will be eating with us."

Blaze stared at Hunter in disbelief. "Are you saying that you expect me to cook for your help?"

"Exactly. Did you think that all you had to do was keep the cabin clean and play with Becky?

You're gonna earn your keep, young lady. Everyone carries his weight on a ranch."

Seething with indignation, Blaze said calmly, "Will you step outside with me for a minute?"

Hunter looked down at her, trying to read her mind. When her face showed none of the emotions that roiled inside her, he shrugged his shoulders and said, "I can give you a couple minutes. Then I've got to go help my men." As they walked out on the porch he added, "If you want to cuss me out, you could have done it inside. Becky wouldn't understand what you were saying."

"But she'd understand this," Blaze said furiously, and threw herself at him. Taken by surprise, Hunter was sent stumbling backward by the force of her attack, and before he could regain his balance, her hard little fists were pounding his chest, her booted feet kicking at his shins.

"Ouch! Damn it, that hurts." Hunter panted, trying to catch her hand, at the same time trying to keep out of reach of the blows to his shins.

"I meant for it to hurt," Blaze grated, breathing heavily.

"You little hellcat"—he gasped—"I don't want to hurt you but if you keep it up I'm going to have to restrain you."

"You lay a hand on me and I'll scream so loud they'll hear me at the fort," Blaze threatened as she continued to swing at him.

Hunter knew that she would do just that, and though she wouldn't be heard at the fort, his men could hear her. Once again, she had pulled one over on him. And since he couldn't catch her hands, all he could do was keep out of reach of her feet and let her pound on his chest until she wore herself out.

Finally Blaze stopped, out of breath. She glared at Hunter; then, turning on her heel, she walked back into the kitchen.

Hunter waited a minute and then followed her. He found Blaze sitting at the table, staring stonily ahead. Guilt stirred inside him. He no longer thought his plan for getting one up on her was funny.

He walked over to the worktable and pulled from the provisions a large paper-wrapped package. Folding back the wrapping, he laid bare a five-pound piece of beef. Giving Blaze a cautious look, he asked, "Could you please have this roasted and ready to eat by sundown?"

Blaze's only answer was to give him a scathing look, then turn her head away.

Hunter stood a moment, uncertain, wondering what she was thinking. When she kept her head averted, he quietly opened the door and stepped outside.

It gave Blaze great pleasure to see that Hunter had a slight limp. Evidently she had gotten in some telling blows.

# *Chapter Eight*

As Saint galloped toward the noise of shouting, swearing, and firing of guns, Hunter could feel his knee stiffening up. "That's all I need," he muttered, "a limp to go with my battered face."

Wry amusement twisted his lips. He had known many women in his adult lifetime, but none had ever attacked him. However, he thought, none had had cause to jump all over him.

Hunter's conscience began to bother him. He was taking advantage of his young wife. He knew that she didn't know anything about cooking. It was pure orneriness that had made him order her to cook for his hired hands, he admitted to himself. All the other ranchers had cooks to prepare the meals for the hired hands.

And there was Becky. Blaze was awfully good to

her, teaching her English, sewing clothes for her. Already the little one adored the new woman in her life. She was Blaze's shadow. And that his wife returned his daughter's affection was easy to see, for Blaze was not one to pretend. If she disliked her little charge she wouldn't try to hide it.

He wasn't sure why he was being so hard on Blaze. With his first wife he'd always acted the gentleman. And look where that had gotten him. He had no wish to repeat the heartache he'd known with Jenny. But if he didn't lighten up, he knew he would lose Blaze.

Strangely that thought did not sit well with Hunter. He pushed back the image of her sparkling green eyes and the recollection of her lips parted with longing as he kissed her.

He was berating himself for caring one way or the other when a cloud of dust churned up by men and bawling cattle came in view. He pulled his hat down low on his forehead in the hope that his battered face wouldn't be noticed.

Blaze was still fuming as she put the supplies away. If Hunter Ward thought he was going to use her like a workhorse, he could very well think again. Cooking for a bunch of ranch hands had never been part of their agreement.

When she had put the last item away, a bag of salt, she had come to a decision that would put an end to her ever cooking for the men after tonight. Hunter hadn't liked the supper she had prepared for him last night, and he was going to like what she put on the table tonight even less. But for now she was going to get back to cutting out Becky's nightgown.

Once she had the soft pink flannel cut out. Blaze took the pieces into the family room to sew together. As she stitched away, Becky sat on the raised hearth playing with scraps of the material left over from her gown, and Blaze planned her supper. When the clock showed almost two she laid aside the sewing and walked into the kitchen.

As she took a nearly new roasting pan from a peg driven into the wall, she thought to herself that Hunter's first wife hadn't cooked too many roasts. Certainly she hadn't cooked for ranch hands. But Hunter had loved her and no doubt anything she did, or didn't do, had been all right with him. She was a fool if she thought he would treat her the same way. In his mind she was only lowly help, and he apparently intended to let her know that every chance he got.

Disregarding Rose's written instructions on how to season the meat and let it roast at a low heat, Blaze put it in the roasting pan and shoved it into the oven. She straightened up, stood a moment, then fed more wood into the firebox. With a satisfied look on her face, she returned to her sewing. She didn't know much about cooking yet, but common sense told her that five hours in a hot oven would reduce the meat to a toughness that would be almost impossible to chew.

Becky's gown was almost finished when it was time to start preparing the rest of supper. Before

Blaze started peeling the potatoes she opened the oven door and looked at the roast. Her eyes glowed and a grin tugged at her lips. As she had expected, the meat was now half its former size.

When she had the potatoes boiling on the stove, she opened two cans of peas and set them to heating next to the other vegetable. Next she stirred up a batch of skillet bread, wondering when she would be able to try the sourdough bread she'd seen in Rose's recipes. She was determined she wouldn't try her hand at that until she was cooking only for her hateful husband and his daughter.

Blaze was sure that wouldn't be too long in the future as she tried piercing the meat with a fork and found it almost impossible to do.

But then again, she thought, she might not be able to bake anything more in the Ward home. Maybe she had gone too far in her revenge. The hot-tempered rancher might throw the meal out and her with it.

Dusk was settling when Blaze caught sight of Hunter and the men riding in. They all looked so worn out she felt a moment's guilt. It wasn't the cowhands' fault that her husband was a low-down polecat.

She watched the men unsaddle their mounts and then turn them loose in the small fenced-in pasture in back of the barn. When they gathered on the porch to make use of the soap and water Hunter had placed there that morning, Blaze, becoming a little nervous, began setting the table. When she heard Hunter tell the men to remove their spurs before entering the kitchen, she put the small roast on the table, grimacing as she added a bowl of lumpy mashed potatoes that she hadn't seasoned. Her nose twitched at the odor of burned peas as she dished them up.

Followed by his men, Hunter stepped into the kitchen and sniffed the air suspiciously. He looked at the meal awaiting them, then darted a dark look at Blaze. The mocking curve of her mouth told him that she had intentionally prepared a meal that was next to impossible to eat.

Damn her, how dare she embarrass him this way in front of his men?

A glance at his help, however, showed Hunter that they wouldn't even know what they were eating, they were so busy ogling the little beauty.

Annoyance creasing his forehead, Hunter begrudgingly introduced his men to her. The bright smile she gave them robbed them of speech, making them blush and shift their feet awkwardly. When she sat down at the table they all scrambled to sit next to her. Looking disgusted, Hunter took his seat at the head of the table. When the noise of scraping chairs subsided, he picked up the carving knife lying next to the roast.

Hunter wasn't surprised that he had to exert pressure on the blade in order to cut through the dry and tough meat. He shot Blaze a look that was so cold, she shivered inside. He looked as if he could cheerfully throttle her.

She managed to give him a sham apologetic

smile and to say sweetly, "You know I can't cook very well, Hunter."

"Yes"—his lips curled contemptuously—"we both know where your forte lies, don't we?"

In the thick silence that followed Hunter's remark, hot tears burned the backs of Blaze's eyes. It was the first time he had ever insulted her in front of other people. She stood up and, blindly taking Becky by the hand, led her into the main room. As she sat rocking the bewildered child, the tears escaping and running down her cheeks, the only sound coming from the kitchen was the clinking of knives and forks.

Back in the kitchen, Hunter was immediately sorry for his uncalled-for remarks to Blaze, and he pretended not to see the dark looks shot his way from his help. The men clearly sided with his wife.

It didn't take long for the men to choke down the meal that Blaze had taken great pains to ruin. When they wordlessly left the table, Hunter scraped the dirty plates. Then, gathering up the cups and flatware, he stacked them on the workbench, telling himself that the action was the least he could do to make up for his insults.

When he went to the main room and stood just inside the door, an uncertain look came over his face. Blaze didn't acknowledge his presence by word or look. Finally he said gruffly, "I'm riding to the fort to see about hiring a cook."

When Blaze made no response, and his daughter made no effort to come to him, Hunter turned and left the cabin. As he strode toward the barn he thought about what a fool he had been. He had learned early on that Blaze was a match for him when it came to outwitting each other. He should have remembered that she would seek revenge. But even had he remembered, he wouldn't have expected her to strike so soon.

And now, because of his reckless tongue, he had to hire a cook and install a range in the bunkhouse until he could get a cookhouse built. All a waste of his time. He wanted to have the cattle rounded up and on the trail within the week, so every hour counted.

"Why couldn't she have gone along with me until the cattle drive was made?" Hunter fumed.

"Probably because you didn't take the time, or give her the consideration, to ask her," his inner voice chastised.

When Blaze heard the kitchen door open and close, she put Becky on her feet, saying, "We'll have our supper now, honey."

The little girl smiled and rubbed her stomach. "Becky hungry."

"Me too." Blaze ruffled the child's bright curls.

In the kitchen she went to the range and took from the warming oven two plates of food she had prepared earlier for her and Becky. Each held a slice of ham, fried to a golden brown, a serving of smoothly mashed potatoes and a helping of peas she had taken from the pan before allowing them to scorch.

As she carried their supper to the table she saw

the dirty supperware Hunter had cleared from the table and stacked on the workbench. She curled her lips and thought scornfully, Does he think a small effort on his part is going to make up for his insult in front of his hired help? The only thing that would please her was if he got down on his knees in front of the men and asked for her forgiveness.

# Chapter Nine

As he entered the barn to saddle Saint, Hunter changed his mind about riding in to the fort to look for a cook. He was suddenly conscious of how tired he was, how sore his muscles were from being in the saddle all day. It had been a long and hard fourteen hours and he didn't look forward to climbing on the stallion again for another long ride.

Besides, his friends would insist that he have a drink with them, and considering the mood he was in he would probably end up having several drinks. And with another hard day coming up tomorrow he didn't need to have a growling stomach and a throbbing head.

Having decided to look for a cook tomorrow, Hunter was about to return to the cabin when he caught sight of his cowhands playing poker through the uncurtained window of the bunkhouse. Maybe he should join them, he thought, let them know he had a pleasant side to him also. He hadn't come off at all well during supper. If cowboys didn't like and respect the man they worked for, they didn't put their hearts into their job.

And God knew he needed their goodwill and all the support they could give him. As it was, it would be nip and tuck getting the cattle rounded up and ready for the trail before bad weather arrived.

As Hunter passed the wagon on his way to the bunkhouse, he saw the packages holding Becky's coat and boots lying on the seat where he had left them. He had planned to surprise the little one with them after supper but had forgotten in his irritation at the meal Blaze had forced on them.

Hunter wasn't entirely welcomed by the cowhands when he entered the bunkhouse. That was apparent from the stony looks he received when he pleasantly asked if he could join them for a few hands.

Finally the drover gave a curt nod of his head and Hunter took a seat that gave him a view of the cabin. He intended to play cards until all but the kitchen light went out. That would signal that Blaze and Becky had gone to bed. He didn't want to have any more run-ins with his wife. He always seemed to lose.

The stiffness gradually went out of the men as Hunter deliberately let them win all the hands.

They had warmed to him considerably by the time he saw through the window that only one light shone in the cabin.

"Well, men," he said at the end of a game, "you've cleaned me out. I'm gonna go hit the hay."

"I expect we should too," Clay Southern said, gathering up the cards into a stack and setting them aside. "We need our rest to fight them cantankerous longhorns again tomorrow. I wish we had a dog to scare them out of the thickets."

"That's a good idea for next spring," Hunter said. "I'll see about getting one."

A couple of the men followed him outside to relieve themselves in back of the bunkhouse. The good nights they called after him were pleasant enough, and Hunter smiled his relief. He knew, however, that if he were to regain their complete respect he'd have to be careful how he treated Blaze in their presence. They would be watching him.

"And I'll be watching them too," Hunter muttered as he retrieved the package from the wagon seat. Already the four men were half in love with the lovely Mrs. Ward. He'd gone down that path before, with Jenny.

Hunter took off his boots in the kitchen; then in his stocking feet he moved quietly about, stoking the fire in the range, then covering the glowing coals in the fireplace with gray ashes. With the packages under his arm, he silently entered Blaze and Becky's room.

He stood beside the bed, looking down at

Blaze's sleeping face bathed in the moonlight flooding the room. She looked so vulnerable, curled up on her side, her hands tucked under her chin. As usual he was amazed that she still had that untouched air about her.

*If only you were the way you look.* Hunter shook his head regretfully as he pulled the covers up over her bare shoulders and laid the packages on the foot of the bed before silently leaving the room.

When the ache in Hunter's loins settled down until it was bearable, he fell asleep, only to dream of a wife who would come to his bed pure and innocent. One that other men did not desire, and one who was quite content to be his alone.

Hunter awakened the next morning just as the sky was turning pink behind the mountains. Remnants of his dream still lingered in his mind in a hazy kind of way. Somewhere in his mental images the pure, biddable wife of his dream turned into the little high-spirited vixen he had married, and he had made such wild love to her he now felt as exhausted as if it had really happened.

After having had such a vivid dream of Blaze, Hunter wondered why he didn't have a full, hard erection. He slid his hand down past his belly and swore in disgust when his fingers became sticky.

"Hell"—he grunted—"this hasn't happened to me since I was a greenhorn kid."

He rolled off the bed and walked over to where a basin and pitcher stood on a washstand. He dared to hope, but doubted, that instead of dust he might find water in the pitcher. His first wife, Jenny, had never bothered to fill it.

Surprised and thankful, he found it full to the top. Also there was a bar of soap lying in a dish, and clean towels and a washcloth hung beside the oval mirror on the wall.

Filling the basin, he dropped the soap in the water and, working up a lather, he washed his face and hands. He was careful not to splatter the floor, for surprisingly Blaze had thoroughly cleaned his room and he liked it that way. If he were careless of it, she was ornery enough not to so much as make up his bed.

After he had soaped the washcloth and scrubbed his private parts, Hunter prepared to shave. He ran his hand over the stubble on his chin and jaw, then took a close look at his face in the mirror. He decided that the dark whiskers would help camouflage the cuts and bruises put there by James Wilson.

After running a comb through his hair, thinking that he needed to make a visit to the barber, he walked into the kitchen. His first act was to fire up the range and set a pot of coffee to brewing. He then went to the larder and brought back a slab of bacon. When it was sizzling in the skillet he cracked a dozen eggs into a bowl and whipped them together with a fork. Putting them aside until the meat was finished frying, he set the table, making as little noise as possible.

When everything was ready to be put on the table, including Blaze's leftover skillet bread, Hunter stepped out on the porch and gave a shrill whistle. Almost immediately the bunkhouse door opened and the men piled out, hurrying toward the cabin. Hunter grinned crookedly. They were probably starving after the mess that had been served to them last night.

Good mornings were mumbled to Hunter as the men sat down at the table and attacked their breakfast like a pack of hungry wolves. Hunter thought it was a lucky thing he had filled plates for Becky and Blaze and placed them in the warming oven. This bunch wasn't about to leave a crumb of food.

The hasty meal was soon eaten, and as the men drank a second cup of coffee, they waited for Hunter to give them the orders for the day.

"We'll begin by combing the foothills for strays," Hunter said. "I won't be able to join you until later in the day. I'm going to the fort to see about hiring a cook and see a carpenter about building a cookhouse. I shouldn't be gone longer than two or three hours."

A mingling of looks came over the cowboys' faces; relief that Hunter's wife wouldn't be preparing any more meals for them, and disappointment that they wouldn't have the pleasure of being around her anymore.

When the men had left, Hunter cleared the table and then wiped it off. Back in his room he stamped on his boots, strapped on his Colt, then settled his broad-brimmed hat on his head. As he left the cabin he took his jacket off the peg beside the kitchen door.

Blaze hadn't awakened at Hunter's stirring around in the kitchen. It was the noise of scraping chairs, men's voices and the clinking of flatware that had brought her eyes open. When she caught the aroma of bacon and fresh coffee she smiled wryly. Her husband wasn't chancing her making breakfast for his men.

And that was fine with her. The news that he was hiring a cook today was better yet.

She eased herself over on her back, careful not to awaken Becky. Gazing up at the ceiling she thought to herself that so far nothing had been said about her having to leave. And since Hunter was willing to go to the expense of hiring a cook, it appeared that he was at least satisfied with the way she was keeping his home clean and tending to his daughter.

She suddenly felt lighthearted. It looked as if things might work out after all. She continued to lie in bed awhile longer, planning what she would make for tonight's supper. She wanted it to be perfect in every way. She intended to prove to Mr. High and Mighty that she could cook. With the help of Rose's recipes, that was.

Blaze sat up in bed, swung her feet to the floor and pulled on her flannel robe, shoving her feet into her fur-lined house slippers. The floors were cold these mornings, and she worried about Becky's little bare feet. Perhaps, until she could get to the fort and purchase the things the child badly needed, the little one could wear a pair of woolen hose, after Blaze made some alterations on them. She could fold over and stitch the toe to the heel, which in turn would give Becky a thick sole to walk on.

Blaze had decided what she would serve her husband for supper. She intended to make another beef roast, only this time she would follow Rose's instructions. It would be juicy and tasty with the herbs she would sprinkle over it. The mashed potatoes would be mashed smooth and the string beans would be cooked with a small piece of salt pork to give them added flavor.

She was ready to go into the kitchen when she saw the two packages lying against the bed's end rail. She bent over them, wondering what was in them and when Hunter had put them there. She didn't like the habit he had of entering her room, especially when she was asleep.

The rustling of the paper as Blaze unfolded it awakened Becky. She sat up, smiled at Blaze and asked eagerly, "Eat?"

Blaze's laughter pealed out. "I believe your stomach is like a sinkhole. It has no bottom." She finished unwrapping the packages and her eyes widened as she gazed down at the little coat and boots. "Look, Becky," she exclaimed, "see what your daddy bought you!"

Becky didn't fully understand Blaze, but when she saw the small garments, she knew they were for her. She stood up in the first nightgown she had ever owned, and jumping up and down she cried excitedly, "Becky wear!"

Chuckling, Blaze helped her into the coat, and then Becky sat down and stuck out her feet to have the boots put on. Blaze looked among the papers for a pair of stockings. There were none.

*Trust a man to forget that,* she thought. *Hunter will have to make another trip to the fort to buy her some.* She grinned. That would make him growl.

Becky was reluctant to give up her coat, but when she was allowed to keep on the boots, which fit her perfectly, she graciously let Blaze help her off with the former garment.

When they walked into the kitchen Blaze was surprised to see the table cleared and the dirty dishes stacked in the sink. The chairs were neatly in place around the table, and the floor wasn't too messy. She had been sure in her mind that the kitchen would take her an hour to set right.

Blaze was about to start her and Becky's breakfast when the decided odor of bacon wafted from the warming oven. When she opened its door she was surprised to see not only one plate filled with bacon and eggs, but two.

*What's he up to?* she wondered, taking down the plates and placing them on the table. *He's not acting human for no reason. He probably wants me to wash the men's clothing next.*

As she and Becky ate, Blaze glanced out the window. The clear sky promised a fair day. An idea struck her. As soon as they finished breakfast she and Becky were going to ride in to the fort and buy Becky's stockings.

The sun had burned away the mist by the time Hunter rode up to the fort. Bridger was sweeping his narrow porch as he swung off Saint's back.

"Howdy, Hunter." The old man paused and leaned on the broom handle. "What brings you in again, and so early?"

"I've decided that I need a cook after all. My kitchen is too small to accommodate four extra people," Hunter said as he looped the reins over the long hitching rail.

*Uh huh,* Bridger thought, hiding his amusement. *The little woman put her foot down, didn't she?* Ol' Hunter was going to be hard-put pushing that one around.

"That means I'll have to get a cookhouse built also," Hunter continued, stepping up beside Jim. "I'll use the same carpenter who built my bunkhouse, but finding a cook might not be so easy. I don't suppose by any chance you'd know of any who's out of work."

"As a matter of fact, I may. Bucky Hayes who's been cookin' for the women at the Pleasure House, has been complainin' that he's sick and tired of makin' meals for a bunch of females who ain't satisfied with what he serves them. Seems like they always want him to cook somthin' more fancy than what he's used to preparin'."

"Maybe his cooking's no good."

"Oh, hell no. Bucky's real good at cookin' hearty

154

meals. The kind cowhands like."

"I wonder if Lucianne would get mad at me if I took away her cook."

"I doubt it. She argues with Bucky about the meals too. She'll probably be glad to get rid of him. That soft heart of hers would never allow her to fire him. Anyhow"—Bridger cocked an eye at his young friend—"why would you care if she does? You ain't got any business visitin' her place anymore, what with that purty little wife of yours waitin' at home."

"It's just that I like the ol' girl," Hunter answered, ignoring the remark about his pretty little wife. "I'm gonna amble over there now and talk with this Hayes. He sounds fine for my men. If that carpenter stops by, ask him to wait until I get back."

All was quiet at the long log building when Hunter knocked on the red-painted door. He imagined that Lucianne's girls were still sleeping after a hard night's work. The trappers and mountain men kept them busy every night. It was rumored that Lucianne was a wealthy lady.

At Hunter's second knock a tall, lanky, balding man, somewhere in his sixties, answered the door. "The whores are all sleepin'," he said, peering at Hunter from pale blue eyes.

"I'm not interested in them." Hunter grinned. "I think you're the one I've come to see."

A frown creased the man's long forehead and his eyes narrowed. "I can't help you that way, mister. I only go to bed with women."

"Me too." Hunter's grin widened. "Are you Bucky Hayes?"

"That's my handle. Are you by any chance lookin' for a cook?"

"Yes, Bridger said you might be interested."

"Who are you, fellow, and would I have to be cookin' for any females?"

"You'd only be cooking for my cowhands, and my name is Hunter Ward."

"Ah, yes. I've heard the girls talkin' about you."

Before Hunter could respond, a feminine voice called from the kitchen, "Who's there, Bucky? If it's someone looking to shake the sheets with one of the girls, send him away."

"It's Hunter Ward, Lucianne," Hunter called back.

"Hunter!" A tall, big-breasted woman with frizzy black hair stepped out into the narrow hall. "You haven't been around here in ages. Have you tired of your young wife already and need some more experienced lovemaking?"

"Lovemakin'?" Bucky snorted. "Is that what you call it? The racket that goes on in the girls' rooms sounds more like ruttin' buffalo."

Hunter winked at Lucianne and leaned down to kiss her powdered cheek. "I didn't come to visit one of your girls, Lucianne. I came to steal your cook."

"You can have him," Lucianne said, then smiled to take away the sting of her words. She was fond of the cranky old man. "All he does is fight with my girls. Let me get dressed and I'll meet you at the fort for a drink or two."

"Sounds good. We haven't had a good confab in a long while. But I can't stay too long. I'm busy getting a herd together to drive to market."

Lucianne and Hunter had been close friends for over eight years, beginning right after she and her girls had shown up one day at the fort. They had been heartily welcomed by the men in the area, but of course the women took a dim view of them.

When the madam disappeared back into the kitchen, Bucky asked, "How many mouths will I have to cook for?"

"Four. Maybe five," he added, thinking that Blaze might not cook for him.

"Fine. Where is your place?"

Hunter gave him instructions how to get to the ranch, then added, "You'll have to cook in the bunkhouse until I get you a cookhouse built. Shouldn't take more than a week."

"I guess that's all right," Bucky groused. "I'll get my duds and ride on out."

Lucianne wasn't long in joining Hunter at the fort. He sat at the bar, a glass of whiskey waiting for her. "So, how do you like marriage?" she asked after swallowing half her drink. "What kind of filly is she? I hear she's very beautiful."

"She is that," Hunter agreed. "And she's awfully good with my little daughter." He gave a short laugh. "Sometimes I get a little jealous of how Becky has taken to her. The little one prefers her company to mine."

"That's only normal if your wife is good to her.

After all, the child doesn't know you any better than she does your wife. I'm sure the little one didn't get any affection from that squaw you left her with."

"Yes," Hunter said unhappily. "When I went off and left her it was the biggest mistake of my life."

"I think the biggest mistake you ever made was marrying her mother."

"That was a big mistake," Hunter agreed. "I hope I'm not repeating the same mistake with Blaze."

"Blaze. That's an unusual name. I used to know a young girl named that. I taught her how to read and write and how to do sums."

Time got away from the old friends as they reminisced about old friends, and the wild parties that had gone on in the Pleasure House. They spoke then of the present time.

"What do you think about all these sod-busters that are coming in?" Lucianne asked. "Do you think they are going to ruin cattle-ranching with their fences and all?"

"I think they've been sold a bill of goods about settling in this region," Hunter said. "The growing season isn't long enough for them to get in any worthwhile crops. And wait until they experience one of our winters. They'll damn near freeze to death."

"If they don't starve to death first." There was concern in Lucianne's voice. "Bridger has carried some of them on the book already and he said that he can't do it much longer. As it is, he's going to be hard-put to pay for the load that's coming in a couple of weeks. That will be his last delivery until next spring and it's just his normal order. He hadn't planned on so many wanting credit so soon."

"I imagine that the ones who make it through to next spring will probably push on to California," Hunter said. "That's why I'm not overly worried about them fencing off the range."

"You're probably right," Lucianne began, then stopped when a childish voice cried out, "Papa, Papa!"

"Becky, where'd you come from?" Hunter exclaimed, pushing away from the bar, then looking past her to where Blaze stood in the doorway separating the bar area from the store. Then, ignoring her, he swept Becky up in his arms and said proudly, "Meet my daughter, Lucianne."

"What a beautiful child, Hunter," Lucianne said, smiling at the little girl riding on her father's arm. "Where is your mother, honey?"

When Becky looked puzzled, Hunter explained, "She doesn't have a good grasp of English yet. Blaze is standing over there in the door."

Lucianne's eyes sharpened and she snapped, "Are you embarrassed to introduce a woman like me to your wife?"

"Don't talk foolishness," Hunter said, and motioned toward the slender young woman who stood watching them.

When Blaze didn't stir from the door, only lifted her chin a little higher, Lucianne turned and looked at her. She made a soft sound of surprise; then, taking a hesitant step toward the still figure, she exclaimed in wonder, "Blaze, is it you? The same little Blaze I used to know, all grown up?"

"Lucianne!" Blaze moved forward, her eyes sparkling. "Is it really you?"

While Hunter gaped at them in bewilderment, the two women threw themselves into each other's arms with joyful cries. "I've thought of you so often, Lucianne." Blaze wiped at the moisture in her eyes. "I missed you so when you left."

"I've thought of you, too, Blaze, wondering where you were, what kind of young woman you had grown into. I cried when I had to leave you."

"So did I. I wouldn't speak to Dad for two weeks."

A sadness came into Lucianne's eyes. "I heard about Luke's death, that Garf Mullen shot him."

"Yes. Dad was trying to protect me from that awful man."

Lucianne lowered her voice. "I guess you know that your husband cleared out the Mullen gang. That they were all brought to justice."

"Yes, I heard that." Blaze spoke in the same low voice. "Do you know if Mullen was killed?"

"I heard that Hunter shot and killed him. Why don't you ask him?"

Blaze shrugged. "The subject has never come up. You might as well know, Lucianne, our marriage isn't a love match. Hunter needed a housekeeper and someone to watch over Becky, and I needed a home. We don't talk much, and never about the past."

"I'm sure that will change in a short time," Lucianne said with conviction, then changed the subject. "How is your grandpa Elisha?"

"Poor Grandpa." Blaze's eyes clouded. "He died in his sleep one night after we joined the wagon train coming west."

"Ah, honey, I'm sorry to hear that. He was a grand old man." Lucianne reached out and touched Blaze's arm. "You've had a hard time of it, haven't you?"

"It hasn't always been easy, but it could have been worse, I guess."

"You're gonna be all right now. You've married a fine man. He'll take good care of you."

Blaze slid a glance down to where Hunter stood, out of earshot of their conversation. He had set Becky upon the bar and was watching them with some bewilderment. When she didn't make a response to her old friend's statement, Lucianne asked with a frown, "Hunter is treating you all right, isn't he?"

"If you mean does he beat me, I can truthfully say that he has never laid a hand on me," Blaze answered, but she was thinking that being abused mentally was sometimes worse than being beaten.

Lucianne looped her arm in Blaze's, and as they walked back toward Hunter she laughingly said so that Hunter could hear her, "Just let me know if this husband of yours don't treat you right. If he steps out of line I'll move you into my place."

When Blaze darted a look at Hunter, she knew from the half sneer that lifted his lips that he was thinking she would fit right in with the other whores living with the madam.

"Hunter might not be too surprised if you did," Blaze responded. "You see, he thinks I was one of the camp women following the outlaw gang."

Lucianne shook her head. "I can't understand why he married you then, thinking you were a woman of low morals."

"He desperately needed a white woman to take care of Becky, to teach her English. Because he was single, the settler women wouldn't allow their daughters to work for him. I was his last hope." After a pause, Blaze said, "He was so arrogant in telling me that he couldn't get anyone else to work for him, I told him that the only way I would take the job was if he would marry me. I never dreamed he'd agree."

"You're such an innocent, Blaze. What man wouldn't want to marry you, to have you in his bed every night?"

"If he thought that," Blaze said with a snap to her voice, "he certainly thought wrong. He still sleeps alone."

"That's very unusual, Blaze. I'm sure Hunter wants you to share his bed, and it's your duty to do so."

"Not if I don't love him," Blaze defended herself. "Anyhow, he hasn't said that he wants me beside him."

"He wants you there all right," Lucianne said

162

with a knowing laugh. "I could feel it coming off him in heat waves."

When Blaze blushed a fiery red Lucianne said softly, "You're still a virgin, aren't you, honey?"

When Blaze mutely nodded her head, Lucianne said with snapping eyes, "I hope someday you can rub that rooster's nose in that fact. Men think they are so wise and they don't know nothin'."

"Isn't that the truth." Blaze laughed at Lucianne's description of men. "But enough of them. I have to buy Becky some stockings and then get on back to the ranch. I'd like to come visit you, though, so that we could chat more."

"You know you'd be welcome, honey, but tongues will wag if you do."

After a short, bitter laugh Blaze said, "They wag anyway. I've grown a tough hide where that's concerned."

"In that case, I'll come visit you too."

"Good." Blaze nodded her head and lifted Becky off the bar. In the store she and Lucianne parted with a hug, and Blaze purchased six pairs of little stockings for Becky and led the child outside.

As Blaze rode homeward with Becky sitting in front of her, the promised candy stick in her mouth, she was thinking with pleasure of the reunion that had just taken place between her and Lucianne. Besides the happiness of seeing her old friend after so long a time, she had a more secure feeling knowing that she could go to her if the need ever arose.

Blaze was wondering about what Lucianne had

said about Garf Mullen having been killed when the ringing of an ax up in the foothills of the mountain broke into her thoughts. Was there a family living up there? One day she and David had taken a ride in that area and the only building they had seen was one deserted, run-down shack with its window broken and its roof sagging. Certainly no one could live in it.

She decided that someone was cutting firewood and she fell back to thinking of Lucianne and when she would see her again.


Had Blaze known that the dilapidated building housed a man and his wife, who had come to the area to spy on her and Hunter, she wouldn't be feeling so contented.

The ax continued to rise and fall as Blaze rode out of hearing distance. The thin woman wielding the blade did so out of frightened determination. Although her arms felt that they would drop from her shoulders in exhaustion, she dared not stop. To do so would only get her another beating.

It didn't bother the once attractive woman in the least when from the shack there came the roar of her husband achieving release with the Indian woman he had been using off and on all morning. She was only thankful. The more he rode his new squaw, the more rest her tired body would get.

And it needed rest badly. Late last spring Pearl Mullen had come down with a severe case of influenza. She still hadn't fully recovered. Sometimes she thought she could feel the life slowly draining out of her body.

Now that it was too late, Pearl knew that she should have left her husband, Cotter, two weeks after they were married, the first time he beat her. But she had stayed on, thinking that she could change him, believing his promise that it would never happen again.

There had been a change, but only for the worse. When Cotter had moved her to Mexico, away from family and friends, the beatings became almost a daily occurrence.

Shortly after settling in a one-room shack, Cotter had fallen in with a bunch of raggedy, hard-core outlaws who lacked any sense of morality.

Her husband had shown his power over her by beating her in front of his new friends. Pearl lived in dread that someday her husband would do as he often threatened: let the outlaws have their turn with her.

She had had three miscarriages in that hot, arid desert, each one weakening her more and more. Then one day a man had ridden in and told Cotter that a lawman had shot and killed his brother Garf.

If her husband was capable of loving anyone, it was his outlaw brother. In a rage he had torn the shack apart, then ordered her to pack some grub. He'd sworn that he was going to find the lawman and shoot him between the eyes. But first he was going to make him suffer.

It had taken them a month to track down the

whereabouts of the ex-lawman called Hunter Ward.

The first person they'd met upon arriving in the area was New Moon, and Cotter had moved her in with them. The woman had hard feelings for the rancher and was eager to help destroy him.

Pearl leaned a moment on the ax handle to draw an arm across the perspiration that had gathered on her brow. She wished there were something she could do to prevent what her husband and the squaw planned: kidnaping Mr. Ward's wife and drawing him into a trap where he would be at Cotter's mercy. How she could help the rancher, she had no idea. She only knew that an innocent woman shouldn't be hurt.

# Chapter Ten

The first person Hunter saw when he stepped outside the fort was Kile West. It took but a few minutes to make arrangements for the carpenter to build a cookhouse. Hunter headed home then, mulling over the fact that Blaze and Lucianne had known each other in the past. It was evident that there was a fondness between them, and he wondered how old Blaze had been when she'd met Lucianne. Had she already been a camp woman or had the madam taught her more than book learning? Maybe she had taught the young girl the tricks of the trade as well.

At any rate, his bride must have lost her virginity somewhere along the way. Otherwise she never would have traveled across country in the company of two single men and then lived with them once they settled in the area.

When the wagon carrying the cookstove and his new cook passed him, Hunter determinedly put Blaze out of his mind and urged Saint into a full gallop. He told himself that he was a damn fool for even thinking about her. As long as she took good care of Becky and didn't shame him by messing around with other men, he didn't care what her past had been.

Blaze had kept her mount at a more leisurely pace because of Becky, and by the time they arrived at the ranch, the new cookstove had been installed in the bunkhouse and Hunter and an elderly man were transporting supplies from the larder room to the long building.

Blaze climbed out of the saddle, lifted Becky to the ground, and then asked Hunter, "When you're finished there, would you please take care of my horse?"

Hunter paused and gave her a suspicious look. It was unusual for her to use such a polite tone with him. What had she hatched up in that brain of hers? "You saddled him, didn't you?"

Blaze smiled innocently at him. "I would unsaddle him also, but Becky is tired and wants to take a nap."

Hunter looked at his daughter. Her bright, sparkling eyes told him that she was far from being sleepy. He decided he would give Blaze the benefit of believing her and muttered, "I'll take care of him in a minute."

When he turned to take the last box of supplies

off the wagon he saw Blaze give Bucky a brilliant smile. There was nothing he could do but introduce them. "This is my wife, Blaze, and my daughter, Becky," he said gruffly.

"I'm right pleased to meet you both," Bucky said, offering a gnarled hand to Blaze and ruffling Becky's hair with the other.

When Blaze shook his hand, he said, "You look mighty young to have a daughter that age, ma'am."

"She's my daughter's stepmother," Hunter said shortly. "Come on, let's get these supplies moved. I've got work to do."

"Yes, sir, right away, sir." Bucky winked at Blaze and then tried to keep up with Hunter's long, impatient strides.

*I like him*, Blaze thought, ushering Becky ahead of her as they entered the kitchen. *He reminds me of Grandpa. Hunter's abrupt manner only tickles him.*

After having coaxed Becky to relinquish her boots long enough to pull on a pair of the new stockings, Blaze got busy cutting out another little dress. Later, as she sat before the fire stitching the seams of the little frock, her mind dwelled on Lucianne.

There was so much she wanted to ask the woman who had been so kind to her over eight years ago. Why had she come to this wilderness fort, of all places? And how well did she know Hunter? Had she known his wife? Had he been so broken up over her death that he had gone off and left his infant daughter to be raised by an Indian woman?

When the clock struck three Blaze decided it was time to get the roast in the oven. The days were growing shorter and sunset would come early.

Placing Rose's instructions on the workbench, she proceeded to follow the directions precisely. Her friend had promised a roast prepared in this manner would never fail to come out perfect. After sprinkling dry herbs over the meat, she put it into the oven. She checked the firebox then, and after a thoughtful moment laid a stick of wood to the moderate fire burning there. The trick, according to the recipe, was to keep an even heat going, not to fire up the stove as she had done yesterday.

Blaze next turned her hand to the preparation of the string beans she would serve with the roast. After carefully reading how to cook them, she cut three thin slices of salt pork from a long slab and placed them in an iron pot. As the cast iron heated she peeled and chopped up an onion. While the onion was turning transparent she opened a can of string beans. She waited a minute; then, turning the slices of meat over, she emptied the beans on top of them and put the pot's heavy lid on. The beans would simmer gently, turning out just right by the time the roast was done.

By the time Blaze got back to her sewing, the flavorful aroma of roasting meat and herbs was wafting throughout the cabin. She rose occasionally to stir the beans, and one time to peel potatoes and put them to boiling.

When it grew dim in the cabin, Blaze knew the sun would set before long and that Hunter would expect his supper to be waiting for him. She folded up her sewing and went into the kitchen. Opening the oven door she found the roast done to perfection. Lifting it out she placed it on the back of the stove to keep hot. She found that the beans were ready to be pushed back beside the roast and that the potatoes were ready to be mashed. After adding a big chunk of butter and some rich milk to them, she set the table.

By now it was time to light the lamp on the table. Why wasn't Hunter here yet? she wondered. She went to the window and peered outside. She was in time to see him following the men into the bunkhouse. An angry glint appeared in her eyes. She had gone to all the trouble of making a perfect meal for him and he was going to eat with his men.

Her lips firmed to a thin line. Not if she had anything to say about it, she decided angrily. She helped Becky into her coat, and, taking her by the hand, she marched over to the bunkhouse. She flung open the door and stood there with arms akimbo. The men, including her husband, who was about to fork a steak onto his plate, stared at her furious face with open mouths.

"Hunter Ward," she said sharply, "your supper is waiting for you at home and your daughter would like to share it with you."

Hunter thought he had never seen Blaze so angry. If he wanted to avoid a slanging match with her in front of his men, he'd better make some excuse for eating with his hands.

With a lingering look at the steak he had let drop back down on the serving platter, he stood up and said as pleasantly as he could, "I thought maybe you'd be too tired to cook tonight, considering your trip to the fort today." He tried not to think about what kind of mess Blaze had prepared for him.

It was a hollow excuse and both Blaze and Hunter knew it. She gave him an icy look, and then turned and stamped outside. Becky looked over her shoulder at her father. Hunter snatched his hat off the floor and followed them. He was boiling mad, and as soon as they entered the kitchen, he almost snarled the words, "Don't you ever embarrass me in front of the men like that again."

"And you keep in mind not to do the same thing to me." Blaze wheeled on him. "It works both ways, you know. I don't care how much you insult me in private, but you'll treat me with respect in public, or I'll leave here so fast you won't be able to see my dust."

Hunter was on the point of yelling, "Why don't you go now?" when he saw Becky clinging to Blaze's legs, a look of pleading in her gray eyes. His daughter understood enough of their shouting to be afraid of losing the woman she so plainly adored.

He stroked a hand over Becky's blond curly

head and said gently, "Shall we eat, little girl? I'm starving." Becky nodded eagerly, understanding the word *eat*. Chuckling, Hunter picked her up and sat her in the chair whose seat had been raised with two boards nailed together. Blaze got control of her temper, too, and began putting supper on the table.

*It doesn't look bad and it sure smells good,* Hunter thought as he picked up the carving knife. *It's juicy too,* he added to himself in surprise as the knife sliced easily through the meat.

When he began to eat, Blaze watched him surreptitiously. She knew that it aggravated him that she had prepared an excellent meal and that he honestly couldn't find fault with it.

When supper was over Hunter left the table, and it appeared he was going to leave the cabin. "Why don't you take Becky into the family room and tell her a story while I clean up the kitchen?" Blaze suggested. "She hasn't seen much of you lately." There was an accusatory note in her voice that made Hunter want to shake her.

But Blaze was right. He hadn't spent much time with his daughter since bringing her home a new stepmother. He helped Becky off her seat and led her into the family room. He sat down and lifted her onto his lap, and with her head nestled against his chest, he began to make up a story about a little girl and her pony.

In the background he could hear Blaze humming some song as she washed the dishes. A contentment he hadn't known since childhood settled over him. He lost the thread of his story and grew silent as he wished things could be different between him and Blaze. If only they could forget the past and stop bickering with each other. If only there were trust between them.

Hunter became aware that Becky wasn't fussing at him to go on with his story. He looked down at her and found that she had fallen asleep. He was smiling tenderly at her little face when Blaze walked into the room. When he looked up at her the soft light remained in his eyes.

As he continued to gaze at her, Blaze gave him a confused smile and sat down in the chair next to him. "I see she's fallen asleep," she said in a half whisper.

"Yes," Hunter answered in a like tone. After a moment he said, "You look tired. I hope you haven't been working too hard."

Blaze was so startled by his statement that she couldn't answer for a second. Had Hunter Ward just showed some concern for her welfare? "I don't imagine that I work any harder than the other women around here," she answered.

"I don't know about that. Every time I ride into town I see a bunch of them in the store chattering away like a flock of blackbirds. They seem to have time for a little entertainment."

Blaze lifted a teasing eyebrow at Hunter and joked, "Do you have something in mind that I would find entertaining?"

Hunter wanted to say that yes, he did. That he'd like to take her to bed and entertain her all night.

But he knew she wasn't thinking along those lines.

Before he could answer, Blaze was saying laughingly, "Maybe you'd like to take me to watch the bull-riding contest that the trading post has every Sunday afternoon."

"No." Hunter grinned at her. "I don't think you'd like that. You wouldn't like the groin strap they put on the bulls."

"What is a groin strap?"

"It's a strap that is put on the rear of the bulls. When it's drawn tight it's painful to his male parts. That's why they buck so hard and try to gore the rider when he is thrown."

"No, I wouldn't like that at all." Blaze shuddered. "That's a cruel thing to do to an animal."

"Yes, I guess it is," Hunter agreed thoughtfully. "I just never thought of it before."

"If the men put themselves in the place of those bulls, that would be the end of bull-riding. Don't you think?"

"I know I wouldn't like it," Hunter said, amusement in his eyes. "What if we have Rose come over and sit with Becky the next time they have a dance at the post? We'll get all gussied up and attend it."

"I'd like that." Blaze's eyes sparkled.

"Good. I'll find out when the next dance is going to be held."

Blaze stood up, remarking that she'd better put Becky to bed. She reached down to slide a hand under the girl's little bottom, and in doing so the back of her hand brushed against the bulge of Hunter's manhood. She blushed furiously when he jumped as though he had been scalded with hot water. She lifted Becky into her arms and, stammering a good night, she left Hunter sitting in front of the fire.

Hunter swore softly as he grew hard.

There would be little sleep for him tonight.

Hunter was in torment as he stretched out between the covers, listening to the rustle Blaze's clothing made as she undressed and then got into her nightgown. He envisioned her naked body and suppressed a groan. He would be willing to give up half his cattle to have that soft body lying beneath him, his hardness moving in and out of her in long, rhythmic strokes, to hear her cries of ecstasy time after time.

He was a long time falling asleep.

And so was Blaze. She kept seeing Hunter's face relaxed in sleep, thinking how gentle he was with his daughter, how much fun he'd been tonight. She envied his first wife, whom he had loved. No doubt he'd been a different man altogether with her.

Finally, impatient with herself for wasting her thoughts on Hunter Ward, Blaze gave her pillow a whack and was soon asleep.

Hunter was in a foul mood as he rode to join the men who had been at the branding fire half an hour already. He had overslept and he had a dull throbbing in his loins.

He topped a knoll and reined the little workhorse in to gaze down at the Wilson brothers' holdings. In the distance he could see them working at building a cabin. A frown creased his forehead. It looked about half-finished. Did they think to lure Blaze back by erecting a building in which she would be comfortable during the long, cold winter months?

And she might go, he thought, his frown growing. She must be hurting as badly as he for a bed partner. Growing impatient with his musings, Hunter promised himself he wouldn't think of his wife again today. He lifted the reins and kneed the sturdy little horse into a basin that was thick with morning mist. He could make out the darker gray of smoke rising from the branding iron fire and rode toward it.

Blaze heard the kitchen door close behind Hunter and gave a big sigh of relief. She was dying to go to the outhouse and she had no desire to be around him this morning. She still felt awkward at discovering the unmistakable evidence of his desire for her. And after their playful conversation, she was not at all certain what her feelings for him were. In some ways, it had been easier just to hate him.

She remained in bed awhile longer, giving Hunter time to walk to the barn, saddle up and ride out. She stared unseeingly at the curtains gently stirring from the light breeze coming through the open window. She was finding it harder than she had thought to live with Hunter, see him every day, and remain indifferent to him.

At last Blaze heard the quarter horse gallop away. She slid out of bed, slipped on her house slippers and reached for her robe at the foot of the bed. Shivering in the morning coolness, she hurried across the floor and closed the window. She checked to see if Becky was well covered up and then left the cabin practically at a run.

When she left the tall, narrow building with its half moon–shaped window, Blaze looked up at the sky. It was a cloudless bright blue. It was going to be a beautiful fall day. There wouldn't be too many of them before the snows and bitter cold arrived. She had already seen several flocks of geese flying southward in their usual vee formation.

On the spur of the moment Blaze decided to take advantage of the sunny day. She would take Becky to watch the branding of the cattle. It would be a new experience for her too.

When Blaze entered the kitchen she found Becky sitting at the table. "Eat?" The little girl gave her a questioning smile.

"Yes, you'll eat." Blaze shook her head in amusement. As she stirred up batter for flapjacks Blaze thought how much she had grown to love the child in the short time she'd been caring for her. She didn't think she could love her more if she were her own daughter.

And that wasn't a good thing. Her feelings for the child would hamper her if ever she thought to leave Hunter Ward.

The sun had burned off the mist by the time

Blaze and Becky rode away from the ranch. She was about to follow the tracks the grub wagon had made when she was distracted by the sound of axes biting into wood. David and James were still clearing their land, she thought. But when she looked in their direction she was surprised to see that the brothers were at last erecting a cabin. Turning the stallion's head, she rode the short distance to where her friends were now struggling a log into place.

"Hey," she called out, pulling the stallion in. "It's about time you started building yourselves a winter home!"

Sweating from his exertion, James grinned and said, "The tent is getting a little cold at night, so we figured we'd better get busy and build us some better quarters."

Blaze's eyes twinkled teasingly at the two young men. "You're not fooling me," she said. "You just waited until you got rid of me to build your cabin. I can just hear the two of you telling each other that you'd freeze me out."

"You know that's not true." David pinched her calf through the material of her skirt. Reaching up to take Becky from her, he said, "Come on down and see how much we've got done."

The half-finished cabin consisted of two big rooms with a floor of hewed planks. Each room had a good-sized window, and a fireplace of fieldstone had been erected in one room. The way the brothers had her checking out every little detail of their carpentry told Blaze how proud they were of their efforts.

She was careful to praise their handiwork highly. "You're doing a wonderful job of it," she said when they walked back outside. "You'll be nice and warm in your new home when the winter winds blow. Your new brides are two lucky women. When do you expect them?"

"Sometime soon," James said. "Before the snow flies, I hope."

"You gonna come over and help us caulk between the logs?" David arched a teasing eyebrow at her.

"I'd like to, but if Hunter knew I was here now he'd raise the roof."

"We know, Blaze." James boosted her into the saddle and David handed Becky up to her. "Maybe you can slip over one day when we get the place finished, let us know if you like it."

"I intend to. Do you have bed linens, blankets and quilts?"

"No, we have to make a trip to the fort to buy all that. There are quite a few things we'd like, but for the time being we'll just buy what we absolutely need," David said. "We've got to be sure we've got enough money for supplies this winter and for crop seed come spring."

"Besides," James put in, "our wives will probably want to have a hand in choosing most of the furnishings."

"I expect you're right," Blaze said. Giving them a wave good-bye, she turned the stallion in the direction of the spot where the branding was taking place.

Blaze heard the cattle before she saw them. When she topped a knoll a few minutes later, she gazed down at the basin where Hunter and his men were working. Everywhere she looked, bawling longhorns milled about. *Good gravy*, she thought, *if my husband isn't already a wealthy man, he's going to be someday.*

She rode on down the small hill and drew rein beside the chuck wagon. In the melee of frantic cattle and swearing men, Blaze watched a cowboy race his horse after a frightened yearling, twirling a rope with a running noose over his head. When he got close enough to the animal, he sent the lasso spinning out over the young steer, snaring it on his first try. The steer went down and was dragged to the branding fire.

Blaze looked away when the hot branding iron was applied to the terrorized half-grown steer. She had been told that it didn't hurt the animal, but she knew different now. She imagined that redhot iron being pressed against her flesh and shuddered.

It wasn't long before the men discovered Blaze's presence and loped their mounts over to greet her. She responded with the same warmth they showed her. She was laughing at some remark made by a cowboy when she heard the pounding of hooves. She looked up and saw the cattle scatter as Hunter's horse thundered through them. Pulling the animal to a rearing halt, Hunter directed a black look at the men and demanded coldly if they had quit work early. His thinly veiled anger sent the men hurrying back to roping and branding.

Hunter turned a contemptuous look at Blaze and lashed out, "I don't want to see you hanging around my men again, distracting them from their work. Now take my daughter and get the hell out of here."

Hurt and confused, Blaze could only stare at Hunter. She had innocently come here only to watch the branding. The last thing she'd had on her mind was to flirt with the cowhands.

A sudden burst of anger replaced Blaze's other emotions. She was getting fed up with this man's unjust accusations, the way he blew hot and then cold, but she wasn't going to argue with him in front of Becky. So, giving him a withering look, she silently turned the stallion's head homeward.

Becky lifted a small hand and gently patted the tears that were running down Blaze's cheeks.

Hunter stared after Blaze. He had hurt her deeply. He had seen it on her face, in her beautiful eyes. Why had he lashed out at her? She hadn't been doing anything to set him off. She had stopped her horse well back from the branding fire where the men worked.

He suddenly knew where his burst of temper had come from. Jenny. His first wife had loved to flirt with his men, and she'd used any excuse to do so.

If he and Blaze were to make a go of their marriage, he must stop comparing her to Jenny. So far she had shown no sign of being man-crazy.

Suddenly Hunter was dead tired. His muscles sagged with fatigue, and his mind was crazed with wanting to make love with his wife.

# *Chapter Eleven*

Bare of all clothing, Cotter Mullen lay sprawled in a jumble of raggedy horse blankets waiting for his breathing to return to normal. He turned his head to look at the equally naked woman lying beside him. The squaw was breathing heavily also. He had never known a woman whose sex drive was as strong as his own. He could vent his lust on her anytime the notion struck him, which was often, and she was always ready to eagerly oblige him.

It had been that way from his first encounter with the woman. He thought back to that day.

He and his wife Pearl, who was always sickly and lay like a board beneath him every time he mounted her, had been on the trail in the Montana Territory, hoping that they were headed for Fort Bridger. It was high noon when he spotted in the distance a line of willows that stretched out of sight. With a thankful sigh he turned his mount in the direction of the lush growth. Willows only grew where there was water. In this case, a river.

They and the horses were in desperate need of water. Their mouths and throats were parched. Day before yesterday they had drunk the last of the brackish water in their canteens and hadn't come across a watering hole since.

He had known it would be useless to use the spurs on their mounts, to try to make them run. The animals were exhausted and might drop dead if forced to move faster. And that he hadn't wanted. Between renegade Indians and rattlesnakes, a man wouldn't last long on foot.

It had seemed ages before they reached the winding river. The horses had their noses in the water before he and Pearl dismounted. Once they gained the ground they threw themselves down on the riverbank and drank deeply of the life-giving water.

It was when Cotter had drunk his fill and stood up that he had seen the squaw standing in the middle of the stream. A wolfish smile sprang to his face as his eyes moved over the wet tunic clinging to her body. His manhood stiffened and pushed against his trousers.

He was unbuttoning his fly as he stepped into the river and waded toward her, rape on his mind.

He was so intent on ravishing her as he grasped her by the arm and started dragging her to shore, he didn't realize at first that the woman wasn't

185

fighting him. Rather, she was hurrying along, as anxious as he to couple. Without ceremony he pushed her to the ground and shoved her single garment up around her waist. She spread her legs and he plunged himself inside her. In a matter of seconds he was exploding deep within her body. He slumped on top of the woman, his full weight making her grunt.

Cotter ignored her discomfort, for he was growing hard again.

A few moments later Cotter was ready to go once more. He lifted himself up on his elbows, and while the woman was still drawing deep breaths of air into her lungs, he began slamming in and out of her. She didn't object to the hard riding she was receiving: instead she lifted her body to meet each hard drive of his hips.

After taking the woman two more times in the next hour, Cotter was finally sated for the time being. He wondered if the squaw had a man. She was the best woman he had ever had and he would like to move her in with him and Pearl when they settled somewhere.

He glanced at his wife, who sat on a large flat rock only a few feet away. He would get no trouble from her if the woman joined them. She hadn't opened her mouth all the time he rode the squaw.

Cotter's lips curled in a cruel smile. She knew better than to complain. She had done so the first time he brought home a whore. After giving her a good beating, he had made her watch as he rode the whore time after time. She had never objected again when he brought a female to their home.

He turned his head and looked down at the woman. Her short tunic was still up around her waist and her legs were spread apart just as he had left them. "What are you called, woman?" he asked.

"New Moon," she answered with a coy smile. "What are you called?"

Cotter took a minute to wonder whether or not to give his real name. Hunter Ward would recognize the name Mullen and become suspicious of him if he heard it.

He said finally, "I am called Deke Meyer." New Moon nodded and he asked, "Do you have a man?"

"No. My husband was killed in a battle with another tribe over five years ago."

"Who do you live with now? Who takes care of you?"

"I live alone in my tepee. For the past five years I took care of a white man's child. He remarried recently and sent me back to my village." New Moon brought a sham look of sadness to her face. "I have no one to look after me now."

"What if I become your man?"

New Moon looked at Pearl, who sat staring out over the river. "But you already have a woman." She looked back at Cotter.

"Bah!" Cotter gave a dismissive wave of his hand. "I wore her out a long time ago. I keep her around to cook and take care of my wants."

"In that case, then, I will be your woman," New Moon said with a wide, pleased smile.

187

Cotter rose and hitched up his trousers. "Are we anywhere near Fort Bridger?" he asked as he buttoned up his fly.

"Yes." New Moon stood up and smoothed down her short tunic. "The fort lies about five miles from here."

Cotter's face became hard and tight. He wanted to shout the jubilation New Moon's words had brought him. The man he sought would soon pay the price for having killed his brother. His voice was calm, however, when he said, "I don't suppose there's a deserted cabin or some kind of building that we could move into around here?"

New Moon shook her head, then a second later said, "There is a sort of hut up in the foothills about two miles from here. It has only three walls and a tin roof. An old trapper used to live in it until he froze to death one winter."

"That will be fine," Cotter said, not planning to hang around the area after he had taken care of Hunter Ward.

Now Cotter sat up among the twisted blankets and pulled on his trousers. They had been living in the hovel for two weeks while he scouted the area. It was time to start putting his plan into action.

On his way outside to relieve himself, he gave Pearl a sharp nudge with his foot as he passed her thin pallet. "Get up, bitch, and make us some breakfast."

\* \* \*

It had been overcast when Blaze and Becky started out for Fort Bridger, but halfway to their destination the clouds were beginning to break up and the sun shone down on them.

Blaze hoped that she wouldn't be too late to give Bridger her Christmas order. Rose had told her yesterday that there would be no more deliveries after the end of the month. After that the weather became too uncertain, the driver wouldn't chance getting caught in a blizzard.

She wanted to order Becky a doll and a woolen scarf to go with her coat. Also a pair of little house slippers, if the catalog advertised them. She was still put out that Hunter hadn't brought the book home with him when she'd asked him to.

"He was probably afraid that I would order something for myself," she muttered under her breath.

Hunter and the men had left on a cattle drive yesterday morning, and she had been lonely at the ranch last night. She had jumped at every little sound, even though the shutters were tightly closed and the door barred with a heavy piece of wood. The only way someone could get into the cabin was to come down the chimney.

Long before dusk she had carried in a plentiful supply of split logs to keep the fire going in the fireplace, as well as to keep the range fired up for cooking.

With her chattering, half in English and half in Arapaho, Becky was company. Blaze affectionately tightened her arms around the little body nestled firmly in front of her, but the child didn't lend a sense of security. And the little girl missed her father, going often to the window to look for him. Blaze had tried to explain why her papa wasn't there, but Becky didn't yet have a firm enough grasp on English to understand that he would be gone a couple of weeks before he could return to them.

Blaze couldn't believe that she missed the hot-tempered man. She asked herself how a sane person could miss someone who could be kind and considerate one minute, then rude and insulting the next.

She thought of the previous morning when Hunter was preparing to leave on the cattle drive. He had swept Becky up in his arms, making her giggle when he gave her a smacking kiss on the cheek.

"Are you going to be a good girl while your dad is away?" he asked, smoothing the curls off her forehead.

Becky bobbed her head up and down, parroting, "Good girl."

Hunter laughed softly and, giving her a squeeze, stood her back on the floor. Then, turning to Blaze, he'd said kindly, "Here is money for supplies. I don't want you to do without while I'm gone." Then his tone had grown hard. "I don't want to hear any talk about you when I get back." Before she could summon a retort, he had left the cabin.

As the stallion plodded along, there grew in

Blaze a determination that someday Hunter Ward was going to eat every insult he had ever thrown into her face. And there had been so many, she hoped he would choke on them.

The fort came into view and Blaze pushed Hunter out of her mind. She was surprised at the number of horses and wagons drawn up in front of the fort. She wondered why so many were there on a weekday as she slid from the saddle and hitched the stallion to a tree a good distance from the other animals. He was a testy fellow, always wanting to fight other stallions.

When she and Becky walked inside the fort, the big room was crowded with people, mostly women and children. They stood about, some talking quietly amongst themselves, some silent, wearing worried frowns. Blaze wondered at the relief in Bridger's voice as he greeted her.

"What can I do for you, Blaze?" he asked.

"I'm hoping that I'm not too late to give you my Christmas order."

"You're just in time. The man will be pulling in any minute now with my new delivery. I'll give him your order and he'll deliver it on his last trip here before winter." He reached beneath the counter and brought up a much-thumbed catalog. Pushing it toward Blaze he said, "It's got some right nice things in it for a body to buy for Christmas."

As Blaze began leafing through the thick book, she said, "I've never seen so many people in here at one time. Is there any reason for it?"

"I'm afraid there is." Bridger sighed heavily. "They know a fresh load of supplies is coming in today and they want to make sure they lay in enough food to get them through the winter."

"That's good for you, isn't it?" Blaze couldn't understand the worried tone in his voice.

"No, it's not." Bridger lowered his voice. "They want me to carry them on the books and I can't afford to. If I give all of them credit, I won't be able to pay for the next wagonload of supplies. Besides, it wouldn't be fair to my paying customers not to have on hand what they might want and need." The old man sighed again. "I'm at my wit's end what to do, Blaze."

Blaze could feel the women's scornful eyes boring into her back. She wondered what the settlers had been thinking of, traveling hundreds of miles across country with their pockets practically empty. How had they planned on getting through the winter?

Blaze's gaze fell on two youngsters, their features pinched as they stared longingly at a glass jar of candy sticks. Her heart went out to the children. Why should they pay for their parents' thoughtlessness?

She continued to turn the pages of the catalog, but her attention was not completely on the items for sale. She was thinking of the money Hunter had given her for supplies just before he left.

When Bridger walked past her, she said to him quietly, "Jim, I would like to speak to you privately."

"Sure, Blaze. We can talk in my living quarters," he said, and walked to the end of the counter, where he pushed open a door. Stepping aside, he let Blaze and Becky enter a big room, then followed them inside. "Have the rocker there by the fire, Blaze," he said, "and the little one can sit on this." He pulled a cloth-covered stool up beside Blaze.

While the old man busied himself with laying a log on the fire, Blaze glanced around the room. It was sparsely furnished, but spotlessly clean. Beneath a window there was a table with a bench flanking each side. On the east wall there was a bed, neatly made up, with a bearskin rug on the floor that would keep Bridger's feet from the cold surface when he rose from bed.

"Now," Bridger said, straighting up and brushing off his hands, "what did you want to talk to me about?"

Blaze handed him the money Hunter had given her. She and Becky could make do without it. "For the sake of the children out there, I want to help the homesteaders get through the winter. I would like to donate beans and flour to the families with children. It's not much, but it would ward off starvation."

"That's right generous of you, Blaze, but I'm surprised that you want to help the women who bad-mouth you all the time."

"It's not for them, Jim. It's for the children. I hate to think of them going hungry all winter."

Bridger thought to himself that this young

woman was as beautiful inside as she was outside. He hoped that Hunter realized what a gem he had married.

"One more thing, Jim: you are to tell no one about this. It is to be our secret. Do you promise?"

"You have my word. I won't tell—" Bridger was interrupted by the sound of heavy wagon wheels. "That's my delivery. I'd better get out there before the women take off with everything."

Taking Becky by the hand, Blaze followed Jim into the store and took up her stance at the end of the counter. As she resumed leafing through the catalog, she glanced occasionally at the women who eagerly eyed the supplies being carried in.

When Becky grew restless and wanted to be with the other children, Blaze picked her up and set her on the counter. She handed her a candy stick and said, "Mama will be finished in just a minute and then we'll go home."

The last of the supplies were finally brought in and stacked behind the counter. Before Jim could finish settling up with the driver, the women crowded around him. Each held a grocery list, all of them talking at once.

Jim held up a gnarled hand and barked, "Listen to me, you women. I can't afford to give you all credit. Now, you women with children, I will let you have enough beans and flour so that with careful handling you should make it through until spring. Your menfolk can hunt deer and rabbit for fresh meat."

When some of the women began to grumble, a

dark, warning look from their husbands quieted them. A big worry had been lifted from their shoulders and they didn't want the crotchety old man to get angry and change his mind.

As the first woman stepped up to the counter, Blaze finished her Christmas list. She had ordered a baby doll, a scarf and matching stockings for Becky, a lacy shawl of blue for Rose and a red petticoat for Lucianne.

She interrupted Bridger long enough to tell him her order and replace the catolog back beneath the counter.

When she and Becky left the store, the women gave her envious looks that she had been allowed to use the catalog. As Blaze rode out of town she didn't notice the man who had stepped outside and stood watching her through narrowed eyes.

They were within two miles of the cabin when Blaze heard the faint howl of a wolf. It seemed to come from the foothills of the mountain, but when she peered that way she saw no sign of the animal. Nevertheless she urged the stallion into a fast-paced trot. She would feel much better when she got to the safety of the cabin.

Blaze's anxiety grew when a series of yowls rent the air, this time louder and nearer. She looked over her shoulder, and fear like a piece of ice settled in the pit of her stomach. A pack of five gray, lean bodies was coming up behind them.

It seemed to Blaze that in the blink of an eye they were surrounded by the snarling, yipping animals. Becky began to cry and push herself closer to Blaze as the stallion whistled his terror, his eyes rolling as he danced about.

Blaze was equally terrified, but she kept telling herself that she mustn't lose control, that her and Becky's life depended on her keeping a firm hand on the reins.

But when the wolves circled closer around the stallion, nipping at its heels and legs, it raised itself up on its haunches and, with a frenzied scream, tore away. As Blaze fought to check its headlong flight, trying desperately to stay on its back, the animal got the bit fast between its strong jaws and ran wild across the range.

Blaze felt that her arms would be yanked from their sockets as she pulled on the reins, trying to slow the breakneck speed of the flashing hooves. She was sure she could hang on no longer, that she and Becky would go flying over the horse's head and be trampled to death, when from the corner of her eye she saw a horse coming up beside her. The rider grabbed the stallion's bridle close to his mouth, and within seconds the animal was slowed down to a walk.

Blaze reached around Becky and patted the animal's trembling, sweaty neck. She looked over her shoulder in the direction from which they had made their wild dash and shivered, although she could barely make out the gray shapes of the wolves who sat looking after them. She returned her attention to the man who had probably saved her and Becky's life.

He was attractive in a hard sort of way, somewhere in his late thirties, she judged. Smiling, she held her hand out to him. The way he returned her smile, she pegged him as being used to attracting women. She didn't care for his sort. She had seen too many of his ilk in the many outlaw camps she had lived in. In fact, he reminded her of someone she couldn't quite place, and she wondered if he had ever been in one of those camps. Maybe when she was younger.

However, she told herself, whether he was an outlaw or a plain cowboy, she owed him thanks. She was sincere when she said, "My daughter and I are thankful that you came along."

"So am I." The man smiled, his eyes caressing her, lingering a moment too long on her breasts. "It's not every day that Deke Meyer has the good fortune to rescue such a beautiful woman."

Blaze let his flattery pass and said, "Well, Mr. Meyer, Becky and I had better get on home. Those clouds to the north look like they're going to pour down water anytime now."

"Do you live near here?" Meyer asked, plainly wanting to talk further with her. "Maybe I should ride along with you just in case the wolves decide to trail you again."

"Thank you, but that's not necessary. Our ranch is just behind that knoll to your right."

Cotter Mullen's eyes narrowed a fraction. Then, maneuvering his mount up to Blaze until their legs rubbed against each other, he said in soft tones, "You didn't tell me your name."

Blaze frowned slightly and was relieved when

the stallion sidestepped, putting some distance between them. "I'm Mrs. Ward," she said, her voice curt.

Cotter quickly lowered his lids to hide his jubilation. As he had expected, the little beauty was Hunter Ward's wife.

When Blaze said, "Thank you again, Mr. Meyer. I have to go now," Cotter smiled pleasantly and let her go. He knew where she lived now, and in the near future he would come visiting.

Blaze felt the bore of Deke Meyer's eyes on her back as she rode away, and a shiver shuddered up her spine. Deke Meyer was a cruel and ruthless man. She had seen it in the coldness of his eyes and the thin line of his lips. She hoped never to be caught alone with the man.

They hadn't ridden far when Becky craned her neck around to look up at Blaze. "Becky no like man," she said. "He bad."

Trust a child to know the character of a man, Blaze thought.

The outlaw remained where he was for several minutes after Blaze left him. He had made a change in his plans. He had thought before only to grab the woman Blaze, and let the stallion carry the kid on home.

But the thought had come to him, Why not take Ward's daughter first and hold her for ransom? He and his squaw needed money. He would demand that the woman bring the money and then he would keep her.

Mullen lifted the reins, a satisfied look on his rough features. Everything was going to work out fine.

# *Chapter Twelve*

Hunter pulled the collar of his black slicker up around his ears. The drizzly rain that had been falling when they broke camp had now turned into a freezing downpour.

The gray, wet range was a dreary sight, he thought as he trailed along behind the cattle. The icy keening of the wind seemed to bite into the very marrow of his bones.

Hunter's eyes felt gritty from only a few hours of light sleep. One of the men had foolishly shot at a deer, and the unexpected boom of the gun had sent the cattle into a headlong flight. Knowing that they would never be able to stop them, he had yelled out to the cowboys, "Keep the hellions moving. When it comes time to make night camp they'll be tired and ready to feed and bed down."

The ruse had worked, but the longhorns had remained nervous and sullen. Consequently, he had been afraid to sink into a deep sleep in case the ornery critters decided to run again.

Luckily, if everything went right he would be meeting the commissary agent tomorrow and the devils would no longer be his concern.

Worrying about the cattle hadn't been the only thing that had kept him from a restful sleep. The woman he was married to insisted on creeping into his mind. Sometimes he would welcome her in his dozing state; other times he would rail at her, asking why she hadn't gone on to California instead of settling in the wilds of Wyoming to live in a tent with the Wilson brothers to see to her needs. And why had she demanded that he marry her, knowing the opinion he held of her?

Now, awake, shivering with hunched shoulders, Hunter asked himself the same question. Why had she insisted on marriage? Had she been shrewd enough to figure out that in the long run it would be to her advantage to marry an up-and-coming rancher?

He berated himself for giving in to her demands and agreeing that neither one of them would fool around outside the marriage. He thought of the years stretching ahead, living like a monk, and knew he couldn't do it. When he got home he was going to tell her straight out that if she didn't share his bed, he was going to make a weekly trip to Lucianne's place. For God's sake, he was only thirty-three years old. Much too young to be put out to pasture.

It hit him then that Blaze would also be free to seek a lover. The thought brought a constriction in his chest, and his hands balled into fists. The vision of her long legs wrapped around a man other than himself was unthinkable.

"But why is it unthinkable?" he asked himself. "She means nothing to me."

"If that is true," his inner voice was quick to say, "why does it make you bleed to think of another man holding her softness, kissing her red lips, murmuring love words to her? You know you have that kind of dream about her, that you would like it to be real.

"I think you are a coward, Hunter Ward. You're too afraid of being fooled again."

"And I think you're loco," Hunter snapped. "I admit that I lust after her, but that is as far as it goes."

But what was the answer to his dilemma? he asked himself. The answer was clear. He wanted Blaze and no other. He wanted a real marriage with her. But before there could be trust between them, he would have to put from his mind all the men she had known. It wouldn't be easy, he knew. Especially when he thought of Jenny and the way she'd betrayed him. Could he do it? He didn't know. He could only give it his best effort.

Hunter was suddenly anxious to get home, to start courting his wife.

*    *    *

Blaze slowly came awake. As she lay in the warm cocoon of her feather comforter, with Becky snuggled up against her, she dreaded throwing back the covers and making the cold dash to the main room. Before, when Hunter was home, he had always risen first and had a roaring fire going in the fireplace as well as one in the big black cookstove. She also missed the pot of coffee that would be waiting for her.

The weather had changed drastically the past two days. It was gloomy, with cloudy gray skies, and a sharp wind that chilled any exposed flesh. But, as Rose had pointed out, it was that time of the year, a forewarning of what was to come later: a winter such as most of the homesteaders had never seen.

Well, she couldn't lie in bed all day, Blaze thought. And besides, she wanted the cabin warmed up before Becky awakened. Gathering her courage and gritting her teeth, she threw back the covers and hurried into her heavy robe, while her feet were feeling for her fur-lined house slippers.

Her teeth chattered as she knelt and rekindled the fire in the fieldstone fireplace, which could hold two large logs if needed on a freezing winter day. Flames bit into the wood, causing it to snap and crackle. She stood up and braced herself to go into the kitchen, which would be colder than the main room. Unlike the fireplace, which kept a little warmth from the banked fire in it, there would be nothing but cold ashes in the cookstove.

Blaze was quite adept at building fires now, and she soon had the stove fired up. She worked the pump handle then, filling the coffeepot with water. When she had added coffee grounds she lifted one of the stove lids and, after placing it on the back of the stove, she set the pot directly on the flames. In a matter of a few minutes the coffee was perking, sending out its sharp aroma.

Blaze stood a moment, holding her chilled fingers over the heat that was already radiating from the cast iron. She walked over to the window then and pushed aside the curtains. Outside everything seemed shrouded in a gray mist. Was it going to rain? she wondered. She hoped not. The days were short enough as it was without being able to set foot outdoors, even if it was only for a short walk around the yard and a trip down to the stables to see if the stallion was all right.

Blaze was ready to turn from the window when the first drops of rain plopped onto the dusty yard. "Darn!" she muttered as more splotches joined the first one. It seemed that within minutes pools of water were forming in low spots. With a long sigh she began preparing breakfast. Becky would be up soon, eager to eat and asking the same question: "Papa be home today?"

The fine, misty rain fell and stopped intermittently, the overcast skies warning that this condition would be the theme of the day. Blaze accepted the fact that she would be housebound all day and wondered what she could do to pass the time.

"I might as well get used to that," she told herself, for when the snow arrived there would be many days when she couldn't leave the cabin.

It was around one o'clock, shortly after she and Becky had eaten lunch, when Blaze heard the sound of hooves splashing through the mud and water outside. She glanced out the window and smiled delightedly. Her friend, Rose, bundled up in a slicker, had come to visit. She hurried to open the door as her neighbor slid off the back of an old, stubborn-looking mule.

"Rose," she cried, "hurry on in and sit by the fire."

"A little heat will feel good." Rose paused in the doorway to shed her slicker. When she had given it a couple of hard shakes, getting rid of most of the water, she handed it to Blaze. "This dampness goes right through a person." As Blaze hung the black garment on a peg behind the cookstove, Rose added as she sat down at the table, "I just had to get out of the cabin for a while or go crazy. Jake has been under my feet all day, makin' my ears ring with his constant beefin' at the weather."

"I sympathize with you." Blaze looked meaningfully at Becky, who was leaning against Rose's legs. "She asks me a dozen times a day when Hunter is coming home."

When the little one gazed up at Rose and asked, "Papa be home soon?" Rose picked her up and sat her in her lap.

"He'll be home any day now," she said, then looked at Blaze for confirmation.

"I look for him near the end of the week," Blaze

answered as she poured them each a cup of coffee and set out a platter of sugar cookies she had tried her hand at the day before.

"Have you missed him?" Rose asked, watching Blaze's face as she sat down.

Blaze pulled the sugar bowl toward her and dipped a spoon in it. "Yes," she said, stirring the sweetener into the dark liquid. "I miss his company, what little I've had of it. And I feel safer when he's in the cabin at night." She smiled faintly. "He always had fires going and a pot of coffee made by the time I got up. I miss that."

"Well now, that's nice of him to do that for you," Rose encouraged.

"Oh, I'm not sure he really does it for me." Blaze laughed. "Maybe he still doesn't trust me to make a decent cup of coffee."

"I doubt that, Blaze. I don't know your husband all that well, but I've got a feelin' that beneath that hard look of his, there's a kindness in him."

"Oh, there is. He couldn't be sweeter when it comes to his daughter. However, I've only seen that side of him on rare occasions."

Blaze took a sip of her coffee and, setting it back down, said, "I shouldn't expect him to be otherwise, considering I forced him to marry me."

"Blaze," Rose said thoughtfully, "did you ever stop to think that if marriage was the only way Hunter could get someone to take care of his home and daughter, there are any number of single women who would jump at the chance to become Mrs. Hunter Ward?"

"No, I haven't, but if he married one of them, he wouldn't be able to treat her the same way he does me. He'd have to treat her like a real wife. Since he's still in love with Becky's mother, he couldn't bring himself to do that."

"I think you're wrong," Rose said and then changed the subject. "Have you heard that Lucianne and all her girls but one are down with influenza? I guess the one who is still on her feet is bein' run ragged takin' care of the others. Accordin' to Doc Hines, Lucianne is pretty bad off. She needs more care than the girl can give her."

"Can't he find some woman who is willing to come in and help out?"

"None have stepped forward, and I guess the doctor doesn't want to ask, them bein' whores and all."

"But they're human beings," Blaze exclaimed indignantly. "They shouldn't be ignored and left to die like sick animals."

Blaze leaned forward. "Rose, would you keep Becky at your place for a few days? I'm going to go take care of the madam until she is well."

Rose looked scandalized for a moment, then relented. Hadn't she, more or less, done the same thing by championing this girl when all the other women in the train had shunned her?

Rose stood up and poured herself another cup of coffee. When she sat back down she said, "I'd be delighted to take care of Becky as long as you want me to. But you know the women's tongues will wag all the more if you move in there. And you must give some thought to how Hunter will take to you bein' there."

"I don't give a snap of my fingers what those busybodies say. And as for Hunter, he and his friends have used Lucianne's girls innumerable times, I'm sure. They're the ones who should be nursing them."

Rose could only say, "Maybe you're right."

"I'll go pack Becky's clothes now," Blaze said, already on her way out of the kitchen. Within ten minutes she had the little dresses and underclothing she had made packed in a leather satchel.

Becky was excited about riding on the mule and going to Rose's for a visit, so there weren't any tears when she and Rose rode away.

But tears smarted the backs of Blaze's eyes as she packed some clothes for herself. She was going to miss the little one. Blaze wouldn't let herself think about how much she'd miss little Becky as she saddled the stallion and swung onto his back. She was about to pass the Wilsons' finished cabin when an idea struck her. She would ask the brothers to keep an eye on the ranch while she was gone.

As the stallion wended his way among the many stumps jutting out of the ground, Blaze heard a pounding coming from behind the cabin. She steered her mount in that direction and reined in when she saw David and James slipping and splashing through mud and water as they worked at fashioning a door to the shedlike building in which their horses would be sheltered from the fierce cold once winter set in.

They both looked up when she cleared her throat. Wide smiles lit up their faces and James said, "It's about time you came visiting."

"You know that calling on you two is out of bounds," she said with a grin, water dripping off her hat brim.

"I take it Ward is still gone, since you're here anyway," David teased as he hammered in the last nail that would complete the door.

"Yes. I don't expect him back until the end of the week. However, I didn't come to visit. I'm in a hurry to get to the fort. Lucianne and three of her girls are down with the flu and need some nursing. The doctor and the one woman who is not ill are worn out from tending to them."

"Good Lord, Blaze, you're tempting the Devil to go there. Hunter will raise holy hell with you," James said, concern for her wrinkling his forehead.

Blaze shrugged. "He's always raising hell with me about something or other. Lucianne is a friend of mine from way back. She needs me."

If the brothers were curious as to how Blaze could be friends with a woman running a whorehouse, they didn't let on. David only said, "I take it you want us to take care of the little girl while you're gone." As he spoke he gathered up the tools and tossed them into the shed.

"No, Rose has taken Becky home with her. I was just hoping you could ride by the ranch every day or so, make sure everything is all right there while I'm gone."

"Sure thing, Blaze," James answered. "I just wish we could help you out when Hunter learns what you're up to."

"I'm afraid I'll have to face him on my own," Blaze responded laughingly as she dug her heels into the stallion's sides and galloped away.

As Blaze rode up to the fort, it seemed as though half the population of the area had braved the rain to come to the trading post on this Saturday afternoon. Beneath the roof of the narrow porch a group of ranchers stood at one end, no doubt talking about cattle, while on the other end homesteaders stood about. Their faces showed many expressions. Some looked hopeful, but most looked doubtful about their future. Blaze wondered how many of them would still be here this time next year.

As she rode past the fort she could see Bridger through the grime-covered window, hurrying about, waiting on his customers. A grim smile curved her lips when one of the women spotted her and hurried to the window. Within seconds four other faces were peering out at her.

Blaze's ears would have burned had she been able to hear what they were saying to each other.

"It don't seem right that a woman like that should snag the most eligible bachelor in the area," Caroline Hank opined.

"I bet Hunter was barely out of sight before she was up to her old tricks," another added.

"Do you suppose she's gone off and left the child alone?" a heavyset mother of two teenage daughters wondered out loud.

"I'm sure she hasn't done that," a young woman, newly married, defended Blaze. "She seems awfully fond of the little one. I heard she had to teach the child English, and that she keeps her clean and well dressed. Rose Hackett told me that Mrs. Ward sewed the pretty little dresses that she wears."

"Ha." Mrs. Hanks snorted. "All put on for her husband's benefit. Who knows what goes on when he's not around?"

The young wife opened her mouth to say that she thought they were all wrong about Blaze Ward, but she was interrupted when Mrs. Hank hissed, "Look! She's going to the whorehouse."

"Why would she be goin' there?" someone asked. "Doesn't she know them women are all down with the flu?"

"I heard tell she's a close friend of that Lucianne," Caroline said contemptuously. "She's probably gonna take care of her."

Bridger had overheard their conversation, and his manner was very cool to those who still had money to trade with. But his building anger found an outlet when Mrs. Hank, whose family had food only because of Blaze's generosity, plunked two bolts of material on the counter and brazenly ordered, "I'll have a dress length off each one of these."

"Look, ma'am, you know you've got all the credit you're gonna get, so forget about any fripperies."

"I would hardly call clothes fripperies," Caroline answered sharply.

"They are when they're unnecessary," Bridger replied just as sharply. "Your two girls are dressed almost as good as Blaze Ward."

"What do you mean, almost as good? In my opinion they are dressed better."

"That's all you know about clothes." Bridger curled his lips. "You couldn't afford to buy the dresses Blaze wears." Bridger didn't know the worth of Blaze's clothing, but when he threw that bit in he figured Mrs. Hank didn't either.

Caroline only snorted, pushed aside the two bolts of material and stamped toward the door. Bridger grinned when the irate woman left the fort, her two sullen-faced daughters following her. The bitch didn't know any more than he did about the quality of cloth and clothing. It pleased him when he saw a couple of the women trying to hide grins. When he waited on them he slipped a jar of strawberry jelly in their packages.

When Blaze stepped into Lucianne's establishment, the odor of fevered bodies, chest ointments and unemptied chamber pots hit her in the face. A bewhiskered, harried-looking Dr. Caleb Hines greeted her.

"I hope you've come to lend me a hand," he said wearily, looking at her out of red-rimmed eyes. "If I don't get a couple hours' sleep pretty soon, I'm going to fall flat on my face."

"I'm here to help you, Doctor." Blaze shrugged

out of her wet slicker and hung it on one of the many pegs driven into the wall, where Lucianne's customers hung their coats while waiting to be escorted to one of the girls' rooms. "Tell me what to do."

"Lucianne is the worst off. All her air passages are inflamed and she's mostly out of her head with fever. She needs round-the-clock care. I hope that I can save her."

Anxiety was in Blaze's voice as she exclaimed, "Let me get started. Where is her room?"

"Right this way." The doctor led her to a door that opened into Lucianne's private quarters.

When Blaze stepped into the good-sized room, she was struck with its opulence. Her feet seemed to sink into the carpet, which was the same blue color as the velvet drapes at the window. A quick glance around the room showed a divan upholstered in a delicate blue-and-white print positioned beneath the window. A fancy table sat between it and a chaise longue, which was a solid ecru in color. On the eastern side of the room there was a rocker beside a small shiny stove. Sitting on the floor next to it was a woven basket full of bright green yarn, and knitting needles stuck into what appeared to be a half-finished scarf. Blaze thought vaguely that Lucianne hadn't always been a whore. The sitting room testified to that.

And so did Lucianne's bedroom, Blaze realized later when she had the time to look at it. But for now her whole attention was on the woman who tossed restlessly on the high tester bed.

"Here are Lucianne's medicines and when she should take them," Dr. Hines said, indicating a fragile-looking table holding an array of bottles, a spoon and two glasses beside a water pitcher. When he had gone over the medication with Blaze, explaining how each one worked on the deadly flu, he said, "I'm going to stretch out on that fancy divan in there and catch some sleep. Lucianne won't need any of this for another couple hours. But call me if you need me."

And so started four days in which Blaze and the doctor worked at saving Lucianne's life. Twice they thought they had lost her, but the spunky woman hung on to the thin thread of life still within her.

On the fourth morning, around two o'clock, the madam passed the crisis and Blaze thanked God for it. Lucianne was very weak, and had lost a lot of weight, but she would live.

In the meantime her girls had recovered and had been up for two days. On the fifth morning Blaze turned the nursing of Lucianne over to her girls. She missed Becky and longed to wear her own clothes again. She felt half-naked in the dresses the girls had loaned her. They showed her knees and more of her cleavage than she was used to exposing.

Blaze found Lucianne propped up in bed enjoying a cup of tea. "Come join me," her friend said with a smile. "I have a nearly full pot and an extra cup. Caleb was supposed to share the tea with me, but I haven't seen the scamp."

As Blaze lifted the teapot and filled her cup from it, she gave Lucianne a mischievous look and remarked with a grin, "I think Dr. Hines is more to you than a doctor. When you were so ill, before your fever broke, he was like a wild man."

"Oh, honey"—the madam laughed—"even as a little girl you were always imagining things. Now, have you come to tell me that you are going home?"

"Yes, I have. I'll leave this afternoon," Blaze answered, spooning sugar into her tea. "I miss Becky and the cabin." She gave a short laugh. "I even find myself missing my grumpy husband sometimes. Why anyone would miss a crabby bear, though, is beyond me."

"When do you expect him home?"

"I don't know, but soon, I imagine. I'd like for Becky and me to be home when he arrives. Have the cabin warm."

Lucianne smiled to herself. Blaze probably didn't know it, but she was falling in love with her husband.

"Blaze, honey," she said, "I'll never forget what you've done for me and the girls. I don't know what we'd have done without you. Caleb was running himself ragged before you got here. Some of us might not have made it without your help."

"I was happy to do all I could, to pay back all the things you did for a lonely little girl. Anything nice and womanly about me is due to your teaching," Blaze said softly, hoping that her husband would understand why she'd spent the last five days at the Pleasure House.

# *Chapter Thirteen*

Hunter knew the little quarter horse was tired. He had been on the trail since early morning, stopping only once to let the horse drink at a shallow river.

Ordinarily he wouldn't push a mount so, but he was in a fever to get home and try to make peace with Blaze. Somehow he must convince her that they should try to make their marriage work, to be husband and wife in the true sense of the word. He was working hard at forgetting her past life.

Six days ago he had met with the commissary agent out of Chicago, at the stockyards where the trains stopped to take on water. The man liked the looks of the longhorns and gave him top price. With the check in his vest pocket Hunter went with his own men to the two-room building behind the water tower. The gray, weather-beaten building had been erected for the convenience of those who still rode the coaches to destinations the railroads didn't yet reach. It had only one door, which led into a room that served food cooked by the manager's Indian wife. The rear room was a saloon of sorts. Besides the rot gut whiskey the man served, there were also a couple of Indian whores. Hunter bought his men a round of drinks, then returned to the front room to be served a bowl of venison stew. With his appetite sated, he stuck his head in the saloon door to tell his men that he was leaving and that if they wanted to, they could remain here for two more days. He reminded them that there was still a working ranch waiting for them on their return.

Hunter hadn't been sure if his men had even heard him. At the time they were bickering over who should go first into the curtained-off cubicle in the back of the room and which of the two women they should take with them. He shook his head. Under normal circumstances the cowboys wouldn't dream of going to bed with such unattractive women. The youngest one had to be nearing forty, and her pockmarked face had one front tooth missing. The other one, somewhere in her fifties, was so fat she waddled when she walked.

But the men were feeling randy, and since there were only the two women available, they turned a blind eye to the shortcomings of the worn-out Indian squaws.

Hunter and the cook left then, heading for

home. Hunter had soon outdistanced the creaking chuck wagon in his hurry to see his daughter and try to work something out with his wife.

There were still a few hours of daylight left five days later when Hunter topped the familiar knoll that looked down on his cabin and holdings.

Everything looked the same as he had left it. Except, strangely, there was no smoke rising from either chimney. Why? he wondered. It was November and the weather was damned cold. He was surprised they hadn't had snow yet.

Suddenly anxiety gripped him. Something was wrong . . . very wrong. His apprehension grew as he neared the cabin. Even if Blaze had taken Becky and gone to visit Rose, she would have left a slow fire burning in the fireplace.

When Hunter stepped into the kitchen, he got the feeling that the cabin had been empty for a long time. There was a dead stillness about it. He laid a hand on the cookstove on his way to the main room. It was as cold as the day he bought it. When he hunkered down in front of the fireplace and sifted the gray ashes through his fingers, there was no life to them. He stood up. No fire had burned there for a long time.

Where were his wife and daughter? He ran his fingers through his hair. What had happened to them? Had a grub-liner come through and made off with them? He could understand Blaze being taken away, but a man wouldn't want to be bothered with a small child.

A thought came to Hunter that made his hands

ball into fists. Had Blaze gone back to the Wilson brothers? Had she taken Becky with her? He doubted that. She had probably taken the child to Rose Hackett.

Hunter left the cabin at a run, his face rivaling that of a storm cloud. He still had enough awareness about him, however, to realize that the weary little workhorse hadn't the stamina to take him to the Wilsons' unless it was at a slow walk. He was too much in a hurry for that. Saint would take him there as though he were flying.

James Wilson was chopping wood in front of the new cabin when Saint galloped up and was pulled to a gravel-scattering stop. "Where is she?" Hunter demanded, glaring down at James.

James leaned on the ax handle, a hint of amusement in his eyes. "By 'she', I imagine you're referring to Blaze."

"You know damn well I am. She and my daughter."

Looking up at his scowling face, James couldn't wait to say the words that would wipe the arrogance off the proud rancher's face. Pronouncing each word clearly so that Hunter couldn't misunderstand him, he said, "Your wife has been living at Lucianne's the past five days." After seeing Hunter go pale, he softened his voice somewhat as he added, "Your little girl is with Rose Hackett."

Hunter wanted to spring at the man who had dealt him such a blow, to beat the mockery off his handsome face. He managed somehow to control himself and, thumping the stallion with his heels, sent it toward the fort at a dead run.

When Hunter drew rein in front of the Pleasure House, he was struck by how quiet it was in the long building. Also, he was surprised by the absence of horses tied to the hitching post. It was nearing dusk and usually a few men would already be here, claiming that they wanted to get the girls while they were still fresh.

Leaving the saddle, Hunter stepped up on the porch and rapped loudly on the red-painted door. He had to knock twice more before he heard light footsteps moving across the room in which he had waited many times years ago.

He hadn't expected Blaze to answer the door and, taken by surprise, he only stared at her a moment, while inside him a battle raged. He wanted to grab her, mold her body to his as he kissed her soft red lips. At the same time he wanted to shake her, rail at her for being a common whore.

His last impulse took precedence. While the startled Blaze stared up at him he said, ice dripping from each word, "So, you are here. I thought maybe James Wilson was lying."

"As you can see, he wasn't," Blaze said just as coldly. "Is that all he told you?"

"Wasn't that enough? What more did he have to tell me? I didn't wait around for him to tell me how many men you've entertained since you returned to your old trade."

"I see," Blaze said in dead tones, wishing she could get her hands on James for not telling the whole truth. But knowing her husband's low opinion of her, she supposed it wouldn't have made any difference if James had told him everything. One way or another, the big, scowling man would have come to the same conclusion.

Still gripping the door, Blaze waited for the condemnation about to be showered on her head. What Hunter said, however, was the last thing she expected.

Passing an insolent look over her body, taking in the short, gaudy dress that barely covered her breasts, he said with a curl of his lips, "I'll be back later to see how Lucianne's new whore performs. How much do you charge?"

Her lips a white line, the muscles in her legs trembling with red-hot fury, Blazed lashed out at him. "You rotten piece of scum. I'm going to tell you something I swore I never would. But it's going to give me great pleasure now to tell you that I have never known a man in the way the Bible describes it. I am a virgin and I intend to remain that way. And furthermore, I'm not returning to the ranch with you."

Hunter's face paled beneath the whisker stubble on his cheeks and jaw. He knew Blaze spoke the truth from the way she flung her fiery words at him. "Why didn't you tell me this the first time I insulted you?" he asked, his voice shaky.

"As if you would have believed me," Blaze answered in a flat voice. "Anyway, it didn't bother me a whit what you thought of me. I've enjoyed watching you make an ass of yourself."

"I've certainly done that," Hunter said wearily,

passing a hand over his mouth and jaw. "But there was so much about you that pointed to your being a loose woman: you were practically living with two single men. I'm not the only one who thought you had loose morals."

"You mean those women who gossip about me? Let me tell you something about them. They never mention how it was their husbands who forced me to travel with David and James. When Grandpa died they were going to leave me behind because there was no man to drive my wagon any longer. They didn't care what could happen to a woman alone. When the brothers, who had no wagon, stepped forward and offered to drive mine, they saved me from God knows what.

"When we arrived here I had no money, no place to go. So I parked my wagon close to their camp-site for their protection. They fed me and looked after my well-being until you showed up. They have always acted the gentlemen toward me. They never thought that I was a loose woman."

"Stop, Blaze," Hunter begged. "You're making me feel lower than a snake's belly. Please come home with me. You must know that things will be different between us from now on. Besides, what about Becky? You're the only mother she has ever known. She will be heartbroken to lose you."

When Blaze still looked as though she was going to carry out her decision not to go home with him, Hunter said, a note of pleading in his voice, "I don't expect you to sleep with me if you don't want to. But if we start out fresh, get to know each other, maybe in time you will change your mind."

The look Blaze gave him said that she doubted that would ever happen, but Hunter pressed on. "What do you say? Will you give me another chance?"

Before Blaze could answer there was the sound of a window opening above them. Lucianne called out anxiously, "Are you all right, Blaze?"

"Please tell her that you're all right," Hunter begged.

Blaze knew she must give Lucianne an answer. "I'm fine," she called. "Hunter and I are discussing whether or not I will return home with him."

There was silence from above for a moment: then Lucianne said, "If you don't want to go back to the ranch, honey, you're welcome to stay here with me."

"I'm happy to hear that, Lucianne. I may take you up on it." An image of Becky's small face appeared before her then. Could she bear to give her up?

"What will you do about Becky if I don't return?" She felt herself weakening.

"I don't know. Hire Rose Hackett to look after her, I guess. She could watch the little one during the day and I'll be with her at night."

"Rose likes Becky, but I don't think she would care to have her around all the time," Blaze said, then made a fast decision, one that had a lot to do with the anguish she saw in Hunter's eyes. "I'll say good-bye to Lucianne and then we'll leave."

A wide, surprised smile curved Hunter's lips. He

couldn't believe that he was getting a second chance.

Riding two horse lengths behind Hunter, Blaze tucked her chin into the folds of her shawl. It was bitterly cold and she was afraid that they wouldn't reach home before it started snowing.

When they reached the place where the trail forked off toward the Hackett place, Hunter rode on past it. Blaze called out, "We have to pick Becky up."

"I'll get her tomorrow. It's growing late and I want to get home before dark. It looks like it's going to snow."

That made sense, Blaze thought, but she needed the presence of the little girl in the cabin. Being alone with Hunter would be nerve-racking. How would they pass the evening? What would they talk about? They knew nothing about each other, had never had more than two or three civil conversations.

A piercing wind had picked up and now Blaze could only think about how cold she was, and how soon would it be before they got home.

The wind grew more fierce, and when they reached the ranch it was whipping the branches of the pines sheltering the sturdy cabin. "I'll put the horses in the barn after I've started a fire in the fireplace and the kitchen stove," Hunter called over the roar of the wind as he slid off Saint's back. Before Blaze could dismount, he put his hands on her waist and lifted her out of the saddle. She was too surprised to thank him.

As they stepped up on the porch, flakes of snow began to fall. "We made it just in time," Hunter said, pushing open the heavy door made of split oak. "I'm afraid we're going to have a full-fledged blizzard. I feel sorry for anyone caught out in it."

"It's almost as cold inside as outside," Blaze muttered, still bundled up as she sat watching Hunter kindle a fire in the large fireplace. When Hunter had flames reaching up the chimney, he went into the kitchen and lit a fire in the big black stove. It wasn't long before she heard him leave the cabin to tend to the horses.

Heat from the fire began reaching out to Blaze, and she rose and went into the bedroom she shared with Becky. She removed her jacket and shawl and whipped the hated dress over her head and flung it aside. Her blue woolen robe lay at the foot of the bed and she slipped it on for the time being. Later she would have a long bath before putting on clean clothes.

With comfortable house slippers on her feet she walked into the kitchen. Now, what to make for supper? she wondered, standing in the middle of the floor, chewing thoughtfully at her lower lip. The meals at Lucianne's had been skimpy and far between because everybody was busy taking care of the sick ones. What she would like was a big steak and a baked potato. She imagined Hunter would like that too.

When Hunter entered the kitchen a short time later, his hat and shoulders white with snow,

Blaze had two potatoes in the oven and was trying to slice a couple of steaks off a side of beef.

Hunter watched her sawing away at the meat, then as he took off his jacket, he said with a grin, "You'd better let me do that before you cut off a finger."

"I'll not argue with you." Blaze handed him the knife with a smile. As he cut easily into the meat she opened a can of corn and poured it into a pan to simmer on the stove. She still didn't know how to bake bread or make biscuits, so she turned her hand to stirring up a batch of skillet bread.

Once the steaks were cut, Hunter leaned against the table watching Blaze move about, enjoying her graceful movements, the gentle sway of her hips. He imagined them cradling his own as he made love to her. When he felt the stirring of an arousual he sat down at the table to hide its bulge from her. She would think him a randy bull.

When he managed to control the throbbing between his legs, he said with a smile, "I see you're figuring out how to organize a meal."

"Yes, with Rose's tutoring." Blaze relaxed a little. Maybe it wouldn't be too bad, spending an evening with Hunter.

Nevertheless, she would feel more comfortable when Becky came home.

As Blaze had hoped, the meal she put on the table couldn't be faulted. Hunter was generous with his praise after he forked a piece of steak into his mouth, chewed and swallowed.

"It's just the way I like it." He beamed at her. "If

you keep feeding me meals like this I'm going to get fat this winter."

Her face flushed with pleasure at his praise, Blaze looked at Hunter's whip-lean body and doubted that. His type of build would never run to fat, even when he was an old man. His boundless energy would see to that.

When the meal was eaten and Blaze started to pour their coffee, Hunter stood up. "Let's have it in front of the fire after we've done the dishes."

"We?" Blaze asked, thinking that surely she had misunderstood him.

"Sure, we. Do you think I don't know how to dry dishes?"

Blaze shrugged. "The only man I ever saw do it was my grandfather."

"I'm sorry about your losing him," Hunter said quietly as he began to stack the dirty dishes.

"Thank you," Blaze said, filling the dishpan with water from a large black teakettle. "I lost my father, too, you know."

"No, I didn't know. When was that?"

Blaze frowned. Was he going to pretend he didn't remember her father being killed? Her chagrin sounded in her voice when she said, "You know when. You were there, at the outlaw camp when Garf Mullen shot and killed him."

Stunned, Hunter paused in drying a plate. "That isn't what the sheriff said when I took his body in."

Blaze relented with an unhappy sigh. "Dad always used an alias. He didn't want my mother's people to know that he had turned outlaw. Mama's parents had begged her not to marry the handsome stranger who worked for them one season."

"How come you didn't go to your mother's people when you lost your father and grandfather?"

"Number one, I don't know where they live, even if they are still alive, and number two, I doubt if they would want Luke Adlington's daughter."

"But shouldn't you at least give them a chance to decide?"

"No. If they wouldn't accept my father, I wouldn't want to know them."

If there was one thing Hunter had learned about his wife, it was that she was a stubborn little soul. Now he also discovered that she was loyal to those she loved. He found himself wanting that same faithfulness from her. No doubt those fine qualities had come from her mother. But then again, maybe there also lived inside her traits of her wild outlaw father. Perhaps she was not to be completely trusted.

Hunter resumed drying the plate. At any rate, he wished that he had known Luke Adlington was Blaze's father. Things would be different between him and Blaze now.

When the kitchen was put to order, Blaze and Hunter carried their coffee into the main room and placed the cups on the table that sat between two chairs. While Hunter laid more wood on the fire Blaze lit the lamp. With their feet propped up on the hearth, they sipped at the hot, strong brew,

229

watching the flames dance and listening to the snow brush against the window. A peacefulness she hadn't known since losing her father and grandfather stole over Blaze. If only it could last, she thought, but knew that it wouldn't. There was no love between her and Hunter, and that was necessary for two people to live in harmony with each other.

The comfortable silence was broken suddenly when from outside came the sound of galloping hooves. "What fool would be out on a night like this?" Hunter muttered, leaving his warm spot before the fire and going to look out the kitchen window.

When he returned there was a relieved smile on his face. "It's the cowhands. I was beginning to be a little concerned about them. I had told them they could stay behind a couple of days after we delivered the cattle, but when the weather changed I was sorry I hadn't insisted they come home with me and Bucky."

"Well, it looks like they changed their minds," Blaze said as the clock whirred, then struck nine times.

Blaze stretched and yawned. "I think I'll take a bath and then turn in," she said.

"A bath sounds good," Hunter said, then grinned crookedly. "I'm sure I smell like a hibernating bear." He stood up. "I'm going to mosey on down to the bunkhouse and soak in a tub of water. Talk to the men a bit."

While Blaze dragged the wooden tub into

Becky's room and filled it with water from the stove, Hunter sat talking to his men as Bucky prepared a bath for him.

"How come you men came home early? Surely you didn't spend all your money so quickly in that flea-bitten tavern."

"Naw," his drover said. "We didn't have time. I got the feelin' that the weather was goin' to turn bad so I insisted we start home the day after you left."

"How was the trip back? I know it was cold."

The drover nodded. "The first five days were cold enough to freeze the balls off a wooden Indian. But we didn't run into snow until about twenty miles back."

"I'm glad you're back," Hunter said. "If it continues to snow like it's doing now, we'll have to haul hay out to the cattle."

He noted that Bucky had a tub of water waiting for him. He stood up, shucked off his clothes and stepped into the steaming water. His men started a game of poker while Bucky made them some supper.

Back at the cabin, Blaze stepped out of the tub and quickly toweled off her shivering body. The warmth of the bedroom had quickly dissipated when the closed door shut off the heat from the main room.

She pulled a flannel gown over her head and, as she shrugged into her robe and house slippers, she glanced down at the bathwater. What should she do with it? she wondered. She wasn't about to drag the tub out onto the snow-covered porch.

She decided that she would leave it where it was for the time being. She would take care of it tomorrow.

That decision made, she opened the bedroom door so the heat could flow back in and then hurried into bed. She was half-asleep as she pulled the covers up around her ears. It had been an emotionally charged day and her mind demanded rest.

The snow squeaked beneath Hunter's feet as he hurried to the cabin. Would Blaze still be up? He hoped so. He would like to spend more time with her.

He found the main room empty. A disappointed sigh escaped him. He'd have to wait until morning to see her again.

A thought hit him then. Maybe she was still awake and he could stand in her doorway and talk to her awhile.

His hopes high, he walked softly down the hall and stopped in front of Blaze's open door. Her lamp was still lit, but turned down low. In its dim glow he saw that Blaze was sound asleep, only the top half of her face showing above the covers. His gaze fell on the tub of bathwater. He stepped inside the room and, after hefting it, carried it out. When he had taken it out onto the porch and tilted it so that the water could drain out, he went back into the main room.

He sighed again. He might as well go to bed. When he had laid more wood on the fire, then banked it so that it would burn slowly all night, he went to bed and dreamed all night of holding Blaze in his arms, making love to her.

A dead silence awakened Blaze. It took her a moment to realize that the wind no longer blew and that snow wasn't brushing against the window. The storm had blown itself out.

As she lay in the warm cocoon of the feather bed, dreading the thought of getting up and braving the cold room, she became aware of the aroma of frying bacon wafting into her room. Was Hunter making breakfast?

Not wanting him to think that she was a lie-a-bed, she pushed back the covers and reached for her robe. As she pushed her feet into her house slippers she noticed that the tub of water was gone. When had Hunter taken it away?

She hurried into the kitchen and found Hunter standing by the stove. He looked up and stared at her.

She has never looked lovelier, he thought, his gaze going over her sleep-filled eyes, her hair hanging past her shoulders in a tangled, curly mass. He couldn't speak for a moment, so great was his desire to sweep her up, carry her to his bed and there make love to her all day.

Blaze saw the desire in his eyes and became confused and muddled. "I'll finish making breakfast," she said in a strained voice.

"That's all right," Hunter said. "I've almost got it done. By the time you've washed up I'll have it on the table."

When Blaze had splashed water on her face and used the towel, she sat down at the table. "I want to thank you for carrying out my bathwater," she said.

"It was no trouble. That's the least a man can do for his wife." He grinned at her as he carried two plates of bacon and eggs to the table.

Blaze reached for a slice of bread, thinking to herself that it was more than he would have done for her in the past. But I must stop thinking of the past, she thought. They would never get along if she continued to remember all that had gone on before.

When Hunter joined her and picked up his fork, he said, "I'm going to get the men started on taking hay to the cattle; then I'll go pick Becky up."

Blaze smiled eagerly. "I can't wait to see her. I've missed her terribly."

Hunter was aware that his daughter was the reason Blaze had come home with him. He wished it weren't so. He would give half his ranch if he had been the reason.

But that was a foolish wish. After the way he had treated her, why would she come back because of him? By the time he finished eating breakfast he had vowed that he was going to change Blaze's opinion of him. Never again would he give her cause to dislike him.

When he had lingered over breakfast as long as possible without being obvious about it, he said, "I'd better be going."

Blaze stood up with him. "I want you to take

along a blanket to wrap Becky up in. She was only wearing her coat and hood when I dropped her off at Rose's. It wasn't nearly so cold then."

A short time later she watched her wide-shouldered husband stride toward the barn, the blanket draped over his arm. *You are a handsome devil,* she thought, *and very likable when you want to be.*

The cabin was pretty much in the same condition as when Blaze had left it to go take care of Lucianne and her girls. But dust had managed to creep inside and cover everything with a fine gray film. It felt good to be dressed in her own clothes again, and she dug out her dust cloth and started in. She broke into song and smiled. She hadn't realized before just how much she loved her home.

When she had the cabin up to her standards, Blaze decided to bake a batch of Becky's favorite sugar cookies. It would be a homecoming surprise for her.

It was around ten o'clock and Blaze had a couple dozen cookies cooling on the worktable when she glanced out the window and saw Hunter riding toward the cabin. She could only see the top of Becky's head, because Hunter had the blanket wrapped around her so securely. She flung open the door just as Hunter lifted his daughter to the ground. Becky tore the blanket from her face and rushed into Blaze's outstretched arms. Her eyes were sparkling with happiness.

"I've missed you." Blaze hugged the little body to her.

"Becky missed Mama too." Blaze received a squeeze around her neck.

Hunter sat looking down on them, thinking how good it felt having his two women home again.

# *Chapter Fourteen*

Cotter Mullen lay in the semigloom of the hut, staring up at its patched ceiling, which was only inches from his head when he stood up and walked about. When a cold breeze stirred the sewn-together burlap bags that made the fourth wall, he knew it was time to find better quarters. Each day it was growing colder. He didn't know how long it would take him to settle with Hunter Ward, so he'd best find something before a wind-driven blizzard came along and completely covered the shack.

As New Moon snored beside him he mapped out a plan that would be ideal if it worked. Unceremoniously he pushed the sleeping New Moon onto her back and crawled between her legs. She grunted as he plunged himself inside her, then quickly came awake and arched her back to receive more of him.

Lying hunched and shivering on a thin straw pallet, covered with only one moth-eaten blanket she had found discarded in the brush, Pearl lay listening to the hoarse breathing and the slapping of bellies coming together from the soft pile of furs that New Moon had brought from her village.

She thanked God that she wasn't the one taking the battering of her husband's body. She didn't even mind that the Indian woman treated her with scorn, ordering her about, and even striking her now and again. She would endure almost anything that would save her from Cotter's cruel treatment.

She knew from previous times that it would be close to an hour before the lusty pair would be sated. She could sleep a little longer before she had to face another day that seemed to have no end.

However, Pearl slept longer than she had intended and was awakened by a hard kick to her side. As she sucked in against the pain of it, Cotter ordered, "Get your ass out of bed, you lazy slut, and make us some breakfast. I'm makin' some changes today, which I'll tell you about after we've eaten."

Pearl pulled on her scuffed shoes with holes in the soles and hurried outside with the thin blanket around her shoulders. As she kindled a fire in the same spot she had used since coming to the hovel, she wondered what her husband had cooked up in that scheming brain of his and in what way it would affect her. Did he plan on going off and leaving her to fend for herself? She wouldn't put it past him. He had worn her out and had no more use for her now that he had New Moon. The Indian was equal to his lustful demands, was even strong enough to hold her own if he should try to beat her.

Although the thought of being left alone on the mountainside was a little bit scary, she would welcome not ever having to see Cotter Mullen again. To be free of his punishing fists.

When the salt pork and beans were hot, Pearl called out that breakfast was ready. As Cotter and New Moon filled their plates, she went and sat down on a tree stump, waiting for them to finish eating. She could then go and eat whatever they had left her. That had been the Indian's dictate and Cotter had readily fallen in with it.

Cotter was still eating when he put a question to New Moon. "Do you think your people would mind if we moved to your village and lived in your tepee? It's gettin' too cold to live here much longer."

New Moon stared into the flames of the cook fire, hiding the crafty look that had jumped into her black eyes. She wanted the white woman out of Cotter Mullen's life, and here, perhaps, was a way of arranging that.

She shifted her gaze to Cotter. "If the worthless white woman wasn't with us I could tell the tribe that you are my man. They would then welcome another hunter to help them find game."

"Good!" Cotter slapped his thigh. "I don't plan on Pearl going with us anyway. I have other plans for her."

Ripples of dread slithered up Pearl's spine when her husband turned his attention to her. What fate had he planned for her? Nothing good, she knew.

What he said was the last thing she expected to come out of his mouth. "I want you to hustle down to the fort and go knock on that Lucianne's door. I want you to convince her to hire you on to work for her."

Pearl stared at him, appalled. "I couldn't bring myself to sleep with the men who go in there, even if she wanted me to."

Cotter's lips curled in a sneer. "You crazy bitch, none of the men who go there would want to buy your services. I meant for you to hire on as a cook, or look after the women who whore for her." The threat of violence was in his eyes and tone when he said, "I don't care how you do it, but I want you in that house before nightfall."

Pearl shook her head in bewilderment. "I don't understand why you want me there."

"Because, you empty-headed bitch, I want you to listen and learn all you can about Hunter Ward and his wife. I want you to learn their habits. When Ward leaves his ranch and when he returns. I want to know if his wife has certain days she goes to the fort. Is it in the mornin's or afternoons?"

"But why do you need more information on Mr. Ward?" Pearl dared to question her husband. "You know where he lives. Why don't you wait on the fort trail someday and have it out with him?" *Shoot him in the back like you have other men,* Pearl added to herself.

Cotter shook his head. "That would be too easy a death for the bastard. I want him to suffer hard and long before I shoot him in the guts. I'm gonna get hold of that little girl of his for ransom money. And when his purty little wife brings it I'll make her do things to me that will rip him apart."

"But Mrs. Ward has never done anything to you. Why make her suffer, Cotter?"

"That don't make no difference. Anyhow, I got a hankerin' to ride that little filly."

Pearl slid a glance at New Moon and said, "I suppose you'll keep her after you've killed her husband." She noted that New Moon's eyes had become black slits as she waited for Cotter's answer.

Cotter's lips curved in a leering smile. "It wouldn't be hard, havin' her around. She's a fiery little piece that I'd enjoy tamin'." When he noticed the sullen look on New Moon's face he hastened to add as he dipped his hand into the vee of her neckline, "She couldn't please me the way my new woman does though. I'll never give this one up."

But as he fondled New Moon's heavy breasts, she didn't respond to him. She was remembering that Blaze Ward had taken one man away from her and that she could take Cotter if she wanted to. A fierce determination grew in the Indian woman's eyes. She would see to it that it never happened.

241

Cotter removed his hand from New Moon and gave Pearl a hard look. "What are you waitin' for? Get on down to the whorehouse."

"It won't work." Pearl tried to reason with him. "Look at the rags I'm wearing. That woman will never hire me. And what do I say when she asks me where I come from, if I have any relatives? And she'll want to know about my bruises, who has been beating me."

"That is a poser," Cotter agreed, not one to look very far ahead.

As he pondered Pearl's questions, New Moon spoke. "She can say that she and her husband were traveling alone to the fort and renegade Indians attacked them. They killed her husband and took her captive. She can say that one of the braves claimed her as his woman and that he beat her a lot."

"Now that's a real good idea, New Moon," Cotter exclaimed with a wide smile. "I'll reward you for it in just a minute." He rubbed a hand suggestively down his fly.

He turned hard, cold eyes on Pearl then. "If you don't convince that woman to hire you and you come draggin' back here, I'll tie you up and leave you for the wolves to gnaw on. Now get goin'."

"Where is the fort? I don't even know which direction to go. And how far is it?"

"Just keep walkin' east and you'll run into it. It's only about five or six miles."

With a ragged sigh Pearl stood up. Gathering the tattered blanket around her, she started out.

\* \* \*

Pearl plodded along, shivering violently in the thin blanket. Her tired legs felt as if she had been walking forever, but rationally she knew only about three hours had passed.

However long it had been, she knew one thing. She couldn't go on much longer. Cotter hadn't given her time to eat any of the breakfast she had prepared, and her meager strength was giving out.

Pearl continued to plod on, stopping often to rest. She grew panicky when she saw that the sun had disappeared behind gray clouds. She could become lost without it to guide her.

With sheer determination she was putting one foot in front of the other when great flakes of snow began to fall. She looked up at the dark, angry-looking sky. Bad weather was on the way and she prayed she would reach the fort before it arrived. She gave a frightened start when from a distance there came the yowl of a wolf. Her fear of being attacked gave her the strength to start running.

Pearl ran and ran until she could run no more. As she sank to the ground, enveloped in a swirl of snow, she saw the shadowy figure of a man coming toward her. She wondered if it was Cotter, coming to check whether she was going to the fort or was running away from him. But as oblivion overtook her she saw an elderly Indian kneel down beside her. *Maybe I'll get lucky*, she thought in a haze. *Maybe he will kill me.*

\* \*. \*

The Pleasure House was in full swing again. Lucianne's girls were fully recovered and were busy taking one man after another to their rooms. The men had been without them for over a week, and the whores were eager to make money again. Everybody was happy.

Everyone except Lucianne. The madam was kept busy cooking, cleaning and washing bed linens. Her once long, buffed nails were broken, and her hands were rough and chapped from scrubbing laundry every day.

And she couldn't see an end to it, she thought dismally as she took a break from washing dirty dishes, pots and skillets. No one wanted to work for her. She wished she and the girls hadn't been so rough on old Bucky. An early dusk had settled in because of the snow, and she lit a couple of lamps before pouring herself a cup of coffee and sitting down at the long kitchen table. She struck a match to a cheroot and relaxed, listening to the shrieks of laughter from her girls and the loud guffaws from the men.

Lucianne was satisfied that there would be no fights among the men. They knew that if they started a brawl, those involved would be barred from ever entering her place again.

In her days as a practicing whore she had seen the insides of many houses practically destroyed by drunken, rowdy customers engaged in fights over women. The first rule she had laid down on setting up her own place was that there would be no battles in her establishment. Rule number two:

If for some reason one of her girls didn't want to entertain a certain man, she didn't have to. Most of the time it was because the man was dirty and reeked of stale sweat. Wry amusement curved Lucianne's lips. That rule had taught the men that they had better be reasonably clean before approaching her girls.

And rule number three: A man would be out on his rump in a hurry if he abused one of the girls.

Lucianne had just put her tired feet up on the chair across from her and reached for her coffee when a muffled thud came at the door. "Damn!" she swore. Some stumbling drunk had come to the wrong door.

She stood up on her aching feet. She would soon send him on his way. She didn't mind if a customer had been drinking a bit before coming to visit the girls; the majority of them came from the tavern, so it wasn't surprising that they'd had a few drinks. But fall-down drunks were never allowed inside.

Lucianne opened the door and stepped backward, staring at the snow-covered Indian staggering under the weight of the woman in his arms. He almost knocked her over as he practically fell into the kitchen.

"Long Hair"—she hovered over the Indian as he deposited his burden onto a chair—"who is this white woman?"

"I don't know," the old man said when he had caught his breath. "I was on my way to the fort to trade some furs for cornmeal when I saw her fall to the ground. I knew I could not take her to my village, so I brought her to you."

"Is she alive?" Lucianne bent over for a closer look at the thin, white face.

"Just barely, I think," Long Hair answered. He was standing behind the chair, his hands on the woman's shoulders to keep her from falling to the floor.

"I wonder if her condition is due to the blizzard or the beatings she's had." Lucianne lightly ran a finger over a blackened eye and a purple bruise on her cheekbone. "I've never seen her around here, have you?"

"No. She is a stranger to me."

"Let's get her to bed. After you've rested a bit, would you please go fetch Dr. Hines to come have a look at her?"

Long Hair gathered the scant weight of the woman into his arms again and followed Lucianne into the small room next to hers, the same one that Blaze had used while tending her. As he laid the woman on the narrow bed, Lucianne opened the connecting door to let the heat from her stove filter in.

"I will go for the doctor now." Long Hair straightened up. "Then I will go parley over the furs with Bridger."

Lucianne nodded. "If you're sure you've rested enough. But Long Hair, you musn't try to get back to your village tonight. The storm is getting worse. You must spend the night here. I'll make you a pallet beside the stove in my room."

Amusement sparked in the old man's black eyes. "Perhaps you are right, but my people will never believe that I spent the night with the madam Lucianne."

"Won't the men be envious of you?" Lucianne grinned at him.

When he left, chuckling, Lucianne began to get the wet clothing off the woman and was appalled at the bruises on her thin body. There were very few spots that didn't have marks from a beating. Some were old bruises, others freshly made.

"Some bastard has taken his fists to you many times, huh, little bird," Lucianne said softly as she pulled one of her flannel gowns over the woman's head and smoothed it down over her inert body. "Maybe we'll find him someday and teach him how it feels to be beaten and kicked."

She had just pulled the covers up around the woman's shoulders when Dr. Hines, followed by Long Hair, stepped into the small bedroom.

"Well, Lucianne"—the stocky man in his midfifties smiled at the woman who had been his lover for the past eight years—"I understand you have another stray to take care of." When he had shed his jacket and hat he said, "Let me take a look at this woman who was foolish enough to go wandering around in a blizzard."

As the doctor began his examination of his new patient, he remembered that he too had once been a stray that Lucianne had taken in. He had been addicted to the bottle, drunk more often than sober. He was unshaven most of the time and his suit was always wrinkled from his having passed out and slept in it.

He had come down with pneumonia that first winter when he wandered into the fort, and it had been Lucianne who had taken him in and nursed him back to health. As he had tossed and raved, in a high fever, she had learned of the devils that pursued him.

He had been an army doctor and had seen too much suffering. To dull the memory of those soldiers he had been unable to save, he had turned to whiskey.

As Lucianne bathed his feverish body and spooned vile-tasting herb tea into him, he had fallen in love with the proprietress of a whorehouse. And by what still seemed a miracle to him, Lucianne returned his love. However, before she would let him share her bed, she made him take an oath that he would never drink again. He had kept his word, and most of his nights were spent in her bed.

After about ten minutes of listening to the woman's heart and lungs, Dr. Hines pulled the covers back up to her shoulders. With a disbelieving shake of his head, he said, "God must have been looking after this one. By rights she should have been dead years ago. Some bastard has treated her cruelly for a long time. At some point in her life she has had four broken ribs that managed somehow to mend, a dislocated shoulder that was never put back in place and scars on her back and legs from a whip being laid on her."

"The poor little thing," Lucianne whispered, tears in her eyes. "Will she live, Caleb?"

"She'll live." Caleb nodded, opening the little black bag he had placed at the foot of the bed. "There's steel in that abused body. There has had to be to survive the kind of life I think she has led. All she needs is a lot of rest and good food. She's half-starved."

Handing Lucianne the bottle, he said, "Give her a tablespoon of this three times a day. It will help build her up." He snapped the bag closed and gave Lucianne a roguish grin. "Do you feel like having company tonight?"

"I'm sorry, Caleb." Lucianne squeezed his arm against her breast. "Long Hair is going to sleep beside my stove tonight. I couldn't send him out in this storm. He would never make it back to his village."

Caleb shot a sour look at the old Indian who had stood back, watching and listening to everything going on. He returned the doctor's stare with a devilish grin.

You old heathen, Caleb thought as he stroked a finger down his lover's cheek. "I did have my mind set on . . ." He broke off when a low moan sounded from the bed. He and Lucianne bent over their patient and found her staring up at them with wild eyes. She grabbed Lucianne's hand and whispered hoarsely, "Are you Lucianne? Please, you must give me a job." Before the madam could answer her, the woman had drifted off again.

"Do you think she wants to be one of your girls?" Caleb asked in disbelief.

Lucianne shook her head. "I hope not. It would be an impossible wish."

"She probably doesn't know what she's saying. After a night's sleep and rest, she'll be more rational. You can learn all about her then," Caleb said, giving a longing look at the comfortable bed in the other room. He sighed resignedly, and after giving Lucianne a warm kiss, left, saying he would look in on his patient tomorrow.

Lucianne stirred beneath the feather comforter, wondering what had awakened her. A wide smile curved her lips when she realized that it was the stillness outside that had roused her. There was no more sound of whistling wind, no slash of snow against the windows. The blizzard had blown itself out.

But it was icy cold in the room, she discovered when she leaned up to check the time on the fancy little clock on her bedside table.

The hands on the pewter face showed it was a little after eight o'clock. She shifted her gaze to Long Hair, who lay sleeping quietly beside the stove. "You old reprobate," she said fondly, "now that it's time to get up, you sleep quietly."

The old man's loud snores throughout the night had wakened her numerous times. She reached down and, picking up one of her fancy house slippers, tossed it at the Indian. As it hit his chest he wakened instantly and sat up.

When he looked at her wild eyed, she smiled at him and said innocently, "You're up early. I figured you'd sleep late, considering all that went on since you got here with the woman."

Long Hair picked the slipper off his bony chest and grumbled, "I would have slept if certain people didn't throw their shoes around."

"I wonder how that happened." Lucianne pulled her arms back under the warm covers. "But now that you're awake, would you mind firing up the stove? We need to get some heat in here. I want to take a look at my guest."

After giving her a look that said he wasn't fooled by her act of innocence, the old man threw back his blankets and, with much grunting from painful joints, rose and began stoking the fire. Only a few glowing coals remained. When they bit into the wood and burst into flames, he went to the window and pushed aside the heavy drapery. The winter storm had done its best to completely cover the fort. Only the roof and part of the main door were visible. Bridger and his swamper were already digging out.

"How does it look out there?" Lucianne asked.

"The worst I've seen in twenty years," Long Hair answered absently, his mind on his hungry people, who had waited in vain for his return with the cornmeal. The little ones would be crying their hunger, and the mothers would try not to hear them. The men, of course, would have put on snowshoes and gone out to try tracking down a deer. But it would be a futile effort. No animal would be out today except maybe wolves. Not even the long-eared rabbit would leave his burrow.

The room had quickly warmed, and as Lucianne left the bed and drew on her robe, Long Hair said, "I go now to the fort with my furs. My people expected me back last night."

"Are things bad in your village, old friend?" Lucianne asked, retrieving the house slipper she had tossed at him.

"Yes, it is bad for my people. As more and more white men move onto our land, there is less and less game to be found. Not enough to put by for the winter." He paused before saying with some envy, "We cannot go to Bridger's and purchase supplies and say, as the white man does, 'Put it on my book. I will pay you later.'"

It was true what the old fellow said, and Lucianne couldn't bring herself to look at his wrinkled face. It wasn't fair that the very white men who had diminished the Indians' game were allowed to buy what they needed with the promise of paying later. It seemed to her that the Indians would be a better risk than the homesteaders, who would probably pull up stakes and leave as soon as the weather warmed and the snow melted. After experiencing the blizzards, they would probably go to California. Bridger was willing to risk losing a pile of money on them, yet would make the Indians pay cash for a five-pound bag of cornmeal. And the furs that Long Hair was going to trade with Bridger were worth ten times the cornmeal.

Lucianne was thinking how shameful that was

when she was struck with an idea. It was so logical she was surprised that one of the ranchers hadn't thought of it.

"Don't go just yet, Long Hair," she said, walking across the floor to her desk. While the old Indian waited she pulled open a drawer and retrieved a pad of paper and a pencil. Returning to the warmth of the fire, she sat down and began to write. A few minutes later when the Indian pulled on his jacket, impatient to leave, she ripped the page from the pad, folded it in half and handed it to him.

"Give this to Bridger," she said. "I have written that you are to be allowed to purchase supplies anytime you need them."

"He won't do that, you foolish woman." He pushed the paper back at her. "In all the years he's been here, he has never let an Indian have anything without paying for it first."

"He'll do it this time, for I'll be carrying your tribe on my book."

Long Hair swallowed, and forgot to hide his surprise as he croaked, "But it will cost you a lot of money to feed my people all winter. How will we pay you back?"

Lucianne looked at the bundle of furs just inside the door. "You will pay me with the furs you trap this winter. The men in your village will now be free to trap instead of hunting. You'll be as well off as the homesteaders who work the soil for a living. Maybe even better off." She smiled at the old man. "I see a better life for you and your people, Long Hair."

Long Hair stared at Lucianne a minute, the complete understanding of what she had said growing in his eyes. There were at least twenty able-bodied men in the tribe. With every one of them laying a trapline, when it came time to bring in their traps at the end of the season they would be able to more than repay Lucianne.

As he put the piece of paper in the top of his knee-high moccasins, he wondered why it had taken a mere woman to think up a way to help his people. Thanks to her sharp thinking, his people would eat every winter, better than they had for years.

Before he went out into the icy cold to fight his way through snowdrifts to the fort, he looked at Lucianne and said solemnly, "This kind act of yours will never be forgotten."

When Bridger saw the elderly Indian step into the store without his usual bundle of furs, he said sternly, "Long Hair, you know I'm not going to let you have anything if you don't have money or furs to trade."

"I would be stupid indeed if I haven't learned that in all these years," Long Hair answered.

"Well, what do you want? I'll not have you hangin' 'round just to keep warm."

"I don't need your fire to keep warm. My heart is warm today." Long Hair produced Lucianne's note and handed it to the storekeeper. As Bridger read the note, Long Hair's grin grew wider while the white man's face grew puzzled and then angry. He knew exactly when the skinny man realized there would be no more furs coming from the Indian who was his biggest supplier.

"Damn the woman," he heard Bridger mutter, but Long Hair kept a straight face when he was asked coldly what he needed in the line of staples.

"I need more than staples," Long Hair answered. "I need what you whites call 'supplies.' I'll begin with a side of beef."

"How are you gonna get all this home?" Bridger asked as the items grew on the counter. "Carry it on your back?" he said with a sneer.

The Indian walked over to a wall where traps and webbed snowshoes hung from wooden pegs. He took down a pair of the shoes and returned to the counter. "I have a travois in Lucianne's horse stable. The snow has a hard crust on it. I will have no problem pulling all this home."

Bridger scowled at the old man. The old heathen was beating him at every turn. He couldn't wait to chew out that Lucianne.

Lucianne's spirits were high as she went to check on her guest. Not only was she helping the starving Indians, but she had just struck a business deal that would more than pay for the food the tribe needed to stay alive. Indians knew the best places to trap furs, and she would be the one selling them to Bridger. He would not short-change her the way he had cheated them over the years.

She found her patient still sleeping, so she went into the kitchen, built a fire in the cookstove and put on a pot of coffee. All was quiet inside and out as she fried bacon and scrambled eggs. The girls would sleep late today. They'd had a busy evening. When she prepared two breakfast plates she gave her patient the bigger amount. She was bound to be very hungry.

Lucianne found the woman awake and sitting up when she entered the small room carrying a wooden tray holding their breakfast. "Good morning." She smiled at the bewildered-looking stranger. "How are you feeling?"

"I'm feeling surprised that I'm still alive," the stranger said, giving her a wan smile from pale lips. "The last thing I remember is falling senseless to the ground, sure that I was dying."

"You were barely alive when an old Indian found you and brought you here. But we'll talk about that later," Lucianne said, noting how the woman's eyes kept straying to the tray. "I've made us some breakfast." She placed the tray on the woman's lap and removed her own plate from it. The way the woman dug into the bacon and eggs, Lucianne hoped that she had prepared enough breakfast. She held back from eating her own just in case.

When the woman patted her stomach and said she felt stuffed, Lucianne poured them some coffee. As they drank it, she began her questions. "What is your name, honey?"

"Pearl Mu—Meyer." Lucianne thought it odd

the way she stumbled over her last name.

"How did you happen to be caught out in a blizzard . . . alone? Don't you have a husband?"

Pearl looked down at her empty plate and said in a voice barely audible, "I did have, but ten days ago six Indians attacked our wagon. They killed my husband and took me prisoner."

"You poor thing." Lucianne squeezed Pearl's hand in sympathy, but at the same time she was thinking that the Indians in the area were peaceful, had been for years. It was unlikely that they would attack this woman and her husband. Unless some of the young braves had turned renegade and the whites didn't know it.

"Were they cruel to you?"

Pearl didn't look fully at Lucianne as she answered, "Yes. I was treated badly. My hands and feet were tied all the time."

Lucianne wondered why there were no marks on Pearl's wrists and ankles. Indians used thin strips of rawhide instead of rope to tie things together. If Pearl had been tied up for ten days, her wrists and ankles would be rubbed raw. She watched Pearl's face closely as she said, "It must have been awful, tied up that way."

Pearl nodded. "Yes, it was. I was never free of the ropes except when I had to go into the bushes to relieve myself. And my wrists were untied when I was given something to eat once a day."

As Lucianne sipped her coffee, several questions went through her mind. The woman was lying, but why? Was she trying to protect a brutal husband?

Caleb had said that many of the scars on her body were old ones. Someone had put them there.

"Pearl"—Lucianne set her cup on the tray—"last night before you fainted away, you asked me if I was Lucianne. You were quite insistent that I give you a job. Why were you looking for me in particular?"

A look of panic shot into Pearl's eyes. It was clear that she didn't remember that short period of lucidity and it bothered her greatly. Her hand shook a bit as she set her cup down and gave Lucianne a strained smile.

"I must have heard the Indian women talking about you and decided that if I ever got away from the village and found my way to Fort Bridger I would ask you for a job."

"How did you manage to get away from your captors?"

Pearl looked away from Lucianne as she said, "In the late afternoon yesterday, when I asked to make a trip to the bush, a brave's told his wife to go with me. I guess she was jealous of her husband's attention to me, for when we were out of sight of the village she hissed at me that I should leave. I struck out running, and you know the rest."

Lucianne wished that she knew what had happened before Long Hair found the woman. There was only one Indian village within twenty miles of the fort. Long Hair's chief, Black Crow, would never have allowed a white woman to be kept prisoner there, nor would he allow her to be beaten.

Pearl's story was full of holes. As Lucianne wondered if she should believe any of it, Pearl asked hopefully, "Will you give me a job?"

Lucianne took a while answering. Something told her that Pearl's presence meant danger for someone in the area. Wouldn't it be wise to give Pearl a job so that she could keep an eye on her?

Lucianne couldn't help the amusement that shot into her eyes as she thought of Pearl's request. "What kind of job are you looking for? You're too old to entertain my customers," she said, adding to herself, *And too worn out.*

A grimace of loathing clouded Pearl's eyes before she answered, "I know that. I meant a job as cook and housekeeper."

It's plain she doesn't like men, Lucianne thought as she answered, "Are you a fair cook, Pearl? My girls are particular about their meals."

"I'm a real good cook, ma'am," Pearl answered, and this time she spoke the truth. Before she'd married Cotter, her mother had taught her how to make all the tasty meals that were put on their table.

"We'll discuss it later. After you've rested and regained some strength." Lucianne smiled at Pearl as she gathered the plates and cups onto the tray. "Go back to sleep now. I'll look in on you later."

# Chapter Fifteen

Blaze stood at the kitchen window, a glum look on her face as she gazed at the white, frozen world outside. If the past week was any indication, it promised to be a fiercely cold winter. Old mountaineers unable to run a trapline anymore claimed they had never seen the like in all the years they had trapped.

The icy cold up in the mountains, where even the waterfalls were frozen, had driven all but the hardy mountain men down to the post. They would wait out the winter, snug in their cabins, hibernating like bears.

Blaze's thoughts drifted to the ranchers. They, like Hunter, worried about their cattle out on the range. Would the animals starve to death? The cattle weren't like deer, smart enough to dig down beneath the snow and find the dry grass there. The ranchers hoped that they could find enough brush to chew on to keep them alive until the snow melted. Hunter was thankful that he had taken the majority of his cattle to market before the storms came. With any luck, the hay his men spread every day would keep his longhorns alive.

In the short time Blaze had spent around ranchers, she had learned much about these men who had settled the Wyoming territory. The constant danger of the frontier had produced bold and brave men, honest and direct.

Like Hunter, she thought, her lips curving softly. He was most of those things. He was brave and honest, at least. She always felt protected in his presence. And his directness had led to many confrontations between them when he used to accuse her of being a whore.

But these days their relationship had changed completely. They talked and laughed together. He kept the porch free of ice and snow so that she wouldn't slip and fall when she had occasion to go outside. He kept the wood box filled, things he would never have done for her before.

The blizzard had done an important thing for them. In the three days they had been housebound they had gotten to know each other. They learned each other's likes and dislikes. For instance, although he wasn't a churchgoing man, Hunter believed firmly that there was a God. His credo was, Do good and forget it; do bad and remember it.

Grandpa had, more or less, taught her the same thing.

With her forefinger she printed out her husband's name on the breath-steamed window and giggled. It was something a teenage girl would do.

Blaze was about to turn from the window and join Becky, who was chattering child-talk to herself in the main room, when she saw a horse and rider making their slow way to the cabin. The horse was breathing streams of white vapor as he labored through snow that sometimes reached his belly.

When he came nearer Blaze gave a glad little cry. The rider was James Wilson. How nice it would be to visit with him again, to joke around and laugh together like they used to. It would be nice to have someone to talk to besides Hunter and Becky and Bucky, the cook. Now that the men were hauling hay to the cattle, Hunter was gone from dawn till dusk. And little Becky, although she was company, could only carry on a conversation at a five-year-old level. And Bucky became tiresome after a bit as he rambled on about the days of his youth, telling her outrageous stories.

When James pulled the tired horse in at the porch steps, Blaze flung open the door, and with a big welcoming smile said, "Tie your horse up at the porch, James, while I pour us some coffee."

"That sure sounds good. I'm near froze."

Still smiling, Blaze filled two cups from the pot that had been keeping hot on the back of the stove, then set out a plate of cookies. When James stepped into the kitchen a few minutes later and pulled off his boots so as not to track up her spotless floor, she asked as he hung his jacket and hat on the wall next to her jacket, "Why didn't David come with you?"

"The cow we bought is ready to drop her calf, and she's having a little trouble doing it, so one of us has to be there to help her if it becomes necessary. We drew straws to see which lucky one of us got to come visit the beautiful Blaze. And of course to see how you fared during the blizzard."

"Keep your flattery to yourself, James Wilson." Blaze gave him a light rap on the head as she sat down at the table. "But I'm very glad to see you. I was in danger of coming down with cabin fever."

"It looks like you survived the storm, at least." James took a long swallow of his coffee.

"Yes, I did. But wasn't it fierce? I was so thankful that you and David were in a cabin instead of the tent house or the wagon."

"So were we," James said with a wry smile. "The tent was blown away and the wagon tipped over on its side."

"Have you been to the fort, heard how the rest of the families made it?"

David managed to get down there yesterday. We had run out of kerosene three days after the storm and were tired of fumbling around in the dark. He didn't hear of anyone having any trouble, but a lot of the men from the wagon train said they were going to California as soon as they could. Claimed that this part of the country wasn't fit to live in, that they didn't want to ever again live through such a brutal winter.

"He checked in on Lucianne and her girls and they were doing fine." James grinned. "He said the girls were complaining about how busy they have been since the storm. I guess that now the men can't get out and around taking care of business, all they want to do is spend their time at the Pleasure House. Lucianne has a new housekeeper and cook. A woman this time."

"Who is she? Anybody we know?"

"I don't think so. I've never seen her before. She looks kinda sickly, David said."

After a slight pause James said, "He didn't run into Hunter anywhere. I guess he's been sticking close to home.

Blaze merely nodded. When Hunter wasn't out working, he spent all his time with her at the cabin. Sometimes she had the feeling that he was trying to court her. "How are things between you and Hunter these days?" James asked.

"Much better. We don't argue anymore. Hunter is actually very attentive to me," she confessed shyly.

James, sipping at his coffee as he gazed out at the pale sun trying its best to warm the frozen land, said suddenly with a frown, "Here comes Hunter now."

"It's unusual for him to come home so early," Blaze said, breathing a troubled sigh. Her pulse raced nervously. Was Hunter going to be angry, finding James here? Although he was now aware that she had never slept with James, he still felt animosity toward the homesteader.

They watched Hunter ride past the cabin and on to the barn. "Maybe I'd better leave," James said. "He's gonna be madder than hell, finding me here."

"No, James, stay right where you are. This is supposed to be my home, too, and I ought to be able to have my friends visit me whenever they wish."

"That's true, I guess, but Ward isn't going to see it that way. He hates the air I breathe."

A moment later James warned, "Here he comes, and his face looks like a storm cloud."

Blaze's heartbeat quickened when she heard Hunter's feet hit the porch and stomp toward the door. He didn't bother to take off his snowy boots. The door flew open and he stood there, glaring at James through narrowed lids. "I thought I made it clear to your brother that I don't want you two coming around here," he said, his voice sharp and clipped.

James looked back at him a moment, then said in tolerant amusement, "As a partner in this marriage, hasn't Blaze the right to have her friends visit her?"

"Yes, she can, as long as it's a woman friend. I don't want any man hanging around here when I'm not home." Hunter jerked off his jacket as though to do battle.

"Look!" Blaze slapped her hand on the table. "James and David stepped forward and offered to drive my wagon and look after me when the other men of the train wanted to leave me in Fort Laramie. That place is a hellhole where nothing but bad could have happened to me. They are my dearest friends and they are welcome to come here anytime they want to."

"Come on now, you two." James stood up and began stamping on his boots. "I only came here to see how you weathered the storm." He pulled on his jacket and set his hat on his head. "I'll be getting back to my place now."

"Thank you for your concern, James." Blaze stood up also. "Say hello to David for me, and bring him along the next time you come to visit."

James gave a slight shake of his head, warning her not to say anymore. Her answer was a stubborn tilt of her chin. When he had left, she turned back to give Hunter a piece of her mind. He had left the kitchen and was now in the other room talking to Becky.

"Of all the times for him to come home early," she muttered as she gathered up the cups she and James had used.

In the main room Hunter was regretting the impulse that had brought him home early. He simply hadn't been able to stay away from Blaze any longer. Was he becoming besotted with her? he'd asked himself as he rode along toward home. He wanted to be with her all the time.

And though they got along famously these days, things weren't progressing fast enough for him. He ached for the day when he could become her husband in all ways. It was wearing him down, living together in friendship only. He had hinted at her sharing his bed, but she had either not caught on to what he was getting at or she had intentionally ignored his innuendos.

A thought had hit Hunter then, one so unwelcome that his knuckles had turned white from gripping the reins so tightly. Could Blaze be in love with another man? If so, was it one of the Wilson brothers she had given her heart to?

He recalled how the three of them had traveled across country together, how they had practically lived together before he'd married Blaze.

Which brother, he wondered, and why hadn't that one married her? He decided that the older brother, James, would appeal to Blaze. He was big and strong, and handsome as hell. And several years younger than he himself was, he reluctantly added. All the single girls around the trading post seemed to be vying for James's attention. And though the homesteader was always pleasant and polite to them, he showed no interest in courting any of them. Was it because he was in love with Blaze?

It occurred to Hunter that maybe Blaze was in love with someone he didn't know. Maybe her love was a member of the old outlaw bunch he had broken up. He remembered that one of the Mullen bunch he had taken in was younger than the others, not a hard-core outlaw yet.

A grim smile touched Hunter's lips. If Blaze was hoping for that one to come for her, she would have a long wait. That young man would spent at least ten years in prison.

As Hunter recalled those outlaws, he remembered the stranger who had entered the saloon just as he was leaving. The man had looked vaguely familiar. Had they crossed paths when he was a lawman? He guessed not, since the man had barely looked at him.

With a self-derisive twist of his lips, Hunter chastised himself for thinking that every stranger he saw was wanted by the law. He was no longer a lawman and must break that habit.

Twenty minutes later excitement built inside Hunter. Just a few yards away was his cabin, smoke coming from its chimney. Inside it would be cozy and warm, smelling of something sweet baking in the oven. Blaze was turning into a fine little cook. He always looked forward to supper.

But all Hunter's good thoughts disappeared in rage when he saw one of the Wilsons' horses tethered to his porch. As he led Saint to the barn and unsaddled him, he told himself that he would soon see which of the brothers his wife was interested in.

Now, half an hour later, Hunter sat with his daughter, wondering if he had made an ass of himself. James Wilson had seemed sincere when he claimed that he had only stopped by to see how they had fared during the storm. Good neighbors did look after each other. He had ridden to the Hackett place to be sure that Rose and Jake were all right. Why had he flown into such a rage when he saw James's horse tied up to the porch? he asked himself.

He knew why, he thought, his mind going back five years. His head resting wearily on the chair back, he relived his short marriage to Jenny. He recalled his anger and hurt when he'd found her in bed with the drifter. He had forgiven her, but he hadn't forgotten. By the time she'd run off to meet the man, he hadn't cared enough to go after her. But Jenny had made him distrustful of all women.

And that had been a mistake, he told himself now. Blaze was in no way like his first wife. Although she was of a fiery nature and had a fast temper, she was honest and didn't have a deceitful bone in her body. If she said something was so, a man could take it as gospel.

Could he make it up to her, get back to the footing they'd been on before his temper had ruined it? Dear God, he hoped so, for he was afraid that she was so upset with him she might go to Lucianne.

He debated going to Blaze now and apologizing. He would ask her to forgive his rash words to her friend. But then he decided it would be best if he stayed out of her sight for a while, let her cool down a bit. He sat on, biding his time.

After a while there came the sound of Blaze starting supper. He wondered wryly if she would make something tasty; or in her anger at him, would she serve up something like she had done when she was learning how to cook?

When Becky sniffed something cooking she slid off Hunter's lap and ran to the kitchen. He was relieved to hear Blaze talking to the child in her usual loving way. At least she wasn't taking her anger at the father out on the daughter.

Of course she wouldn't do that. Hunter scolded himself for thinking that she would. He knew that Blaze dearly loved the little one. Her affection for the child was his one hope that she wouldn't leave him.

It was growing dark and Blaze had lit the lamp in the kitchen when Becky came running in to tell him that supper was ready. When he walked into the kitchen he gave Blaze an uncertain look, but she had her back turned to him as she forked pork chops from a skillet. The only way he knew she was still upset with him was the stiff way she held her back.

Hunter was relieved when Blaze sat down at the table. At least she was going to eat with them.

The pork chops were crispy on the outside, tender and juicy on the inside. The mashed potatoes were whipped smooth, and the gravy to pour over them was free of lumps. The baked squash, smothered with butter, was tender and tasty.

"As usual, you have made a fine meal, Blaze," Hunter ventured. "Everything is mouthwateringly good."

"Thank you," Blaze said coolly, not lifting her gaze to him.

For the rest of the meal only Becky talked. It didn't seem to bother her that her parents only answered her in monosyllables.

When the strained meal had been eaten, Hunter remained at the table as Blaze stacked the dirty dishes to be washed. Maybe they could talk while he dried.

That hope was dashed when Blaze said coolly and firmly, "I don't need you to help with the dishes. You can go join Becky in the other room."

Dismissed so curtly, Hunter felt that all he could do was go sit with his daughter. At least she wasn't mad at him.

What is taking her so long to straighten up the kitchen? Hunter wondered when an hour had passed and Blaze hadn't made an appearance. Suddenly he understood what she was doing. She was killing time until she could put Becky to bed. She was still angry and didn't intend to spend any time with him.

When the clock struck seven, Becky's bedtime, Hunter knew his assumption had been right, for almost immediately Blaze walked into the room, announcing with a smile at Becky, "It's time for bed, little love."

His daughter gave him a wet kiss on the cheek, then slid off his lap and took Blaze's hand to be led to bed.

Hunter waited, drumming his fingers on the chair arm. He would give Blaze ten minutes to get Becky settled, and then he was going to talk to her, even if he had to force her to listen to him. He wouldn't be put off any longer. He wouldn't be able to sleep a wink, not knowing what she had in mind.

When the allotted time was up, he walked quietly to Blaze's open bedroom door. He could only stand and stare. Blaze stood in front of the mirror, brushing her hair. In the lamplight behind her he could clearly see the outline of her breasts through the thin material of her nightgown every time she lifted her arm. When she caught his reflection in the mirror she spun around and in a half whisper demanded, "What do you want?"

"I want to talk to you. I need to talk to you."

"About what?"

"You know about what. The way I acted toward James before."

Blaze laid the brush down and stepped out into the hall, leaving the door ajar about a foot.

Giving him a cold look, she said, "Well, what have you got to say about how you acted?"

"I acted like a total fool when I saw the two of you sitting so cozy at the table, having coffee together. It ran through my mind that James would like to take you away from me and Becky, that he would like to marry you."

"If I had wanted to marry James, you wouldn't be my husband now."

"Why did you marry me, Blaze?"

Blaze thought a minute, then, dimpling, said, "I wanted to get revenge for all the mean things you'd said to me. I wanted to make your life miserable," she teased.

"You succeeded, you little witch." Hunter

grinned down at her. "I have never been so miserable in my life."

"But I thought that when we were on good terms you were content," Blaze said, serious now.

"In a way I was. I enjoyed every minute of our time together. But sitting in front of the fire at night and talking just wasn't enough. I know that you're not experienced in the way of men, but you must have known that I wanted to be a husband to you in all ways." Hunter stroked a finger down her cheek. "I never even got a good-night kiss from you."

"I'm not a mind reader."

"Well, I'm asking you right out, Will you forgive me for my bad behavior and give me a makeup kiss?"

"I guess I can do that." Blaze smiled and lifted her face to Hunter.

Hunter lost no time in taking advantage of her offer. With a groan he drew her to him, molding her slenderness to his hard body. She grew tense a moment, but when he tilted her chin and laid his lips on hers she seemed to loosen up a bit. Hunter began then to move his lips, to deepen the kiss. When he felt her relax and press into him he dared to slip his tongue between her lips. She started at his action but didn't draw away from him.

Encouraged, Hunter began to undo the buttons of her gown. When he had the garment open to her waist, he pushed it off one shoulder, baring her breast. With a sigh he left her lips to trail tiny kisses down her throat until he came to the firm breast. He cupped it in his hand and rubbed his thumb against its nipple. When he lowered his head and settled his mouth over the pebble hardness, Blaze gasped and pressed herself closer to him.

Hunter was breathing fast. He had wanted her to be soft and willing when he made love to her, for her to feel the same fever pitch of desire that was scorching through his veins. And it had happened. She wanted him. He scooped her up in his arms and carried her to his bedroom.

"Hurry into bed before you freeze," he urged when he had pulled the thin gown over Blaze's head.

Blaze was far from being cold as she laid the covers back and slid beneath them. She had never felt so hot in her life. Hunter had stirred a fire in her that was hotter than a summer sun.

"Are you lighting the lamp?" she asked at the rasp of a match was followed by a small flame.

"Do you mind if I do?" Hunter asked, touching the flame to the lamp's wick. "I've waited so long to make love to you, I want to see it all happen."

Before Blaze could answer he was kneeling on the edge of the bed, pulling the covers off her.

Hunter caught his breath at the perfect body waiting for his touch. His hand trembled as he reached out and stroked a firm, pink-tipped breast, then with a feather touch moved down her rib cage. He paused at her waist a moment, then reached down to rest his hand on the crisp curls that protected the part he was aching to bury himself in. Slowly he slipped a finger between her feminine lips. His pulse raced. She was hot and moist, ready for him.

He stood up and tore off his clothes. His heart pounding in anticipation, he knelt beside Blaze, and, parting her legs, he positioned himself between them. When she made no move to wrap them around his waist, he lifted them there himself.

What was the best way to introduce a virgin to her first act of lovemaking, Hunter wondered as he hung over Blaze. Should it be one sharp shove of his hips after he had entered her, or should he go slowly?

When Blaze gazed up at him, her eyes full of trust, he hated the thought of hurting her. She was so slender; he was so large. There was no way he could keep from hurting her.

With a regretful sigh he took his hardness in his hand and guided it to the place that was waiting for him. With a whispered "I'm sorry, Blaze," he plunged inside her with a powerful shove of his hips.

Blaze's sharp cry of pain, the shudder that shook her body, made Hunter swear softly. Full of remorse, he held her close. "I'm sorry to hurt you so," he said. "It couldn't be helped. But the pain will go away soon and you will enjoy yourself."

"You mean it's not over?" Blaze whimpered.

"Not yet." He caressed a soft kiss across her brow. "It won't hurt anymore. I'll go slow and easy. You'll like it, I promise." He dropped his head to pull a pink nipple into his mouth.

As Hunter gently and slowly suckled her, Blaze couldn't utter a word. She could only lie beneath him as wave after wave of surrender passed from the suction of his mouth to the hardness firmly inside her. She was overcome with sensations she had never known before.

She made no objection when Hunter began to move his hips, sliding slowly and carefully in and out of her, at the same time drawing her nipple between his lips in rhythm with his long, deep thrusts.

Blaze felt the warmth inside growing hotter and hotter, and suddenly it seemed as if she was leaving her body, soaring out in space. She heard Hunter groan hoarsely as his body shuddered. He then went limp, his breathing hard and fast as her body took his weight.

As his breathing calmed down, Hunter lifted part of his weight off Blaze and asked softly, "Are you all right? Do you still hurt?"

Blaze shook her head. "I don't ache, but I'm a little sore."

"Did you like it?"

"Yes." She blushed, not knowing if she should have liked it.

Hunter gave a pump of his hips. "You want to do it again?" He smiled down at her.

"Could we?" Blaze looked at him in surprise.

Hunter chuckled at her innocence. "We can do it as often as we like."

"Oh, I didn't know that." She smiled up at him, then wrapped her arms around his shoulders as Hunter began to rise and fall on top of her.

# Chapter Sixteen

"New Moon, get up and put more wood on the fire." Cotter Mullen gave her shoulder a rough shake.

The Indian woman drew the back of her hand across her mouth, wiping away the spittle that had drooled from between her lips. "You do it," she said sullenly. "I've done it all night."

"And you'll do it all day." Cotter glared at her in the dim light filtering through the smoke hole where the poles came together at the top of the tepee. When she opened her mouth to protest again, Cotter grabbed her arm and, twisting it behind her back until she cried out, growled, "Do you want more of what you got the last time you disobeyed me?"

New Moon silently shook her head. Since moving into her lodgings, where the heavy snow kept them prisoners in a small area, she had learned the other side of the man she knew as Deke Meyers. He was truly evil, a man who delighted in inflicting pain on her. Before it had been his wife who received his meanness. Now it was her turn. He beat her savagely at least once a day, for no reason she could see.

The one she had received yesterday had been the worst beating to date.

On rising that morning and going to the chief's lodge for their share of food, she had been sternly informed by Black Crow that her man must leave the comfort of his warm fire and lay a trapline like the rest of the village men had done. The chief said that if he didn't start bringing in furs soon, there would be no food for them.

New Moon shuddered as she relived telling Deke what Black Crow had said. He had gone into a rage and had beaten her so cruelly, she feared he had broken two of her ribs. And as if that weren't enough, after he had exhausted himself beating her, he had spent close to an hour using her in every demeaning way he could think of.

As she left the warmth of the furs to feed the fire, she asked herself the same question she had put to herself since he'd begun beating her. Would she be better off without him? It had been five years since she'd had a man of her own. She was reluctant to give him up. Besides, would he leave willingly? She never knew what to expect of him.

There was one thing, however, that never varied

and that still pleased her: his driving lust. She wasn't surprised when he ordered, "Get back here now and pleasure me." As she bent over him she told herself that if he didn't care for her he wouldn't want to lie with her so often.

She ignored the little voice that said sneeringly, "Foolish woman, he would lie with a sheep if nothing else was available."

When he was finally through with her, New Moon moved out of his reach and asked, "Are you going to lay traps today?"

"Yes, damn it, I'm gonna lay some traps and you're gonna help me. You know more about trapping than I do."

New Moon knew that meant she would be doing all of the work while he sneaked back to the tepee. Any furs that were brought to Black Crow would be ones she trapped, although Deke Meyer would take the credit for it.

While New Moon lived with the evil inside Cotter Mullen, Pearl went about her duties, often breaking into little songs from her youth. She hardly resembled the woman Long Hair had carried to Lucianne's Pleasure House. Most signs of the bruises on her face and body had faded, and her sunken cheekbones and bony hips were beginning to fill out a bit from the nourishing food she ate every day.

As she had convalesced Lucianne had worked at making her four dresses. The garments were fashioned from fine, soft wool in bright colors. Pearl took great pains in her care of them. She had worn rags for too many years not to appreciate her new finery.

Pearl had taken up her duties a week ago, cleaning and cooking and mothering Lucianne's girls. They in turn acted like loving daughters to her. She would have known complete happiness and contentment if not for one thing. She mustn't forget why she was here. She was to spy on her new friends, find out all she could about Hunter Ward and his wife. So far she had learned nothing about either one of them. The rancher hadn't visited the Pleasure House and she hadn't heard his name mentioned by the girls or the men who visited them. And since she hadn't left the Pleasure House since arriving there, she knew nothing about Mrs. Ward. She lived in dread of the day Cotter would appear, demanding to know what she had learned about the couple.

The sun had dipped below the horizon and Pearl was lighting the kitchen lamps when Lucianne came into the room. "Before you start supper, Pearl, would you please go to the fort and bring me back a spool of white thread? I'm mending the girls' undergarments, which have been torn by overeager men."

Pearl had dreaded leaving the security of the Pleasure House, and night was coming on. Was Cotter out there somewhere waiting for her?

Lucianne saw her hesitation and said gently, "You have to go outside sometime, honey. There are no Indians around here who would harm you."

Pearl knew this, but what Lucianne didn't know was that there was a man, much worse than any Indian, who might be out there ready to use his fists on her when she had nothing to report to him. Nevertheless, she slipped her arms into the jacket Lucianne held for her.

In the fading light Pearl walked as quickly as she could on the snow-packed path leading to the fort. She breathed her relief when she came to the back door of the fort, the one the girls used when going there to drink and dance, to have a little entertainment before their work began. She took hold of the latch and was ready to push open the door when the chilling sound of her husband's voice arrested her hand.

"Not so fast, bitch. Get over here." Cotter ordered, his tone saying that she had better obey him if she knew what was good for her.

Fear of what lay ahead had her knees knocking together as Pearl joined her husband beneath the heavy foliage of a big pine. Grabbing her arm and giving it a twist, he growled, "This is the third night I've stood out here, freezing, as I waited for you to stick your nose out." His grip tightened. "From now on I want you out here every night around this time. Now"—he turned Pearl loose—"what news do you have?"

Her face as white as the snow she stood in, Pearl cowered away from the man she hated with all her being. "I'm sorry, Cotter, but I don't have a thing to report. Hunter Ward hasn't been near Lucianne's, and I haven't heard anyone so much as mention his name."

Pearl had barely finished speaking when Cotter pulled back a fist to hit her in the face.

"Don't hit my face." Pearl held up her arm to ward off the blow. "Lucianne will want to know who put the bruise there."

"I guess you're right," Cotter agreed, but his eyes glared hatred at her. Then, as Pearl breathed a soft sound of relief, Cotter added, "She won't see this though," and hit her hard in the stomach with his fist. While she was bent over in pain, he said before disappearing into the darkness, "You'd better have something to report to me the next time I see you."

# *Chapter Seventeen*

Christmas was a week away and almost everybody in the area was preparing for it. As Blaze strung garlands of popcorn to be entwined with pine boughs that Bucky had cut from the big pine at the corner of the cabin, she regretted that her handiwork couldn't go on a tree for Becky instead of decorating the mantel. The little one had never had a Christmas tree. Being in New Moon's care since she was born, she didn't even know there was such a thing as Christmas, a decorated tree, gifts from Santa Claus.

Blaze smiled wryly. In truth, she wanted a tree for herself almost as much. She had never had one either. It had always depressed her when the outlaw gang was riding through some town and she would see through the windows trees all bright and shiny, with strings of popcorn and red berries and colorful bows tied on the branches.

Bucky had told her that usually, weather permitting, Jim Bridger had a party for the folk living in the vicinity. But this year, what with the unusually heavy snowfall, he had canceled it. Outlying ranchers wouldn't be able to come in for a month or so. The owner of the trading post didn't think it was fair to have a party when so many of the children couldn't attend. The grouchy old man was always fair, the cook had said, then tacked on, "Exceptin' for the Indians. He always cheats them on the price of the furs they bring in."

Had Bridger's Christmas order made it in before the snowfall? Blaze wondered as she set to work hanging the green and white garlands along the mantel. She would be really disappointed if Becky didn't get the doll she had ordered for Christmas. She would ask Hunter to check with Bridger the next time he went to the post.

Hunter, she thought, a sadness coming into her eyes. Although they made exciting love every night, he had yet to say those three all-important words: *I love you.*

They were back on their old friendly footing in the daytime, although Hunter went to town a little more often now. That hurt her feelings also. When he'd been working at getting her to share his bed, he'd hung around the cabin more.

She gave a bitter little laugh. Now that he was sure of her, it seemed he felt that he didn't have to court her anymore.

Over the past month, she had come up with two reasons why he wouldn't say the words she so wanted to hear. The first one was that he couldn't forget she was the daughter of an outlaw, and was unworthy of his love. The second one, and probably the right one, was that he had loved his first wife so much, there was no love left for any other woman.

Blaze blinked away the moisture that had gathered in her eyes. Should she settle for what Hunter was capable of giving her? Would her love for him sustain their marriage? She had heard of marriages where neither partner loved the other, yet those marriages had lasted, producing many children.

But were those husbands and wives happy? she couldn't help wondering.

At any rate there was nothing she could do to change her situation. She had known for almost a week now that she was expecting Hunter's baby. Luckily, so far she had managed to wait until he was gone in the mornings before losing her first cup of coffee. The morning sickness and sore breasts were the only indications that she was expecting. Otherwise, she had never felt better. Her eyes sparkled and there was a glow to her skin. And this morning she hadn't been sick at all.

She had been spending a large part of each day sewing baby clothes, but she always made sure they were put away in Becky's room before starting the evening meal.

Blaze had just sunk down in her favorite rocker

to work on one of the tiny garments when she heard a complaining female voice outside. She recognized it as Lucianne's immediately. With a glad smile on her lips, she quickly shoved the tiny gown under some yarn in her work basket and hurried to open the kitchen door.

She stood on the threshold, a tickled smile on her lips as Lucianne yelled at Bucky, who stood in the doorway of the cookhouse laughing at his one-time employer's predicament.

"You old reprobate," Lucianne was yelling at him. "Come make this ornery critter stand still so I can dismount."

Blaze remembered that Lucianne had never gotten along with horses, and when it appeared that Bucky wasn't going to do her bidding, Blaze called out, "The mare won't stand still because you're sawing on the reins. Just drop them and she'll stand still."

"Ornery critter," Lucianne said again, but this time she was referring affectionately to Bucky, who had relented and come to help her out of the saddle.

"Ornery mistress," Bucky grumbled. "Pulling the bit into her tender mouth."

"Oh, I didn't mean to hurt her," Lucianne cried, and the little mare received so many loving pats that she snorted and actually swung her head to dislodge the hand that was giving her so much attention.

"What's in the packages?" Blaze asked as Lucianne untied two bulky boxes from the back of the saddle before Bucky led the little mare to the barn.

"Don't ask me." Lucianne puffed up the two steps to the porch. "When Bridger found out I was coming to visit you he asked me to bring them along. Said he kept forgetting to send them out with Hunter."

"I know what they are!" Blaze's eyes sparkled. "It's Becky's Christmas presents. I kept meaning to ask Hunter if they had come in."

"Are you two fighting again?" Lucianne frowned.

"Oh no. Hunter stays home every night. But he's been working so hard, most times he falls asleep in his chair until bedtime."

"A regular old married man, huh?" Lucianne laughed. "They are all—" She broke off as Blaze suddenly put her hand to her mouth and dashed out onto the porch.

Lucianne followed her and put a bracing hand on her forehead as she lost her coffee. A few minutes later when she led Blaze back into the kitchen, Becky came running up, crying, "Mama sick again?"

"Again, Blaze?" Lucianne asked as the trembling girl rinsed out her mouth. "Have you vomited before?"

"Yes," Blaze said wearily as she sat back down. She pushed the damp hair off her forehead. "You might as well know. I'm expecting."

"You are?" Lucianne smiled. "How do you feel about it? What does Hunter have to say?"

"I guess I'm happy. As for Hunter, I haven't told him yet."

"When are you going to tell him he's to become a father? You can't hide a fact like that too long."

"I'll tell him before long," Blaze said. "I'm just not ready yet."

Lucianne looked at Blaze and shook her head. "I know you're not telling me everything, but I'll not pry." She went on to talk about doings at the post and local gossip. Before she left she said, "Take care of yourself, Blaze. The morning sickness will let up in a few more weeks."

Hunter was preparing to leave the post when the door opened and the same stranger he had seen there before walked into the tavern. When the man walked past him without a glance, Hunter slapped his hat on his head and left the tavern. He wasn't aware that the stranger watched him go with hate-filled eyes. Nor did he know that shortly after he mounted Saint and rode off, the newcomer finished his drink and silently left.

Hunter was partway home when Saint stiffened under him and pricked up his ears. Hunter sat forward and listened. Although he heard no sound other than the squawking of a blue jay, he felt the presence of someone close by. He drew his Colt and slowly twirled the cylinder, checking that it was loaded. Then putting the gun back in his holster, he started the stallion forward at the same plodding gait on the path of trampled snow. His eyes constantly moved as he tried to spot the man, or men, who might be waiting in the semidarkness to take a shot at him. He had made many enemies during his five-year stint as a territorial marshal. It could be any one of them dogging his trail.

Hunter knew when he was no longer being followed. The stallion's muscles had relaxed, and his own sixth sense gave him no further warning. Nevertheless, he was relieved when the cabin came into view. The lamplight shining through the kitchen window was a welcome sight.

# *Chapter Eighteen*

Blaze stretched and yawned in the warm cocoon of the feather bed, then suddenly sat up. It was Christmas morning. She couldn't wait to see the pleasure in Becky's eyes when she looked at her first doll.

Surprised that Hunter was not beside her, Blaze lay a moment, listening for sounds that he was making coffee in the kitchen. She smiled, waiting to see if he would come back to bed for a little while, as he often did on these cold mornings. When after a few minutes she heard nothing but the ticking of the mantel clock, she rolled over in bed, wondering where on earth Hunter could have gone so early on Christmas morning.

A serene silence hung over the land as Hunter rode along. The cold air stung his cheeks and pinched his nose, and he hunched against the chill as Saint plodded on.

Hunter had slipped out of bed, careful not to awaken Blaze, just as the sky was showing a rosy pink in the east. He had an errand to run before she got up. He was on his way to pick up two Christmas gifts, one for Blaze and one for Becky. For his daughter he had chopped down a small, perfectly shaped pine tree yesterday and left it beside the trail to be retrieved today. It would be the little one's first Christmas tree.

The other gift, for Blaze, was her little mare, Beauty.

He hadn't known at the time what made him keep Blaze's mount when he had turned all the other horses belonging to the outlaws over to the sheriff. He hadn't known either why he had kept the animal hidden out on the range. Then when he and Blaze started getting along together, sharing the same bed, he slowly realized he had been keeping Blaze's pet because it belonged to her. He had realized at the same time that the mare would make the perfect Christmas gift to give to her. He had rounded up Beauty and taken her to the Hacketts' and asked them to keep her until today. Christmas morning.

He rode past the tree he had cut down. On the way home he would drag it along behind Saint.

When Hunter reached the little cabin that Rose and Jake had built, he was thankful to see it was still dark inside. He wouldn't have to lose any time talking to them.

Beauty greeted him with a soft whinny and nudged at his shoulder as he slipped a lead rein over her head. He led her outside, then, mounting Saint and leading the mare, he left the barnyard.

It took but a moment to tie the tree behind Saint and they were off again.

The sun was barely rising when he rode up to his barn. He dismounted and quickly untied the tree, then led Beauty into the warmth of the stables. He led Saint in next and unsaddled him. Then with a wide board, a hammer and a couple of nails, he went outside and nailed the piece of wood to the tree's trunk. He quietly took it into the house and set it up in a corner near the hearth. He built up the fire in the fireplace and then started a fire in the cookstove.

He had a pot of coffee almost brewed when he heard Blaze stirring in the bedroom.

He went and stood in the kitchen doorway to watch the expression on her face when she saw the tree. Last week she had admitted she would like a tree for herself, that she had never had one. It saddened Hunter to know that his wife hadn't had much of a childhood. Hunter didn't have to wait long before Blaze entered the room, her arms full of packages.

She gave a start, seeing him standing there so quietly; then she smiled and said, "Merry Christmas, Hunter."

"Merry Christmas to you too, Blaze." He returned her smile as he crossed the room and took her into his arms and kissed her. "Do you see anything different in here?" he asked when he released her.

She took a slow look around the room, then gasped her pleasure when she spotted the tree. "Oh, Hunter." She clasped her hands to her breast. "A Christmas tree!" As she walked around the pine, inspecting it, Hunter picked up the packages she had dropped. "As soon as I finish making breakfast, I'll get to popping more corn and making little bows out of ribbon."

"I'll make breakfast and you can start right now."

Blaze had a lapful of bright little bows when Hunter came and told her that breakfast was ready. As she sat down at the table, she prayed that she wouldn't have to vomit the minute the coffee hit her stomach. It hadn't happened the last two mornings, but it might this morning. She took a cautious sip of the strong brew. Her stomach gave a couple of lurches, then settled down.

A pale rising sun bathed Hunter and Blaze through the window as they ate the breakfast Hunter had prepared. When they talked it was in low tones, so as not to awaken Becky. They had almost finished the meal when Hunter said, "I've got a Christmas gift for you."

"You have?" Blazed looked at him, surprise in her voice and eyes. "Where is it?"

"It's out in the barn. Stay here and I'll bring it to you. You might want to put on your jacket. It's too big to bring into the cabin." He grinned boyishly. "I could bring it into the kitchen, but I don't think you'd want me to."

A Christmas gift, Blaze thought excitedly as she pulled on her boots and then reached for her jacket. It would be the first one she had ever received. So many Christmases had come and gone unnoticed in her lifetime. On the run from the law, her father and grandfather had had all they could do to escape the men who followed them.

She recalled how on one Christmas when they were safe in an isolated hideout, Grandpa had told her a story about baby Jesus. How the baby had been born in a manger, how wise men had come bringing him gifts of gold and jewels. Grandpa had ended his story by saying that remembering the birth of Jesus was the right way to celebrate Christmas, not with gifts and decorated trees.

Blaze walked out onto the porch just as Hunter stepped through the barn door, holding the reins of the mare that followed him. She stared at the animal, rubbed her eyes and stared again. She must be mistaken, she thought. It couldn't be her little pet Beauty. She had thought never to see her again.

Blaze walked slowly down the steps, still unable to believe her eyes.

"Beauty, where have you been all this time?" she asked softly as the little mare whinnied a low greeting and nudged her head against Blaze's shoulder.

Her arms around the little animal's neck, Blaze looked up at Hunter with shimmering eyes.

"Where did you find her?"

"I didn't find her. When I turned the outlaws' horses over to the sheriff I kept her. After I resigned from my marshal's job I brought her here to the ranch."

"I couldn't wish for a better Christmas gift," Blaze said, but thought to herself as she rubbed the spot between Beauty's eyes that there was one thing that would please her even more: hearing Hunter say that he loved her.

She looked up at him and said awkwardly, "I don't have a gift for you. I never dreamed that you'd have one for me."

Hunter dismissed her words with a motion of his hand. "I didn't really give you a gift. After all, the mare was already yours. I just returned her to you."

"Oh, how I wish I could race her across the range, feel the wind on my face and in my hair as I yell like a wild Indian."

"Is that what you used to do?" Hunter asked with a smile.

Blaze's cheeks pinkened a bit. "I know it's childish for a grown woman to do that, but yes."

"I don't think you should be embarrassed about it," Hunter said softly. "I've done the same thing, and not always in high spirits. Sometimes I race the wind out of rage and frustration."

"I've done that also," Blaze said in a low voice.

"What if I throw a saddle on your pet and you take her for a ride?" Hunter suggested. "She needs the exercise. You know, of course, that you can't run her on the narrow path cut through the snow."

Blaze's eyes sparkled. "Yes, I know. I'll get my scarf and gloves while you saddle her." She stood a moment, watching Hunter lead the little mare away, puffs of vapor escaping its nostrils in the frigid air. She smiled wryly. She would freeze her tail off, but the ride would be worth it.

"Becky is still sleeping," she told Hunter a short time later as he led Beauty up to the porch. As he took hold of her waist to boost her into the saddle, she added, "Don't let her open her gifts until I get back."

Blaze didn't ride far in the freezing weather. When she turned around, the mare had difficulty maneuvering in the deep snow banking the narrow path. In all, hardly half an hour had passed before they were approaching the cabin again. As Blaze stepped up on the porch she could hear Becky crying hysterically.

"What's wrong?" she asked Hunter, who looked ready to cry out of frustration himself.

"She was afraid you weren't coming back." Hunter answered as his daughter slid off his lap and threw herself at Blaze, wrapping her arms around her legs.

Blaze picked the sobbing child up and, holding her close, explained gently, "I only went for a short ride on the little horse your Papa gave me for Christmas. You were still sleeping and I didn't want to wake you up."

Becky lifted her tearstained face and stared accusingly at Blaze. "Becky thought Mama never coming back. You wake Becky next time."

"I will, honey, I promise," Blaze said gently, using the heel of her hand to wipe away the tears on the small cheeks.

"Now," she said, setting Becky down, "let's go see if you have any Christmas gifts under the tree."

Becky ran from the kitchen, crying excitedly, "Becky got a horse too?"

Blaze and Hunter followed the little girl, amusement on their faces. "Becky got something better than a horse," Blaze said, and lifted the lid on the box holding the doll. "See, a baby doll." She lifted it out and held it toward the awestruck little girl.

As Becky, her eyes shining, hugged the doll to her chest, Hunter put his jacket on and went to the barn. When he returned he carried a red sled under his arm. "It's a sled," he explained when Becky looked at it questioningly. "When it warms up a little later on, Daddy will take you for a ride on it."

Darkness was about to descend as Pearl took the path to the fort. The snow made a crisp sound as she walked along. Her boots were new. Lucianne's girls had given them to her on Christmas morning a week ago. She lifted a red-mittened hand to stroke the matching scarf covering her head and shoulders. They were Lucianne's gift to her.

Pearl loved Lucianne and her "soiled doves" and would do anything within her power for them. Her fervent wish was to stay with them always. But that would depend on Cotter. If he wanted her to go with him after he had accomplished his evil deed, there was nothing she could do. He had threatened to do harm to Lucianne if she didn't obey him. She would walk through fire to save that kindhearted woman from suffering.

Her heartbeat quickened as she came to the pine where she knew Cotter would be waiting for her. Again she had nothing to report to him about Hunter Ward. Then he would beat her, being careful not to mark her face.

"It's about time you got here," Cotter growled as Pearl stepped beneath the large tree. When she made no immediate response he demanded, "Well, do you finally have something to report?"

Trembling inside at what was to come, Pearl shook her head. "I haven't heard a word about Hunter, but I saw his wife at the fort yesterday."

"What time of the day was it?"

"Between one and two o'clock. She was telling Bridger that it was the first time she'd been out since the blizzard, but now that the snow has melted some she would be coming in more often."

"Is that all?"

"When she left the store she stopped at Lucianne's for a short visit. I have a feeling that they're old friends. When she left she said that she would visit longer with Lucianne next week."

"Did she have the child with her?"

"No. I heard her tell Bridger that Hunter was home with her."

"What about Ward?"

"I've only seen him once since Christmas."

Cotter didn't say anything for a moment as he stared down at the ground. Then, muttering, "Keep your eyes and ears open," he strode off in the direction of the Indian village. Pearl stared after him, not believing that he hadn't taken his fists to her.

# Chapter Nineteen

It was near the end of February and Hunter was sitting in the cookhouse mending bridles and reins. He often spent time there when heavy snow prevented his getting out on the range to check on his cattle.

There had been another blizzard in January just over a week after Christmas. The storm had lasted two days, laying another foot of fresh snow on the old. Everyone had stayed indoors unless it was absolutely necessary to brave the howling blizzard. A man couldn't see more than three feet ahead of himself.

A smile flickered in Hunter's eyes. Although he and the other ranchers worried what the new additional snow would do to their cattle, being housebound hadn't bothered him. In fact, he had welcomed the storm and wished that it would last longer. It gave him the excuse to stay in the cabin and be around Blaze.

He had often wondered what she did all day in the cabin. He had learned that she passed the time much as he imagined other wives did. She swept the floors, dusted the furniture and did a lot of baking. In between, as Becky followed her about, she taught the little one new words.

Hunter lifted his head and listened when the shrill whinnies of his stallion reached the cookhouse. Bucky grinned and said, "Blaze's little mare has come into heat and that big feller wants to get at her."

"Yeah," Hunter agreed, "and I've got to make damn sure he doesn't. Blaze would have my hide if that happened."

"How come? Then two would make a damn finelooking foal."

Hunter grinned. "I don't think she'd like the idea of her little pet having a fling with that ornery stallion of mine."

"I wouldn't doubt it." Bucky grinned too. "Women can get some crazy things in their heads."

No more was said between the men. Bucky got busy preparing some sourdough batter, and Hunter continued mending a bridle. Their minds, however, were thinking things they didn't express. Bucky was remembering when he was a young stallion, never getting enough of sleeping with a woman, and Hunter was thinking how he felt like going over to the cabin to make love to his wife right now.

Back in the cabin Blaze finished hemming a tiny gown. As she neatly folded it she wondered if she would have time to cut out another one before Hunter left the cookhouse and came to the cabin for lunch.

A look at the clock told her that if Hunter stuck to his usual habits, she'd only have about twenty minutes. Not nearly enough time to spread the material on the table and cut out the shape of a baby garment.

A wry look came into her eyes. If Hunter should catch her doing that, she could tell him that she was making clothes for Becky's doll. He probably wouldn't know the difference.

Blaze broke off her thoughts when Becky, who had dragged a chair to the window and was looking out, suddenly cried, "Rose come to visit us."

"Are you sure, honey?" Blaze came to stand behind her. A wide, pleased smile curved her lips. It was Rose, bundled up to her eyes and wearing a pair of her husband's trousers. Blaze had learned that during a Wyoming winter, style was forgotten. Keeping warm took precedence over everything else.

"I knew you couldn't bring the little one out to visit me," Rose said as Blaze swung open the door, "so I have come to visit you."

"We're so happy to see you!" Blaze took hold of her friend's arm and pulled her inside. "Come over by the stove and let me help you off with your jacket. You must be half frozen."

"It's not as cold as you might think," Rose said, unwinding the heavy scarf from her head and neck. "There's no wind and the air is very dry. But I'd have come today regardless of the weather. I think if I hadn't got out for a while I might have gone crazy and started after Jake with a butcher knife."

"I understand your feeling," Blaze said laughingly as she poured them some coffee. "I've been shut in all winter. I'm going to the fort Saturday, even if I have to ride in a blizzard."

"How's my little girl?" Rose asked, picking up Becky, who had come to lean against her. Settling the little girl on her lap, she said, "My, what a big girl you're getting to be. Since I saw you last you must have grown two inches and put on ten pounds."

She looked up at Blaze. "You look like you've gained a few pounds too. When a person doesn't get enough exercise the fat piles up fast."

Blaze made no comment, but inside she wished that her situation were as simple as that.

"Now," Blaze's eyes twinkled as she sat down, "has Jake been to the fort and heard any gossip?"

"There's a bit." Rose put Becky off her lap. "A couple trappers are courting Caroline Hank's daughters and she is having a fit about it. She's as poor as a churchmouse, but thinks her girls are too good for a pair of lowly trappers. She wants some rancher's sons to come calling. It's my belief that she ought to thank God that any man would want them. They giggle all the time, they're wasp-ish like their mother and not at all attractive. Both run to fat and the youngest one has a cast in her right eye."

"I noticed on the wagon train coming out here that they gossiped a lot," Blaze said. "And come dark, the oldest one was always slipping off to meet some man or other. Caroline spent most of every evening looking for her," Blaze added with amusement.

"That's another reason Caroline should be thankful that her girls may snag a husband. That oldest one is going to come up with a big belly one of these days and Mrs. Uppity Hank won't like that one bit."

After a slight pause Rose said, "The fort is full of talk about John Jackson and that young girl married to Yancy Davis. Her name is Bess. Re-member how she had to do all the work on the trail? Had to find her own firewood, build the campfires while that no-account Yancy sat on his rump watching her, never lifting a hand to help her? I never believed this, but the talk on the trail was that when they went to bed, he made her do all the work there too.

"Anyway, to get back to my story. John Jackson has been slipping over to the Davis place every time Yancy goes to the fort. Bess lets him know it's all right for him to come by closing the cur-tains at her kitchen window. John hightails it over there then and stays until they see Yancy coming home. He slips out the back door and walks the short distance to his cabin.

"Everybody knows what's going on, but no one bothers to tell Yancy. He's not at all liked and it tickles the folks that his wife is putting the horns on him.

"Other than that, everything is pretty humdrum, I guess. Everybody is waiting for spring to come."

"Hunter thinks most of the homesteaders will move on once they can travel," Blaze said.

"Jake thinks so, too, from what he hears. Their plans are to go to California."

"But you and Jake won't be going, will you?" Blaze asked anxiously.

"No, we're staying. Jake picked out a good piece of land with a small stream going through it. We can live nicely off it. There is the Indian scare though."

"What about them? I haven't heard anything about an uprising," Blaze said, a worried frown on her forehead.

"It's said that some of the young braves from Black Crow's tribe have been raiding the home-steaders and ranchers. They steal anything they can get their hands on, including cows and horses. They haven't killed anyone yet, but they so hate the white man, it's feared that may happen next."

"Oh dear, if it's not one thing it's another." Blaze sighed. "Hunter says that Black Crow is a fine, honorable man who wants to get along with us. He must feel terrible about what his braves are doing."

"He may not know. He's quite old and probably

stays close to his fire. Jake thinks that when the weather warms up and Black Crow gets around again, all this trouble with the young men of his village will come to an end."

"I certainly hope so," Blaze said, and then their talk turned to the mundane trivia of living through a Wyoming winter. Blaze bragged that she could now bake a perfect pie.

"I should be able to," Blaze laughed. "Apples have been the only fruit I've been able to get my hands on. Luckily Mr. Bridger still had several bushels left in his storeroom. Besides the pies, I have made apple cobbler, apple tarts and applesauce. I even put some in Becky's oatmeal one morning and the little minx looked up at me and said sadly, "Mama's little love is tired of apples."

"I don't doubt it." Rose laughed. "After my sixth pie Jake refused to eat any more. Desserts around our house have been mighty slim this winter."

"Since you can't bake much, how have you been spending the days?"

"I've been making a quilt. The wedding ring pattern. It's not going to be real pretty, I'm afraid. All I have to work with are drab colors: mostly material from Jake's trousers and shirts that have worn out at the knees and elbows. It will be nice and warm to crawl under next winter, though."

"If you want to make a quilt out of bright colors, why don't you ask Lucianne for her girls' discards? You'll have one of the brightest quilts around." Blaze laughed. "They only wear silks and satins. All the colors in the rainbow."

"Do you think she would give them to me? I don't know her to speak to. We've only nodded at each other when we pass on the street."

"Of course she would. Lucianne is the nicest, sweetest person you could ever meet."

"I think I will then. I'm just about finished with the one I'm working on. I've never made one out of silk and satin before. I bet it will be lovely."

After a short pause in which Blaze refilled their coffee cups, Rose said, "You look a little peaked, dear. Aren't you feeling well?"

"Oh, yes, I feel fine. I guess I've lost my color over the winter."

Rose waited a minute, then asked, "Are you sure you're not expecting?"

"What makes you ask that?" Blaze almost dropped the coffeepot as she returned it to the stove.

"I don't know." Rose shrugged. "It's just that you have the look my sister always got when she was expecting another baby. And you have put on weight."

"Oh, dear," Rose exclaimed when Blaze covered her face with her hands and started crying. "Did I guess right?" She pulled Blaze's hands away.

"Yes," Blaze sobbed, tears running down her cheeks.

"And you're not happy about it?" Rose asked, perplexed.

"I am and I'm not. You see, Hunter doesn't love me."

"Of course he does. Why wouldn't he? You're

307

beautiful, you keep his home clean, you cook him good meals. And what about the loving way you take care of little Becky?"

"None of that matters when he's in love with a dead woman."

"Has he told you that?" Rose asked doubtfully.

"No, of course not. He's too smart to come right out and say so."

"Have you told him about the baby?"

"No, I haven't, and I don't intend to." Blaze wiped her eyes. "Come spring I'll be leaving with the settlers when they pull out."

"Blaze, honey, you'll be making a big mistake. You have no idea how hard it is going to be raising a child by yourself."

"I know it won't be easy, but I'll manage."

"I wish I could stay longer and talk you out of your foolish thoughts, but dark is coming on and I want to get home while there's still daylight. But I'll be back soon and we'll thrash this thing out."

Blaze only nodded her head, wishing there really was some way to work out her problems.

# Chapter Twenty

March had arrived and the snow was shrinking. There was definitely less snow on the ground than there had been two weeks ago, Blaze thought, standing on the porch wrapped in a shawl, taking deep breaths of the pure, pine-scented air.

But I mustn't think that spring has arrived, she told herself. Bucky had said yesterday that they would get more snow, maybe even another blizzard. He had added that he remembered one bad storm coming through in early May.

Blaze decided suddenly to take advantage of the rare mild day to ride to the fort. She was low on maple syrup, and maybe she would visit with Lucianne awhile.

She stepped off the porch and hurried down the path to the cookhouse. She would tell Hunter that he would have to sit with Becky while she was gone.

Only Bucky was in his kitchen when Blaze pushed open the door and stepped inside. She smiled at him in greeting and said, "I thought Hunter was here. Has he gone to the fort?"

"Naw, he said he was going to try and find his herd, see if he had lost any over the winter. He rode off about an hour ago."

Darn, Blaze thought. She really had her heart set on going to the fort. She gave Bucky a speculative look. Becky liked the old man . . . maybe he would keep an eye on her in the cookhouse for a while.

Bucky caught her looking at him and left off peeling a pan of potatoes. "What are you cookin' up in your head, young woman?" he asked. "I get real nervous when you get that glitter in your eyes."

Blaze chuckled. She had gotten to know the sour old man and knew that his bluster hid a very kind and caring heart. He sometimes made her nervous, the way he could almost read her mind.

"I need to ride to the fort to get syrup, and since Hunter isn't around, I was wondering if I could leave Becky here with you while I'm gone."

"Oh, well, if that's all you want, bring the little monkey over." Bucky resumed peeling potatoes. With a crooked grin he said, "I thought maybe you wanted one of my secret recipes."

"Oh, I know you would never give me one of those," Blaze said solemnly, her eyes twinkling with silent mirth. They both broke out laughing then. Bucky wasn't known for fancy cooking.

It took Blaze about twenty minutes before she started down the path to the fort. It had taken most of that time to coax Becky into staying with the old cook. She had finally succeeded by promising the little girl that she would bring her back a candy stick.

Beauty stepped along at a fast clip, wanting to run, but wise enough to know that the snow was too deep for that. There was a chill in the air that crept through Blaze's clothes. She was thankful when she spotted the fort about half a mile away. She made up her mind that her trip would be a short one. As the day turned to night it would grow colder, and the temperature would be freezing when the sun went down. Her visit to Lucianne wouldn't last long.

A little later, when Blaze stepped into the store, she found that two other women had taken advantage of the nice day to do some shopping: Caroline Hank and Maybelle Potter, the pair who kept the gossip about her going. When they looked down their noses at her, she tried to ignore the snub.

She chatted with Jim for a few minutes, and then took the can of syrup and the candy stick and left to visit Lucianne.

The woman who answered her knock on the back door was a stranger to Blaze. She wondered who the haunted-eyed woman was and why she looked startled for a moment when she gave her name.

The stranger was pleasant, however, when she said, "Come in and warm up."

Blaze stepped into the short hall and smiled when Lucianne called from the kitchen, "Is that you, Blaze?"

"Yes, it is," Blaze answered, following the woman into the big warm room.

"I've been thinking about you, honey." Lucianne helped her off with her heavy jacket.

"You have? What have you been thinking?" Blaze smiled and sat down in the chair the woman pulled away from the table for her.

"This is Pearl Meyer, my new cook and house-keeper," Lucianne said before answering Blaze's question. When she had sat down across from Blaze, she asked, "How is your morning sickness? You're looking fine."

"I'm feeling well," Blaze said. "After a few weeks I stopped losing my breakfast, just as you said I would."

Lucianne studied her young friend's face and saw the sadness far back in her eyes. "Have you told Hunter about the baby yet?"

Blaze shook her head. "I've decided not to tell him. I . . . I'm going to leave him once the passes open up in the spring. I think I'll go on to Califor-nia with the settlers."

"Oh, Blaze, how can you do such a thing? Hun-ter loves you, and you can't deny him his own baby. Look at what a wonderful father he is to Becky. He would be thrilled to know he's going to be a father again."

"No, you're wrong. He loves Becky's mother, not me, and that makes all the difference in the world."

A short silence grew as Lucianne studied her young friend's face through lowered lids. Then she asked, "Has Hunter ever talked to you about his first wife?"

"Hah!" Blaze gave a short laugh. "He'd never discuss his precious Jenny with me. Did you know her?"

"Let's just say that I knew of her."

"I expect she was very beautiful."

"Not as beautiful as you," Lucianne said. "She was dark while you are very fair."

The subject of Jenny Ward was unanimously dropped when Blaze said with a soft smile, "I think I felt the baby move this morning. There was a little flutter in my stomach."

"You probably did. You're about far enough along to start feeling movement."

"How would you know, Lucianne? You've never had a baby," Blaze teased.

"That's right, but I was the eldest of eight children; my ma had one every spring just like a cow. Ma would hardly be over having one before Pa, the mean bastard, would be putting his seed in her again. Having them so close together weakened her and she died delivering the eighth one, a baby boy. That made five boys and three girls.

"Ma was buried but a week when he brought home a new wife. She was only thirteen, still playing with dolls. She had no idea what to expect in the marriage bed, unlike us kids. We knew all about that. We'd heard it, seen it, all our lives.

"I can still hear poor little Pansy crying as that old bastard kept after her all night.

"The next morning she was so ashamed, she couldn't look us kids in the face. I helped her a little by telling her that what had gone on in the bedroom the night before was what happened between a husband and wife, and that she must expect it to happen again, that in time she would get used to it.

"She lay around all day, too weak to do anything. My sisters and I fed her a lot of beef broth to strengthen her for what lay ahead.

"Pansy was expecting after the first month of marriage. She lost that baby in her third month because she was so young and that old bastard wouldn't leave her alone.

"When I was fourteen, Pansy died during a sixth miscarriage. We buried the poor little thing next to Ma. When Pa went off to marry yet another young girl, I took my two sisters, ten and twelve, and, stealing what money there was hidden under a floorboard, we left. I had no idea where we were going, but we ended up in Cheyenne, a wild place then." Lucianne sighed. "I guess I don't have to tell you how I supported myself and my sisters.

"They're doing just fine. I kept them pure and they married fine young men. One has a small ranch and the other is a newspaperman.

"Each sister has a couple children, ready to get married themselves. Once a year I scrub the paint off my face, get dressed in respectable clothing and go visit them." A proud smile lifted Lucianne's lips. "My nieces and nephews are crazy about their aunt Lucianne. They think I'm a dressmaker."

Blaze looked at the madam with warm affection. What a kind, decent woman, she thought before saying, "Actually, then, in a way you have had babies. Certainly you have taken care of them. What happened to your brothers, and is your father still living?"

"I don't know. I don't know anything about any of them. Once the girls and I left we never looked back. I hope that my brothers grew up to be fine, decent men. As for that old man, he's probably still alive, making life miserable for some poor woman."

A burst of laughter coming from outside silenced Blaze and Lucianne. Blaze's face lost its color. She had recognized the male laughter. It was Hunter's.

Against Lucianne's protest, she rose and went to the window, where she could get a partial view of the Pleasure House's front door. She felt a jab of pain in her chest when she saw her husband sharing a laugh with Lucianne's youngest and prettiest prostitute. Had he been in bed with her all the time his wife sat in the kitchen drinking coffee?

Blaze turned to Lucianne, who had followed her to the window. Giving her an accusing look, she asked, "Why didn't you tell me he was here?"

"I swear to you, Blaze, I didn't know. There must be an explanation why he's here. Maybe—"

"Hah!" Blaze cut across Lucianne's words. "There's only one reason he's here, the randy wolf."

"Now, Blaze, you don't know that," Lucianne argued as Hunter tipped his hat to the young whore and then strode off toward the fort.

"I'm not an idiot. I know what I saw," Blaze said furiously. She shrugged into her jacket and was out the door, with Lucianne calling after her not to do anything rash.

Blaze slammed the door behind her so hard, it rattled. She achieved what she intended. The noise it made carried to Hunter, who was almost at the fort's door.

He turned his head and saw Blaze coming toward him, fury twisting her features. "Ah, hell," he swore under his breath.

He'd come to the fort this afternoon in a celebratory mood, but it looked like he'd have little to celebrate once Blaze got through with him.

It had taken him over two hours to locate his cattle earlier. Instinct had led them to a small valley sheltered from the worst of the winter weather. There were windswept areas where they had been able to find patches of dry grass. The herd was rib thin, but it didn't look as though he had lost too many animals. If there wasn't another hard blizzard, the rest of them would make it. He relaxed and turned Saint's head toward home, reaching into his vest pocket for his sack of tobacco. The small white bag was almost empty, and he had no more at home.

He turned the stallion's head in the direction of the fort. He was halfway there already and he might as well pick some tobacco up now.

As he'd opened the door to the store, he'd knocked a young prostitute on her read end. Her arms full of packages, she'd glared up at him.

Hunter grinned and reached down to help her up. "Why don't you watch where you're going, Nancy?" he teased.

"Why do you have to bang open a door like the Devil was after you?" the young woman scolded as he pulled her to her feet.

Nancy had often chatted with Hunter when she saw him in the fort having a drink with friends. She'd smiled up at him and asked with twinkling eyes, "Do you want to help an old friend home with her packages? I'll see that you're well rewarded for it."

"Now, Nancy, behave yourself. You know I'm an old married man, but I'll help you home anyway," he'd said, taking her purchases from her.

"Anything been happening in your life lately?" Hunter asked as he walked behind her.

"Nothin' excitin'," she answered, "but there's been a few funny happenin's. For instance, one of my customers couldn't perform when I took him to my bed. He got mad and said it was my fault and wanted his money back. I told him to go whistle up a tree, and he said if I didn't give him the money he'd send his wife over to get it."

They'd both been laughing uproariously when they reached Lucianne's big house, but from the look on Blaze's face as she bore down on him now, his wife wouldn't share the joke.

Glaring up at him, her hands clenched into fists, she hissed, "I guess you know you have broken the pledge between us. I warned you I wouldn't be made a laughingstock among the folk here. From now on you can take your pleasure in some other woman's bed. And I'll play the same game you do. They can snicker behind both our backs."

"Damn you." Hunter grabbed her wrist. "I didn't break our promise. I was only helping Nancy home with her packages. I went as far as the door and then . . ." His words trailed off. Blaze had turned around and was walking briskly away, her back ramrod straight.

Hunter stared after her, grating out under his breath, "Just try cozying up to another man, lady, and I'll kill him."

# Chapter Twenty-one

It was a crystal-clear night. The whiteness of the snow was almost blinding under a full moon when Blaze stepped through the kitchen door to stand on the porch and gaze out over the range.

She pulled her knitted shawl closer around her shoulders. She felt sad and lonely and she knew why. The time was fast approaching when she must leave the ranch, Becky and Hunter.

She loved all three, but only Becky seemed to love her back. The land, of course, had no feeling for her one way or the other. It just lay there to be used or abused. And Hunter had never pretended that he loved her, she reflected dejectedly. There had been a time when she foolishly thought that maybe, after a while, he would at least develop an affection for her.

319

She knew now it would never happen. Instead of growing better, their relationship had grown worse since she had caught him with the young whore. Hurt and jealous, she had moved back into Becky's bedroom, and now he left the cabin as soon as he finished eating supper. Whether he went to the bunkhouse or rode to the fort, she didn't know. She had thought to ask Bucky a few careful questions about how his boss spent his evenings, but pride kept her from doing it. The cook was a shrewd old man and probably wouldn't be fooled, no matter how cautiously she put her questions to him.

If Hunter was spending his evenings at the fort, Bucky would feel sorry for her, and she didn't want his pity. She could live with the gossip-mongers, their dislike of her, but pity would be more than she could endure.

The baby kicked inside her and Blaze laid a loving hand on her stomach. Come September she would have a little person who would love her unconditionally. It wouldn't care that she wasn't perfect. It wouldn't compare her to someone else.

Becky called her from inside the cabin and a gentle smile curved Blaze's lips. That little one loved her completely and would be crushed for a while when her mama left her.

"But no more than I will be," Blaze whispered to herself as she returned inside.

All the time Blaze had stood on the porch, Hunter had stood in the shadow of the bunkhouse watching her. What was she thinking about as she gazed out over the white land? he wondered. Was she thinking of leaving him? God, he hoped not. What would he and Becky do without her? As her name suggested, she had lit up his home with warmth and love. He didn't think he could go back to the cold, empty life he'd led before.

He carried his gloom with him when he entered the bunkhouse, and the cowboys silently sighed. Their boss, lately, took all the pleasure out of their poker games with his long face.

Two nights later the calm of the ranch was broken. It was around midnight and everyone was sleeping soundly, with the exception of the cook, who was suffering stomach upset. It was brought on by his own cooking, or so the cowboys ragged him.

Bucky was sitting in the dark at the long table where he had just finished drinking a glass of water with baking soda stirred into it. The full moon lit up the outside well enough that he could see the cabin and bunkhouse, but caught up with the pain in his gut, he paid them no attention. After a while he belched a couple of times and felt a little better.

Maybe now he would be able to go to sleep, he thought as he rose from the table with a wide yawn. He rinsed out his glass, and as set it on the workbench, a movement outside caught his attention. He leaned forward to see if a deer had wandered into the ranch yard and gave a start. It was no animal that was peering into Hunter's bedroom window. It was a man. Who was he and what was he up to?

Bucky's first thought was to go to the door and call Hunter. He realized then that if he did that, the man would run away and they wouldn't know who he was or why he was sneaking around in the middle of the night peering into people's windows.

"I'll take care of the bastard," Bucky muttered, pulling on his boots and shrugging into his jacket. As he carefully opened the door, praying it wouldn't squeak, he picked up the heavy club he always kept leaning against the wall. He would slip up on the man and knock him out with a blow to the head.

Bucky's plan went well until he was about three feet away from the man, who was still staring intently through Hunter's window. Then, stumbling in the semidarkness, he accidentally stepped off the shoveled path onto the unbroken ice-crusted snow. It made such a cracking noise in the silent darkness that the man whirled around, saw him, and lunged at him.

His heavy weight knocked the much lighter Bucky backward, and as he fell his head hit a large rock on the edge of the path. When he lay unmoving where he fell, the man ran off, disappearing into the night.

Two hours later Clay Southern, Hunter's drover, came riding home from the fort, where he'd had a few drinks and visited the Pleasure House. He was whistling softly as he made his way toward the barn to put up his mount when he saw the crumpled figure lying in the snow. He quickly dismounted and hurried to the inert body. "Hey, Bucky, old fellow," he exclaimed, recognizing the elderly cook. "What are you doing layin' out here in the snow?" He felt Bucky's limp wrist for a pulse. He found it, but it was weak. When he gathered the old man in his arms to carry him to the cookhouse he saw the blood on the rock.

When a fast glance around the immediate area showed the footprints of someone running away from the cabin, it was clear to him what had happened. The old fellow had seen a prowler and had gone after him with the club he still had clutched in his hand. It was clear also that Bucky had lost the battle.

After Clay had groped his way through the dark kitchen and on into Bucky's living quarters, he set the unconscious cook on the bed and tugged his jacket off him, then pulled off his boots. Since Bucky only had on his long underwear and no socks on his feet, Clay laid him on his side on the bed, facing the wall so that his head wound was accessible. Pulling the covers up around the bony shoulders, he added another blanket he found lying on a shelf, and then hurried to the cabin to tell Hunter that he thought Bucky was near death.

A gray, misty dawn had arrived when Hunter and Dr. Caleb Hines left the sickroom and walked into the kitchen. "Is he gonna make it, Doc?" Hunter asked as the doctor pulled on his heavy Indian blanket jacket.

"It's too early to say yet, Hunter. Both his lungs are congested and his age is against him. He's going to need around-the-clock care for the next twenty-four hours, if he makes it that long."

"He'll get good care," Hunter said, concern for Bucky in his voice.

"If you don't mind, I'm going to send Lucianne out here to give you a hand."

"She's welcome to come, of course, but I don't think it's necessary. Blaze and I can take care of the old fellow."

Hines shook his head. "Maybe you could take a twelve-hour shift, but Blaze couldn't. You forget that she has your daughter to take care of. When would she get any sleep and rest? And somebody has to take over the cooking for your hands." He knew from the startled look that came over Hunter's face that he had not thought of that.

Dr. Hines took a stocking cap out of his pocket and pulled it over his head and added, "I'll send Lucianne right over. Despite the way she and Bucky used to argue, she's real fond of him and would want to help nurse him back to health."

The doctor was gone then, leaving Hunter to mull over his words. He soon came to the conclusion that Hines was right. He and Blaze couldn't do it alone. Blaze would have her hands full cooking three meals a day for the cowboys.

That is if she agrees to take on the job, he thought as he blew out the lamp whose light was no longer needed. He started walking toward Bucky's bedroom, thinking that he might as well find out right now Blaze's feelings about spending most of her time cooking. Just then the door swung open and Clay Southern entered the kitchen.

"How is the old feller?" Clay asked in the low tones that were used around sickness.

"Not very good, I'm afraid. He has pneumonia and Doc doesn't know if he'll pull through or not."

"That's a shame," Clay said, shaking his head. "Now that it's daylight, me and the hands are startin' out to track the bastard down."

Hunter looked out the window and swore softly. "From the looks of the sky, it's gonna start snowing anytime now. If it's heavy enough, it will cover the tracks the bastard left."

"Maybe it will hold off long enough for us to find him," Clay said and quietly closed the door behind him.

Hunter took a long breath and prepared himself to ask Blaze about cooking the meals.

When he entered the room, Blaze was sitting on the edge of the bed laying a wet cloth on Bucky's forehead. "How's he doing?" he asked, going to stand beside her.

"He's burning up with fever." Blaze looked up at Hunter, concern in her eyes. "Do you think he's going to make it? What did the doctor say?"

"Well." Hunter sighed. "He said that Bucky is real sick and he didn't know if he would make it or not. He's sending Lucianne out to help us with him."

"That's very thoughtful of him, but do you think we'll need her?"

"I think so," Hunter said, then, squaring his shoulders to do battle with Blaze, he said, closely watching her face, "you won't be able to help much with the old man, for I'm afraid you'll have to take over the cooking for the men."

Blaze shook her head, opened her mouth to protest, but before she could speak Hunter said, "I'll help you, of course. It won't be too hard for you, I promise." He laid a hand on her shoulder and coaxed, "I'll do all the cleaning up after meals."

"But what about Becky?" Blaze asked, feeling herself weakening. She guessed it would be the logical thing for her to take over Bucky's job. It would be easier than that first time she'd attempted to cook for the men. She knew her way around a stove now.

"I think it would be safe to bring Becky here," Hunter said in answer to her question.

"All right, I'll do the cooking," Blaze said, "but I don't want to hear any sneering remarks from you if I fail at it."

"You won't fail. You're a real good cook, Blaze." He grinned then and teased, "I won't say a word if you burn the biscuits and your gravy is lumpy."

When she gave him a weak smile he said, "I'll go get Becky now."

"Be sure you dress her warmly and bring along

some of her clothes. You'll find them in the middle dresser drawer."

Just as Hunter stepped outside the door, it began snowing. The flakes were big and plentiful. In just a short time they would cover all traces of Bucky's assailant. "Damn," he swore. "We're gonna have to worry about that polecat for God knows how long."

# Chapter Twenty-two

"I think I'll go home tomorrow," Lucianne said, fingering her hair as she watched Blaze put a four-pound roast into the oven. "My hair is badly in need of the curling iron. All the frizz is gone out of it."

Blaze closed the oven door and sat down across the table from her friend. In her opinion, Lucianne looked more attractive without the frizz and the paint on her face. She looked like a respectable married woman.

But the paint and tight curls and gaudy dresses were the trademarks of prostitutes. All of it was as necessary to them as an apron was to a homemaker.

"I'll miss you"—she looked fondly at Lucianne—"but I understand you have a business to run." Her lips lifted in a crooked smile. "Your girls are like children in a way and need you to direct them."

"Nancy has been doing a fine job of it the past week. However, when she brought me clean clothes yesterday I could tell she was getting tired of riding herd on the others. She's been having trouble with Mona. If you remember, that one is lazy. She not only shirks her share of the cooking and housecleaning but she also entertains only two or three men a night, leaving the other girls to take up the slack, and that's not fair to them."

Nancy, Blaze thought as Lucianne talked on. The girl had been here three times, bringing Lucianne clean clothes and reporting what went on in Lucianne's absence. She was vibrant and fun-loving and Lucianne's most sought-after prostitute. It wasn't surprising that Hunter would desire her too.

"Isn't that right, Blaze?" Lucianne asked, breaking in on Blaze's disturbing thoughts.

"I'm sorry, Lucianne, but my mind wandered a moment. What were you saying?"

"I was saying that now Bucky is coming along fine, you really don't need me here."

Blaze nodded. "He's doing remarkably well. But so grumpy and ill-tempered I'm ready to choke him."

"Caleb is letting him get up tomorrow. Maybe his mood will improve once he's out of bed."

"Well it had better; otherwise I'll go home and leave Hunter to do the cooking and looking after him."

"You can't do that." Lucianne laughed. The cowhands would raise the roof if they had to eat Hunter's cooking. You've spoiled them with the fine meals you put on the table, besides being so pretty for them to look at. It's going to be hard enough for them to go back to Bucky's plain fare.

"But I worry about you and Hunter. Who was that man who Bucky caught peering into Hunter's window? I ask myself if he was looking for Hunter, or for you?"

"I doubt he was looking for me. Unless maybe he's one of those men who like to secretly spy on women."

"I hate to think that we have a man like that living among us." Lucianne shivered. "It gives me the creeps just thinking about it. It's too bad Hunter's men lost his tracks in the new snow that fell."

They left off discussing who the man could be when Bucky called out crossly, "Lucianne, you promised to bring me a cup of coffee."

She shook her head in annoyance as she stood up. "The old devil knows damn well I did no such thing. I think I'll pour the coffee over his head."

Blaze smiled at Lucianne's threat, knowing she wouldn't carry it out, and said, "He can get his own coffee tomorrow."

"Yes, he can, and by the end of next week he can take over the cooking again."

"I certainly hope so. I want to get home too. I haven't minded the cooking; Hunter has been a big help, cleaning up after the meals. It's just that I miss being in the cabin, keeping it clean and all."

330

"You're going to miss all that when you leave, huh, honey?" Lucianne said gently as she poured a cup of coffee for Bucky.

"Yes, and I don't know how I'll ever be able to leave Becky."

"I still think you and Hunter can patch things up between you."

"Good grief, Lucianne"—Blaze spoke sharply—"are you so blind that you haven't noticed how cool he is toward me, that we never talk to each other?"

"Yes, I've noticed all that, but I've also seen the way he looks at you when you're not aware of it."

"You mean how he'd like to tear off my clothes and take me to bed?" Blaze sniffed. "I'm aware of those looks, the randy wolf."

"No, I don't mean that. He looks at you the way a man looks at a woman he's in love with. I admit he'd like to take you to bed. I've seen that look in his eyes also, but love and desire often go together, Blaze."

"You're way off the mark, Lucianne. If he loves me the way you claim, why does he visit Nancy all the time?"

"I'm not aware that he does." Lucianne looked surprised. "And I'm sure I would know it if he did. Nancy would be bragging about it."

"Not if he visited her secretly and told her not to tell anyone."

"I give up," Lucianne exclaimed angrily. "Think what you want to." She picked up Bucky's coffee and stamped into his room.

331

*   *   *

Hunter sat on the top step of the porch, watching his daughter play in the snow. He laughed with her when she stepped into a snowdrift that came up to her waist. Only once had he had to rescue her, for she was a gritty little child and managed to wade through the snow to where it only came to her knees.

He looked at the sled marks crisscrossing the area between the cabin and the outbuildings. Every day since this last storm he had bundled Becky up, set her in the bright red sled and spent an hour pulling her around in it.

He never took her out of sight of the cabin, though. There was a man out there somewhere who meant him harm and was probably capable of hurting him through his daughter.

Who was the man? Hunter looked out over the white landscape. Bucky couldn't tell who it was in the darkness. He said all he knew was that the man looked mighty big as he lunged at him.

There were several big men in the area, two of them being his trapper friends. He knew it was neither of them, and he couldn't believe that any of the other big men he knew would prowl around his cabin and peer into his bedroom window.

Hunter also worried about Blaze. She could also be in danger from the man. He hadn't had to worry about her during Bucky's illness; she had been kept busy in the cabin. But the old man was coming along fine, and any day now Blaze could be moving back to the cabin. She liked to ride into the fort at least once a week, and it wouldn't be wise for her to do that since the incident of the prowler.

He would like to accompany her, but doubted she would want him to. Well, he would just trail along behind her to see that she came to no harm. His stomach knotted, thinking of her being taken by his enemy.

He had thought—hoped—that since they'd been thrown together so much the past week, he would be able to convince her that she was wrong about Nancy; that they could get back to their old relationship.

It hadn't happened. Blaze avoided him all she could in the two-room cookhouse, speaking to him only when she had to.

Hunter's attention was caught by two riders going toward the fort. The Wilson men, he thought darkly. There was always the chance that Blaze might go to them. The brothers would take care of her. Especially James. That one was crazy about her and would kill any man who presented a danger to her.

The thing was, it would kill Hunter to see Blaze living with another man.

*I've got to stop thinking about it,* he thought; *otherwise I'll go crazy.*

Hunter stood up and called to Becky that it was time to go in. As she came toward him, her eyes sparkling and her nose and cheeks rosy from the cold, he remembered the pale, shy child he had found on his return home after his long absence. What a change had been wrought in his daughter, and it was all because of the woman he loved with all his heart.

# *Chapter Twenty-three*

It was the first day of April. The snow was melting where the sun hit it all day, and meltwater was beginning to make its way down the mountains.

But spring was arriving in fits and starts. It would be sunny one day, then cold and gloomy the next, as though Mother Nature were warning people that winter wasn't completely over yet; that she might play a trick on them by flying in on the back of a blizzard. It wouldn't be an unusual occurrence, old-timers said. They recalled getting a heavy snow as late as May.

Hunter had the feeling that Blaze was planning to leave him. As he sat on the top rail of the corral, his boot heels hooked on the rail below, he wondered what he could do to stop her. For two days now she had been washing and ironing. She had placed his and Becky's clothes in their usual drawers, but had left hers, neatly folded, on top of the dresser. That action told him that later she would put them in a valise. He had seen a sadness on Blaze's face when she looked at Becky sometimes that added to his conviction that she would be leaving soon. She loved his little daughter, and it would hurt her to leave the child.

"Why do you sit here brooding about it?" his inner voice asked. "Why don't you march up there and tell her how you feel about her? Tell her that you love her and that you want her to stay."

"She'd never believe that I love her."

"You could try to make a deal with her. Why not offer her a wage like you do with your other help? If she agrees, you'll have the time to convince her of your love."

"I'll put the proposition to her right now," Hunter muttered, stepping down from his perch, eager to put his plan in motion.

He took one step, then froze. James Wilson was riding up to the cabin. His heart thudded against his ribs. Had the handsome farmer come to take Blaze away today? When had they made their plans? he wondered, standing rooted to the ground, trying to make up his mind what to do. He hadn't been off the ranch since Bucky was attacked and neither had Blaze. He didn't think there had been any notes passed between them. His men were in awe of Blaze's beauty, but their loyalty would be with him. They would never involve themselves in deceiving him.

"I'm going up there and order that bastard off my property," Hunter thought when Blaze came to the cabin door and stood in its opening, smiling at their neighbor. He hung back when James didn't dismount. He and Blaze spoke briefly, and then Wilson rode away.

What had they said to each other? he wondered, his hands unconsciously balling into fists. Had James been checking when Blaze would move back in with him and his brother?

When Wilson had ridden out of sight, going toward the fort, Hunter returned to the cabin. The aroma of spicy apples baking greeted him as he stepped into the kitchen. Blaze was rolling out pie dough to start another one.

Forcing himself not to let his voice show what he was thinking, Hunter said, "I saw Wilson here before. What did he want?"

Blaze looked up at him, a streak of flour smudged on one cheek, surprised that he spoke so calmly. He hated James. Why wasn't he shouting as he'd always done before if James came around?

"He wanted to know if I needed anything from the store," she answered finally.

"That was neighborly of him." Hunter spoke so matter-of-factly, it made Blaze blink at him.

"Do you need anything from the fort?" Hunter asked after pouring himself a cup of coffee and sitting down at the table, careful not to get in the way of the rolling pin or the bowl of sliced apples waiting to be put in the pie shell.

Blaze hesitated a second, then, looking away

from Hunter, said, "I do need a couple of things, but they are of a personal nature."

Her answer pleased Hunter, gave him hope. If she loved the farmer, there would be nothing too personal for her to ask Wilson to bring to her.

"It's a fair day; why don't you ride to the fort and get what you need? Some fresh air would be good for you; put the roses back in your cheeks."

*Since when has he worried about my health?* Blaze was too stunned to speak for a second before she answered, "I think I will. It will feel good to get out of the cabin for a while. I'll go as soon as this pie is baked." She had placed the piece of rolled dough over the apples she had ladled into the pie tin while they talked and was now crimping the edges together.

"I can keep an eye on it," Hunter offered. "Just tell me approximately how long it should bake so I know when to start checking on it."

"Well," Blaze answered, taking the finished pie out of the oven and sliding the new one in to take its place, "after about half an hour, start looking in on it every few minutes. When the crust looks like this one, take it out."

"I can do that. Take your apron off and get ready to go." Hunter rose and walked to the door. "I'll be right back. I want to tell a couple of the hands to go check on the cattle."

Hunter wanted to speak to his drover, but not about the herd. He wanted to tell Clay Southern to secretly trail along behind Blaze when she rode off to the fort. That prowler was still out there somewhere and Hunter would take no chances with Blaze's welfare. And at the first opportunity he was going to ask her to stay on with him and Becky under whatever conditions she would accept.

As Blaze rode along, oblivious to the fact that she was being followed, she pondered Hunter's changed attitude toward her.

She still hadn't made up her mind where she would go when she left the only real home she had ever known. She didn't want to think about it, but knew that she must. She would have a baby in September and she had to think of its welfare. She had come to one decision, however. She must go far enough away that Hunter would never learn that he was a father again. She wouldn't put it past him to take their baby away from her.

Lucianne wanted her to go to Cheyenne, where she had friends who would look after her, but that was too close. Hunter went there on business sometimes.

The fort loomed up ahead, and Blaze pushed her worrisome thoughts aside for the moment. They would, of course, come back to her the minute she was alone.

When Blaze stepped into the store part of the fort, she was greeted by Caroline Hank and Maybelle Potter. What was going on? she wondered. Why were her two worst enemies being pleasant?

When she reached the counter and the group of women who were talking there excitedly, she wasn't long in discovering why Caroline and May-belle had done a complete turnaround from their usual treatment of her.

"I just couldn't believe it when James and David helped those two young women off the stage and then introduced them as their wives," one of the women was saying. "It turns out that they were already married when they joined the wagon train. They had come ahead to claim land and to build a cabin before their wives arrived. Both the young women were upset that their trip out here by train and stagecoach had been delayed until now by the weather."

"Did you know they were married, Blaze?" Caroline Hank asked.

"Of course I knew," Blaze answered impatiently. "They told me before we left Fort Laramie."

Blaze turned her back on the women then and asked Bridger in low tones if he had any baby yarn.

Bridger answered in the same hushed tones, "It's over there with the rest of the yarn."

"Would you go get me a couple of skeins of white and keep it hidden from them?" She jerked her head toward the women, who were still chattering about the brothers.

"Why sure, Blaze," Bridger said, curiosity in his eyes.

"I'm knitting a scarf for Hunter," she lied. "I want it to be a surprise."

"Are you sure you want white? Wouldn't a dark blue be more appropriate?"

"Maybe, but I like working with white."

When Bridger picked up a small sack and went to do Blaze's bidding, she looked around the store, her eyes lighting on New Moon. The Indian woman was glaring hatred at her, her lips a sullen, bitter line. Who had been beating her? Blaze wondered, noting a cut lip and an ugly bruise on New Moon's cheekbone. Who had taken his fist to her, an Indian or a white man?

Bridger nudged her back and, when Blaze turned around, he handed her the sack. "I hope Hunter will be surprised and pleased," he said, smiling at her.

"Me too," Blaze answered. Ignoring the women, she walked toward the door, thinking that Hunter would be surprised, but hardly pleased, if he knew what she was really going to do with the white yarn.

Clay Southern, who had secreted himself in the tavern, finished his drink, and then waited a couple of minutes before he followed Blaze.


New Moon trudged along in the cold as she returned to her village. Her breathing was shallow because if she took deep breaths it hurt her lungs. She feared her man had broken another rib when he'd beaten her last night.

The Indian woman knew now that she must get away from him before he killed her in one of his rages, but she wasn't sure how she could escape. She feared that she would only be free of him when he tired of her and went away. She sighed.

That wasn't likely to happen until he had settled his grudge against Hunter Ward. His inability to do that so far had made him mean and short tempered.

New Moon was cursing the day she had ever met Deke Meyer when the Indian village loomed ahead of her. As rib-thin dogs came barking toward her, she lifted the leather flap of the wigwam and stepped inside. She saw at a glance that Deke was in a black mood, that when she told him Bridger wouldn't sell her any whiskey he would erupt into violence. She gave him a wan half smile as she advanced to the fire burning in the pit lined with rocks.

"I think it's colder today than it was yesterday," she ventured, kneeling down and holding her hands out to the heat.

A nervous tension gripped her when Deke made no comment for several minutes. A stony silence always preceded the beatings she received from him.

New Moon was beginning to tremble when he said in deadly tones, "I don't see no whiskey bottle." She started to edge away from him, but he caught her by the hair and dragged her back beside him. "Well," he grated, "where's the bottle?"

New Moon's words were barely audible as she said, "Old Bridger said nothing but food on the bill."

Cotter came up on his knees, hovering over her, his face distorted with rage. "Bitch, why didn't you offer to go in the back room with him, spread your legs for him? He'd have let you have the whiskey then."

New Moon shook her head. "Bridger is not like that. He would have laughed at me."

"Well, I'm not laughin', am I?" When New Moon only looked at him helplessly, he slapped her across the face with the back of his hand. She toppled over onto her back, her nose broken and bleeding. While she lay there dreading what would come next, Cotter stood up, jerked on his jacket and stamped out of the tepee.

With pain-filled eyes and tears running down her cheeks to mingle with the blood trickling from her swollen nose, New Moon crawled across the mat-covered floor to the opening of the tepee. She lifted the corner of the heavy buffalo-hide flap and peered out. Her gaze fastened on Deke, who was slipping along behind the hut that held the pelts the village men had trapped all winter. Soon they would be taken to the woman, Lucianne, their benefactor. Thanks to her, this had been the first time in New Moon's memory that her people hadn't gone hungry in the winter.

The battered woman knew what Deke had in mind. He would break into the hut and take enough skins to buy him the whiskey he was determined to have. If he was caught stealing from the tribe, he would die a painful death. The number-one law of the tribe was never to steal food from each other, and the cache of furs meant food for the village.

As New Moon watched, Deke reappeared, looking cautiously around, the front of his jacket bulging with pelts. When he disappeared in a stand of pine a few yards away, she crawled back to the fire, muttering, "You got away with it this time, but you won't if you try it again. From now on, night and day a watch will be put on the hut."

# *Chapter Twenty-four*

Icicles two feet long hung from the cabin's eaves where the snow was melting off the roof. As Blaze hurried from the barn where she had given Beauty a helping of oats, she looked up at the clear blue sky and thought that maybe spring was finally arriving, that there would be no more snowfall.

It was reported that all the passes were open now and that the coaches were coming through regularly again. All she had to do to leave Fort Bridger was to pack her clothes and catch one of the departing coaches. The thought that she would never again see Hunter or Becky brought moisture to her eyes.

Lately Becky seemed to sense that something was going to happen, something that would interrupt her newfound peace and happiness. She would hardly let her mama out of her sight, and at night, even in her sleep she clung to Blaze.

"It is going to take all the courage I possess to leave her." Blaze sighed sadly. "But she will have her father, who loves her dearly. He will see to it that she will soon forget me."

Hunter will be glad to see the last of me, she thought unhappily. Ever since the snow began to melt she had caught him looking at her from beneath hooded eyes. What was he thinking then? she wondered. That spring would never come so that he could be rid of her and install Nancy in her place?

Well, that time was near at hand and he would get his wish. He would have Nancy to warm his bed, without having to promise love he could no longer give. Next week she was going to buy a ticket that would start her on the trip to California.

When Blaze opened the cabin door and stepped inside she found Hunter sitting at the table as though waiting for her. When she had taken off her outerwear and hung it up, he said, "I would like to talk to you, Blaze."

Blaze was startled for a moment. Couldn't he wait until all the snow was gone before sending her off? Now that she wouldn't sleep with him anymore, it seemed he was eager to be rid of her. She sat down across from him and before he could speak she said, "I know what you're going to say, so I'll answer your question before you ask it. I intend to remove my presence from here next week."

"I wasn't going to ask you when you plan on leaving," Hunter protested, a sound of alarm in his voice. "Though I guessed that you were planning to go. I want to make a deal with you."

"What kind of deal?" Blaze looked at him suspiciously.

Hunter was silent a moment as though searching for the right words. Then slowly he began. "I've been thinking that since I'll have to pay some woman to take care of Becky, whether here or in the woman's home, why not give you a wage to care for her? She loves you."

*But you don't,* Blaze thought after she recovered from her surprise, *and therein lies the problem.* Loving him the way she did, it would be unbearable to live in the same house with him, year after year, her youth slipping away.

"I'm sorry," she said finally, "but it wouldn't work. I'll be leaving next week as planned." Once he knew of the baby, he would never let her go.

Becky came running into the kitchen then and crawled up on her lap. As Blaze burried her face in the child's soft curls, she missed the despair that darkened Hunter's eyes.

"Where will you go?" Hunter asked after several seconds had passed.

"To Cheyenne," Blaze lied unhesitatingly.

"I'll give you enough money to last you until you get settled and find a job."

"Thank you."

"What kind of job will you look for?"

"Taking care of children, I suppose, or maybe

working as a housekeeper for some wealthy family." Blaze hesitated a moment and said, "Or maybe I'll meet some man and fall in love with him. Maybe even marry him, once you've divorced me."

Hunter didn't make a comment, but had Blaze looked at him, she would have read on his face that he had no intention of ever giving her a divorce.

Lucianne answered the knock at her back door and smiled at Long Hair and the young brave who stood looking at her. A travois was attached to the younger man's shoulders. It was piled high with prime furs.

"My nephew White Rabbit and I have brought you our winter catch," Long Hair said. "Do you think they are enough to cover what we have out on your bill this winter?"

"They are more than enough, old friend." Lucianne ran her eyes over the furs, knowing that she could get double what Bridger was used to paying the Indians. "Take them on to the fort and I'll be there to dicker with Scrooge as soon as I get dressed."

Long Hair and White Rabbit grinned when Lucianne said *Scrooge*. They had never heard the word before, but from the tone Lucianne used in saying it, they felt sure it wasn't complimentary to old Bridger.

The fort owner was eyeing the furs avidly when Lucianne entered the store, her expression saying that she was ready to do battle. Over the winter she had talked to the trappers who came to visit her girls and she knew the worth of each different fur.

"Well, Jim, let's get down to business," she said, marching up to the counter. "Get out your paper and pencil and we'll go over each pelt, decide its worth."

"That's not how I do it with the Indians," Bridger protested. "I give them so much for a load."

"I know that." Lucianne curled her lips down. "But these are my furs and you will give me a decent price for them or I will have them shipped to Cheyenne."

It was obvious from Bridger's face that he wasn't at all happy with the way things were going. Nevertheless, he knew there was nothing he could do about it if he wanted the fine pieces of fur. So, giving Lucianne a sour look he pulled paper and pencil from beneath the counter and carried them with him as he walked over to the pile of pelts.

As Lucianne and Bridger haggled over the price of each fur, Long Hair and his nephew stood with stoic faces as if everything going on had nothing to do with them. But deep within the black eyes there was a glitter of amusement and high regard for the woman who was getting the better of old Bridger.

They waited patiently while Lucianne and the fort owner totaled up the long list of the furs they had brought in. They shot hopeful looks at each other. Would there be any money for them when their bill with Lucianne was settled? They would be happy with just a little; enough to buy the children some of the candy sticks and rock candy displayed in a glass case, some beads for the women and ammunition for their rifles. That last was sorely needed for the fresh meat they must hunt and kill during the months until trapping season arrived again.

When finally Lucianne turned to them, the business between her and Bridger finished, Long Hair and his nephew couldn't control the wide smiles that lit up their faces. The number of greenbacks she handed Long Hair was more than he had seen in his lifetime. While she looked on, a wide smile of her own crinkling the corners of her eyes, the old Indian began to move about the store, looking thoughtfully at items he had never dreamed of being able to buy.

His purchases began to grow on the counter. Bolts of brightly colored calico were piled next to boxes of rifle cartridges, two new rifles, shiny beads and buttons, needles, spools of thread and scissors, pots and pans, bags of candy and a wide-bladed hunting knife.

When it looked as if Long Hair had finally finished, he walked over to a rack that held women's headwear, everything from slatted bonnets to ones decorated with cloth flowers and tall feathers. He reached up and took down a bonnet that Bridger had tried to sell for two years.

As Lucianne wondered which of the Indian women would be the recipient of the excessively ornate, ugly creation, Long Hair walked over to her and solemnly set it on top of her curls. She sneezed as an accumulation of two years' dust flew from the feather that tickled her nose. She peered through the offending plume, not knowing whether to laugh or cry. A glance at Bridger's tickled grin made her do neither. She settled the bonnet more securely on her head and said gravely, "Thank you, Long Hair. It is beautiful."

The old Indian nodded his head, then turned to Bridger and asked proudly, "How much do I owe you, Jim?"

It was Lucianne's turn now to send the annoyed Bridger a devilish grin. It was the first time an Indian had called him by his first name. *Get used to it, mister,* she thought. *From now on the Indians are going to live as well as most of the white men around here. Probably better than the homesteaders. If there are any of them still around,* she added to herself. Already three families had loaded up their wagons and pulled out, headed for California. The Hank family had left yesterday, and she could hardly wait to tell Blaze that her old enemy Caroline was gone. With that gossipmonger gone, maybe Lucianne could convince her young friend to stay on in the community.

Maybe I'll ride out to the Ward ranch today, she thought, then looked up at the sky as she left the fort. She frowned at the dark clouds gathering in the north and decided that she would go tomorrow. The darkened sky indicated that they might get a late squall. Although it would be of short duration, it could be fierce, and a person could become lost in it and freeze to death.

Lucianne entered her back door to avoid her girls. She must get this horrible hat off her head and hidden before they saw it. Otherwise, there would be no end to the teasing she would receive from them.

But as she entered the kitchen, she found all four of her girls sitting at the table drinking coffee. They stared at her pop-eyed a minute and then burst into roaring laughter.

Lucianne glared at them a second, then stamped out of the room, their hilarity following her. When she entered her room she took off Long Hair's gift and carefully placed it in a hatbox. She would never wear it, but she would always prize it over all her other ones. It had been given to her with respect.

# *Chapter Twenty-five*

The sun was lifting on the eastern horizon when Blaze came slowly awake. She lay on her side, staring at the wall opposite her. Today she was riding to the fort to purchase her ticket; it was the first step toward changing her life.

What lay in the future for her? she wondered. She hoped profoundly it would be better than her past. She had known little happiness and contentment in her nineteen years. Before Hunter there had always been the uneasiness of hiding from the law, the fear that her father might be shot and killed by some posse that was chasing the Mullen gang.

Then there was the short time spent with Hunter, taking his insults, falling in love with him, knowing that he would never return her love.

There had been no happiness there.

Would she ever meet a man who would love her for herself, look beyond the beauty that had been the bane of her life, not just lust for her as Hunter did?

And if she should meet such a man, would she love him in return? Could she ever drive Hunter out of her mind? She was afraid she couldn't. There would be the child they had created together to always remind her of him.

Blaze heard Hunter moving around in the kitchen and waited until she smelled brewing coffee before sliding out of the warm bed. She hurried then to pull on her robe and slide on her house slippers. She wanted to catch him before he left the cabin, to tell him that she was going to the fort today and that he would have to stay home with Becky.

Hunter was sitting at the table, waiting for the steaming cup of coffee to cool enough to drink. He thought how lovely and desirable she looked with her curls all tumbled and her cheeks sleep-flushed. He answered her polite good morning. As she walked to the stove he got a side view of her, and thought that she was gaining weight. Not enough excerise during the winter months, he imagined.

When Blaze joined him at the table, she reached for the sugar bowl and said, "I'd like to ride to the fort today. Can you stay home with Becky for a couple of hours?"

Hunter looked away from Blaze to hide his

alarm. Not fifteen minutes ago he had sent his men out, three to check the cattle and one to ride fence, to look for spots where the weight of the drifting snow might have broken it over the winter. He didn't want Blaze riding alone, for he couldn't help thinking that danger still lurked somewhere on the range. That there had been no more evidence of a prowler snooping around didn't mean that he wasn't still out there somewhere biding his time.

He thought hurriedly, then said, "I have to ride into the fort myself to buy some new rope, but we could leave Becky with Bucky and ride in together."

"Do you think he'd mind?"

"Naw, he loves having her around. She gives him someone to tell his long-winded tales to." Hunter grinned. "It doesn't matter that Becky is talking her child-talk at the same time."

Blaze smiled too. She was aware of that. She had seen it happen many times. "I wanted her to get some fresh air today. Do you think he would mind taking her out for a little while?"

Hunter shook his head and grinned. "That one can talk outside as well as inside." He stood up. "I'll go tell him while you get Becky up and dressed. Bucky will give her breakfast."

Forty-five minutes later Becky was happily eating flapjacks in the cookhouse, and Hunter had his stallion and Blaze's mare waiting at the porch. It hadn't snowed last night, as some had feared it would, and according to the bright sun overhead it promised to be a fair day.

The wind was sharp, however, and Blaze kept her face buried in the fur collar of her jacket. She was glad that she had remembered to tell Bucky to dress Becky warmly before taking her out.

Neither spoke as they rode along. Both had the same thing on their minds: three more days and Blaze was leaving. While she wondered what life had in store for her, Hunter wondered how he could exist without her in his life.

When they arrived at the fort, the Potters and another family, their wagons piled with their belongings, were just pulling out. "You folks leaving us?" Hunter asked as he swung out of the saddle.

"We sure are," Mr. Potter answered. "You couldn't pay me to live in this frozen wasteland another winter. We're off to California where the sun shines every day."

Hunter could have told him that only happened in the desert and that the rest of the state had a lot of gloom and cold rain in the winter. He didn't warn them of this, though. He was too glad to see them go and wished that all the other homesteaders would do the same. They were a blight on the land with their fences and rude little shacks.

As Hunter followed Blaze into the store, they were greeted by Lucianne. "I was just getting ready to ride out to your place," she said, a small sack clutched in her hand. "I just ran in here to get some candy sticks for Becky."

"It will only take me a minute to take care of my

business, and then you can ride to the ranch with me," Blaze offered.

"Thank you, honey, but you know how I hate to ride. You come to my house. Pearl baked a chocolate cake yesterday. We'll have a slice with a cup of coffee."

"Sounds real good." Blaze smiled and, linking arms, they walked toward the Pleasure House.

Hunter watched them go, a bleak look in his eyes. Blaze would confide her plans to the older woman and they would discuss her leaving over their coffee. When they entered the madam's back door, he entered the store. His nose twitched at the rancid odor of the untreated furs brought in by the trappers and mountain men. Bridger's customers would have to put up with that smell until the raw pelts were baled and shipped off in the wagon that would be sent for them out of Cheyenne. In the meantime Bridger would have few women customers. Male relatives would be doing the shopping.

As he walked toward the tavern entrance, the busy Bridger looked at him long enough to say, "You see them clodhoppers leavin', Hunter? Just like rats desertin' a sinkin' ship, they've been pullin' out ever since the weather broke.

"Yeah, I saw them and I hope that they all leave," Hunter said as he passed on into the tavern room.

The big room couldn't hold another half dozen people, Hunter thought to himself as he elbowed his way through drunken trappers, rough mountain men and Lucianne's girls, there to help the men spend their money.

Greetings were called out to Hunter as the bartender poured him a glass of whiskey. As he sipped the raw liquor he thought to himself that there was no other brand of men who could celebrate an event like a bunch of trappers. Their carousing would last for days. Fights would break out from old grudges, over the whores or simply because one man stepped on another's toe. He couldn't believe that one time he had been a part of such carrying on.

He still liked his rowdy friends, enjoyed their company when they weren't drunk, but somewhere along the way he had lost the wildness that had once been a big part of him. His only desire now was to settle with Blaze and his daughter, tend to his ranch, build up his herd.

Hunter stared gloomily into his glass. He might as well forget about living with Blaze for the rest of his life. In order to get over his loss of her he would throw himself into making a success of his ranch. Finishing his drink he left the tavern unnoticed and, passing through the store, walked out onto the porch to wait for Blaze.

"Pearl looks preoccupied today," Blaze said when Lucianne's new housekeeper had served them the cake and coffee and then left the kitchen.

"Yes, she's been that way for the past two weeks; all nervous and jumping at the slightest noise. I think something is going on and I can't figure it out."

"In what way?"

"Well, she always takes a walk after the supper dishes are done, to get some fresh air, she claims. Last evening I asked her if she would put some kerosene in the lamps before she left and she became so upset she actually started wringing her hands, so I told her they could wait until she got back. She dashed out the door like the Devil was on her tail. I became suspicious at her strange behavior and peeked through the curtains to watch just where her walks took her. When she came to that big pine between here and the fort she suddenly ducked beneath it. She hadn't stayed there more than ten minutes when I saw her coming back."

"Do you suppose she has found herself a beau?"

"I don't think so. Why would she hide that?"

Blaze shrugged. "It was just a guess."

"Well, all I know is that I don't like her recent strange behavior. I have a feeling nothing good is going to come from it."

"Like what?" Blaze asked.

"I don't know. I just have this feeling. It's like an omen." Lucianne rubbed the gooseflesh on her arms.

"Now don't go jumping the gun, Lucianne. I can't believe that Pearl would be involved in anything that would hurt you. She likes and respects you too much."

"You're probably right," the madam agreed,

then said, "Let's talk about you. Are you still determined to go off to California?"

"Yes, that's why I came to the fort today, to get my ticket for boarding the coach."

"Does Hunter know you're leaving?"

"He knows."

"What does he say about it?"

"Nothing. He did ask me if I would stay on if he paid me a wage. I turned his offer down and nothing more has been said about it."

"I wish you would at least move in with me until the baby comes. I hate to think of you delivering it with no one to hold your hand in labor."

"Don't worry about me, Lucianne. I've never had a mother to help me."

"I know that, honey, but that doesn't make it right. Make sure you send me your address as soon as you find a place to live. I'll try my best to be with you when your time comes."

"I'd like that, Lucianne. I am a little nervous about delivering the baby, but I'd understand if you couldn't make it."

When Lucianne started to pour her another cup of coffee, Blaze put her hand over her cup. "The way it's clouding up out there, I'd better get my ticket and hurry home before it starts raining."

Her longtime friend helped Blaze into her jacket, and then they fell into each other's arms, tears in their eyes. When they pulled apart Blaze left with no further words.

As she hurried along toward the fort, Blaze saw Hunter standing outside as though he was waiting for her. He'll have to wait a little longer while I get my ticket, she thought.

She had just stepped up beside Hunter when a wild cry drew their attention to a rider coming toward them, laying his quirt on his horse.

"That looks like Bucky's horse," Hunter exclaimed, stepping to the ground.

Blaze's heart began to pound, for as the rider raced closer she saw that it was indeed the old cook. Why had he left Becky alone at the ranch?

She stepped down to stand beside Hunter when Bucky pulled in the heaving horse.

"What's wrong, Bucky?" Hunter demanded, his voice hoarse with the fear that gripped him. "What's happened to Becky?"

"She's gone, Hunter. She just disappeared in a minute's time."

"What do you mean, she disappeared?" Blaze asked, white faced.

"An hour or so ago I bundled her up and took her outside just like you said. We was playin' Cowboys and Indians when I remembered the pot of beans cookin' on the stove. I went into the shack to see if they still had enough water in them. They did and I came right back outside, but the little one was gone.

"I swear to you, Hunter, I wasn't gone half a minute."

Hunter and Blaze were mounted and racing away before the old cook finished talking. His shoulders sagging, Bucky dismounted and stepped into the store. He spoke to Bridger about

361

Becky's disappearance, and fifteen minutes later ten men were mounted and racing toward the Ward ranch. When they pulled up in front of the cabin, the dark clouds that had hung overhead for the past two hours opened up. Rain, in a torrent, came down in sheets.

A few hundred yards away, Hunter swore savagely. The hoofprints he had picked up disappeared in seconds in the onslaught of rain. He bowed his head and unashamedly cried hopeless tears. Where was his little girl? Was she frightened and crying?

Finally Hunter managed to push away his panic and to think logically. Why would anyone want to steal his daughter? Was there a man out there somewhere who hated him so much that he would take his bile out on an innocent child? What kind of monster was he?

When Hunter rode back into the barnyard and he saw his friends who had come to help search for his baby, he hadn't come up with one name.

"What with the rain, I'm afraid we're not going to be any help to you, Hunter," his friend Travis Carter said, water dripping off his hat brim and shoulders. "We figured we could help you hunt down the kidnapper, but his tracks are gone now."

"I know," Hunter answered tiredly, "but thanks for coming."

"We'll be back tomorrow to help you look more if you want us to."

"It would be no use, Travis." Hunter swung out of the saddle. His shoulders bowed dejectedly, he led the stallion into the barn, and his friends silently turned their horses around and rode off in the direction of the fort.

After Hunter rubbed down the stallon with a gunnysack and threw a horse blanket over him, he left the barn, dreading to enter the cabin. There would be no little girl running to him, no laughing, childish voice calling out to him.

When Hunter opened the kitchen door it was as he had expected it to be, silent and somber. Blaze sat at the kitchen table, her face pale as she stared at her clasped hands on the tabletop. She lifted anguished eyes to him and grated out, "Damn this rain to hell."

Hunter made no response to her damnation of the weather, only laid a comforting hand on her shoulder as he walked to the stove. When he lifted the lid off the big cookstove, he was thankful there were still a few live coals glowing inside it. He fed them some wood shavings from the wood box, then added small pieces of wood. Putting the lid back on he pulled the half-filled coffeepot forward to heat up.

"Why don't you go get out of those wet clothes? When you come back the coffee will be hot."

Blaze nodded and, like a sleepwalker, she rose and left the kitchen.

Hunter watched her go, knowing that she was hurting badly. He wished that he could put his arms around her, comfort her. I want her to comfort me as well, he thought on his way to his room to change into dry clothes himself.

When Blaze returned to the kitchen, dressed in her gown and robe and toweling her rain-soaked hair, Hunter was there ahead of her. He had changed into dry trousers and a flannel shirt and heavy socks.

"I've reheated the chili from last night," he said, ladling some into a bowl. "Although we're not hungry," he said, placing the chili in front of Blaze, "we've got to eat, keep up our strength so that we can continue to search for Becky."

When Hunter sat down across from her, Blaze obediently picked up her spoon and dipped it into her bowl.

"Where could she be, Hunter?" Blaze asked when she couldn't force any more food into her mouth. "Who could have taken her? Could it have been a bear?" Her face etched with suffering, she had a hard time voicing that terrible thought.

Hunter shook his head. "No animal made away with her, Blaze. Becky would have screamed and Bucky would have heard her. It was a man. He slipped up behind her and clapped his hand over her mouth, making it impossible for her to cry out."

"I don't suppose you have any idea who the man is?"

"I have no idea. I've wracked my brain and can't come up with anyone. As soon as I've finished eating I'm going to ride over to the Indian village and talk to Black Crow, ask him and his braves if they've seen any strangers around, or anything that looks suspicious."

The rain continued to pound down outside as they talked, and after Hunter lit the lamp on the table he said, "I'm going over there now. Why don't you lie down for a while? This has been a terrible shock for you."

"I couldn't sleep," Blaze answered wearily. "I'll wait until you get back. Maybe you'll have some news."

Blaze sat on in the gloom that held the cabin in its grip, agonizing thoughts going through her mind. Where was Becky? Was she crying for her mama? Was she cold? Was she being mistreated?

# Chapter Twenty-six

"Shut that damned kid's mouth up. I'm tired of listenin' to her blubberin' and carryin' on," Cotter order New Moon as he crawled off her. "Someone is gonna hear her and come to investigate the racket she's makin'."

When New Moon rose out of the pile of furs and walked out of his reach she said sullenly, "I don't know why you brought her here in the first place."

"You don't have to know—" Cotter sat up and dragged on his trousers—"but I'll tell you. The kid is number one in my three-step plan. Number two, she will bring Ward's wife here when I leave a note telling her to bring me some ransom money in exchange for the young'un. Number three, Ward will track his wife here and I will make sure he dies a slow, painful death."

New Moon went and squatted down in front of the rain-soaked Becky and spoke to her in her native tongue. The little one stopped crying immediately as she cringed away from the Indian woman, a terrified look in her eyes.

"What did you say to her?" Cotter asked, relieved that the crying had ceased.

"I told her that I would kill her mama if she didn't shut up."

"Maybe you ought to get her out of them wet clothes. She won't be any good to me if she dies from pneumonia. But first, I don't suppose you have any paper or a pencil around here?"

Surprisingly to Cotter, New Moon nodded that she did. In the five years she had lived in the Ward home she had pilfered those items, along with other small objects she thought wouldn't be readily missed. She dug into a woven reed basket and brought out a pad of paper and a pencil. Cotter took them from her and, sitting down in front of the fire pit, he laboriously began to write his ransom note.

Half an hour later he folded the sheet of paper, a pleased smile on his face. It wouldn't be long now before he could finish the job he had come here for. When Hunter Ward lay dying at his feet from a gut shot he would go, leaving behind his whining wife and the Indian bitch who no longer interested him.

Stretching out on the bed of furs, he looked at New Moon and ordered, "Get me some supper. I have to go somewhere when it gets dark."

It was several hours later when Hunter returned to the cabin. His trip to the Indian village had proved futile, but he had spent some time searching the woods anyway.

When the door opened Blaze gave a frightened gasp, then calmed down when she saw it was her husband. His face was almost as white as the piece of paper he held in his hand. "What is that?" she asked as he groped for a chair and sat down.

"A ransom note, I think," Hunter answered in a shaken voice. "I just found it on the porch." He held the scrap of paper up to the lamp and began to read out loud. "Ward, I have your daughter. For five hundred dollars you can have her back. Send your wife with the money to where the trail forks between the Indian village and the post. She is to come at nine o'clock tomorrow morning. If you or anyone else follows her, your kid is dead."

As Hunter crumpled the note in his hand, Blaze asked, "Do you have that kind of money?"

"Just barely. I still have most of the money I made from the cattle drive." He sat down at the table. "I won't let you go alone, you know."

"But, Hunter, you'll be chancing Becky's life if you come with me."

"He won't know I'm around until it's time for me to kill him," Hunter said grimly. "I'll work out a plan before tomorrow morning."

He blew out the light and helped Blaze to her feet. They needed each other tonight, not in a physical sense, but to draw comfort from each other's presence. Blaze made no objection as he led her to his room. Stretched out in bed, they clung to each other as they prepared to wait the long hours till morning.

Blaze heard the clock strike seven the next morning and came awake. Yesterday's events came to mind immediately. How had Becky fared through the night? Was she hungry? Was she terribly frightened? Of course she was. She was only a little girl.

As she dressed in warm clothing she smelled coffee and heard Hunter moving around in the kitchen. When had he left the bed? Had he slept at all?

When she walked into the kitchen and looked at him, it was obvious from his red-rimmed eyes that he hadn't slept a great deal.

They smiled a wan good morning to each other as Blaze walked to the sink and splashed water on her face. "Have you thought of a plan?" she asked after Hunter had placed ham and eggs on the table.

"Yes," he answered as they both sat down to the meal. "As soon as I finish eating I'm going to ride to that fork in the trail he wrote about. I know where it is. There's a big pine there and I intend to climb it, hide myself in its branches. I'll be able to see when he meets you."

"Will you shoot him then?"

"I thought about it, but we need him alive until he leads us to Becky. I'll hide in the tree until it's safe to follow the two of you."

"Do be careful," Blaze said a short time later as Hunter pulled on his jacket.

"Don't worry about me. Make sure you're careful," Hunter said, wishing that he could kiss her. But he was afraid to do it.

Forty-five minutes later Blaze left the cabin with a bag full of green backs and walked to the barn to saddle Beauty.

Morning mists still hung in the low spots as Blaze rode along, hunched into her jacket. The rain had finally ceased, but it had left a bone-chilling dampness in its wake.

She was filled with anticipation and apprehension. She looked forward to holding Becky in her arms again, but she knew it wasn't going to be that simple. She, like Hunter, hadn't voiced the thought that the man might take the money she was carrying, and then kill her and Becky.

Blaze was nearing the forked trail when Beauty lifted her head and snorted uneasily. *He's nearby*, Blaze thought with a shudder. *He's probably watching me right now.*

Her heart beating so loudly it hammered in her ears, she came to the forking of the trail. No one was waiting for her. She wanted to look for Hunter up in the tall pine that stood there. She knew she mustn't. The man could be watching her.

Blaze grew stiff and cold as the minutes passed by, and Beauty was restless, stamping her hind hooves impatiently at being held in. When Blaze judged she had been waiting around fifteen minutes, Beauty began shaking her head and side-stepping. Some person or animal was nearby, Blaze thought, leaning forward to pat the arched neck and speak calming words to the mare. When she straightened up, a startled gasp escaped her. A man stood a few feet away.

"You!" she croaked, recognizing the stranger she had met once before.

"Yes, me. I bet you never thought to see me again."

"I never thought about it one way or the other." Blaze frowned down at him. "Who are you, and did you write that ransom note?"

The man watched her face closely as he said, "I wrote the note, and my name is Cotter Mullen."

A shiver of cold shock raced up Blaze's spine. No wonder the man had reminded her of someone that one time she had met him out on the range.

"Are you Garf's brother?" Blaze asked, trying to keep the alarm out of her voice.

"That's right." Cotter's eyes mocked her. "Did you bring the money?"

"I did, but I'm not going to give it to you until I see the child and am satisfied she is all right."

"I could take it away from you, you know," Cotter growled.

Blaze gazed down into the man's evil-looking eyes, saw the threat in them and prayed that Hunter was up in the tree watching. She was trying hard not to look up among the branches when Cotter said gruffly, "I've not beaten the brat, if that's what you're afraid of. Follow me and you can see for yourself."

Blaze's first thought as Cotter took the trail leading to the Indian village was that Black Crow was in on the abduction of Becky. She remembered then that Hunter had been to the village the night before and decided it was unlikely that Black Crow was involved in the kidnapping.

She felt more sure of it when Cotter skirted the village and came in behind a tepee that sat apart from the others. It was plain he didn't want the Indians to know that he was bringing her here.

But what was he doing in an Indian village? When she had dismounted and Cotter pulled back the flap of the tepee and stepped aside for her to enter, his familiarity with the Indian abode suggested to her that he lived there.

It was so dark in the hide structure that at first all Blaze could see were the flames in the fire pit. Then she made out a small body rushing toward her, crying out, "Mama, Mama!"

She caught Becky in her arms and hugged her fiercely. She gently removed the clinging arms from around her neck then and, looking down at the small, tear-streaked face, asked softly, "Are you all right, honey? Did the bad man hit you?"

Becky shook her head. "But New Moon scare me. She say if I not stop crying she go to cabin and kill you."

Blaze lifted her head to look for the Indian woman. When she saw her standing off to one side, she hardly recognized the woman. New Moon had lost so much weight her fringed tunic hung on her body. Her cheeks were sunken and her eyes had been blackened recently. She looked half dead. When and how had the Indian hooked up with Cotter Mullen? Blaze wondered.

She almost felt sorry for the woman until she remembered how cruel she had been to the little girl who still clung to her.

"Are you satisfied that the brat is all right?" Cotter stood looking down at her and the child.

"You haven't beaten her, but New Moon has scared her half to death."

"She'll get over that, so you can give me the money now."

Blaze took the bag from her waist, where she had tied it, and handed it to him, thinking that soon she and Becky would leave this place and be back with Hunter, the nightmare forgotten.

Cotter grabbed the money and then said to New Moon, "Get the kid's coat on."

"I'll do it," Blaze said as Becky looked at the Indian woman with fearful eyes. She picked up the small garment that had been laid beside the fire pit to dry, and helped Becky into it. When she had done up the buttons and tied the scarf around her head, she stood up and took Becky's hand.

"Come on, honey," she said, "let's go home." She started walking toward the tepee's door, but Cotter stepped in front of her.

"You're not going anywhere, missy," he said with a growl.

"Why not? You have the money you asked for. Aren't you going to keep your bargain?"

"Sure I am. I'm gonna take Ward's daughter

partway home right now. But I didn't write anything about letting you go."

"What do you mean, you'll take her partway home? She's too young to find the rest of the way home," Blaze protested, Becky's safety uppermost in her mind.

"I know that," Cotter snapped impatiently. "I'm gonna take her within a mile of the cabin, then fire off a couple shots. That will bring Ward comin' to investigate."

"Why are you keeping me? Hunter has no more money to ransom me."

Cotter looked at her with a leering smile. "I don't want any money for you, pretty little filly." Grinning wolfishly, he let his gaze drift over Blaze's slender body. "I just want you . . . in my bed. And when Ward finally figures out where you are, I'll be waiting for him. I'll make him watch while you pleasure me, and then I'll shoot him in the gut."

"Oh, my God!" Blaze gasped.

Grinning evilly, Cotter handed his gun to New Moon and said, "If she tries to leave, shoot her."

He grabbed Becky's hand and pulled her away from Blaze, hurrying toward the door. She ran after them, crying out, "Don't be afraid, Becky; he's taking you to Papa."

As the flap closed behind them she could hear Becky crying, "Mama come too! Mama come too!"

Bucky stepped out of the cookhouse and closed the door behind him. As he stood scratching himself dejectedly, thinking he would never forgive himself if Becky wasn't found, there came on the still morning air the sound of two shots. It was a range signal that someone was in trouble. He hurried over to the cabin, but was surprised to find it empty. Were Blaze and Hunter the ones who had fired the shots?

He returned to the cookhouse, grabbed his jacket, clapped a hat on his head, then hurried to the barn at a half run. Within minutes he had saddled a horse and was racing it in the direction from which the gunshots had come.

His heart gave a jolt of relief when he came upon Becky's small figure sitting on a tree stump. She was a woeful-looking little thing when he climbed out of the saddle and rushed to her. Her eyes were red and swollen from crying, and her teeth, whether from fright or cold, were chattering. He grabbed her little body up close to his bony chest and, mopping her face with a none too clean kerchief, murmured soothing words to her. "You're all right now, honey. You're safe with Bucky."

He rocked her back and forth until she stopped sobbing, then asked softly, "Who brought you here, honey?"

"The bad man. He yell at Becky all the time."

"Do you know where your mama and papa are?"

The curly head nodded. "I know where Mama is. The bad man and New Moon has her in a funny-looking house."

A tepee, Bucky thought. Blaze must be in Black Crow's village. But where was Hunter? Had the unknown man shot and killed him? He must get back to the ranch as soon as possible and alert the men.

"Let's get you to the cabin and warm you up, honey," Bucky said as he stood up and lifted Becky onto the saddle. "I'll bet you're hungry too," he added, climbing up behind her.

"Becky very hungry."

Hunter had been watching from his perch in the tree when Blaze arrived at the rendezvous point. She had looked so cold and alone, he'd wanted to call to her, to let her know that she wasn't alone, but he'd been afraid the man might be nearby, watching her.

His body had jerked erect when a man, leading a horse, stepped from behind a clump of pines. When he'd heard the name Cotter Mullen, he'd realized why the man had looked familiar the couple of times he had seen him: he was Garf Mullen's brother, come to take revenge for his death. He heard Cotter ask Blaze if she had brought the money, and he'd nodded his head in silent approval when he heard Blaze say she wouldn't give it to him until she saw whether the child was all right.

When they'd disappeared out of sight, Hunter climbed down from the tree and stretched his stiff muscles. For a moment he wished it had been possible to hide a horse nearby, for it would take time—time Blaze and Becky might not have—to walk to the Indian village, if that was where Cotter was holed up.

He thought that he had covered a mile when he heard hooves coming up the trail. He jumped behind a pine whose branches swept the ground, just as a big horse came around a bend in the trail. Cotter held the reins and sitting in front of him was little Becky. Hunter swore under his breath as he saw big tears rolling down her fat little cheeks. His first impulse was to step from behind the tree and shoot the man in the heart.

But what if he should miss and hit Becky?

Hunter had told himself that Cotter would probably take her close enough to the ranch buildings where someone would find her. He must think of Blaze also. This might be his only chance to get her; he could come back later to deal with Cotter.

Now, half an hour later, he was nearing the Indian village. The tracks he followed, however, didn't lead directly to it. They veered off, skirting the main group of dwellings. He walked on until the prints took him to a tepee that sat several hundred yards from the others. No wonder Black Crow hadn't known of Becky's presence last night. He hoped that Blaze was alone, but thought that probably Cotter had left someone to watch her.

He was coming up close behind the buffalo-hide structure when he heard galloping hooves approaching. Cotter was returning, he thought bitterly as he threw himself into some tall brown weeds and listened intently.

"Well, your brat is probably home by now," Cotter said as he entered the tepee and sat down next to Blaze. "I left her about half a mile from your cabin and shot twice into the air. I hid in the trees until I saw an old man ride up and hurry to her."

*Bucky,* Blaze thought. *God bless him.*

She gaped in disbelief when Cotter suddenly pulled New Moon down onto the pallet of furs and said with a leer, "You watch closely now to see what pleases me. Later on you'll do the same thing."

Her face red with embarrassment, Blaze stood up and turned her back on what was going on. She clapped her hands over her ears so that she wouldn't have to listen either. All the time she wondered where Hunter was and prayed that he was close by.

Blaze imagined that Cotter had sated his lust when he ordered New Moon to get up and cook him something to eat.

She watched the Indian woman drag herself off the furs, kneel beside the fire pit and kindle a fire in it. When Cotter went outside she asked, "Why do you stay with that brute, New Moon? Why don't you tell your chief how cruelly he treats you?"

"I am ashamed for my people to know. Chief Black Crow warned me that Cotter was evil when I first brought him to the village." She sighed. "I didn't believe him."

New Moon looked at Blaze and to her surprise said, "The wall of the tepee behind you isn't pegged down. I never got around to doing it after my husband died. It is plenty loose for a person to crawl under it. Cotter plans to start for Mexico tomorrow morning, taking you with him. If you hope to live to be an old woman, you will slip out of here the first chance you get."

Blaze started to thank her, then closed her mouth when New Moon held a finger to her lips and whispered, "He is coming back."

For the sake of the baby growing inside her, Blaze forced herself to eat some of the flat cakes New Moon had made from cornmeal and baked over the hot coals of the fire pit. She looked at Cotter with loathing when he started talking about what would happen when they got to Mexico. "You'll grow to like me, pretty little girl, once your husband is out of the way. You'll see. It won't be long before you'll welcome me to your bed."

"Never in a million years," she snapped, and, leaving the fire, she walked over and sat down, her back to the unfastened wall.

Cotter's only response was a barking laugh as he stretched out on the furs and closed his eyes. Five minutes later, when he began snoring, Blaze reached behind her and started feeling for the bottom of the unpinned leather wall.

Everything was fastened tight to the ground. Had New Moon played a cruel trick on her? With tears of frustration gathering in her eyes, she was ready to give up when her fingers suddenly touched cold soil. Her heart jumped and beat rapidly. Escape was just minutes away.

Blaze's fingers went still when a warm hand

closed over hers. Hunter. He was out there. All she had to do was roll beneath the loose hide and she would be with him.

She was ready to lie down and roll herself to freedom when the snoring stopped. She looked fearfully at the pallet, then relaxed her tense muscles. Cotter still slept. He had only turned over on his side. She turned back to make her escape and found Hunter squirming his way into the cone-shaped room. Covering her mouth to smother her glad cry, she fell into his arms when he came up on his knees.

As they hugged each other fiercely neither saw that the sleeping man had awakened and was now standing only feet away, a gun trained on them.

Hunter sprang to his feet when his enemy said with a sneer, "Now ain't that a touching scene."

Hunter's first thought was to go for his own gun, throw himself to the side and shoot Cotter before he could pull the trigger. He saw then that the wily outlaw had the gun trained on Blaze. Cotter would shoot her before Hunter could get his own shot off.

"I knew you'd be out there somewhere." Cotter's eyes shot hatred at Hunter. "I knew you wouldn't let your purty little wife 'come alone. And that's good, because before I'm through with you, you're gonna wish that I shot you the minute you crawled in here."

His gun still trained on Blaze, he walked over to her and jerked her to her feet. Holding her against him, the gun now held to her head, he ordered,

"Back down on your knees, Ward. New Moon is gonna tie you up."

As Hunter sank helplessly to the ground, he said, "You have no cause to harm my wife. She's never done anything to you."

"I'm not gonna harm this purty little girl. I'm gonna give her pleasure while you watch."

To show his intentions, he laid a hand on Blaze's breast and painfully squeezed it. At her cry, Hunter tried to get to his feet, but New Moon had just finished tying his ankles together. Tied hand and foot, he could do nothing but watch through rage-filled eyes as Cotter ripped Blaze's shirt open and clawed one of her breasts free of her camisole. "Ain't that a beauty?" he said, fondling the quivering flesh. "How does it taste, Ward? You must have had it in your mouth a hundred times since you married her."

When Hunter's only response was stony silence, Cotter lowered his head, saying, "I guess I'll have to find out for myself." When his lips closed over the shrinking flesh, and Blaze began to pummel his face with her hard little fists, Hunter lost all control.

"You low-life bastard, I'll kill you, see if I don't. I'll hunt you to the end of the world and smash your ugly face to a pulp; then I'll gut-shoot you so that you die a slow, agonizing death."

Cotter flung Blaze aside, and came at Hunter, snarling, "I'm gonna make you eat them words, mister."

He was upon Hunter then, hammering at his

face with both fists again and again. Hunter felt his lips and eyes swelling, and his vision dimmed. He didn't know how much longer he could hang on.

Then, mercifully, Cotter stood up, growling, "I'll be back to give you some more later on. I think it's time I soften up your little wife some. I don't like her high-toned attitude. When I finish knocking her around a bit, she won't be so high-and-mighty when I crawl between her legs."

Hunter managed to come up on his elbows in time to see Cotter walk up to Blaze and hit her hard across the face with the back of his hand. She let out a cry and fell to the floor. He came down beside her and continued to slap her face. Hunter felt each hard blow that was delivered to her. He knew that soon she would pass out.

He began to struggle against the rawhide strips that bound him. When they slipped off his wrists, to his surprise he realized that New Moon had barely tied him up. He shot the watching Indian a look of thanks. She, in turn, came and stood in front of him, blocking Cotter's view of him, giving him the chance to untie his ankles, which were bound in the same loose way. As he got up on his haunches, New Moon stepped away.

On his feet then, but tottering, Hunter drew his gun and said in a voice that made Cotter grow cold, "Stand up, you bastard, and meet your maker."

Cotter sprang to his feet, wild eyed. "New Moon," he cried, "keep my gun on him. If he moves a muscle, shoot him."

It was a standoff, Hunter knew. If New Moon shot and killed him, only God knew what misery and shame would come to Blaze. He looked at the Indian woman and the gun trained on him. Death was in her black eyes. He started to look away; then his heartbeat quickened.

New Moon was slowly turning the gun on Cotter. He held his breath as he watched her finger tighten on the trigger. As he wondered if she would have the nerve to squeeze it, smoke and fire belched from the barrel. The bullet hit Cotter in the chest. The color slowly left the outlaw's face, and his eyes filled with knowledge and resignation. His lips loosened and his jaw dropped as he slowly sank to his knees, then fell facedown.

The bruised and battered New Moon walked over to Cotter's still body. She stood looking down at him a moment, then spat on his head. As Hunter watched her, his feet held fast to the ground, she looked up at him and said woodenly, "I've been wanting to kill him for a long time, but could never get up the nerve."

She sank slowly to the ground then, her own face a death mask, a rattle in her chest. Released from his frozen stance, Hunter rushed to kneel beside her. He raised her head to help her. Her limp body told him that she was beyond help. She had gone to meet the Great Father. He laid her head back down and straightened out her body. He was crossing her arms when he heard the soft thud of unshod hooves coming up to the tepee.

Indian ponies, he thought, jumping to his feet and opening the flap at the entrance. Black Crow and three young braves sat looking down at him.

"We heard shots," the chief said, stepping inside. He looked at the two bodies on the floor, then at Hunter. "The woman is from my village. Did you kill her?"

Hunter shook his head. "The many beatings she received from Cotter Mullen finally caught up with her. But before she died she put a bullet in him."

"That is good," Black Crow said soberly. "She revenged herself. We will bury her in the way of our people. She will rest beside her husband."

When two of the young braves climbed off their ponies and picked New Moon up and put her across the chief's horse, the old man asked. "Will you be burying the man, Hunter Ward?"

"Hell no. He's an animal. He doesn't deserve to be buried. Let the buzzards and wolves gnaw on him. I only want to get my wife home."

Black Crow nodded approval, then kicked a heel into his horse's side and the little animal moved out.

Hunter watched them leave, his blood pumping with new life. He couldn't wait to get home, to straighten out everything between him and Blaze. He hurried to where she lay and knelt down beside her. When he lifted the hair off her face he closed his eyes a moment, as if in pain. Her lip was cut, both eyes were rapidly turning black and both cheeks were bruised. But he felt her wrist and found the pulse strong and steady.

He stood up, and, finding a clay pottery bowl, he filled it with water from a leather jug hanging on a post. As he tenderly bathed Blaze's face, he felt her features to see if any of the delicate bones had been broken. It was a great relief when he found that her beautiful face had only suffered cuts and bruises. When she stirred and moaned he said softly, "Everything is all right now, Blaze. Cotter is dead. New Moon shot him."

Blaze's swollen eyes slitted open. She gazed up at him a moment, then started to cry. "Oh, Hunter," she sobbed. "It was awful having his hands and lips on me."

"I know, honey." He lifted her up so that she lay across his thighs. "It's over now. Try to put it behind you. Button up your shirt and let's go home."

*Home*, Blaze thought, *what a beautiful word*. When her trembling fingers fumbled with the buttons, Hunter moved her hands and finished the job for her. As he helped her into her jacket, she glanced at Cotter's sprawled body and shivered. She asked then, "Where is New Moon?"

Hunter didn't take the time to tell her the whole story. He only said, "Black Crow took her to be laid to rest."

Outside, he helped Blaze to mount Beauty, who still stood beneath a tree where she had been tied. Cotter's stallion was nearby, and after a moment Hunter climbed onto the animal's back, and, nudging him with a heel, he led off.

\* \* \*

Blaze awakened around twilight at the sound of Bucky greeting Lucianne in the cabin kitchen. "My old friend Long Hair just told me that Blaze and Hunter have found Becky," Lucianne was saying excitedly. "Where are they?"

"I've been watching Becky, Blaze is asleep and Hunter is out working with his men." After a pause he said, "I reckon I can go wake Blaze up."

"I'm up, Bucky," Blaze said from the doorway; then she stiffened. Nancy was with Lucianne. Didn't the woman have any shame? Couldn't she wait until tonight to see Hunter when he came to visit her?

Both visitors were staring at her face with horror-filled eyes. "Oh, Blaze, you poor little thing," Lucianne cried, standing up and rushing across the floor to clasp her in her arms. She tenderly ran a hand over Blaze's face. "How badly that brute has beaten you."

"But that's all he did to me, Lucianne, and I am very grateful."

"Amen to that," Lucianne said soberly as she led Blaze to a chair at the table. Sitting down next to her then, the madam said, "Nancy came with me. She wants to say good-bye to Hunter."

"Oh?" Blaze said stiffly, "Are you going somewhere, Nancy?"

"She's taking the stagecoach to Wichita, Kansas, tomorrow morning. Thanks to Hunter's help, she is going to get married when she arrives there."

"And just what does Hunter have to do with that?"

Lucianne gave Nancy a reproachful look and said, "I only found out this morning that this fellow Nancy has been pining for for the past year is a lawman Hunter knows well. They have worked together a few times hunting down outlaws. Hunter has been able to track down the fellow in Kansas and has gotten the two of them back together again."

Blaze looked at Nancy as if for confirmation. A smiling Nancy nodded her head. "Tom and I had a foolish argument and he rode away. But thanks to Hunter we're all made up and this time next week I will be a married lady."

A wave of happiness flooded through Blaze. Hunter had been true to his vows, after all. Some of her elation began to fade away then. He still hadn't said that he loved her.

Bucky pushed away from the table. "I gotta go stir up some dough for biscuits," he said. "The men will be coming in soon, and, as usual, they will be starving."

Lucianne gave Nancy a meaningful look and said, "Why don't you go with Bucky? If you're going to get married, maybe it's time you begin learning a little about cooking."

When the door closed behind the pair, Lucianne looked at Blaze and said hopefully, "I guess after what you and Hunter have gone through, you've got all the differences between you ironed out."

"No, not really. I know now that I was mistaken in thinking he and Nancy were sleeping together, but he still hasn't said a word about love."

"Blaze," Lucianne said impatiently, "when are you going to stop singing that old song? It's plain to everyone else that the man is crazy in love with you."

"Then why doesn't he say it? I know why, and so do you. He's still in love with his first wife." Blaze looked at Lucianne, her eyes daring her friend to deny it, but wishing that she would.

Lucianne heaved a long sigh. "It's not my place to tell you, but it looks like Hunter isn't going to, and I think that you should know about his first marriage.

"If Hunter ever really loved Jenny, his feelings for her died shortly after they were married." For the next ten minutes Lucianne told everything there was to tell about Hunter's failed marriage. When she finished, Blaze was filled with bittersweet emotion. Her heart bled for all that Hunter had endured, but she knew a happiness beyond belief for herself. For the first time she believed that her husband truly might love her.

When Lucianne said good-bye shortly after that, she left a smiling, happy woman behind.

Blaze paced around for a while, eager for Hunter to get home. Finally she couldn't stand waiting for him inside. The walls seemed to be closing in on her. She grabbed Becky's hand, saying gaily, "I think Bucky has some cookies for you."

"I love Bucky's cookies," Becky said in a singsong voice as she trotted along behind Blaze. They reached the bunkhouse and Blaze ushered the little girl inside, calling out, "I'll be back in a minute, Bucky."

As Blaze walked along in the brisk air, she lifted her bruised face to the western sky to let the last rays of the sun warm it. She came to the corral and took a sugar lump from her pocket when Beauty came running to her. As the little mare took the sugar from her palm, a wind came up and the baby kicked inside her. Rubbing her stomach, Blaze wondered when its father would get home. She couldn't wait to see him.

The sun was ready to set when Hunter topped the knoll a quarter mile from the ranch. When he saw the slender figure leaning against the corral, stroking the arched neck of a horse, he instantly recognized that it was Blaze and her pet. His heart gave a great lurch and he started Saint down the hill, his eyes never leaving his wife. He laughed when the wind blew her skirt around her legs, then whipped it against her body. His amusement was suddenly choked off when he saw the slight mound of her stomach outlined against her clothing.

His wife was with child . . . his child.

He gave a big whoop of exuberance and raced Saint toward Blaze. Blaze caught sight of Hunter then, and with a glad cry started running toward him. Hunter slid off the moving Saint and ran to meet her.

They met in a flurry of laughter and wind-whipped skirts. For a few moments all they did

389

was hold on to each other. Then Hunter found Blaze's lips and claimed them tenderly, demanding a response from her.

Blaze responded with her own hunger, and the kiss went on and on.

Finally, out of breath, they pulled apart, and looking into each other's eyes said in unison, "I love you."

On their way to the house, their arms wrapped around each other's waists, they paused at the bunkhouse long enough for Hunter to stick his head in the door and call to Bucky, "Do you mind if Becky spends the night with you?"

Bucky's only answer was a grin.

"Do you have to?" Hunter complained huskily when they walked into the cabin and Blaze said she was going to take a bath. "I'm desperate to make love to you."

The look Blaze gave him said that she was of the same mind. "I have to, Hunter. I have to get the smell of that man off my body."

"I'm sorry, honey, I didn't think of that. Take all the time you need. I'll fix your bath for you."

Blaze didn't linger in the tub of water too long, but she vigorously scrubbed herself while she was there. She was anxious to get into her husband's arms, to know again the bliss his body could give her. It had been far too long.

When she had toweled off, she blew out the lamp and entered the bedroom she would share with Hunter the rest of her life. In the moonlit room, she saw that Hunter was already in bed, propped up on an elbow, waiting for her. He was bare to the waist, and when she glanced at the end rail she saw his undergarments folded over it. Excitement stirred inside her. He was also bare from the waist down.

When she pulled a gown from the dresser, Hunter said huskily, "Don't put it on, Blaze. I would only have to take it off you as soon as you get in bed."

She dropped the gown, and Hunter thought he had never seen anything more beautiful than his wife as he watched her come toward him. He turned back the covers for her to slide in beside him.

As Blaze came into Hunter's arms and he held her close, his hand stroking up and down her back, Blaze knew that she must tell Hunter about the baby they had conceived.

Slowly then, his hand moved to rest on her stomach. "We must be careful not to hurt this little one," he said softly.

"You know!" Blaze leaned back to look into Hunter's face. "But how? Only Lucianne and Rose knew about the baby."

"I was watching you when the wind blew your skirt. I saw and recognized the change in your body." He dropped a kiss on her forehead and whispered, "I hope you give me a son."

Blaze bucked her hips at him and said saucily, "Maybe I will, and maybe I won't."

"That's the last thing on my mind now," Hunter said hoarsely as he pulled Blaze beneath him.

The bed creaked in slow rhythm as Hunter carefully thrust in and out of his wife. He was finding that this leisurely way of making love had a satisfaction to it that he had never experienced before.

When he rode the crest of ecstasy later he knew with absolute certainty that he had never climbed so high before.

# Epilogue

On an August night five months later Dr. Hines helped Blaze to deliver a healthy baby boy, whom she named Jory.

Over the following years Blaze presented Hunter with two more sons, and then a little daughter. He was often teased about how his sons looked like their mother while the daughters looked like him.

Becky loved her new siblings. When she was sixteen she married the son of a rancher, and a year later made Blaze and Hunter grandparents.

Lucianne married Dr. Hines and turned her business over to one of her girls. She never curled her hair or painted her face again.

Jim Bridger died in his sleep when he was eighty-three.

## Norah Hess

David Wilson's mail-order bride left him and went back east after six months of marriage. She did not like the rugged life of the West.

James Wilson's marriage lasted, and he sired a son and two daughters.

The Wilson brothers continued to be close friends with Blaze. And everyone knew that married life had, indeed, mellowed Hunter when he gave his blessing to a marriage between his second daughter and James Wilson's son.

# Sage · NORAH HESS

## Winner Of The *Romantic Times* Lifetime Achievement Award!

**"Norah Hess not only overwhelms you with characters who seem to be breathing right next to you, she transports you into their world!"**
**—*Romantic Times***

Jim LaTour isn't the marrying kind. With a wild past behind him, he plans to spend the rest of his days in peace, enjoying the favors of the local fancy ladies and running his bar. He doesn't realize what he is missing until an irresistible songbird threatens his cherished independence and opens his heart.

Pursued by the man who has murdered her husband, Sage Larkin faces an uncertain future on the rugged frontier. But when she lands a job singing at the Trail's End saloon, she hopes to start anew. And though love is the last thing Sage wants, she can't resist the sweet, seductive melody of Jim's passionate advances.

_3591-X                              $4.99 US/$5.99 CAN

**_Storm_**
**_NORAH HESS_**

"Norah Hess not only overwhelms you with
characters who seem to be breathing right next
to you, she transports you into their world!"
—*Romantic Times*

Wade Magallen leads the life of a devil-may-care bachelor
until Storm Roemer tames his wild heart and calms his
hotheaded ways. But a devastating secret makes him send
away the most breathtaking girl in Wyoming—and with her,
his one chance at happiness.

As gentle as a breeze, yet as strong willed a gale, Storm
returns to Laramie after years of trying to forget Wade. One
look at the handsome cowboy unleashes a torrent of longing
she can't deny, no matter what obstacle stands between them.
Storm only has to decide if she'll win Wade back with a love
as sweet as summer rain—or a whirlwind of passion that will
leave him begging for more.

\_3672-X                                          $4.99 US/$5.99 CAN

# NORAH HESS

After her father's accidental death, it is up to young Fancy Cranson to keep her small family together. But to survive in the pristine woodlands of the Pacific Northwest, she has to use her brains or her body. With no other choice, Fancy vows she'll work herself to the bone before selling herself to any timberman—even one as handsome, virile, and arrogant as Chance Dawson.

From the moment Chance Dawson lays eyes on Fancy, he wants to claim her for himself. But the mighty woodsman has felled forests less stubborn than the beautiful orphan. To win her hand he has to trade his roughhewn ways for tender caresses, and brazen curses for soft words of desire. Only then will he be able to share with her a love that unites them in passionate splendor.

\_3783-1                                                   $5.99 US/$6.99 CAN

# WINTER LOVE
# NORAH HESS

"Norah Hess overwhelms you with characters who seem to be breathing right next to you!"
—*Romantic Times*

*Winter Love.* As fresh and enchanting as a new snowfall, Laura has always adored Fletcher Thomas. Yet she fears she will never win the trapper's heart—until one passion-filled night in his father's barn. Lost in his heated caresses, the innocent beauty succumbs to a desire as strong and unpredictable as a Michigan blizzard. But Laura barely clears her head of Fletch's musky scent and the sweet smell of hay before circumstances separate them and threaten to end their winter love.

_3864-1                                    $5.99 US/$7.99 CAN